ANGEL
SAGE
HEX

Copyright © 2014 S.A. Huchton
All rights reserved.

Except as permitted under the U.S. Copyright Act of 1976, no part of this
publication may be reproduced, distributed, or transmitted in any form
or by any means, or stored in a database or retrieval system,
without prior permission of the publisher.

Book design by Inkstain Interior Book Designing
Text set in Cochin LT.

The characters and events in this book are fictitious. Names, characters, places,
and plots are a product of the author's imagination. Any similarity
to real persons, living or dead, is coincidental
and not intended by the author.

ISBN-13: 978-1499635430
ISBN-10: 1499635435

THE EVOLUTION SERIES, BOOK 3

EVOLUTION: HEX

S. A. HUCHTON

East Baton Rouge Parish Library
Baton Rouge, Louisiana

If I fly, it is with wings you helped me grow.
If I rise, it is on your shoulders I stand.
If I succeed, it is with your faith I believed.
If I fall, it is your hands that help me up.
To my friends and family, if I am a superhero,
It is with the cape you gave me.
Thank you.

CHAPTER 1

THE CHAINS rattled against the metal bed frame. The sound they made, the heavy clunking clink, echoed through the thick fog surrounding her.

Candace pulled on the cuffs again, making the sound, listening as it bounced off of the unseen walls. The noise kept her company. She didn't know how long it had been since she heard another person's voice.

When screaming didn't work, she switched to pleading. When that failed, she tried tears. Nothing made a difference. The fog remained, the silence as heavy and impenetrable as ever.

Whatever that stuff was, it wasn't steam. It didn't collect anywhere, or speak to her the way water molecules did. In fact, there was barely a whisper of water anywhere. The dust in her bones testified to how long it had been since she last tasted fluids.

Candace stared up from her position on the cot. She couldn't even form the fog into amusing shapes to pass the time, so, instead, she spent her hours mulling over how she got into that situation. The last moments replayed in her head in slow-motion; the weird disorientation, the last ditch attempt to stop whatever that woman was doing, the explosion... Whenever she got to that part, she flinched. Jackson's traces were all over those flames. He attacked her. He tried to kill her.

She frowned to herself. Maybe he succeeded. Maybe that unending limbo was all that waited on "the other side." However, the torturous effects of dehydration said otherwise. Death wouldn't be that miserable, unless it was Hell. Possible, given that she'd violated the whole "thou shalt not kill" rule on more than one occasion, but she always imagined Hell would be worse, if it existed at all.

Speculating was stupid, though. Candace wasn't dead. She couldn't be.

One memory at the end of the whole Aspen affair haunted her. It consisted of three parts: a face, a voice, and a light. She was pretty out of it at that point, but there was no mistaking the guy with blond hair and red highlights. His face was burned into her brain. What did he do when he slung Candace over his shoulder? Clearly he brought her to her current location, but not by any conventional means.

And then there was the voice. She heard it in her nightmares whenever she drifted off to sleep. The absolute anguish in Jackson's cry when he screamed her name constricted her throat and threatened to bring tears. Were she not so dehydrated, she probably would've sobbed like a baby. The guilt he must be feeling, knowing he was the one responsible for knocking her senseless… Every piece of her hurt for him. If she could, she would give the world to let him know it wasn't his fault. She was okay.

Oddly, she *was* okay. Her head should be pounding. Her body should be screaming at her with every movement. Yet, she felt fine, not a bruise or scratch anywhere she could detect. She would trade "okay" for the chance to see him again, to let him know she was alive, even for one more moment to say the words always with her.

I love you.

The light was the last thing she ruminated on. Well, not only the light, as there was more to that part than simple illumination. The sensations that went with it, the shifting, expanding of everything she was, was that the HEX guy's power? What was it? What did he do?

Candace knocked her head back against the thin mattress and cursed. She wished whoever was holding her would get on with it already.

"I'm bored," she called up into nothing, her voice scratchy. "Whatever you're going to do, could we hurry it up? If you don't kill me soon, I'm going to die of boredom or dehydration."

More silence.

She sighed. She didn't really expect that to work.

"If you think I'm stupid enough to try and fight my way out of here, you should really raise your expectations of me. I'm smarter than I look."

Nope again.

"I imagine this is probably what Kristie feels like. Y'know, minus the chains and she gets sexy alien books."

Two heartbeats passed.

A new sound, a hollow clang, reverberated off the walls. Thrilled by the prospect of something different, Candace held her breath.

But that was it: the clang, and then nothing.

She went back to staring at the milky miasma, thinking. The clang was something, at least, but whether it was her cue to shut up or a hint that she was on the right track, she couldn't be sure. Still, nothing else elicited a response from whoever was holding her. So maybe they were waiting, but for what?

She decided to try again.

"If there's something you guys want to know, maybe you should try, oh, I dunno, asking? It's amazing what happens when you…" Her words disappeared in a yawn. "Sorry," she said, her speech slurring. What the hell? "When you attempt to be…" Attempt to be… what? What was she going to say?

Sleep crashed down on her, and the world faded from foggy gray to completely black.

"…WITH US yet?" A voice prompted Candace to peel an eyelid open, the other following unevenly.

Candace immediately squinted against the harsh light, but her body was slow to respond. Each twitch of her muscles felt like moving through syrup.

"Can you hear me?" A woman spoke, but Candace couldn't get her vision to track a face. Every time she tried, her gaze drifted around the room to settle on something, but she was distracted by a bright color or interesting shape the next second.

"Hello?"

Her tongue lolled out of her mouth when Candace attempted to wet her dry lips. Nothing worked the way it should. Most likely she looked like a mental patient.

"Mica, I think you need to back off on the chemicals. She's too drugged to respond."

Drugged? Oh, what the hell?

"I'm not…" Candace started to say, but lost her train of thought. Damn, she couldn't even keep hold of her brain.

After a few minutes, some semblance of control returned, and she blinked a few times. A woman sat in front of her, with golden cocoa skin and the silkiest, blackest hair Candace had ever seen. She reached out a hand to touch it, but the jerk of chains stopped her. Really? Drugged out of her mind and still chained up, huh? Whatever.

"What's your name?"

She giggled. "Candace. You have pretty hair." She pulled on the chain some more, watching as the length of it moved, collecting in a puddle on her leg and stretching out again.

"What's your last name?"

She giggled again. "Why, you wanna take me to dinner? Sorry. I'm already spoken for."

The woman sighed. "Mica, is this really necessary? Can't

we just talk to her over the PA in her cell?"

"Boss says face to face," a man said from somewhere outside of Candace's line of sight. She dropped her head to one side and tried to see over the back of the seat. Nope. Just chair. "Besides, it's kind of funny."

"It is funny." Candace giggled, then looked back at the woman. "See? Mica thinks it's funny. You should smile more. It's funny."

"What's your last name?"

"What's yours?" She stuck out her tongue.

"Mich, just play along. You'll get more out of her that way," Mica said.

"Mitch?" Candace asked.

The woman frowned. "It's Michele."

"Do you like Mich better?"

"Not really," she said flatly.

Candace nodded appreciatively. "Yeah, I get that. My cousin nicknamed me Candy Cane when we were kids, and I still can't get rid of it. Jackson calls me Sugar Plum, but he's the only one. I used to hate that, too, but whatever. It's kinda cute now. Especially when he whispers it." She giggled. "Sorry. TMI?"

Mich didn't look amused. "What's your last name?"

Candace made a serious face. "Bristol. What's yours?"

"What's your ability?"

When she tried to cross her arms, the chains jerked taut, and she got distracted playing with them again.

"Candace?"

"Hmm?" She looked up.

"Your ability?"

EVOLUTION: HEX

"Clearly not super strength," she said with a sigh, frowning at the chains as they went up and down. Up and down. "Why am I chained up? I don't wanna hurt anybody."

"Because you killed two of our people already."

Candace tilted her head back to the ceiling and considered it. "I did? Oh, right. Wait, no. That's not right."

"What's not right?"

"Two. Not right."

Mich snorted. "I'm pretty sure it's two."

Candace wobbled her head from side to side. "Nope. Not two." She held up a finger, staring at the lines of her fingerprints for a moment before she remembered what she was doing with it. "Portland. Your nutso mistake killed a shitload of people and our team leader before I snapped his neck." She whipped out another finger, and then a third. "San Jose. I dunno what those guys were doing, but they killed one of my friends before I took out that trash, too." Her pinky joined in on the body count. "And then your little fire in the snow. That was pretty awful." Candace shivered. "She was screaming about killing everybody. I couldn't…" The memory choked off her words. Even through the haze of drugs, the guilt over that death hit hard. She swallowed and continued. "So, by my count, Mitch, four. Not two."

"Five," Michele said, her voice hollow.

"Five?"

"Think hard."

Candace scrunched up her face and stared at the floor. "Five? But Kristie's not dead. At least, she wasn't when I saw her before Aspen. I dunno. They might be really mad now, and if I'm not there to keep them from being horrible to her—"

"Not Kristie."

Candace's scowl deepened, and she scratched her chin against her shoulder. "Five?"

"Five."

"But you're not talking about Adrian."

"Who's Adrian?"

"He's..." she started, then slumped back in her seat. "He was my boyfriend."

"Unstable?"

Candace nodded, unable and unwilling to relive that incident.

"That's quite the body count, Candy Cane."

"Don't call me that, Mitchell," she growled back.

"Mitchell?" Mica chuckled from behind.

Michele's eyes narrowed. "Your unrelated death notwithstanding, we're still at five. You took out Desiree before Chuck grabbed you."

"Who's Desiree?"

"The one with the head missing from her shoulders."

Candace winced. So her last ditch effort hit the mark after all. "Everyone was attacking each other. I only had one shot. I didn't know if I hit anything or what happened."

"Congratulations then."

Candace lapsed back into silence, absentmindedly playing with her chains and trying to ignore the IV jacked into her left arm.

"What's your ability?"

"Water manipulation," she mumbled.

"I told you," Mica said.

Lifting her eyes, Candace studied Michele's face. "Where am I?"

"Like I'm going to tell you that."

"Well, can you tell me how long I've been here?"

Michele considered it. "A little over a week."

Her heart dropped into her shoes. "A week?" She sighed. If Jackson hadn't lost his mind already, he was probably close to it. Candace chewed on her lip. "What are you going to do to me?"

"For now?"

Candace waited.

Michele leaned back in her chair and crossed her arms. "Ask you questions, mostly. That's against my better judgment, but what the hell do I know? The Boss wants to keep an ANGEL in a cage, that's her prerogative."

Candace perked up. "Dr. Ferdinand?"

Leaning forward again, Michele stared at her. "And what do you know about Dr. Ferdinand?"

Struggling to think through whatever they were pumping into her system, Candace knew she shouldn't be telling them all of that. She needed to hold a few cards to her chest. "Not much. She used to work with Dr. Poznanski."

"And that's all?"

Candace shrugged. "And she's behind HEX. That's it." She yawned and worked her tongue in her mouth. "Can I have a drink? I'm dying of thirst."

"You're not dying of anything," Michele said. "And, no, I'm not giving you shit."

Candace scowled. "I already told you I don't want to hurt anybody."

"And yet, you've still killed six people in... how long now?"

"I didn't have a choice. I don't want to hurt anybody," she repeated.

"Sure thing, killer."

Wincing, Candace closed her eyes. Strategy was what she needed, not tears or regrets for actions she couldn't take back, but she couldn't think straight. "It would be monumentally stupid of me to try fighting my way out. I don't even know where I am or how many people are around. I wanted to be an ANGEL to protect and save, not for an ability to kill. I didn't ask for that."

"And yet, here we are."

What else could she say? Words weren't going to conjure trust out of thin air. "I don't know what you want."

"Could you kill me now?"

"What?" Candace's mouth fell open. "What... why would you ask me that?"

"Could you do it or not?"

As high as she was, Candace wasn't even sure. Tentatively, she searched for her connection. It was there, but garbled. If she concentrated hard enough, she might be able to get through. "I don't know. Maybe. That's the wrong question, though."

Michele snorted. "The wrong question? And what, pray tell, is the right one?"

After scratching her chin on her shoulder again, Candace shrugged. "The right question is whether or not I want to."

The smirk Michele gave her was slightly reminiscent of Jackson's. "So do you want to?"

Candace shook her head. "No. Killing is an easy answer, but not necessarily the right one."

"You were right about one thing," Michele said.

"I'm right about a lot of things," Candace replied. "Are you referring to something in particular?"

Michele looked over Candace's shoulder and flicked her chin. "That you're smarter than you look."

Her mouth opened to shoot back a retort, but the words scrambled in her head. Michele's face swam and spun in Candace's vision, but only for a moment before the darkness closed in again.

TIME PLODDED on in a cycle of being bored and staring into the fog of her cell, and drugged-out question and answer sessions. The only way for Candace to mark the passing of days was when Michele wore different clothing. By her count, she was up to two weeks at least, counting the time before their first conversation.

That day, or that night, whatever it was, Candace awoke in her cell free from chains. Ironically, she missed the sound they made. It was strange how she was used to it.

Another change was the tray of food greeting her when the medication wore off. Even though she hadn't eaten or drank anything since her arrival, she wasn't starved or on the verge of death by dehydration. Candace supposed they fed her intravenously while she was out or something, otherwise she would've died a week ago.

Along with the food was a five-gallon jug of water, which she didn't hesitate to pour down her throat as quickly as she could manage without drowning. Only when she was down to the last of it did she question the purity of the fluids.

Candace snorted a laugh. She spent two weeks in and out of drugged stupors. It was dumb to worry about that.

The ever-present fog must have something to do with her periods of unconsciousness. Each one was preceded by that heavy clang, so she reasoned they were pumping something into her cell to knock her out. She waved away the haze in front of her face, irritated. What was that stuff, anyway?

After she ate, she sat on the floor, leaning up against a warm, metal wall. Candace closed her eyes and pulled her knees up to her chest, leaning her head on her folded arms. For the first time, she allowed herself to cry. Really cry, not the fake tears she used before to try getting their attention. They seeped out of her, silently shaking her shoulders.

Her heart ached. Would she ever see Jackson again? Her fingers drifted up her right arm, tracing the pattern of scars on her skin. Over and over. C. Swirls. J. Swirls. C. Swirls. J. Swirls. She memorized the texture, remembering his touch, desperate for any trace of him. Jackson was burned into her soul as much as he was her body. Was he all right? Did he know she was alive?

The air stirred, and she froze, not daring to breathe. Without looking, she knew she was no longer alone.

"Giving up?" His voice wasn't familiar.

"Been there, done that," she said, not moving an inch.

"We were wondering when you'd finally break."

Candace took a deep breath and lifted her head. "Who

said I was broken?"

Blond hair. Red tips. He was crouched in front of her, close. What was his name again? God, those stupid drugs. Her brain was mush.

"Your tears tell me plenty, Candy Cane."

When he used her nickname, she scowled. "You don't get to call me that. You have to earn it."

He snorted and pushed a hand back through his spiky hair. "What would you rather I call you? Sugar Plum?"

Something in her snapped. Faster than he could blink, her fingers wrapped around his throat and she pulled his face within an inch of her own. "Only one person has that privilege, and you aren't him." She shoved him away and sank back to her position against the wall.

He chuckled as he regained his balance. "That wasn't very nice, sweetheart. You really should rethink that hostility."

"Newsflash, Precious. You don't get to tell me what to think. Don't call me that again, or I'll kill you for real next time."

"I'd advise against that."

Candace burst out laughing. "Really? You're kidding, right? I'm trapped in a windowless room, wandering through drug-addled interrogations whenever the hell someone gets a wild hair to screw with me, and I've been chained up in more or less solitary confinement for what I guess is over two weeks now. The people I care about more than anything in the world might think I'm dead, and there's no indication when, if, or how I'll ever get the hell away from you people. So, tell me, *Chuck*." She paused as his name finally emerged from her memory. "What else are they gonna do to me? Torture me? Kill me? Fine. At least that's something different."

The mischievous grin spreading across his mouth sent a ripple of doubt through her confidence, but she refused to let it show. Even as he reached out and brushed the side of her face with his fingertips, Candace didn't flinch.

"You're pretty when you're sleeping, but I like you better when you're feisty."

Despite the urge to recoil from his touch, she stayed put. "I bet you say that to all the girls."

God, he actually laughed. "You are a tough one, huh, Candy Cane? All right, fine. I can see I've got my work cut out for me, but I'm willing to give it time."

Ugh. She might actually throw up on his shoes.

Chuck stood and held out a hand. "Come on then."

"As tempting as it is, I think I'll pass."

"I wasn't asking."

"I see you've hit on the problem, Precious."

"You have a meeting."

"Sure I do," she said, not budging an inch. "But I'm not going anywhere with you, creepshow."

"You have a thing for flattering nicknames, huh?" He sighed and planted his feet. "Look, there's only one way out of this box, and that's with me. I mean, I can always let them knock you out again and then cart you out of here after that…" He paused and grinned. "Actually, I didn't mind that so much. You can't complain about where I put my hands then."

Again fighting back the urge to vomit, she stood. "Do

you have trouble finding girlfriends? I can't imagine why. Rapist is such a flattering color on you."

The muscles in his jaw twitched violently, and he yanked her over by the arm. Candace kept her face impassive, not about to show him the terror threatening to consume her self-control. She had every means of defending herself, but if he was the only way in or out of that room, she couldn't risk killing him.

With one hand on her forearm, the other snaked around her waist, pulling her against his chest. "Ready to go for a ride, Candy Cane?" he whispered in her ear.

She bit down on her tongue. If she opened her mouth to speak, she'd puke for sure.

As light erupted around them, she pinched her eyes closed. Again there was the feeling of expanding, shifting, displacing from herself and within herself. Her knees wobbled, but Chuck held her tight.

It was over in seconds.

When he let her go, Candace opened her eyes. He smirked at her, and she blinked.

He was gone.

CHAPTER 2

WHERE THE hell did he go? How?

"Have a seat, Miss Bristol," a woman said, interrupting Candace's ruminations.

Candace turned slowly. She was in a windowless office filled with file cabinets and bookshelves of binders. Behind her, she saw a woman sitting at the desk and another man in one of the guest chairs. The man she didn't recognize, but the woman could only be one person.

She was older than the photos Candace saw during Dr. Poznanski's briefing, but there was no mistaking her. Dr. Emily Ferdinand smiled pleasantly, her salt-and-pepper hair draping around her shoulders. She wasn't dressed like a doctor, at least, not like any of the doctors at the ANGEL Project Headquarters. Candace couldn't recall seeing any of

EVOLUTION: HEX

those scientists in t-shirts and jeans.

"I see you already know who I am, then," Dr. Ferdinand said with a coy smile. "Roger told you about me?"

Candace chewed her lip, unsure of how to deal with the situation. While she never considered coming face-to-face with the head of HEX before, that wasn't how she would've pictured it. The woman seemed far too nice to be a bad guy.

"Confused, hmm?" the man said, his voice smooth as butter. He was about twenty-five, but heavy-set, and it aged him some. When he pushed his thin, brown hair away from his eyes, their unusual darkness indicated he was a Super.

"Why am I unchained and not drugged out of my mind?" Candace asked, backing up a pace.

"Would you rather be?" Dr. Ferdinand asked.

Candace grimaced. "No, but why now?"

The man crossed one leg over his knee and leaned on the back of his chair. "We're pretty sure you're not going to go on a killing spree."

"Only took you two weeks to figure that out, huh?" Candace said flatly. "Sorry. Not buying it. All I'd really have to do is take her out, right?" She flicked her chin at Dr. Ferdinand, then stopped. "But, for all I know, you guys have a mimic too, so that might not even be her."

Dr. Ferdinand chuckled. "Not that I blame you for being a little paranoid, but you're overthinking this. Have a seat, Candace."

"I think I'd rather stand."

She shrugged. "If you like."

Candace shifted her weight from foot to foot. "So, why am I here? I mean, not in the general sense, I get that.

Prisoner of war and such. Why am I in your office?"

"I thought it was time we had a little chat," she said. "I think you've got the wrong idea about me."

Choking back a laugh, Candace stared at her. "The wrong idea? Uh, okay. I'll bite. I suppose there are two sides to every story."

"Sure you don't want to sit?"

Candace cast a suspicious look at the as-yet unidentified man.

"Oh," Dr. Ferdinand said. "I forgot you don't know our Mr. Wentz. Candace Bristol, Alonso Wentz. Alonso, Candace. There. Better now?"

"Not really," Candace said, and looked at him. "What are you?"

"An empath." He cracked a smile.

Wonderful. She was barely used to Deborah and Chloe, now she had some strange dude all up in her business.

"Not a fan, eh?" he said.

She made a face.

"Amazing," he said, studying whatever she was projecting. "How is it that you're so... loud?"

She was definitely not telling him that.

He sighed and shook his head. "Secrets don't make friends."

"I'm not your friend, in case you forgot," she said.

"Candace," Dr. Ferdinand said, motioning to the empty chair. "Really, we're not your enemy."

Realizing she wasn't going to let up about having a seat, Candace relented, leaning as far away from the empath as she could. "You'll excuse me if I don't believe that. Friends don't typically lock each other up in escape-proof boxes and drug them senseless at random intervals."

Dr. Ferdinand frowned. "I am sorry about that, but we had to ensure our own safety."

"Well," Candace grumbled. "I guess it's not like you had anyone that could counter my water abilities."

"Oh, we have that," Dr. Ferdinand said.

Candace sighed. "No, trust me. You don't. Even if they're better than Kristie, it wouldn't matter."

"And what makes you say that?"

"I'm stronger than ninety percent of the ANGEL Project, maybe more." Candace gave her a sweet smile. "I'm special."

"Clustered neurons?" Dr. Ferdinand asked.

Candace nodded. She'd leave it at that.

Alonso snorted. "There's more to it."

She glared at him. "I'm not lying."

He inched toward her, his proximity unnerving. "I didn't say you were lying, I said there was more to it."

Dr. Ferdinand leaned forward on the desk, looking worried. "What did he do to you?"

"Do to me? Who?"

"Dr. Poznanski," she said. "What did he do to you?"

Grimacing, Candace realized she couldn't avoid telling them, not with the empath in the room. "Another round of treatments. I'm a SAGE. SecondAry Genetic Enhancement. With you guys killing ANGELs like you are, we didn't have a choice. We had to up our game."

Dr. Ferdinand paled. "He put you through a second round?"

"I volunteered."

"Why? Why take that risk?"

Candace closed her eyes and gritted her teeth. "Because I was tired of seeing people die. Like I told Mitchell, I became an ANGEL to protect. But you mentioned something about a wrong idea. Any time you want to start with that, I'm all ears."

With a slow, sad shake of her head, Dr. Ferdinand digressed. "You've spoken with Kristie, I take it?"

"A bit."

"And what did she tell you?"

"Not much." Candace shrugged. "That you let these guys," she said, wiggling her fingers at Alonso. "Walk around free until you order them to go make trouble for the ANGELs. That you unleash psychologically unstable genevos into the general population to do their worst. And I get the impression you suck people in like a cult, so there's that, too."

Dr. Ferdinand sighed and leaned back in her chair, thinking it over. "We're not a cult, Candace. Our members feel like family because we offer a kind, loving environment for everyone."

"Yes," Candace nodded. "Until you order them to their deaths. Do you serve Kool-Aid at the going away parties?"

"Everyone knows what our mission is. They go into it with open eyes."

"Right. Your mission," Candace said. "And what would that be, exactly?"

"To expose the corruption and lies of the ANGEL Project, mostly," she said. "Secondary to that is offering genetic enhancements to the public at large, to foster understanding that our members are still human and can function in normal society, and shouldn't be excluded from it."

"Offering enhancements to the public at large? That's stupid and dangerous. You should know better than anyone that the treatments aren't compatible with everyone's genetics."

"Which is why we don't hide it when it doesn't work," she explained. "If the public is educated, they'll know it's not a perfect process."

Candace took a deep breath and rubbed her forehead. "That's the most ridiculous thing I've ever heard. You think exposing people to some of the most violent, mentally unstable people on the planet, purposely putting them at risk, is the best way to educate them? All that does is instill fear and cause pain, which will ultimately result in hatred for gen-evos in general."

"And you have a better alternative?"

Sighing, she realized that she did. "Those 'mistakes'… you're essentially sending them off to die. You're letting other people dispose of what you broke. Innocent people are dying as a result. If the unstable is going to die anyway, save everyone the trouble and take responsibility for it."

"You're suggesting euthanizing them?"

It sounded callous, but, really, was there another option? Unstables were non-functional. Their only purpose was causing death and destruction. "I am. If they can't be rehabilitated, it's better for them and everyone else. I wouldn't want to live that way."

"Your precious ANGEL Project would disagree with you." An edge of bitterness tinged her words. "Is that what you think they do?"

Candace paused. It wasn't something she thought about before. "I don't know, but I guess you're suggesting they don't."

"They don't," she said, no longer smiling. "Despite their highly touted screening process, they have their fair share of 'mistakes' too."

Shadowy suspicions teased at her. "You're saying they keep unstables somewhere?"

Dr. Ferdinand nodded.

"Why?"

"Good question, but I think you're better equipped to answer that than I am."

"How would I know?" Candace asked. "It's not like I've seen…"

But she had. She *had* seen something. Maybe it wasn't solid proof, but there was no other way to explain it.

"Miss Bristol?"

Candace stared at the desk, thinking back to November. "For our final testing, we run through a setup they call the Gauntlet. It's a life-sized recreation of an urban street, and a test of how you'll react in a real-world situation. The people in the streets are all digital, but the main challenge…" She swallowed hard, and when she spoke again, her voice wasn't so steady anymore. "The main challenge is a live person. An unstable."

Dr. Ferdinand made a disgusted noise. "So Roger found a use for his 'mistakes' after all."

EVOLUTION: HEX

The anger, the fear in the man's eyes as he raged at her in the Gauntlet, Candace saw it clearly. Who had he been before? Could such a person be made whole again?

"Which is worse, Miss Bristol?" Dr. Ferdinand asked. "A long life as a captive practice dummy, or a short one as a lesson to others?"

Gritting her teeth, Candace kept her temper in check. "I'd prefer death. Either way, you're using people to your own selfish ends. You have your reasons, so do they. You both assume your way is the best, that it's for the good of all, but you're wrong."

"You think it's better to value one over the good of many?" Dr. Ferdinand asked, eyebrows raised in genuine surprise.

Candace shook her head. "No, but when there's a better way for everyone, you only do anything else because you've rationalized what's best for you. It's selfish."

Dr. Ferdinand didn't look happy with Candace's reasoning. It always sucked when someone called her out on her own bullshit, so she imagined that was the cause behind her expression.

"So that was the only unstable you saw at the compound?" Dr. Ferdinand said, changing the topic.

Candace nodded.

"What was the unstable like? Appearance, ability, that sort of thing."

She shouldn't be answering their questions so freely. It was stupid to give up so much information to an enemy. Candace studied the face of Emily Ferdinand. Her expression was open, honest, with a hint of desperation.

Desperation? That was strange. Why would her eyes bore into her with such an earnest need?

Her eyes.

Her eyes were not the eyes of the genetically altered. They were normal, natural as the day she was born.

"I have a question for you, before I answer any more of yours," she said.

Dr. Ferdinand folded her hands and waited.

Already knowing the answer, but hesitant to ask, Candace pushed forward. "You didn't use yourself as a test subject, did you?"

Her brow creased as she took in the question and what it implied. "No. Is that what he told you?"

Candace answered with another nod.

Dr. Ferdinand's face pinched, and she released a long breath. "You've been lied to, Miss Bristol, and not only about that."

After everything Candace saw and heard since joining the ANGEL Project, the news wasn't shocking. Between Deborah's warning after the fallout from Adrian's death, to her discovery of the torture of Kristie Burke, a few more unpleasant realities only added to her pile of suspicions.

It was time to get to the truth.

"I'm listening."

CANDACE STARED up into the swirling fog of her cell, replaying every part of the conversation with Dr.

EVOLUTION: HEX

Ferdinand.

Maybe she wasn't being honest. Maybe her story wasn't true. Maybe everyone was lying to her so she would pick their side.

Candace wasn't convinced *any* side was the right one. There was so much gray area, the uncertainty was suffocating.

"I wasn't the first GEF test subject," Dr. Ferdinand said. *"It was my son."*

Her son, taken and subjected to genetic modification without her knowledge or consent. That kind of total betrayal by a partner, someone she worked with for years, using her own flesh and blood... it was no wonder Dr. Ferdinand took the steps she did after that.

The only thing consistent in the two stories of how the government came to control the GEF formula was the destruction of the original research facility. Dr. Ferdinand's son was responsible for that, and the entire building was demolished in the struggle to get him under control.

What Dr. Ferdinand didn't know was what happened to him after that. The man Candace fought in the Gauntlet wasn't him, although there were some similarities in ability. When Candace described him, Dr. Ferdinand's shoulders sagged, disappointed. Understandably, she was desperate for some sign that he was still alive.

The whole day left Candace feeling like she was standing on a crumbling rock suspended above a canyon. One wrong step and she'd plummet into an abyss. While she had her suspicions about the ANGEL Project before, she had little in the way of evidence to back it up. At that moment, she didn't know what to believe. With all she heard that day, could she take that as truth? If she did, what would that mean if she ever got out of there?

If she had to choose, where would she fall?

If she chose wrong, could she deal with those consequences?

And then there was Jackson.

When Candace discovered they were torturing Kristie, he tried to talk her out of getting involved. If he knew what she knew, what would he say?

"Don't put yourself in the middle of it, Sugar Plum. Stay out of it. Stay alive."

But it wasn't as easy as survival. Candace couldn't live in that morally ambiguous place he seemed so comfortable in. If her loyalties changed, how would he align himself? Would he stand with her? The thought of suddenly being his enemy...

Taking a deep breath, she stepped away from the unknowable what-if. He wasn't there to ask, and he didn't know what Dr. Ferdinand said.

What was the reality of the HEX program? It wasn't like she had concrete proof they lived as happily as they said they did. Outside of the one meeting that day, all of her encounters with those people involved a heavy amount of sedation, chains, mistrust, and violence.

The line between enemy and ally wasn't a line at all; it was a fuzzy, ever-shifting radius of complexity and situational dependency.

The whole thing gave her a headache, and her dehydration didn't help with that.

"Hungry, Candy Cane?"

Candace refused to flinch when Chuck's breath brushed

her ear.

"What do you want?" she said, continuing to stare up into the fog.

"I want to take you out."

Yeah, right. Only if they drugged her within an inch of her life. "Pass. I just got comfortable."

"There's a shower and a fresh change of clothes in it for you."

Sighing, Candace sat up and slung her legs over the side of the cot to face him. "Resorting to bribery, eh, Chuck? Not satisfied with waiting until they drug me again?"

He smirked at her. "No skin off my nose either way. I kinda like you a little dirty."

She didn't give him the satisfaction of a smart reply. "What do you want?" she repeated.

"I told you, I want to take you out. Dinner? Maybe a movie?"

She snorted. "It's a bit early for Stockholm Syndrome to set in, Chuck. You can't take me out of here without your boss's say so."

"Who said I don't have it?"

"So Dr. Ferdinand gave you permission to take me out, huh? I'm not stupid. Why would she do that?"

Chuck shrugged and shoved his hands in the pockets of his baggy jeans. "Because we're not your enemy. So what do you say, Candy Cane? Wanna get out of here?"

Candace crossed her arms and considered him. As best she could tell, he was totally on the level. It was tempting. She hadn't taken a shower since the morning before Aspen, and her clothes were pretty rank. Still, the thought of spending more time with that guy turned her stomach.

"Where?"

A slow grin spread across his mouth. "Where do you want to go?"

"Somewhere you won't take me, so I'll ask again. Where?"

"What's your favorite kind of food?"

Hang on. He was serious. He actually wanted to take her out somewhere? Like, away from HEX?

She weighed it carefully before answering. "Mexican."

He stepped in front of her and placed his hands on the cot, one on either side of her legs, leaning in close to her face. "I can make that happen, but you have to do one thing for me first."

Candace leaned back, away from him. "What?"

"Promise me you're not going to try anything stupid like running away or, I don't know, killing me."

"Now where's the fun in that?" she said. "I thought you were the type of guy who liked to take risks."

"Are you gonna promise or not?"

She cocked her head to the side and thought. "Depends."

"On what?" he said, lifting an eyebrow.

"On whether or not you keep your hands to yourself."

"I gotta touch you to get you out, Candy Cane."

Candace kept her expression nailed down to perfectly placid.

Rolling his eyes, Chuck pushed away and held out his hand. "Fine. I'll behave if you do."

She stood and took his hand, trying not to cringe at the feel of his skin. His palms were clammy. "Then I promise not to kill you, Precious."

Chuck pulled her against him, hands carefully placed on her back, and the world shifted into light.

CHAPTER 3

THE ROOM wasn't all that different from her room back in California, albeit a little smaller. Candace had yet to see a window anywhere in the place. Where the hell was she, anyway?

Chuck dropped her there and left, saying he'd be back in exactly one hour. She sighed and looked around, then groaned when she saw the clothes they left for her.

A dress and heels. And baby pink, at that. Seriously?

With no other choice, Candace scooped up the clean things on the bed and marched into the bathroom.

The shower was nothing short of heavenly. At least it gave her the chance to completely refill the tank, to which her body responded by being unable to stand for ten minutes. After she was clean and rehydrated, she discovered they even left her makeup and hair products in the small cabinet over the toilet. Not about to encourage Chuck, she went easy on everything, opting for a simple loose braid and the basics as far as her face went.

She scowled at herself in the mirror. Pink. Why pink? She sighed and tried not to think about it.

When she emerged from the bathroom, Chuck was waiting. His baggy jeans and t-shirt were gone, replaced by gray slacks and a button-down shirt. She crossed her arms and fixed him with a look. "This isn't a date, Precious. I don't know why you're going to all this trouble."

He grinned at her. "All what trouble?"

"All that trouble," she said, waving at his clothes. "You didn't have to pretty yourself up for me."

Chuck continued grinning.

"What?" she grumbled.

"I changed my mind. I like you better clean."

"Well, I haven't changed *my* mind. I'm still not interested, Chuck."

He held out his hand, beckoning with his fingers. "We'll see. Let's go."

FOUR SHIFTS later, they were standing in front of a small adobe building trimmed in teal paint. White Christmas lights dripped from the edges of the roof, sparkling in the fading sunlight.

Candace looked around. "Where are we?" Wherever it

was, it looked like the middle of nowhere.

"Domingo's," Chuck said. "Best Mexican restaurant this side of the Rio Grande."

"Yeah, but where?"

"Boron, California."

Her stomach clenched. California. So close to home. So close to *him*.

"Shall we?" Chuck said, opening the large wooden door for her.

The food was every bit as amazing as he said it would be, but she didn't really enjoy it. While he made small talk, asking about her hobbies, her family, Candace spent her time trying to figure out some way to send a message to the ANGEL Project that she was alive. The problem was twofold. One, she was in the middle of nowhere with no guarantee that anything she did would be noticed. Two, she had to do it without Chuck knowing what she was up to. Whatever she was going to do, she needed to do it soon.

"So what do you want to do next?" he asked as he counted out cash to pay the bill.

Candace shrugged. "Use the bathroom," she said. "Am I allowed?"

"You're not going to flush yourself down the toilet or anything, are you?" he said with a chuckle.

If only. "Not my preferred method of escape, no." She slid out of the booth and headed for the restroom.

Locking the door behind her, Candace leaned up against it to think. There had to be something she could do. Orange light from a streetlamp trickled in from a tiny window above the toilet, prompting her to climb onto the tank to get a look outside. It wasn't easy in a dress, but stepping out of her pumps at least made it possible.

It wasn't much of a view. A few dusty homes and the back of a strip mall took up most of what she could see. When she craned her neck to the farthest edge, she could see a small, sandy field dotted with scrubby patches of grass and a skeletal tree.

Maybe someone would notice, even if it wasn't a lot to work with.

For the first time in weeks, Candace submerged herself in her connection. As she tapped into a deep, deep aquifer, she smiled. There were memories of Big Sur in the water. Touching her right shoulder, she traced the pattern of scars through the fabric of her sleeve. *Be swift. Be silent.* She called to the water, bringing it up from the surface to carve away at the dry earth. C. Swirls. J. Swirls. C. Swirls. J. Swirls. *Mark this place. Let them know I was here.*

Opening her eyes, she peeked out the window. She couldn't make out much, but there were definitely marks in the empty lot. It would have to do. She was out of time.

Stepping back into her heels, she flushed the toilet and hurried out to catch up with Chuck.

"CAN I ask you something?" Chuck asked after taking a bite of his ice cream cone.

Candace swallowed her mouthful of hot fudge sundae and nodded. "Sure."

EVOLUTION: HEX

"Why haven't you tried to run? I know you could, if you wanted to."

She stared out the window of the all-night diner, onto the street of some tiny town in Utah, their final stop of the night. "I told you I wouldn't."

He took another bite. "Yeah, but why? It's not because you love my company."

Shifting her gaze back to him, she had to admit that the night wasn't terrible. However, there was more to it than that. "Because I haven't made a decision yet."

Chuck lifted an eyebrow. "And what decision is that?"

Thinking, Candace shoveled hot fudge onto the melting ice cream. "I haven't decided what the truth is yet. I don't have enough information."

"Information about…"

"About everything," she said. "I don't know who to trust or what to believe." When he didn't reply, she looked up. "I'm not going anywhere until I figure it out."

"And when you do?"

She shrugged. "I don't know. Guess that depends on what I decide." Draining the last of her water, she excused herself for one last bathroom break.

Fortunately for her, every place they went that night was in a remote location with plenty of open space out of sight of the front of the building. Along with the restaurant in California, they hit up a movie theater in Nevada, and a pretty little park in Arizona before their last stop. She left her mark at every one, hoping against hope that her message would reach the ANGEL Project or, more importantly, Jackson. Even if the ANGEL project found her symbols, would they tell him? They would know that once he heard about them, nothing in the world would keep him from trying to find her. There, she left his brand in a public park behind the diner. Surely someone would see it.

"Time to get back, Candy Cane," Chuck said when she met him up front. "Had enough freedom for one night?"

With a sour look, she turned and walked out the door, him on her heels. "You have a funny definition of freedom, Precious," she said as they walked into the parking lot. "You might want to invest in a dictionary."

"Hey now," he said, taking her hand and pulling her to him. "I took you anywhere you wanted to go tonight."

Candace shook her head. "There's only one place in the world I want to be, Chuck, and none of these places are it."

The world lit up and shifted twice before they were back in the dorm room again. He hesitated to release her when they landed, his face pinched. "Where would you rather be?"

Squirming out of his grasp, she looked at him, arms folded across her stomach. "It's not a place," she said. "It's a person. A someone. Wherever he is, that's always where I'd rather be."

"And he's an ANGEL," he said. The muscles in his jaw twitched.

Candace nodded.

Chuck stepped close to her, his face relaxing. His eyes softened, their mirror-like gray catching the light. Gentle fingers reached up to trace the side of her face. "I could help you forget him, you know."

She brushed his hand away and shook her head. "Sorry, Precious, that's not how it works. Not with him. Not ever. I can't forget this kind of thing, and you can't replace it."

Something in his smile made her take a step back. It wasn't a friendly smile, or even a kind smile. It was plastic, like a mask hiding the forked tongue of a snake.

"So, what, I don't get anything for my trouble tonight?"

Candace narrowed her eyes at him. "Nothing's changed, Chuck. Don't kid yourself to think it ever will."

A shifting of his features betrayed the battle raging inside him. The tiniest twitch of muscles gave it away. Eventually, he backed down, apparently not willing to confront a fully hydrated, seriously next-level water manipulator on his own. With one last mechanical nod of his head, he vanished, leaving her alone in the silent room.

AS SHE explored the room that night, Candace was surprised to find it stocked with basic clothing items, including pajamas, jeans, socks, underwear, and plain t-shirts. She rid herself of the pink terror as soon as possible, burying it in the back of a drawer, hoping to never see it again.

She laid awake for a long time, thinking, since there was nothing better to do. Deep in meditation, she allowed her connection to speak to her, telling her the twists and turns of the pipes running through the building. Eventually, she traced it outside, hoping to get a read on where in the world she might be, but the best she could do was a taste of rocks and the bitter cold of winter wind. The HEX compound could be anywhere from California to Maine.

At some point she drifted off to sleep, but woke with a pounding heart and gasping breaths not long after. Candace stared up at the ceiling, sucking in air. It wasn't a nightmare that disturbed her sleep. It was something else. The tingles in her toes reminded her of... of...

She pinched her eyes closed and choked back a sudden sob.

Jackson.

She felt him as clearly as if he were beside her, holding her, his breathing as ragged as hers from their shared passion. How could she feel that? For her connection to him to be firing up so strongly, so powerfully, it would require something big happening on his end. Something to make him drop his guard. Something that would leave him open and vulnerable.

But he wouldn't.

He *couldn't*.

Not that. Not with someone else. Not Jackson. Not with everything between them.

Tears slipped from her eyes, and she curled up into herself, clutching the pillow. It was a dream. It had to be. Surely it was just a new nightmare sent to punish her for her misdeeds.

Nightmares. Only nightmares. That must be it.

That *had* to be it.

EVOLUTION: HEX

SOMEONE POUNDED on the door. Candace cracked open an eye, still exhausted from her night of fitful sleep. Grumbling, she threw off the covers and shuffled across the room.

"Well, good morning, Candy Cane." A dark-haired guy, maybe two years her senior, grinned at her. His voice was familiar, but she wasn't awake enough to place it. "How's about breakfast?"

She rubbed the sleep out of her eyes and blinked at him. "What? Breakfast? Who are you?"

He chuckled, the sound of it also familiar. "Ah, right. I forgot you haven't actually seen me yet." He stuck out a hand. "Mica Reynolds: resident drug dealer."

Candace shook his hand absentmindedly, then stopped. "Wait, you're Mica?"

"In the flesh," he said, his smile broad and impossible to dislike.

When Candace fully took in his appearance, his resemblance to Michele was startling. They shared the same golden cocoa skin and pitch black hair. "Are you and Mitchell twins?"

Mica laughed at the nickname. "We are. You better watch it with that Mitchell business, though. My sister already doesn't like you much, and pissing her off more probably isn't a good idea."

Candace rolled her eyes. "Right. Because everyone else has been so warm and welcoming." Her eyes narrowed in suspicion. "Speaking of, why are you here and being so nice to me?"

Shrugging, he shoved his hands in the pockets of his

jeans. "You've got a sense of humor, Candy Cane. It's been a while since I've heard anyone give Mich a run for her money with the witticisms. Besides which, I can't really blame ya for what you did with the ANGEL Project before you met us. I don't think you're an enemy. I mean, the one in Portland was totally understandable. I don't even really begrudge you San Jose. Those two were way off the reservation and kind of dodgy anyway."

God. It was way too early for that conversation. "And what about Kristie?"

He made a face. "She's not dead, though her stupid ass probably should be."

"And Aspen?"

Mica sighed and scratched the back of his head. "Yeah, well, that's a bit of a gray area, isn't it? I mean, you guys were responding to an attack, so I guess I can't fault you. I dunno. It's stupid to blame soldiers for following orders when that's what they're trained to do. It's the order-givers I have a problem with, not the soldiers."

Well, at least someone there was reasonable. Candace yawned and held the door open for him. "You may as well come in. I gotta get cleaned up if you're dragging me out in public."

"Dragging you?" Mica chuckled as he walked in. "You don't have to if you don't want to. I just thought you might want to get out of here before Chuck comes back again."

With a hand on one of the drawers, Candace paused and looked at him. "Comes back again? For real?" She shook her head and sighed. "That guy can't take a hint, can he?"

"Well, since he got dumped he's been getting kind of

desperate," Mica said, then hastily followed it up with, "Not that you're not, y'know…" He coughed nervously and scuffed his foot along the carpet. "You know what I mean. I think he's convinced himself you're easy pickings because you're an outsider."

At that, Candace burst out laughing. "An outsider, huh? That's one way of putting it. I imagine that however many there are of you, most of them would love to take me out, and I don't mean on a date."

"Twenty-six," he said.

She looked up from the drawer of socks. "What?"

"There's twenty-six of us, not including doctors and stuff."

"And stuff?"

He waved at her to hurry up. "We can talk about all that over breakfast. The Boss gave me the go-ahead to fill you in on a few things, so the sooner you're done there, the quicker we can get to it."

Candace rushed through her morning preparations, not even bothering with makeup. After ten minutes, she was finally awake and ready to have a real conversation.

As Mica led her out of the room, the first time she went anywhere without being shifted by Chuck, she got her first real look at the layout of the building. It wasn't particularly fancy or spotlessly clean, but it wasn't claustrophobic or uncomfortable.

"So, I know you won't tell me where we are, but maybe you can confirm a few things for me," Candace said as they walked.

"Sure thing," he said. "What do you want to know?"

Her list was about a mile long, but she went for the obvious first. "Are we underground? I mean, there's no windows, and judging by the pipes I'm pretty sure that's what's going on here."

"The pipes?"

She nodded. "I did some exploring last night. I followed the water around. Er, not physically. You know, sensing it."

"Right. Gotcha," he said. "Yeah, we're underground, but not as far as you were when you were in the cell before. We're roughly six stories down, I think."

"Wow," she said. "That brings up all kinds of questions that you probably won't answer, because eventually I'd figure out where we are."

He grinned. "An abandoned mine, Candy Cane. We repurposed it. Put up walls, ran pipes, wired it for electricity, the works."

"What kind of mine?" she asked, trying to be sneaky. Gold might mean a California location, coal could be Colorado or, hopefully not, something further east, and silver would be more likely in the Southwest.

"Nice try," he said, smirking. "You really are smarter than you look."

She made a face at him, but gave it up. "How far down was my cell?"

"Far enough that by the time we walked you breakfast, someone else would have to be headed down with your lunch."

She stopped in the middle of the hall. "Seriously?"

Mica nodded, a wave of dark hair falling across his forehead. "Yep. That's why Chuck had to get you and why we weren't worried about you escaping. Even if you found the door, you'd be wandering around in the dark for days. You'd be more likely to die before we found you."

Candace swallowed past the lump of fear in her throat. "You guys don't mess around, huh?"

"Couldn't take any chances," he said, then prodded her along. "It wasn't personal, but we weren't sure what you'd try when we brought you around."

"Speaking of that." She looked at him out of the corner of her eye. "What was with the fog in there? What was it? Is that what you used to knock me out, or was it something else?"

"Ah, now that's a question I can definitely answer," he said, positively glowing with pride. "The fog in your cell was my doing. Pretty cool, huh?"

"Depends on what it is. Do I have to worry that I've been poisoned?"

"Nah," he said. "That stuff is totally harmless. It's just condensed air, really. To make sure you had enough of it in case something collapsed. We pumped in knock-out gas when we needed to."

"Well, that's reassuring," she said blandly. "So why are you so excited about it?"

"That's kind of what I do, Candy Cane. I see chemistry, as in, how atoms talk to each other. I commune with electrons, if you will."

She giggled. "Commune?"

Mica shrugged and guided her down a hallway to their left. "Well, I can't do what a lot of us do, in that I can't force elements to do things, like how you control water. I see the communication between elements and substances, and understand how to put things together to make other things, but I can't control their movement. I suppose you could say I'm a chemistry eavesdropper."

"That's..." She turned it over in her head. The potential for his ability was incredible.

"Anticlimactic?" he suggested.

Candace shook her head. "No, not at all. That's actually pretty awesome and insanely useful."

When he looked at her, his expression was a mix of uncertainty and curiosity. "You really think so?"

"Oh sure," she said, nodding vehemently. "You could pretty much make anything I can think of, right? Everything is chemistry and you can understand all of it without having to spend eons doing equations to figure it out. You've basically got the key to understanding the universe in your head. I think 'awesome' might be an understatement."

When he smiled, his entire face lit up. If her words had that much of an effect on him, how undervalued was he there? Mica's ability was awe-inspiring. How could he not know that?

"Thanks, Candy Cane," he said. "I mean it."

"Well, you're welcome," she said. "I mean it, too."

When they rounded the next corner, the smell of food set off loud rumbling in her stomach. How her metabolism processed so much so quickly never failed to surprise her.

"Morning, Graham," Mica said as they pushed open the swinging door leading into a large kitchen. "What's for breakfast?"

A tall, thin, black man turned away from the stove, smiling until he saw Candace. "Liver and onions," he said, his face rigid. Pots and pans rattled menacingly on a rack hanging above the butcher block island in the middle of the kitchen.

Mica stepped in front of her and crossed his arms in front of his chest. "Graham," he said, his voice low and calming. "You need to relax. She's not going anywhere, so you may as well get used to it. I promise you she's okay. She's good people."

Graham's shoulders rose and fell as he took deep breaths. "You could have warned me, Mica. I'm not prepared for her this morning."

"You knew she'd be here sooner or later."

"This is a mistake, bringing her in this soon. I don't trust her."

Irritated to be talked about like she wasn't standing there, Candace bit down on her tongue. It would only cause trouble if she opened her mouth.

"Not to be harsh," Mica said. "But it's not really your call, G. Mich doesn't like her either, and even she green-lighted this."

Graham said nothing, instead glaring at Mica.

"So what's for breakfast?"

"Hashbrown casserole, apple dumplings, and sausage."

Mica groaned. "Oh man, you're killing me, G. You know I could eat those dumplings until I'm sick, right?"

"By all means," the cook said, not giving in to the flattery. "You be as sick as you want."

Without wasting another moment, Mica grabbed her arm and pulled her through the kitchen into a room with four large dining tables and a buffet. He didn't give her the chance to look around at the few people sitting down to eat, shoving a plate and utensils into her hands.

"Graham's all right, but he might not ever like you much," he said, then lowered his voice to a whisper. "Stephanie was his girlfriend."

Candace nearly dropped her plate. "She was... oh my God."

"Yeah," Mica said, already helping himself to food. "I think that went well, though, all things considered."

Candace stared at the food, hesitant to take any of it. She killed his girlfriend in Aspen. If the situation was reversed, she doubted Graham would still be breathing.

"Eat, Candy Cane." Mica nudged her. "Graham's an amazing cook."

She swallowed and closed her eyes, willing herself not to cry. "I didn't want to, Mica. I didn't..." She let her words drop, unable to continue.

"Whoa, whoa," he said, setting his plate down and grabbing her by the shoulders. "Candy, you don't have to explain it to me. I get it. You were a good soldier. He'll see that eventually."

His face blurred through her tears. "I'm an awful person. Why are you being so nice?"

"You're not an awful person," he said. "And as for the other, well, I have a soft spot for blondes."

Candace choked and backed up a pace. "You what?" Her face heated beneath the cool wetness on her cheeks.

Mica grinned. "Gotcha."

She scowled at him and swiped at the escaped water. "That's not funny."

He chuckled and picked up his food. "Kinda is. Get your breakfast, Candy Cane. We've got a big day ahead of us."

CHAPTER 4

"AND HERE'S the medical facility," Mica said, pushing open the door.

The tour of the HEX compound left Candace in awe. That they turned an abandoned mine into such a vast facility made her head spin. "How did you guys do all this? I mean, it had to have been expensive and really time-consuming. This is crazy."

"It didn't start out like this, you know," he said, pausing in a small waiting room. "Dr. Ferdinand used to work out of a mobile lab. She traveled around and picked up people here and there. Once she had a handful of altered folks in her contingent, they started looking for a home base."

"So," Candace said. "Other Supers helped build all this. Telekinetics, earth movers, that sort of thing?"

Mica nodded. "Exactly. Graham was one of the first and had a big hand in it. That guy can literally move boulders with his brain."

"He's a telekinetic then," she said.

"Yup."

"How long have you been with HEX?" she asked.

Mica paused and thought. "About two years now, I think. Dr. Ferdinand found me and Mich when we got into a bad accident and ran off the road. Graham was actually responsible for saving us. He kept our car from falling off the edge of a canyon. Once Asia patched us up, the Boss asked if we were interested in becoming part of the group."

"Your parents didn't have anything to say about that?"

His expression soured. "Our parents haven't had a say in our lives for a long time. Mich and I hit the road when we were sixteen and never looked back. We'd been gone for a year and a half when HEX found us."

So they were runaways. She didn't know what to say to that. Not once in her life did she consider running away from home. Even after so much had changed, she still missed her mom. Had her email from the ANGEL headquarters gone through? Did her mom think she might be a casualty in Aspen? What did she know? Her blood drained into her feet, making her dizzy. What if they told her mom she was dead?

"Are you okay?" Mica asked, his eyebrows bunched together.

She shook her head to clear it. "Yeah, I'm fine. Sorry. I got lost in thought for a minute."

"You sure you're okay?"

"Positive. What's next?"

EVOLUTION: HEX

He sucked in his lips and narrowed his eyes at her, looking unsure about her words.

Candace smiled. "Really, I'm fine."

"If you say so." He sighed. "Okay, so, here's the thing..." Scratching at his chin, he looked at her. "You trust me, right?"

Her eyebrows lifted. "Trust you? Well, that depends on what I'm trusting you with."

Mica led her out of the waiting room and down the hall, pausing in front of a door. "Dr. Ferdinand wanted me to ask if she could have a sample of your blood. She wants to study it to see how the additional treatments affected your system."

Candace balked. "Wait, she wants my blood?"

He nodded. "I'm not trying to pull anything over on you, Candy. She's just curious."

Frowning, Candace doubted it was only curiosity driving it. "Curious to see the effects or curious to see if she can replicate it?"

Mica shrugged apologetically. "I can't tell you for sure, Candy. I'm not a mind-reader. She told me she wanted to check your stability and what changed in your DNA. That's it."

It wasn't like they couldn't force the blood draw if she didn't cooperate. Really, what choice did she have? But if she allowed it, it would be another step in the direction of getting them to trust her, to let their guard down. With a sigh, she relented. "All right. I don't know what good it will do her, but I'll let you. Have I mentioned that I'm really sick of needles?"

He chuckled and opened the door to an exam room. "I

totally understand. It'll only take a minute, I swear."

While it was quick and painless, Candace couldn't help wondering if she wasn't paving the way for more tests in the future. What would be next, a brain scan? Full body imaging? It didn't sit well with her. What if HEX developed the formula to create SAGEs of their own?

Worse, what did it mean for her loyalties? She hadn't given them information that was overly damaging to the ANGEL Project so far, but doing anything other than staying silent and unresponsive could brand her as a traitor. More than ever, she wasn't convinced HEX was an enemy. Perhaps they were in the field, but even that was uncertain. Their methods were flawed, but the ideas behind them weren't. Not completely.

"You've been awfully quiet since the clinic, Candy Cane," Mica said over a bite of lasagna. "Anything you want to share?"

She shook her head. "No, just thinking."

He hummed thoughtfully. "What about?"

"Stuff."

The response garnered her a raised eyebrow, but little else. "Well, if you need to talk it out…"

"I'll let you know."

They ate in silence for a while, Candace thankful that he didn't press for answers. She didn't have any to give him, anyway.

"Can I ask you a question?" Mica asked.

She looked up from her salad. "I suppose."

"You talked about your cousin a lot during those interrogations, but you haven't said who he is. I was wondering if you'd tell me his name. Would I know him?"

"Personally?" She smirked. "I doubt it."

He gave her a flat look.

Was it smart to tell him? Probably not. But it wasn't like you couldn't figure it out by looking at pictures. "Gabriel Vandermeer."

Mica's jaw went slack. "Gabriel Vandermeer? As in, Pavo Team Gabriel Vandermeer?"

"Don't tell me you couldn't guess that. We could pass for brother and sister we look so much alike."

He snapped his mouth closed. "Yeah, I suppose I can see that. It didn't occur to me before." Mica shifted in his seat, the tiniest hint of color in his cheeks.

Gradually, Candace interpreted his reaction. A grin crept across her mouth, smug as a cat. "For what it's worth, I think you two would get on pretty well. You have a mutual fondness for teasing me."

His eyes snapped up to hers, wide with surprise. "I wasn't... I didn't mean..."

"Uh huh," she said, chuckling. "You have a weakness for blonds, right?"

"Yeah, well..." He sighed and went back to picking at his food. "Hardly matters. Your cousin is all over the place in teen magazines and interviews, not to mention he's an ANGEL. He'd probably kill me on sight."

"Mica?"

He looked up again, some of the spark gone from his eyes. "Yeah?"

"For what it's worth, I wouldn't let him kill you." At that, his smile returned, albeit a little less bright than it had been.

"Also..."

"Hmm?"

"Don't believe everything you read," she said cryptically.

Candace left it at that, opting to take a long drink of water instead. Her words left him speechless, more or less the effect she was going for. If Gabe figured it was fine to meddle with her love life, why not return the favor?

The problem of HEX versus ANGELs remained, however, and her momentary good mood dimmed considerably. Even if she got out of there, it would be right back into ANGEL Project control — back to a life hidden away from the world, obscured with lies.

And what of HEX? They weren't any more to blame for carrying out Dr. Ferdinand's orders than she was for obeying Dr. Poznanski and General Jacobs. But what would the ANGEL Project do with those Supers? Kill them? Torture them? Brainwash them? She hated any of those options, but would anyone listen to her? After proving her theory with Kristie, had they adjusted their practices permanently? Granted, she only accomplished what she did with Jackson's help, but...

Jackson.

The thought stopped her cold and her fork clattered to the table. Memories of the sensations that woke her in the night flared into white hot pain. How far would he go to find her? What line would he cross? The thought of him taking his manipulation of Kristie to that extreme was nauseating.

She pushed away from the table and stood.

"What's wrong?" Mica asked. "Where are you going?"

Candace picked up her plate and tried to keep it

together. "Back to my room. I..." She swallowed. "I didn't sleep well last night."

He gave her an odd look, but didn't comment. Instead, they cleared their dishes and he walked her back.

"Any chance you can keep Chuck out of my hair for a while?" she asked as Mica unlocked her door.

"Sure, Candy Cane," he said with an understanding smile. "I'll see if Graham has a shopping list for him. That'll keep him busy for a few hours."

Nodding, she stepped inside. "Thanks," she said.

"No problem," he said. "Someone will be back for you at dinner."

When he was gone, Candace curled up in bed, fighting back the urge to vomit, to scream, to throw things in frustration. What she needed was to calm down and think it through. How could she get out of there without putting every one of them in danger? Was it even possible? The moment the ANGEL Project located her was the moment every last person in that place would face death or a lifetime of misery.

There had to be a way to spare them.

BREATHLESSNESS.

Tingling.

Racing pulse.

And then came her tears. There was no mistaking it. The ache in her heart was undeniable.

Jackson was with someone else.

Torn between wanting to die and wanting to run to him as fast as she could, Candace was paralyzed, trying to steady her breathing through the tears. Did he know she could feel him that way? If he did, maybe he would've waited, hesitated, thought twice.

But, no. Maybe he thought she was dead. Maybe he needed the comfort of someone else's arms.

He waited two weeks.

Two weeks.

She punched the mattress, her anger overtaking the soul-crushing sadness. She had to get out of there. The longer she stayed, the worse it would be for everyone.

And if it continued, if she had to feel much more of that, she might not want to leave. She might not be able to face it. Even as it was, how was she going to look him in the eye?

Candace sat up and slung her legs over the bed, rubbing her face. Getting out meant alerting the ANGEL Project to her whereabouts, and she still didn't have a solid plan. There was a chance she could leave one of her marks outside the mine entrance, but HEX would immediately know about it, would probably get rid of it, and then shove her back in that cell. She didn't even know what the outside looked like, let alone where to place Jackson's brand.

With a sigh of disgust, she stood and paced the room. There had to be some way.

She was so deep in thought, the sudden banging on the door nearly gave her a heart attack. When she opened it, Michele was standing there, looking none too pleased.

"With me. Now."

EVOLUTION: HEX

"Are you my date tonight, Mitchell?" Candace said with a sweet smile.

Rather than reply, Michele turned on her heel and stalked down the hall. Candace hurried after, not sure where they were going, but thinking she was meant to follow. They didn't head to the kitchen, and instead Candace found herself in Dr. Ferdinand's office again.

The Boss was behind her desk, frowning at the screen of her laptop. Michele all but shoved Candace into a chair, then took up a post in front of the door.

Dr. Ferdinand looked up, slowly turning the computer until Candace could see the picture and news article. All of her humor died the moment she took it in.

MYSTERIOUS MARK APPEARS IN PUBLIC PARK

And there in the photo, just as she imagined it would look, was Jackson's brand, carved in the dead grass of the Utah park behind the ice cream parlor.

"I assume this is your doing?" Dr. Ferdinand asked.

Candace swallowed hard and nodded. "It is."

"Why?"

She took a deep breath and met the doctor's stare. "To let them know I was alive. Well, not so much them. Just one person, really."

"Oh, well if that's all, mission accomplished," Dr. Ferdinand said, grimacing. "The ANGEL Project is all over the place now, looking for you. Anything else I should know?"

Candace crossed her arms. "As in, did I leave any markers

here?"

Dr. Ferdinand nodded.

"No. All I wanted to do was let them know I was alive. I haven't given away your location. However..." She stopped, considering the wisdom in what she was about to do. She wasn't coming up with any answers on her own. Maybe that was her chance.

"However?" Dr. Ferdinand prompted.

Closing her eyes, Candace made a decision. "I don't think it's me you have to worry about giving you away."

"Oh, really," she said. "Please explain."

"If she hasn't already, it's only a matter of time before Kristie tells them about this place."

"And how would you know that?"

"She's the one that told us about Aspen," Candace said. "She developed an affinity for..." She swallowed back a surge of bile. "For my boyfriend. He used that to our advantage. With me gone, he'll be desperate to find me, and..." Could she say it out loud? Voicing her suspicions might make them true, and she desperately wanted them not to be. "Anyway, I'm pretty sure he'll get what he's after. If he hasn't gotten the location by now, I think you've got a few days, tops, before he does."

"Oh, Kristie..." Michele murmured from the back of the room.

Dr. Ferdinand rubbed her forehead, frowning. "That girl has problems. I wasn't sad to see her go, to be honest, but I never thought the ANGELs would let her live. If I had..." She sighed. "It doesn't matter. Kristie isn't strong. She was loyal to Dimitri and Caleb, but once they were gone she was difficult to manage. It's entirely possible she'll psychologically destabilize if she's pushed any more. If what you're saying is true—"

"It is," Candace said. "I know him. There's nothing he wouldn't do to find me." Exactly *what* he had done would be a matter of discussion for another time. She couldn't deal with that at the moment. "I need to leave, and I don't want people getting hurt."

"You know I can't just let you go, Candace," she said. "They won't leave us alone if we set you free."

"I know," Candace said. "There's another problem too, though it's more my problem than yours."

"And what's that?"

She chewed her lip as it played out in her head. "Going back means I'll have to lie to them. After everything I've learned, it's different than when I first signed on to the Project. I can't go back and not try to change things, and that's dangerous for me."

"You want to change things?"

"Don't you?"

Dr. Ferdinand sat back in her chair and studied Candace. "So what are you proposing?"

She shook her head. "That's the problem. I don't know. I've been thinking about it a lot. I don't know how I'm going to get out of here and maintain that I'm still an ANGEL through and through. If I'm walking around free as a bird, they'll never buy it. They'd have to rescue me. But, again, I won't ask anyone here to put themselves in danger on my account. No one here would do that for me, anyway. I don't think anyone but Mica gives a crap about me. I mean, why should they? I've killed their friends, their girlfriends, and for what? Someone else's war, that's what. So, you see where I might be hitting the wall with it."

Dr. Ferdinand's gaze shifted to Michele. "What do you think? It could be the opportunity we've been waiting for."

Opportunity? What was that about?

"It's too risky," Michele said. "How do you know we wouldn't be killed on sight?"

"Can you think of a better way?" Dr. Ferdinand asked.

"I'm sorry," Candace interrupted. "What opportunity? What are you trying to do?"

Dr. Ferdinand looked back and forth between her and Michele. After several moments, she finally spoke. "We want to get HEX inside the ANGEL compound."

Candace paled. "You what? Why?"

She lifted an eyebrow in response.

Candace shook her head. "I won't condone needless killing. If that's what you intend to do, I won't support it."

"You know there might not be another way."

"I don't believe that. Killing is the easy answer, but not necessarily the right one."

Dr. Ferdinand said nothing.

Candace picked at her nails and considered the problem. "Look, what is it you really want? To find your son? I mean, he might not even be in California. For all I know, they hold people at the Virginia compound too, and who knows where else. If that's what you're looking for, are you willing to risk other people to get it? If so, they need to know the truth."

Michele lowered herself into the seat beside Candace, her expression strange. "You don't think someone needs to do something about what's going on at the ANGEL Project?"

"Oh, I do," Candace said. "But there has to be a better way to go about it. I mean, what if the other ANGELs knew what I know now? Some of them would have something to say about that. Not to mention the problem with being kept like a pet rat in a cage. A few of them might be happy to live that way, but I can think of more that would rather be *in* the world saving it, than standing to the side and taking orders. Right now, it's my word over everyone else there. Either the other ANGELs don't know, or won't tell. The Supers are sheltered, shielded from all of this. I'm going to be under constant scrutiny when I get back. They'll want to know everything I learned or saw here. If they think for one second I'm not on board with their program, that's it. I'm done. So if you expect others to take a bigger risk than that, you'd better have a really good plan. Otherwise, you might as well pack up and run."

Michele leaned forward on the armrest, her face bereft of any malice. "Do you think you can protect us? Like you did Kristie?"

"Us?" Candace stared. "As in, you're volunteering?"

"Do you think you can or not?"

She chewed on her fingernail. Could she make that kind of promise? She didn't even know how safe *she* would be when she got there. "Honestly?"

Michele nodded.

"Honestly, I want to say yes, but I can't see the future. I don't want anyone to get hurt more than they have been already. I could lie and say sure, without a doubt, but that's not who I am. I'll do my absolute best. That's all I can promise. That's more than you'll get from them if they catch you unprepared here."

Michele's gaze was so intense, so piercing, Candace almost couldn't breathe.

"You'd better be sure about this, Candy Cane." Michele's voice echoed in her head.

Candace jumped up and skittered away, out of her seat. "How did you do that? How are you in my brain?"

The cryptic smile on Michele's face said everything. "How else would I know you're telling the truth?"

Well, great. First empaths, then a mind-reader? That would be her luck. "How did you do that?"

She shrugged. "The same way you move water. I'm just firing off a few synapses in your brain that tell you that you heard something. I can't make you do stuff so chill, okay? I can see your motivations, but only read your thoughts in a vague sense. So I know if you're lying and sort of why, but it's more like pictures than exact words. Get it?"

"That doesn't make me feel any better."

"Well, tough," she said. "I've been doing it from the start with you, so no need to be weird about it now."

"Sometimes ignorance is bliss, you know," Candace grumbled.

"Ladies," Dr. Ferdinand said. "Can we focus?"

Candace slowly sank back into her chair. "So what do you suggest we do?"

"I'd like to leave a small contingent of HEX behind and give away the location," Dr. Ferdinand said. "Most of us will clear out and make it look like this was strictly a holding facility. Those we leave behind won't be ones that could put up much of a fight anyway, as I'll need most of the physical abilities to rebuild elsewhere. The people here will be easily subdued. Do you think the orders will be to capture alive or kill on sight?"

"The orders were to capture alive up through Aspen. I can't make any promises as far as some of the ANGELs go, though. If they're upset enough, any reason to fight will provoke them. They've lost friends and loved ones, too," Candace said.

"It would be easy enough to say we want to flip sides," Michele said. "Being hunted by the government does get old after a while. So does living in a hole in the ground."

"Do you think you can be convincing?" Candace asked.

"Please help us! We're prisoners here as much as she is!" Michele's voice rattled inside her mind, accompanying a plaintive look.

Candace pinched her eyes shut and rubbed her temples. "Okay, I get it. Please quit with that. It gives me a headache."

Michele smirked. "Yeah, I think I can convince them."

"I'm thinking you and Mica," Dr. Ferdinand said. "Perhaps Lucie and Tori as well. And maybe Naveen?"

"Naveen?" Michele said. "You think he's ready?"

"He's eager to do something. You know that."

"But he's never used his ability in a fight. What if he can't keep it together under pressure? He could get himself or others killed."

"What does he do?" Candace asked, curious.

"Temperature manipulation," Dr. Ferdinand explained. "Specifically, he displaces heat, freezing things."

"Hmm," Candace murmured. "That could be tricky. What if…" An idea sprang to mind. "How are Mica's acting skills, Mitch?"

"Good enough he's fooled me more than once." She chuckled.

"Well, what if he sets off some of his knockout gas inside the compound? If he could find a way to warn the ANGELs ahead of time, they might think he really is a traitor. If Mica hands them the keys to the kingdom, so to speak, they probably won't do much to him once he's been captured."

"That has the added benefit of no one getting hurt in a fight," Dr. Ferdinand said. "I can work out the details with him, see how he feels about it."

It was a start, but it was still working without a safety net. "So, what's the backup plan? What if I can't protect anybody once we're back in California? I'm not comfortable with the risks once we're there."

Dr. Ferdinand shrugged. "Chuck's the backup plan. He can pop in and out from a hundred miles away if he has someone to lock on to. If it's someone he knows, he can find them and get them out easily enough."

Chuck again. The chance of him dropping in on her with no warning was not something she was comfortable with. "How will he know if he needs to pull people?"

"Me," Michele said. "I can send him short status updates remotely. Even if I'm locked up, I can tell him what's going on."

"And you can run messages to me through her as well, Candace," Dr. Ferdinand added. "If they let you resume ANGEL status, that is."

"I can't make any promises on the time frame for this. We might be looking at months or more," Candace said. "Any changes that happen will have to be gradual or they'll suspect something. I won't be a party to mass murder."

"I understand."

"And you understand that if I don't like the way things are going, I'm done, right?" Candace wasn't ready to completely give up her loyalties yet. The line was too fuzzy. "I won't screw you over, but I won't let this turn into another one of your *mistakes*."

"We understand each other completely then, Miss Bristol," Dr. Ferdinand said. "I'm willing to give your methods a chance."

Candace let go of a held breath. "Thank you."

"We'll discuss this more in detail once I've had some time to think on it and plan with the others," she said. "Michele, would you mind taking her for dinner?"

Michele stood and waved Candace towards the door. "C'mon newbie. We're being dismissed. You hungry?"

The knots in her stomach said otherwise, but Candace nodded anyway.

CHAPTER 5

"THIS ISN'T going to feel good."

Candace nodded and closed her eyes. "I'm ready. Just do it."

The HEX woman, Tori, took a deep breath and set one hand on Candace's forehead, the other resting on her shoulder.

When Candace asked why she didn't wake up with wounds from Aspen, Michele introduced her to Tori Drake. The Super had the ability to speed up and reverse healing in the body. It explained why Candace awoke without pain in the cell, clearing up some of her confusion.

As they staged Candace's captivity for the ANGEL raid, they had to reverse some of that. In order to make everything as convincing as possible, she had to look the part of a prisoner, which meant a small amount of mistreatment, including not showering or changing clothes for three days. To further the illusion, she was about to relive the damage she took in Aspen.

The pain crept up on her slowly, her body rewinding, the wounds reopening. Candace pulled at the restraints holding her to the bed, trying not to cry out as the dull ache bloomed into full-blown agony inside her skull. Her shoulder was little more than an annoyance in comparison.

When Tori broke contact, the pain dimmed to throbbing pulses of discomfort. Candace took several deep breaths before opening her eyes.

Tori's face was pinched, worried. Her dark blonde hair hung past her face as she bent to examine her work.

"Is it too bad? After three weeks of healing, the worst of it wouldn't be there, so you're lucky that I don't have to take you back any further," she said, her large, dark eyes meeting Candace's.

"I'll get through it, pending I don't have to wait too long. Any word from Mica on the timeline?"

Tori shook her head and stood, checking the flow of the IV line. "Nothing yet. He's been gone for two days now. I'm worried something's wrong, but Michele says it's fine. I was just told to be ready, not when it's coming."

The five days since initial planning were a whirlwind of activity interspersed with multiple devastating instances of feeling Jackson. The periods of connection mostly occurred during sleep, but once or twice took her out at the knees in the middle of preparing the compound for the raid. Candace nearly dropped a medical monitor once, prompting some uncomfortable questions from Dr. Ferdinand. It was all she could do to not break down into tears.

That day had been quiet, however, and a foreboding sense of urgency replaced some of the ache in her heart. Either Kristie gave in, or Mica finally got through. Whichever it was, Jackson's tension was seeping into her. The ANGELs were on their way.

As she watched the slow drip of the IV hooked into her arm, Candace was a giant ball of nerves. She wouldn't be awake for the attack, as everyone in the compound would be knocked out, and knowing she'd be unable to fight or defend left her uneasy. There was no way for her to protect anyone should things not go according to plan.

Hours passed with nothing for her to do but worry. When the hiss of gas reached her ears, it set her pulse racing. She panicked, but it didn't last long.

Within seconds, Candace was out cold.

EACH BEAT of her heart throbbed in her head. Candace groaned.

"Ah, I believe she's coming around. Mr. Clusky, best go let Mr. Lawrence know before he rips something out of the wall."

Her eyes flew open. She knew that voice.

The familiar sights of the ANGEL compound's clinic greeted her, quickly followed by Dr. Poznanski's face.

"Well, hello there, Miss Bristol," he said, smiling. "Nice

to have you with us again."

Candace swallowed. "I'm... back?" she said, looking around. "How? When?"

Before he could answer, the door burst open, and Jackson ran in, instantly on her. His lips felt like fire as they closed over hers, not wasting a moment on words.

At first overcome with relief, Candace stilled in his arms as realization bore down on her. Every instance of connection with him while she was with HEX exploded in her head, and she couldn't hide the tears. Face pinched, she pushed him away.

He had been with someone else.

Jackson opened his mouth to speak, but she put a hand up, silencing him. She shook her head and looked away.

"Candy, I—"

"Not now. I'm not talking to you about that yet. I can't."

His face paled. "What..."

"I know, Jackson," she said, unable to more than glance at him. "But there are other things I need to deal with first. I think you should go." She swallowed past the hurt and tried to focus. Her head was pounding, and he wasn't helping.

Dr. Poznanski set a hand on his shoulder and gently pulled Jackson away. "She's right, Mr. Lawrence. We have to see to her injuries, and she needs to be debriefed. Now that you've seen her, you need to go."

Stunned, Jackson backed out of the room, his mouth working at silent arguments but unable to voice them. Finally, he gave up, turned and left.

Candace choked back a sob. The hurt in his eyes was so raw, so ragged, if she thought about it much more she was sure she'd go running into his arms. There were other things to do first, though. She needed to know the situation before she could figure out how to proceed. The line she walked was little more than a thread, and one misstep could cost her everything.

"First off," Dr. Poznanski said, pulling up a stool beside her cot. "Welcome back. We thought we lost you after Aspen."

"I'm not that easy to kill," she said, the joke falling flat as she spoke.

"Well, they did give it the old college try, didn't they?" He chuckled. "The injuries you sustained could've been life-threatening, but it looks like they treated you at least a little. Is that correct?"

Candace sighed. It was showtime already. "I don't really know. They kept me unconscious for about a week as best as I can estimate. After that it's pretty fuzzy too. They were drugging me pretty heavily for interrogation purposes." When his eyebrows lifted, she hastily carried on. "There wasn't any pain involved, but I couldn't think clearly. I think that went on for about a week before I convinced them I wasn't going to go on a killing spree."

"Yes, about that," he said. "You didn't put up much of a fight it would seem."

"If they thought I was going to kill them, they wouldn't have let up on the drugs, never mind me getting any useful information."

"And did you?"

Candace rubbed her forehead and winced. "Any chance I can get something for this headache before we go into that?"

Dr. Poznanski smiled and nodded. For the first time ever, his expression gave her little comfort, not after everything she'd learned.

It wasn't hard to fake her way through the exam and medical assistance as far as her healing injuries were concerned. They expected her to be tired and irritable after three weeks away. Finally, they left her alone with an IV of saline solution and nothing but peace and quiet.

Though she wasn't physically tired, Candace closed her eyes and relished the moment of reprieve. It might be the last she got before the situation got more complicated.

Two hours in, the door cracked open, and Gabe's head appeared. With the uncertainty of everything else in her life, finally, there was something that was simple.

He grinned when he saw her. "Hey, cuz."

It was easy to smile for him. "Hey yourself. Good to see you didn't forget about me."

As though nothing changed, Candace slid to the side and curled up against him when he laid beside her. Gabe was her lifeline. When the world was a giant mess, he would always be her safety net. The feel of his arms as they surrounded her in a hug settled her nerves.

"Are you okay?"

She nodded against his shoulder. "I mean, I've been better, but I'll heal. It wasn't as bad as it could've been, but I'm glad to be back."

"I bet. You must've been glad to see him again."

Ouch. How was she going to explain that one? "Yeah, I guess."

Gabe paused, then pulled back to look at her. "You know he was a mess without you."

"Didn't stop him from…" The words died on her tongue. That wound was still fresh.

"Candy Cane?"

She lifted her eyes to his, fighting back tears. "He was with someone else, Gabe. I felt it. I…"

His eyebrows shot up into his hairline. "What? Jackson? No way. No way would he have…" He trailed off, cold anger replacing his shock. "I'll kill him, Candy. If you don't, I will. I swear to God if he—"

She shook her head fiercely, pain lancing through her skull. "No, don't. I mean, maybe I'm wrong, but I think I know who and why. I just… it's complicated, okay? What he did—"

"You're telling me you're okay with him fu—"

"No," she interrupted. "I'm not. I'm not okay with that at all, but there's more to it than what you think. I don't know everything yet, though, so I can't say for sure."

"I don't care what his excuse is. He hurt you."

She sighed and sat up, dangling her legs over the edge of the bed. "If it was who I think it was, he was doing it to help me."

"Hold on," Gabe said, sitting up beside her. "You think it was with the HEX girl?"

Candace nodded.

"Why would you think that?"

"Because she likes him," Candace said. "He was the one that got her to tell us about Aspen. I was there. I saw how she reacted to him. Some of my feelings for him seeped into her because we were connected by water."

"And you think he would've gone that far with it?"

Pinching her eyes shut, she tried to keep the mental images of Jackson and Kristie at bay. "I think he was desperate and couldn't think of anything else."

He was quiet for a while, considering it. "So, what are you going to do?"

She shrugged. "I don't know. I have no idea what the situation is, so I can't make that call yet."

"Well, at least that explains why they decided to let her out of her cell. No wonder they were so sure she'd behave."

Candace jerked and stared at him. "They what?"

Gabe nodded. "Yep. About a week ago they let her out for the first time. Jackson was with her every second. I thought it was because he could counter her ability, but maybe that wasn't the case?"

Son of a bitch. That would complicate things even more. How would Kristie react to her being back? And since the girl had a taste of Jackson, would she be able to let him go?

Covering her face with her hands, Candace grumbled unintelligible curses into her palms.

Chuckling lightly, Gabe rubbed her back. "Welcome home, Candy Cane. I missed your drama."

WHEN SHE walked into Dr. Poznanski's office, she wasn't prepared to see Mica sitting there, too. Candace came to a halt inside the door, unable to hide her surprise.

"Not to worry, Miss Bristol," Dr. Poznanski said, misinterpreting her hesitation. "This is Mica Reynolds. He's an ally."

"Yes," General Jacobs added. "Without his help, your rescue would have been a very different situation."

She slipped into the role of cluelessness. "And how's that, exactly?"

"Sit, and we'll explain everything," Dr. Poznanski said, motioning to a chair.

Candace eased into the seat, warily shifting away from Mica. "As far as I know, all he's done is drug me into oblivion on multiple occasions."

"Sorry about that," Mica said, grinning. "Keeping up appearances and all."

"Uh huh."

"We initially got the location from Miss Burke, thanks to Mr. Lawrence's assistance," Dr. Poznanski said. Candace fought down the urge to vomit. "When Mr. Reynolds reached out to us, we used him as confirmation of the information. Courtesy of his chemical concoctions, the entire HEX compound you were being held at was flooded with a knock-out gas, subduing everyone inside. All that was left for us was retrieving you and taking the others into custody."

Candace fidgeted. "How many others? Where are they now?"

The General cleared his throat. "You were being guarded by a small contingent of five individuals, including Mr. Reynolds. Aside from him, the others are being held here."

"And what about Dr. Ferdinand? Have you found her?"

EVOLUTION: HEX

Dr. Poznanski shook his head. "No. She wasn't one of them."

Candace chewed her lip, wondering what to say next. At that point, she was playing everything by ear and needed to be cautious.

"Did you have any contact with her while you were being held?" the General asked.

"Some," she said. "But, like I told Dr. Poznanski, I was drugged for a majority of the time and it all sort of runs together."

"And yet you somehow managed to get out and leave those marks," General Jacobs said, raising a suspicious eyebrow.

She nodded. "One of the HEX members has a teleportation ability. He got permission to take me out one night. I thought if I let him, I might have a chance to get word to you, but I had to be careful."

"But you didn't leave a mark at the holding facility." The General's disdain for her wasn't surprising. She needed to convince them all she was still on the ANGEL side of the fence.

"Correct. It would have given me away, but they probably would've killed me for it," she said. "That, and with my head finally out of the fog, I thought I might be able to collect information for you if I ever got out. Those marks would at least have told Jackson, or maybe Gabe, that I was still alive."

"Your cousin was the one to identify it first," Dr. Poznanski said. "Mr. Lawrence confirmed. It was the first time in the two weeks following Aspen he had a conversation with us without setting something on fire."

Jackson must've been at the end of his rope if they weren't doing anything to find her. Really, what could they have done? Without knowing if she was alive, coupled with not knowing where to look, their hands were tied.

"Do we know where Dr. Ferdinand might be now?" Candace asked. "I only saw her a few times, but I didn't get much more from her than a bunch of questions."

"We have a few leads, but nothing solid," Dr. Poznanski said. "Mr. Reynolds wasn't there for her departure. We suspect his absence raised alarms and caused her to pack up."

She nodded, then frowned. "But why leave me behind? I mean, why not keep me as a bargaining chip at least?"

"She's looking to disappear again," Mica said. "Her army isn't large enough to take on the ANGELs yet, so she's still building. Holding on to you would make it harder to cover her tracks and give us more reasons to go after her."

She narrowed her eyes at him. "Us?"

Mica's smile shone like the sun. "Us. I'm an ANGEL now."

Fighting off the urge to grin was one of the hardest things she'd done in weeks, which was saying a lot. "Huh. Congratulations, I guess," she said, pinching her lips into a grimace. *Be convincing. Be convincing.*

"We believe Mr. Reynolds' unusual gifts with chemistry will be very helpful to the ANGEL Project's mission," Dr. Poznanski said. "And even Miss Nasik agrees he's sincere in his desire to join us."

Interesting. If Deborah gave him the all-clear, how much

did she know? Or did Mica really want to be an ANGEL after all?

"How did you even get in here?" Candace asked. "I mean, it's not like you could just walk up to the building and knock on the door."

"I talked to Chuck," he said, shrugging. "He told me where you guys went that night, so I tracked down one of your marks they hadn't found yet. Anonymous media tips are a magical thing."

"Mr. Sokol was looking into your marks, Miss Bristol," Dr. Poznanski said. "That's when Mr. Reynolds came forward."

"Which one?" she said, looking at Mica.

"Boron," he replied with an amused grin.

"That was my first mark. How come no one found it before?"

Mica shrugged. "No one in that little town pays any attention to anything. If they saw it, they didn't care."

It sounded believable enough, but there was much of it she didn't have a part in planning. Dr. Ferdinand wanted her to have some plausible deniability. At least, that's what she said. It was likely she had plans of her own on top of what they discussed.

The remainder of the debriefing consisted of Candace telling them very little. Since she was a prisoner, most of what it made sense to offer up was what she knew about the HEX members' abilities. She excused her vagueness, blaming it on her injuries and lack of clear thinking during the majority of her captivity. General Jacobs didn't look completely convinced, but at least he wasn't openly hostile.

When she stepped out of the office, Mica went with her.

"So, where are you headed?" he asked.

She glanced down at her clothes and sighed. Cleaning up meant going to the room she shared with Jackson. She still wasn't ready to face that.

"I don't know."

"Don't you have a room here?"

"Yes, but... it's complicated," she said.

Mica ran a hand through his hair. "Look, I know you don't trust me, but I swear I'm on your side. Ask Deborah if you don't believe me."

Oh, she definitely planned on doing that, but not until she could get a shower. They had to be extremely careful. They needed to pretend like they weren't friends. "We'll see."

"You can ask me anything you want to know."

"Hmm," she murmured and headed out of the clinic, Mica on her heels.

"So where are you going?"

"Why are you following me?"

"Because..." he trailed off, his steps slowing. "Because I think you might be the only one here that will give me a chance."

Candace paused, frowning. They were in full public view, and she had to make it convincing. "Look, Mica, was it? It's not like we're friends or anything. I'm a pretty forgiving and open-minded person, but, seriously? You spent the majority of the last few weeks pumping who-knows-what into my body and bombarding me with questions. As much as I'd like to, I can't just snap my fingers and get over it."

He scuffed his foot along the floor, staring at the tiles. "I know. And I get that. I just... do you think you can give me a shot? I want to make up for it if I can."

Candace crossed her arms and watched him. He was either a master actor, or he really did mean it. "You don't seem like a terrible person or anything, but I've got a lot of shit to deal with right now. You're not my first priority, got it?"

"So you'll give me a chance then?" he said, hopeful.

Turning on her heel, she sighed. "Yeah, I guess. Just, give me some breathing room, all right? Find someone else to hang around for a while."

When she walked away, he didn't follow.

CHAPTER 6

CANDACE KNOCKED, hoping someone was in the room.

The door opened, revealing the shocked face of True Clemmons. "Candace?"

"Hey, got a—" her words were cut off as True wrapped her in a hug.

"Oh my lord, sugar, I've been worried sick!"

Candace chuckled and returned the embrace. "I missed you, too." She winced at the pain in her shoulder. "True," she said with a wheeze. "Can you ease up just a smidge?"

True dropped the stranglehold abruptly. "I'm so sorry! Are you hurt? Here, come on in and tell me."

"Thanks," Candace said. "I'm okay, still healing, though. I was hoping to ask you for a favor or two."

"Anything. What do you need?"

"First? A shower and some fresh clothes, if you have any to spare. Nothing fancy, I just..." She sighed. "I'm not ready to go back to my room yet. That's the second thing. I need some advice."

True's forehead bunched, worried, but she didn't ask any questions. "You got it. Go get started on your shower, and I'll toss some things in after I hear the water running for a bit."

Good as her word, clothes were waiting for Candace when she finished cleaning up. True really had the best things. The beautiful light blue sweater and dark wash jeans fit like they were made for her body. Hair still wet, Candace emerged from the bathroom, curling the steam around her hands and sending it off in spirals to the ceiling.

"When did you get that ability?" True asked as she watched on, amused.

"About a month ago," Candace said. "A few days before Aspen."

True patted the mattress beside her. "Come talk to me, Candy Cane. What's on your mind?"

She sank down on the bed, the small comfort of the shower fading. "I need some advice. Do you know much about what's going on with Kristie?"

True grimaced. "The crazy ass HEX girl? The one who's attached herself to Jackson's hip? That Kristie?"

Candace nodded.

"They let her out last week for the first time, right about when they discovered your little marks. It was just for dinner the first day, then all the meals the next. Two days ago they let her out completely, pending someone is with her at all times. That someone is almost always Jackson. I take it this is a problem?"

"Jackson and I share a connection, like next level with the imprinting," Candace explained, rubbing her forehead. Her headache wasn't going away. "I can feel extremes from him, like fear, anger, or when... you know."

"Hang on, you mean like during sex?"

She nodded.

"So what's the... oh," True said, realizing where it was going. Her jaw twitched, and her eyes started to darken. "Candy Cane, if you're telling me he was sleeping with that nutjob I will—"

"That's what I'm telling you, yes, but it was a means to an end, I'm pretty sure. At least, I was sure that's what it was when it started. Please don't do anything. I'm just trying to figure it out."

True sucked in a series of deep, calming breaths. "So that's how they got the location of the HEX compound."

"That and confirmation from the other guy, Mica."

"Candy, I never suspected for a minute he had feelings for anyone but you," True said. "Jackson's barely been holding it together since Aspen. He put all the blame for your capture on himself. No one could talk to him for two weeks after that."

"So he found a way to do something about it," Candace said. "The thing is, I hate it more than I can tell you. That level of manipulation on his part, to say nothing about him sleeping with someone else... True, it's killing me. Even if he did what he did to try and save me, I can't just walk back in there like it's okay." A tear escaped and slid down her cheek. "What do I do? If it was you and Amir, how would you handle it?"

She leaned forward on her elbows and considered it. "I dunno, Candy Cane. I guess the best place to start is to talk it out. I don't have a clue what's going on in Jackson's head, but if it was me and Amir there would be many, many conversations about it."

Candace lapsed into silence, thinking about the whole situation. Really, what else could she do? She had to talk to him eventually. At last check, all her stuff was in his room... unless he'd moved her out, which wasn't out of the question considering everything else he'd done.

"Did you have dinner already?" Candace asked.

"Nope. Hungry?"

"Starved."

"Can I do something about your hair first?"

"My..." Candace touched her still-damp strands. "You want to fix my hair?"

"Are you kidding?" True grinned. "I've wanted to get my hands on it since you showed me the floaty thing it does."

Candace giggled, despite everything. "All right, though I think you'll be disappointed. It doesn't do a damn thing I tell it to."

SHE WAS finally home.

Sitting with True, Amir, and Gabe made everything so

much easier to bear. It was like stepping into a favorite pair of broken-in sneakers: comfortable, with a perfect fit.

At least, it was until they had company.

"Hey now!" a loud, male voice called from halfway across the dining hall. "Who's that in my seat?"

"Shit…" Amir cursed under his breath. "I forgot about him."

Candace turned to see who he was talking about and promptly whipped back around.

Christian Markov, the original poster boy for the ANGEL Project, was headed their way. Should she leave? Stand her ground? What was she supposed to say to him? How was she supposed to act?

"Well, I was going to complain about a seat thief," he said as he stopped beside her. "But I think I'm willing to overlook it in this case." Not bothering to ask, he elbowed his way onto the bench across from Candace, pushing Amir and True to the side. "And who might you be?"

Torn between telling the asshole off and the screaming fangirl in her head, Candace forced a smile. "Candace Bristol," she said.

"A pleasure to meet you, Candace," he said, flashing her a fifty-watt grin. "I'm Christian Markov, but you probably know that already. You can call me Chris."

Holy crap. They weren't kidding when they said he had an ego. "Nice to meet you. I've heard quite a bit about you," she said as calmly as she could manage. "I wonder if you'd apologize to my friends, though. We were in the middle of a conversation when you pushed them aside."

He blinked at her, as though her words were in a foreign

language. "What?"

"My friends," she said. "You were rude. You should apologize."

Gabe was choking on laughter. She kicked him under the table.

Candace didn't think she ever saw a person more confused than Christian Markov was at that moment. He studied her, as though trying to figure out if she was being serious. Her quick glance at Amir and True revealed amused expressions on both of their faces.

"Well?" she asked.

Christian blinked a few times, then turned to them. "Uh, sorry, guys. Didn't mean to butt in."

"No problem, Chris," Amir said, biting back a laugh.

When Christian looked away, True tossed Candace a quick wink before she resumed eating.

"So, Candace," Christian said as his sparkling blue eyes locked onto her again. "Are you this infamous water bug I keep hearing about?"

"I don't know." She looked at Gabe. "Am I infamous around here?"

"Seems fitting." He grinned and stuffed a bite of salad in his mouth.

That was so not helpful. She gave him a look of reproach and turned back to Christian. "I suppose that's the best I can do for an answer, sorry."

"But you manipulate water right?"

She nodded, wary. "Yes, why?"

Christian leaned forward and gave her the most winning smile he could muster. "Well, I've got a little plumbing problem, and I was wondering if you might help me out."

There was so much tension at the table that no one even dared to breathe. As calmly as she could, Candace leaned toward him with a shy smile. Encouraged, Christian edged forward, his head precisely where she wanted it.

"I think I might have a solution for you," she purred.

"And what might that be, sweetheart?"

With a flick of her finger, every drop of water in the glass below his face shot straight up into the air, hitting him dead on. Christian flew back, coughing and sputtering, tipping over the edge of the bench.

Candace stood, lifting her tray and stepping to the side of the table to leave him with some last words. "That should help flush you out, Chris." She smiled sweetly, turned on her heel, and left, peals of laughter following her graceful exit.

OUT IN the hallway, Candace leaned up against the wall, trying to calm her racing heart. Christian Markov, the ANGEL that saved her years ago, made a pass at her, which she answered by sending water up his nose. It was not how she expected their first meeting to go. There would definitely be fallout later.

The problem with leaving the dining hall the way she had was that she didn't know what to do with herself after. Normally she'd eat and go back to her room, but, at the moment, that meant facing off with Jackson and confronting what he'd done.

EVOLUTION: HEX

The situation wasn't going to fix itself. It was time.

One foot in front of the other, Candace made her way down the hall to their room. Nearly there, voices carried from around the corner.

"You can't mean that. Just 'cause she's back doesn't mean anything's changed between us."

Candace came to a screeching halt, plastering herself to the side of the hall.

"You know we can't keep doing this, Kristie. I told you from the start, it was never a permanent thing."

"C'mon, Sunshine," she said, her voice low and throaty. "One more, for old time's sake?"

"Kristie—"

"She'll never know. I can do that thing you like. You know the one."

Ready to vomit if she had to listen to any more, Candace stepped into the open. "Yeah, Sunshine," she said, staring them down where Kristie pinned Jackson to a door. "She could do that thing you like. Seems silly to pass up the opportunity."

"Candace? Candace, I—" Jackson started, pushing Kristie to the side.

Candace held up a hand. "Save it." Turning around, she headed back the way she came. "You have fun with your new toy."

"Candace!" he called as he ran after her. "Candace, please stop!"

Nothing in that world or the next was going to stop her hasty retreat. Having suspicions was one thing, seeing him with her, right in front of her, was another. She was going to lose it for sure.

When his hand closed on her arm, she whirled and tossed it off. "Don't touch me," she hissed. "Don't you dare."

"Candace, listen to me, please," he said, begging. "You have to know, I only—"

"You don't get it," she cut him off. "I don't care. You never should have gone that far with her. Never. Why would you do that to me? To *us*? Did you think I wouldn't find out? Did you think I wouldn't feel it every time you… you…" God, she was so mad she couldn't even say it.

"Sugar Plum, please listen to me." He reached out to grab her again, but she dodged him.

"Don't call me that."

"Are you kids causing trouble again?" Gabe strode up, stopping beside her. "You gonna give him the Markov treatment too, Candy Cane?"

She gave him a warning look. "You still without a roommate?"

Gabe arched an eyebrow. "For the moment. Why?"

"Candace, don't do this," Jackson said. "Let me explain."

She hooked her cousin's arm and pulled him in the direction of his room. "I don't need an explanation, Jackson. Since I already know exactly how much you enjoyed fucking someone else, by all means, I won't stop you."

Gabe leaned in close. "Candy Cane, I think you need to calm down a little."

"I'm fine," she snapped back at him.

"Oh really," he said, pausing to open his door. "Candace, you barely let him say two words."

She stood in the middle of his room and wrapped her

arms around her stomach, trying desperately not to cry. "He didn't need to say anything, Gabe. I caught him. With her. Everything I thought might be true, actually turned out to be. I thought maybe there was a chance I was wrong. Maybe he wasn't with her like that. But he was. He was! I just... I can't..." Hysterical sobs cut through her tirade, and she dissolved into tears as Gabe's arms closed around her shoulders.

"Shh," he whispered, smoothing her hair. "Easy now. Easy."

"Every time I look at him, I'm going to see her, too," she bawled into his chest, overwhelmed by hurt and sadness. "I don't know how to not do that."

"It'll get better, Candy Cane. Give it time."

But they didn't have time. Everything was going to change, and she was going to make it happen. It was inevitable, and she would be behind it without Jackson beside her. She was stronger knowing he was with her; it made the world bearable. If she couldn't get past it, what then? Life without Jackson wasn't a life she wanted.

Gabe let her cry it out, patiently holding her until the sobs abated to sniffling whimpers.

"What do you want to do, Candy?" he asked.

"I can't do that again," she said with a hiccup. "I can't see him again tonight. I can't. I know I'm such a pain in the ass. I'm sorry."

He stood in front of where she sat on the edge of the bed. "Give me your badge."

"Why?"

"I'll go get some of your clothes. You can stay until you

work this out, okay?"

Her lip trembled. "You'd do that for me?"

"Of course, Candy Cane. I'll talk to him. I'll tell him what's going on."

Swallowing, she unclipped her badge and fingered it for a moment, hesitating. "Are you sure?"

Gabe took the badge from her and briefly touched the side of her face. "I'm sure. You know there's nothing I wouldn't do for my favorite cousin."

"I'm your *only* cousin," she mumbled half-heartedly.

"That too," he said with a wink. "Okay, I'll be back in bit."

When he was gone, Candace laid back on the bed with a tired sigh, rubbing her dried out eyes. It shouldn't be that hard. Jackson hadn't done what he did for himself, he did it for her. To save her. To find her. She knew that was the truth, but she couldn't get the feel of it out of her head. Knowing he felt those things with someone else was too much to get over in one night. Maybe she could eventually, but not yet.

Gabe was gone for nearly an hour before he came back with a box of her stuff. He set it on the desk and fished something out of it.

"I thought you might want to go for a swim," he said as he tossed her black bathing suit at her.

"Not if he's going to corner me the second I leave the room," she said.

"He won't," Gabe said. "I talked to him. He doesn't like it, but he's willing to give you some space. It'll give him time to lose the psycho, too."

Candace frowned. "Psycho? True called her crazy, too. What's the deal with that? Did Kristie do something?"

Sitting down on the edge of the bed, Gabe shrugged. "Not really, but there's something about her. I dunno. Ever meet one of those people where you just know they're wound super, super tight, and one more thing happens and they'll snap?"

"Yeah, I think I get what you mean."

"It's like that with her," he said. "There's this weird spark of crazy in her eyes. If she goes, Candy, it'll be bad. Someone with your power destabilizing is a scary thought."

"She doesn't have my power," Candace said. "Well, not like now. She's not nearly that strong. In fact, I'm pretty sure I was stronger than her even before the SAGE treatments… Wait." She paused, studying her cousin. "Did you already start the second round? I totally forgot. Weren't you supposed to—"

"They pushed it back after Aspen," Gabe said. "But now that you're here again, I imagine they'll start us up in a few days."

"They pushed it back because of me?"

"They needed Tobias to track you. They couldn't risk taking him out of the field if something surfaced, which it did. Nicely done with the marks, by the way. Clever. Anyway, I think they would've given you another week or two, tops, before they started us up. They almost pulled me from the plan."

"They did? Why?"

He smiled and pushed some hair behind one of her ears. "Jackson wasn't the only one worried about you."

She dropped her gaze to the floor. "I'm sorry you had to go through that."

"It wasn't your fault, Candy Cane. You pretty much saved all our asses out there. Whatever that HEX woman was doing, we were going to kill each other over it. You stopped her."

"Desiree," Candace mumbled, not even thinking about it. "Her name was Desiree. She generated a field of disorientation."

Gabe stilled beside her. "Did they tell you that?"

Shit. Don't flinch. Don't make a big deal out of it.

Candace nodded. "I don't remember too much through all the drugs they had me on, but a few details stood out. They wanted me to know exactly who I killed and who they were, to make me feel guilty, I guess. Not that I needed any more reasons. I didn't even know for sure if I'd hit that woman or not. It was a last ditch attempt before I completely lost it."

"Well, for what it's worth, you saved our lives," Gabe said, taking her hand. "I think that's what made it so bad for us, knowing that you saved us and were taken prisoner as a result. Jackson had it the worst. He blames himself because he hit you with that fireball at the end."

"It wasn't his fault," she said. "He wasn't thinking clearly. No one was. Not a day's gone by that I didn't remember the sound of his voice screaming for me. That was the last thing I heard before I woke up in a cell. Knowing that he probably put that on himself… it was more than frustrating because I couldn't do a damn thing about it. That was why I left those marks. I wanted him to know I was alive. Not the ANGEL Project, just him. Well, you too, but you know what I mean. Only two people would have known that symbol."

"Can I ask you a question?"

"Sure."

"Why'd they let you out?"

She grimaced. "One of the guys there, Chuck, had a little crush on me. He talked them into letting him take me out to the edges of civilization for a date."

"So why not kill him and run?"

"I thought about it," she said with a sigh. "But you know how it is. We're never off the clock. When they took me off the drugs, I thought maybe I could collect information on them, figure out where they were, how many they were, any plans they had, that sort of thing. I didn't want it all to be for nothing. Also, I was in a dress and heels; not exactly great attire for making an escape in the dead of winter. I was trying to be smart about it."

Gabe snorted. "A dress and heels?"

"Yeah. Pink ones at that," she said, frowning. "It was almost as bad as that stupid marshmallow coat in Aspen."

"Aw, that coat wasn't so bad." He chuckled. "And pink is such a flattering color for blondies like us."

She rolled her eyes. "You're hilarious, Mr. Pinstripes. You can keep your pink. I'll stick with blue, thanks very much."

He laughed again and shooed her off the bed. "More for me. Anyway, you go for your swim. I'll leave the door unlatched for you for when you're done."

Candace leaned down and kissed his cheek. "Thank you

for everything. I mean it."

"Don't even worry about it. I'm sure you'll do something awesome to make it up to me later," he said.

Smiling, she rolled her eyes. After snagging a towel, she left him with a wave and headed for the pool.

CHAPTER 7

SHE STRETCHED and tried to work the ache out of her muscles. Sharing a room with Gabe wasn't the most comfortable arrangement she ever had. When her cousin produced a sleeping bag and extra pillow the night before, she insisted she be the one taking the floor. Her body thanked her for that sacrifice with a sore neck, a stiff back, and a cramp in her calf that wasn't cooperating no matter how much water she drank.

As Gabe snored away in bed, Candace crept out of the room, returning to the pool for another swim. It was early, the sun not even cresting the horizon, when she took her first laps. They were beautiful, restful, peaceful laps…

Until she sensed Jackson's heat getting closer.

Quick as she could, Candace jumped out of the pool and

dashed for the locker room. She barely made it. Little more than a second or two after the door closed behind her, she heard the men's door bang open. After a few minutes, she finally heard the splash of water as he entered the pool. Closing her eyes, Candace connected with the liquid surrounding him, passively tracing the contours of his body, matching them to her memory of him. She ached to touch his skin again, but the moment she considered it, Kristie's face intruded on her thoughts, driving the hurt in her heart a little deeper.

With a sigh, Candace resigned herself to suffering through another day without him. Returning to Gabe's room, she showered and dressed, heading for breakfast before her cousin so much as rolled over.

The upshot to cutting her swim short was that she was nearly first in line for waffles that morning. Nearly, as only one person was ahead of her.

Candace tried to keep her voice steady as she told the servers what she wanted, but it was a challenge as Marissa Hayden was tray to tray with her.

Marissa took up residence at a small table at the back of the dining hall. Candace hesitated, but decided it was time. She had to say thank you.

"I don't mean to bother you," Candace said as she hovered beside the table. "But would you have a minute?"

Marissa looked up, dark, almond-shaped eyes taking Candace in. "You want to sit with me?"

Candace shifted her weight. "If that's okay. I don't want to bug you."

She shook her head. "It's not a problem. It's just that

most people here don't want anything to do with me. You can sit if you like."

Confused, Candace set her tray down and lowered herself into a seat. "Why wouldn't they want anything to do with you?"

Shrugging, Marissa cut into her waffle. "It's mostly to do with Christian, I think. They sort of lump us together."

"That's kinda stupid. I mean, now that I've met Christian I get why they all said to avoid him, but—"

"Oh!" Marissa interrupted. "You must be who he was ranting about last night." She giggled. "The water bug?"

Candace winced. "He was ranting?"

Marissa beamed. "He was. It was awesome. Candace, right?"

"Candace Bristol, yeah," she said, extending her hand. "It's nice to see you again."

She shook her hand, but paused mid-motion. "Again? Have we met before?"

Breaking the contact, Candace stuck her hands in her lap and blushed. "Once. Briefly. You probably don't remember. It was years ago."

"Well, now that you mention it," she said, scrunching up her face as she studied Candace's features. "You do sort of look familiar. How many years has it been?"

"Almost five," Candace said. "It's okay if you don't remember. I was a dumb kid who got caught in a surprise attack."

Marissa sat bolt upright. "The fountain in Des Moines? That was you?"

Candace's jaw flopped open. "You remember that?"

"Of course!" she said, excited. "You were one of my first rescues, plus, I have an eidetic memory. Wow. This is amazing. You're an ANGEL now?"

"First round SAGE, actually," Candace said, sure she was eight shades of red. "I can't believe you remember Des Moines."

"You're that Candace?" Marissa said. "The one they just broke out of HEX?"

She nodded.

Marissa giggled. "Is it wrong of me to feel insanely proud of myself? I've been hearing all these stories about what you've done in the last few months, and I can't help feeling like I might've had a hand in that."

To say that Candace was stunned would be putting it lightly. Marissa looked ready to go full-on fangirl. "I'm not all that amazing, really. I mostly came over to tell you thank you. Without you and Christian, I'd be dead for sure."

"Thank you?" she asked.

"Well, yeah," Candace said. "You left before I got to say thank you that day. When I heard you guys were coming for SAGE treatment, I figured it was my chance. Although, I think I'll probably hold off on thanking Chris after last night." She frowned and muttered. "Plumbing problem. Jesus."

"Plumbing problem?"

Her mood soured as she recalled his comment. "He wanted me to help clean out his pipes," she said. "I did, but probably not the way he intended."

At that, Marissa burst out laughing. "Oh my God, he didn't!"

"He did."

"That's so totally a Christian thing to say," she said, still giggling. "He's kind of stuck in his past glories as far as that goes. It used to be all he had to do was look at a girl, and they'd fling their panties at him. I couldn't handle it. Once he was in the limelight, his ego was off the charts. I was done with the whole thing after about six months."

"So, you two were together for a while?"

She snorted. "Him, me, and every other girl who would give him ten seconds of her attention. Yeah, we were. We haven't been for a long time, though."

Marissa was nothing like Christian, thankfully. If anything, she was the opposite, content to be alone with books and away from the attention that came with being an ANGEL. Candace chatted with her for a good hour or so, and they developed a mutual admiration for one another.

"I guess you've probably been to the library by now," Candace said. "Have you talked to Deborah much? She's been looking for other people to discuss books with." Taking Marissa to the library would be an excellent excuse to see Deborah, and maybe get a read on how much she knew about Mica.

"I've mostly been keeping to myself, but I've seen her around," Marissa said. "She seems pretty nice, but I've never really been comfortable around empaths."

"I know what you mean," Candace said. "But Deborah's really sweet. I've gotten to know her pretty well. I think you'll like her."

"Well, if you aren't busy this morning, would you introduce us? I'm terrible with that kind of thing."

Candace smiled. "I'd love to. Are you done eating?"

"Sure am."

They picked up their trays and headed out, chatting about things they read recently as they dumped their dishes. Marissa pushed open the door to the dining hall, motioning Candace through. Not paying attention, Candace continued talking, slamming face first into the one person she was trying to avoid.

"Whoa there, Sugar Plum," he said, his voice low and soft as he steadied her on her feet.

Her heart dropped into her shoes as she scrambled backwards, out of his reach. All knowledge of words evaporated from her head. His touch was enough to fry her brain. Before she could think of anything to say, Jackson backed up and stepped aside to let her through.

All but running, Candace skittered past him, not sparing a glance for Kristie, who was somewhere behind him.

"Hold up, Candace!" Marissa called as she tried to catch up. Candace slowed, allowing the veteran ANGEL to fall into step beside her.

"What was that about?" she asked as they rounded a corner.

Candace took a deep breath and tried to calm down. "It's a long story, and complicated."

"But that was Jackson, right?" Marissa asked. "I thought someone said you guys were a couple?"

"We were. Are. I don't know. It's complicated."

"I see," she said.

Candace didn't offer anything else on the subject, and they walked the remainder of the distance to the library in silence.

OF ALL the emotions raging through her like white water rapids, Candace didn't expect to add total panic to the mix. Yet when she walked into the library, seeing Mica chatting up Deborah sent her into a tailspin of doubt and confusion.

Immediately, Deborah's eyes snapped up to find Candace. There was approximately zero chance the empath couldn't see the uncertainty or fear.

However she interpreted Candace's reaction, it prompted her to jump up from her seat behind the desk and rush over, taking her hand. Instantly, Candace was flooded with a heady rush of endorphins.

"Turn it down, please," Candace said, her words slurring slightly.

Some of the fog cleared as Deborah pulled her in for a hug. "Sorry, I was erring on the side of caution. How are you? Are you okay? What can I do to help?"

Candace giggled. "Slow down. I'm fine. It's just..." she peeked around Deborah's shoulder. "What's he doing here?"

"Who, Mica?" She threw him a backward glance. "We're talking, that's all." She leaned in close. "He's on your side, Candace. And so am I."

Even with Deborah's calming presence, Candace's knees threatened to give out on her. Was she saying she knew about the plan to make changes? Or was it a simple statement of loyalty?

"Marissa, right?" Deborah said, leaning around Candace to smile at the other woman.

Marissa nodded. "You're Deborah? Candace says you're the person to see when it comes to books."

Deborah giggled and Candace couldn't help grinning. She had missed the sound of it.

"That would be me," Deborah said. "You read pretty widely, I noticed. Do you have a preferred genre?"

It wasn't that Candace wasn't interested in the discussion, but her attention was elsewhere. Mica was watching her with a half-curious, half-amused expression on his face. With Deborah deep in conversation, Candace easily slipped from her grasp and floated over to him, the emotional high slowly ebbing away.

"I see you found someone else to hang on to," she said.

Mica smirked. "Funny, considering it was your hand she was holding a minute ago."

"Yeah, well, that's a long story. This place isn't easy for me to visit. She knows why. She's looking out for me."

"Ah," he said, fidgeting with a thin silver band around his wrist. "So, I wanted to ask you something, but I think you'll probably say no."

Candace waited for the question.

"Well, Deborah's not much for physical training, you know, aside from the gym equipment. I saw there were some trails around here, and thought they might be good for running. Do you know much about them?"

"A bit," she said. "Why?"

"Do you think you could go for a run with me this afternoon?"

"Why, do you need someone cheering you on or something?"

He continued fussing with the bracelet. "No, but I don't think I'd feel comfortable out there on my own yet."

Candace snorted. "Oh, so you're looking for a bodyguard, is that it?"

Mica shrugged as he turned the metal strap a third time. "That, and I'm not sure how much they trust me yet."

"What is that?" she asked, pointing to the thing around his wrist.

"A tracking device," he said with a sigh. "I have to wear this for the foreseeable future. I don't want them to freak out if I take off running because I want some cardio and fresh air."

Candace considered the request. Would it look suspicious if the two of them spent that kind of time alone? If Mica was trying to make her look bad, that could definitely do it.

"Fine, but I'm bringing someone with me."

He raised an eyebrow. "What, you think I'd try something with you? How big of an idiot do you think I am?"

"I think I'd rather not be alone with someone who kept me in a chemical stupor for weeks, if it's all the same to you."

"Whatever," he said. "I just gotta get out of here for a little while. Bring who you want."

"I will," she said, lifting her chin. "Meet outside the pool at two o'clock. We'll go from there. Think you can handle two miles out and back?"

"Candace, just because I'm a chemistry nerd doesn't mean I can't hang with a Physical for a run. Don't worry about me."

Already using ANGEL slang, was he? Clever boy. She

nodded and turned away, heading for the door. "Great. See you at two then."

"TELL ME again why you agreed to this," Gabe said as they pushed through the door to the outside. "It seems awfully trusting on your part."

"Second chances, cuz," she said, taking in a deep breath of chilly February air. "Besides, Deb says he's okay and, really, of all the people I met there, he was probably the least hostile. I'd go so far as to say he was nice. Don't you dare tell him I said so, though. He might be an ANGEL now, but I think I'll keep him at arms' length for a while yet."

They were a few minutes early for the run, and Candace took the time to stretch out her muscles. When Mica stepped out to join them, he jerked to a halt, his jaw slack and eyes wide.

Candace bent and touched her toes, fighting back the urge to laugh as she hid her grin. Damn, did it feel good to meddle. No wonder Gabe liked it so much.

Composed, she straightened and rolled her neck. "All right, I guess we're all accounted for then. Mica, this is my cousin and general pain in the ass, Gabriel Vandermeer. Gabe, this is Mica Reynolds, recent turncoat and self-proclaimed chemistry nerd. Do you boys need to warm up more or—"

The door banged open again, the person joining them killing her question before it was out of her mouth.

EVOLUTION: HEX

"Been a while since I was on a group run," Jackson said. "Thanks for the invite."

Gabe made a big show out of using a tree to steady himself as he stretched out his thighs, avoiding her white-hot death stare.

"Come on, Mica," she said, seething between clenched teeth. "You set the pace, I'll keep up."

Mica swallowed nervously, but did as she said. The moment he was beside her, she was in motion, adjusting her stride and speed to match his longer legs and slower pace. After five minutes of uncomfortable silence, Mica cleared his throat.

"So, uh, maybe next time you should keep it between us," he whispered.

Her jaw ached from keeping it welded shut for so long. "No good deed goes unpunished, it seems."

"You're this Mica I've heard about then," Jackson said, easily catching up to them and falling in beside the former HEX member. "Your thing is chemistry, huh?"

Candace dropped back, falling in beside Gabe. Let Mica talk to him. Then she wouldn't have to.

"What the hell, cuz?" she hissed at him. "Why did you invite him?"

Gabe sighed and made a face. "Because you need to talk to him, Candy Cane."

"And you thought this was the appropriate venue for that conversation?"

"Kristie doesn't run. It's almost the only time she leaves him alone. Besides which, I think you might owe me a little explanation too, hmm?"

She choked. "An explanation? What are you talking about?"

Gabe gave her the "you're not fooling anyone" look and motioned to Mica, a good twenty feet ahead of them. "Explain."

"I have no idea what you're talking about."

"Bullshit, Candace. You're meddling."

"I don't meddle," she said with a sniff.

"Not normally, but you do like to get even."

Candace rolled her eyes.

"And if you're meddling the way I think you're meddling, that means you've got a hell of a lot more you'd better tell me about the last three weeks."

"Maybe I'm just doing you a solid, Gabe. Maybe you should just take it for what it is and see where it goes."

"Candace…"

She shot him a look of warning. "Not now. Not with him here." She angled her head towards Jackson. "You've got yourself to blame for that one."

With that, she kicked it into gear and sprinted ahead, passing everyone and letting the breeze take her.

After five separate forks in the trail, she slowed to a walk to rehydrate before heading back. A bitter cold wind gusted up, knocking her ear wrap off of her head, forcing her to stop and pick it up. Someone else grabbed it before she could get to it, however.

"You're not easy to track," Jackson said, handing her the item. "I checked four other trails before I found you."

"Looks like I still need to work on that then," she said as she snatched it away. "Since apparently I can still be found when I don't want to be."

"Candace, please talk to me," he said as she stepped around him. "You have to."

"Just like you had to fu—"

"I am begging you, Sugar Plum, please, please don't hate me for that." The absolute anguish in his words constricted her lungs, stopping her.

"I…" Jackson started, but his voice caught. "It was the only way I could think of to get you back."

Her hands dropped to her sides, balling into fists. "Did you know?"

"Did I know what?"

She couldn't look at him. "Did you know that every time you did that with her I could feel it?"

He sucked in a sharp breath. "No."

"I can count them, Jackson. They're burned into my head as much as this mark on my arm. Every. Last. One." When he didn't respond, she continued, turning to face him. "Did you think I wouldn't find a way to get back to you? Did you think I wouldn't use every trick in the book to get out of there? Well, every trick except one. There's a line you don't cross, Sunshine, and it only took you two weeks to get there."

The wind stung the tears on her cheeks, but she didn't move to wipe them away. Let him see. Let him know exactly how much she hurt.

But damned if the look on his face wasn't the same as her own. Only his expression held more guilt and shame than she'd ever seen another person hold on to.

"It was my fault they took you," he said, so soft she

barely heard it over the breeze. "I tried to kill you, and they took you from me for it."

How many times had she wished she could hold him, to tell him that wasn't his fault? Candace never once blamed him for what happened in Aspen. He didn't know what he was doing— none of them did. Even she was losing her grip on reality when she went all in on that last attack.

"I will never tell you that was your fault, Sunshine," she said. "Never. Your scream was the last thing I heard that day. That wasn't you out there."

When he took a step toward her, she inched back and flashed her palms, stopping him. "Don't. Don't come any closer. I..." She pinched her eyes closed and swallowed. "I love you, but I can't do this yet. This kind of hurt... You can offer me a million explanations and a thousand pleas for forgiveness, but this kind of hurt isn't going to go away that easily." Looking at him one last time before turning around, she shook her head. "Especially not when she's still hanging all over you, reminding me every time I see her of what you did to save a princess that didn't need you to."

As she ran back to the compound, the only sound that followed her was the crunching of dead grass and leaves beneath her sneakers.

CHAPTER 8

CANDACE WAS laid out on top of a picnic table when she heard them laughing. She sat up to take it in as they approached, both of them smiling uncontrollably.

Searching her memory, Candace couldn't remember the last time Gabe looked so happy. He was practically glowing as Mica said something, finishing a funny story with a loud laugh.

Rather than ruin the moment, Candace hopped down off the table and let them be. At least someone could find a little peace.

Candace took her shower and dressed slowly, not seeing any particular reason to hurry. When she emerged from the bathroom, Gabe was back, scowling at her from the edge of the bed.

Surprised by his expression, she couldn't keep it out of her voice. "What's the matter? Why are you mad?"

Gabe stood, walked over, then pulled her into tight hug. "Thank you, Candy Cane."

It took her a moment to realize he wasn't angry, but eventually she smiled and hugged him back. "You're welcome. Now don't say I never gave you anything."

"You know you've got a lot of explaining to do."

"Don't ruin this, Gabe. Let it be, okay?"

He pulled back and held her at arms' length. "Why?"

Her forehead wrinkled as she looked at him. "Because I think you need this, whatever it ends up being, and I think he does, too."

"And what makes you think it's anything?"

She gave him a bland look. "Because he's cute and totally blushes whenever I mention you. And by the look on your face when you guys were talking after the run. And by the fact that you're thanking me. You wouldn't be thanking me if it wasn't something."

Candace broke away and stepped into her shoes, focused intently on tying them. "I'll see if maybe they haven't given away my old room or something. You don't need me in your hair any more."

"You're not going anywhere, Candy Cane."

She leveled her gaze at him. "Don't be gross. I'm not gonna stick around and watch you be all lovey-dovey mushy face with Mica. Yuck."

He crossed his arms and planted his feet. "Candace, it's not like that. You don't have to leave."

"And when you start SAGE treatments? What then, cuz?

No way. I am not going to be that sort of inconvenience."

"Well, so long as you're going there, I guess I will too," he said. "He has his own room. If it comes to that, which is pretty presumptive on your part, you don't have to go anywhere."

"Interesting choice of words," she said with a snicker.

"Now who's being gross?"

"Fine," she said. "I won't leave. You might regret that later, though."

"Maybe," he said, standing. "Let me grab a shower quick and we'll go get dinner."

"Nothing about your showers are quick, Gabriel. I highly doubt that now that you have a reason to pretty yourself up you'll be any faster."

"Ha ha."

Candace flopped back on the bed, happy she'd done something right. Still, other things gnawed at her, Jackson aside. Curious, she closed her eyes and focused.

Where are you, Mitchell?

She repeated the thought over and over, picturing Michele's face and wondering if it was even working. Candace had no way to know if it would do any good, but she figured she could at least try.

"About time, Candy Cane. Thought you forgot about us."

She jerked as the voice sounded in her brain. It gave her an instant headache.

"You'll rewire for this eventually. It gets easier."

Great. Looking forward to it. How are you? Everyone holding up okay? Anything I should know about?

"So far, no injuries to report. Plenty of questions. They don't

know what to make of me. No telepaths here?"

Not as far as I know. There's a lot of that going around, though.

"*How's Mica?*" There was a distinct note of worry in Michele's question. Did she have trouble reading her twin brother?

He seems okay, but I'm confused as hell. Did he tell you anything about Deborah?

"*He did. She knows about us down here and that you want to make changes. She wants to help. Told me herself. That girl has seen some serious shit, but hasn't been able to do a thing about it. She's on our side, Candy.*"

Distantly, Candace heard the water turn off in the bathroom. *I need to go, but ping me if anything happens, okay?*

"*You got it. Oh, and tell Mica congratulations for me.*"

What?

"*Just do it.*"

Fine. Whatever you say, Mitchell.

"Are you sleeping already?" Gabe asked as he emerged from the bathroom.

Candace opened her eyes and sat up. "No, I was just thinking. Are you done primping? I'm starving here."

With an exasperated sigh, he laced up his shoes and pulled her to her feet. "Come on, then. I wouldn't want you wasting away to nothing."

WITH MICA sticking close to Gabe, Candace opted to sit elsewhere during dinner. Marissa sat at a table in the back again, providing an excellent excuse for Candace to get away from the Pavo Team and pretending not to trust Mica.

They talked about books mostly, and Candace was grateful for the opportunity to shut her brain off. Halfway through the meal, someone pulled a chair up to the end of the table. Christian Markov straddled the seat backwards, elbows leaning on the edge beside her and Marissa's trays.

"What's with people here, anyway?" he said, chewing on a toothpick. "They're all so hostile."

Candace coughed to cover her laugh as Marissa gave him a placating smile. "They're not so bad when you get to know them, Chris."

His eyes drifted to Candace, traveling down her face and over her body. She met his stare with one of her own. "Thinking about the next offensive thing that'll come out of your mouth, or are you about done with that?" she said.

Christian flipped the toothpick with his teeth. "Offensive? I thought you could use the compliment."

At that, Candace nearly choked. "Compliment? You're kidding, right? You think pretty highly of yourself, don't you? I don't care how long you've been an ANGEL, Chris, you talk to me that way again and you'll end up with a permanent plumbing problem."

"Touchy, touchy," he grumbled.

"I'm not touchy," she said. "I just don't appreciate being approached like some screaming high school girl you assume wants to wrap herself around your body. News flash, no one wants to be approached that way. When you figure that out, you might get a little further with the people here. No one likes an egotistical asshole."

Candace stabbed at her grilled chicken and chewed for moment before looking up. Christian stared at her, stunned. Marissa wasn't any less shocked.

"Don't tell me no one's ever told you that before," she said after swallowing. "Are you not familiar with the word no?"

"They think I'm an egotistical asshole?" he said, blinking.

Holy crap. He really didn't know. "Well, yeah," she replied. "I mean, maybe not all of them, but if you treat everyone the way you treated me, Amir, and True last night, what else would you expect?"

His gaze shifted to Marissa. "Is that right? Does everyone think I'm a jerk?"

Marissa sighed and her expression softened. "They don't hate you or anything, but, well…"

"And you didn't think to say anything until now, huh?" He scrubbed a hand across his forehead.

Unbelievable. No one *ever* told him off before? What kind of charmed life was he leading in the Virginia compound? "Are you saying that everyone just let you walk around thinking you were superhero number one for the last few years? I have a hard time believing that."

Christian was very quiet for several long minutes. Eventually, Candace went back to her dinner, not sure what else to tell him. She didn't want to hurt the guy's feelings, but if no one was going to tell him how awful he was to people, she'd throw herself on that grenade.

"I'm sorry, Candace."

Fork halfway to her mouth, she nearly dropped it. "What?"

When he looked at her, his eyes never drifted from her

face. "I'm sorry I used that line on you. You're right. That was pretty shitty of me."

A quick glance at Marissa told her the other woman was as confused as Candace was. He seemed honestly apologetic. She nodded briefly. "Apology accepted. Thank you."

"You're a SAGE, right?" he asked.

"I am."

Christian and Marissa shared a look before he spoke again. "So, we were wondering, could you give us the rundown on what to expect? No one's really told us much."

She clamped down on her inner fangirl, trying not to flip out that the original ANGELs were looking to her for advice. "As far as the process goes? Well, it's a lot like the first time through, only they strap you down and a machine delivers the doses. The pain is on a whole new level, though. I know it's been a while since you guys were through it, but you'll remember fast. It's instant and absolute. You'll scream. I don't care how tough you think you are, you'll feel like you're dying. It sucks."

"How long does it last like that?" Christian asked.

"Forever and a day," she said, chuckling. "I don't know, I wasn't really watching the clock. It's possible that it's worse for me than most because of the wiring in my brain. The first treatment, I went in at eight that morning and barely made it back to my room before midnight. I spent a lot of that time rehydrating, though, so, again, special case here. Jamarcus could probably tell you a bit more about it, too. I think of all of the first round SAGEs, you'll have the best luck approaching him."

"Thanks, Candy," Christian said. "I appreciate the heads

up."

Was that the same guy who hit on her last night? What an abrupt transformation.

"What about your ability?" Marissa asked. "Were the changes immediately noticeable?"

Candace thought back. "Not too much until the next morning, really. The changes in my hair and eyes were the big ones until I tried out my ability in a training room. That and my connection was way stronger than before. I'm constantly aware of all water around me at all times. Every molecule has its own unique voice." She giggled. "It gets crowded in my head sometimes."

Christian flipped his toothpick again, grinning at her. "I'm excited to see what changes I get. Super strength and reflexes are great and all, but I'm wondering what the next level will be."

"Oh, I'm sure you'll have a whole new list of reasons to feel like a big shot," she smiled back at him.

"Like I need more proof that I'm awe—" His quip cut off mid-sentence as his toothpick burst into flames, and he dropped it with a yelp. "What the hell?"

Instantly irritated, Candace slowly turned in her seat, knowing exactly who was responsible. When her eyes met Jackson's, her scowl deepened. "Sorry about that, Chris. Looks like someone's having problems controlling himself again."

Jackson stalked over, his expression murderous. "Making new friends, Sugar Plum?"

"Not your concern," she said. "Apologize. Now."

Kristie appeared at his side, snaking an arm through his.

"Apologize for what?"

Candace pushed back from the table, disgusted. "For being a hypocritical prick, mostly." She picked up her tray and walked away.

When his hand touched her shoulder, she lost it.

"Candace, don't. I'm—" His apology was cut off as she snapped the cord taut.

"I warned you, Sunshine. Don't touch me."

Frozen in place, Jackson couldn't follow her as she dumped her tray and left. Who the hell did he think he was, getting pissed over a conversation with Christian while he was screwing around with another girl? Let him think the worst. Jerk.

A minute later, she finally released her hold on him, unable to stand the feel of the water in his body a moment longer. But as she fled down the hall to Gabe's room, the sound of someone gasping made her stop.

Around the next corner, Chloe was propped up against the wall, clutching her chest, her breathing shallow. Rushing over, Candace reached out to touch her.

"Don't," Chloe wheezed. "I'll be okay. Can you back up a bit?"

Hands up, Candace took two giant steps backwards. "Better?"

"Candy, you know I want to be there for you, but you make it really tough for me sometimes, you know that?" She let out a weak laugh. "You always sucker punch me when my guard's down."

"Sorry," Candace said. "I swear it's not on purpose."

After a few more steadying breaths, Chloe straightened

and faced her. "I know. It's not your fault. I was actually coming to see you, if that means anything."

"Coming to see me?"

Chloe nodded, smiling sadly. "I wanted to say goodbye."

"Goodbye?" she said. "Why? What's going on?"

"I'm leaving in the morning," Chloe explained. "They finally approved my transfer."

"Transfer?"

"To Virginia. They decided to let me go with Andrew at the last minute."

Candace smiled. "That's great, Chloe. Really. I was worried about you two and how that was going to go for you. I'll miss you for sure, but I'd rather know you're happy."

Tentatively, Chloe took her hand, a trickle of fuzzy relaxation causing Candace's shoulders to droop. "Man, you two with this emotional high thing. You guys must be convinced I'm completely bonkers or something."

"Sorry," Chloe said. "This is kind of for me, too, to be honest. I want to talk to you, but I can't when you're that upset. Is it okay?"

She shrugged. "Whatever. I'm just along for the ride."

Pulling her down the hall, Chloe led her to the female rooms and inside one of them. "We can talk in here," she said. "Instead of out in the hall. There's no need for everyone to know about your problems, right?"

Candace giggled. "Oh, I'm pretty sure they already know about my issues with Jackson. If they didn't before, anyone that was in the dining hall tonight does now."

Chloe squeezed her hand and sighed. "Look, I know what he did was pretty bad, Candy, but you should give him a chance to make it up to you."

Shaking her head, Candace was in no mood to entertain anything of the sort. "Nope. He replaced me. He doesn't need me anymore."

"You know that's not true."

Candace glared at the floor.

"I've never seen anyone as desperate as Jackson was since…"

When Chloe stopped, Candace looked at her. "Since when?"

"You know when."

Wincing, Candace looked away. "You mean Adrian."

"Yeah."

"So what you're saying is I inspire self-destructive, kamikaze-style crazy in my boyfriends? Well, that's reassuring."

"I think you inspire a lot of things in a lot of people," Chloe said. "But love always brings out extremes. Jackson explodes, you implode. You're both hurting is the point. There's only one way to fix it, but you have to give a little. I know he's willing to do whatever it takes. Are you?"

"Could you?" Candace pinched back tears. "She's still hanging all over him, Chloe. I don't have a chance when every time I look I see her giving him moony eyes and snuggling up to him. All I can think about is how I could feel him when he was with her. I know he thought he was helping, that it was the only way, but that's part of the problem, too. He was only thinking about himself and what he wanted. It never occurred to him that I would either find out about it or experience it firsthand."

Another wave of soothing endorphins eased the hurt.

"There's more to her still hanging around him than you think," Chloe said. "I won't argue your reasons for being upset, as I think they're definitely valid, but there's more to this Kristie situation than whether or not he likes her. For what it's worth, he doesn't. He can't stand her."

"Then why keep her around?"

"He doesn't have a choice. The higher ups haven't decided what to do about her yet. Both Deborah and I are worried she'll become mentally unstable if Jackson breaks it off clean. Dr. Poznanski wasn't sure what to do about that since you were gone. Even as strong as Jackson is, Kristie has the same power you do. If she snaps, people will die."

"But you don't know for sure that she will."

"One hundred percent? No. But that's why Jackson's been trying to ease away from her gradually. Did he not tell you any of this?"

Candace resumed glaring at the carpet.

Chloe sighed. "You didn't give him the chance, did you?"

She shook her head.

"Candy, you know as well as I do that people are always more complicated than they appear on the outside. You should have at least given him that much."

"It's not that easy," she said. "The whole thing makes me angry and upset and hurt and I just can't let go of it."

Chloe rubbed her back in gentle circles. "I know, I know. You'll get there, Candy Cane."

"Chloe?"

"Hmm?"

Candace sighed and squeezed her hand. "Thank you. I'll try to remember this next time."

"Next time what?"

"Next time he freaks out about me talking to another guy."

"He's worried you're looking for payback, huh?"

"Likely," Candace said. "I was just talking to Christian and Marissa, it's not like I was sitting in his lap or anything."

"What did Jackson do?"

When Candace told her about the toothpick, Chloe giggled. "Sorry," she said. "I can't feel too bad for Christian. He's kind of a jerk. Why were you talking to him?"

"Long story," Candace said. "I don't think he's as bad as everyone thinks, though. Oblivious, for sure, but you know how people are. Layers and all that."

"Yeah, layers." Chloe turned her head to study Candace. "So, what are you going to do now?"

Candace shrugged and stood up, breaking away from the empath. "Right this second? Go for a swim."

"And after that?"

She made her way to the door and rubbed her eyes to clear the fog some. "I don't know. I'm taking things as they come."

Chloe stood and crossed to her, hugging her tightly. "Well, if you need someone to talk to tonight, you know where to find me."

"Thanks, Chloe," Candace said, returning the embrace. "But in case I don't see you, have a safe trip. Tell Hector and Andrew I said hi and to look out for each other, okay?"

"I will. And Candace?"

"Yeah?" she said, stepping into the hall.

"Mitchell says the birds are freaking out."

Speechless, all Candace could do was nod dumbly as the door closed. Chloe knew too? If so, what did she intend to do with the information once she left?

Every time she turned around, a new complication cropped up.

And what did Michele mean about the birds?

CHAPTER 9

CANDACE LOCKED the bathroom door and sank down to the floor. After a few deep breaths, she focused her thoughts on Michele, hoping to get some answers about the cryptic message from Chloe.

"There you are. About time."

When I said ping me, I meant directly. What the hell, Mitch? Chloe too?

"It's not as easy as that. You've got some weird stuff going on in your head. I can't initiate unless I'm looking at you. And yes, Chloe, too. You can't keep a secret from an empath. They can smell a lie a mile away."

What's the deal with the birds? I have no idea what she meant.

"It's Lucie. She's freaking out because she can't hear any birds from her cell."

Birds?

"She communicates with birds. That's her ability."

So what do you want me to do here? If I walk into Poznanski's office —

"Find a way to come visit us. They have to be ready to start the full-on interrogation process by now."

How's that going to help with the bird problem? It's not like I've got a parakeet or something handy to bring down with me.

"The first step is getting you in the room to talk with her. Bring Mica if you want. You can make the rounds or something."

Tonight? Exactly who the hell was in charge? If Mitchell expected her to just go along with whatever…

"No, not tonight. I'll try to keep Lucie calm, but you need to make it tomorrow if you can. The girl just needs to get outside. She doesn't care about much else except her birds. If you get her access, she'll be your friend for life."

That's a tall order, Mitchell.

"Can you do it or not?"

Candace scowled at the tub and considered it. *I don't know about getting her outside, but I can probably get in to see her tomorrow. Maybe the rest of you too. I'll let you know.*

"Holler if you need anything."

Actually, I have another question for you.

"What's that, Candy Cane?"

How much do you know about Kristie? There's some concern she could go nuclear. Can you get a read on her at all?

There was a pause in the silent conversation, and Candace wondered if she was gone.

"I haven't been able to reach her at all. Not a good sign. What are they gonna do with her?"

Chloe said they didn't know yet, but no matter what happens I'll probably be pulled in. Even unstable she can't hurt me. No one else can counter what she can do.

"I'm sorry, Candace."

For what?

"You were right about a lot of stuff."

Anything specific you're referring to this time?

"About leaving others to clean up our mistakes. What Dr. F does with unstables isn't right. I'm sorry that you're paying for it."

Don't get all sappy on me now, Mitchell. Nothing's set in stone yet. She might be fine.

"I doubt it, but I hope you're right about that, too."

Anything else?

"Nope. See you tomorrow?"

I'll do my best.

CRANKY AND sore from another night on the floor with Gabe snoring loudly beside her, Candace made her way to the pool extra early for her swim. Hopefully she'd be able to get more than a few laps in before Jackson showed up.

After thirty minutes, she finally sensed him. She hesitated. Maybe she should ease up on him a little. Chloe was right. If Candace never even gave him the opportunity to speak, how would anything ever get better?

Before she could decide what to do, she felt him on the other side of the door. Completely losing her nerve, Candace threw up her camouflage and sank down into the water, plastering herself in the corner.

She watched him hover by the edge, scanning the room warily.

"What are you waiting for, Sunshine?" Kristie said, coming into view. "You owe me a race."

Let it go. Just let it go.

As they jumped in, Candace considered leaving while they were distracted, but morbid curiosity drove her to watch the situation unfold.

The water stirred around Jackson. Candace felt what Kristie was doing. Still, she maintained her focus, keeping hold of her camouflage while the usurper explored every inch of Jackson's body.

"Kristie," he said, pausing at the edge of the pool. "I told you before, you need to stop."

She swam up to him, leaning on the ledge beside him. "But why? She's made it pretty clear she's done with you, Sunshine. Why fight it? I'm every bit as good as she is, and you know it."

Don't move. Don't breathe. Let it play out.

"Why do you care, Kristie? I already told you we're done."

"And yet, here you are anyway. With me. Still."

"Someone has to be with you, you know that."

"Hmm," she said, drifting closer. "I can't help but notice you haven't gone out of your way to find me a new babysitter. Why don't you just admit you like me, Sunshine?" She reached out, her fingers crawling up his chest.

Jackson brushed them off. "Kristie, I can't give you what you're looking for. I was honest with you from the start. Even if she never talks to me again, it won't matter. I can't give you something that belongs to someone else."

Kristie frowned at his arm, hatefully tracing the lines of his brand. "I could help you get over her if you let me."

Candace was nearly at the end of her patience, ready to lose it on that chick if she didn't back the hell away from him immediately.

"Won't happen," he said. "Now, are we swimming or what? I need to get in at least ten more laps, and I don't need your tricks trying to distract me."

She pouted and turned away from him. "You used to like my tricks."

Jackson didn't respond, instead taking off down the lane for the other end of the pool.

"Satisfied?" Kristie whispered.

Candace jerked. Did she know she was there?

"If you think I'm giving him up, you're very mistaken." Kristie shot her a sidelong glance, sniffed, then dove under water, shooting along the bottom.

Heart racing, Candace took a quick glance at Jackson's progress before jumping out of the pool and racing for the locker room. It was stupid to think she could hide from someone with a water ability. Hell, maybe even Jackson knew she was there. Was he putting on a show for her, or had he meant what he said?

Kristie was undoubtedly trying to rattle her. Everything about that scene was done to elicit one response from Jackson and another from her. Kristie was doing her damnedest to cause Candace as much pain and suffering as she could without direct confrontation. After all, she'd never win in a fair fight; Candace could kill her with little more than a thought. Kristie was aiming for the emotional jugular.

Disgusted with the whole situation, especially since Jackson caused it, Candace went about the rest of her morning routine in a grouchy haze. Rather than go for breakfast first, she decided to see Dr. Poznanski the moment he got in. It was time to get back to work.

AT SEVEN thirty, Dr. Poznanski strolled up to his office, not looking the least bit surprised Candace was waiting for him.

After showing her in, he seated himself behind his desk and booted up his computer. "I assume you're here to discuss our new prisoners?"

She nodded. "I am. I'd like to see what we're dealing with and if I can help, if you'll let me."

"Do you intend on taking the same tactic with them as you did with Miss Burke?"

"If you mean do I intend on bringing Jackson in again, no. Not in the slightest."

He leaned forward on the desk. "What are you looking for this time around?"

"Looking for?" Candace considered it. "Well, I'm not really sure. If nothing else, I might be a familiar face. I can't say that they'll trust me, but they're probably pretty sure I won't kill them. I'm not going in there for revenge. Mostly, I think I want to see if any of them will turn the way you tell me Mica has."

"But you don't fully trust him."

"Of course not," she said. "Even if he was doing it on orders, he still spent weeks drugging me. I talked to Deborah about him, and she says he's on our side. I'm not quite there yet with the trust, though."

"Do you know who we're holding and what their abilities are?"

Candace chewed her lip and let her gaze drift to the ceiling. "I'm assuming you got Mica's sister, Michele. She was always there during interrogation. I think she's an empath or something."

"Telepath," Dr. Poznanski said. "That could be dangerous for you."

Candace grimaced. "Great. Because empaths don't weird me out enough already. Who else?"

"One is a rather disturbed young woman by the name of Lucie Renier. Mr. Reynolds says she communicates with birds."

"But you don't know?"

"We've not tried to verify it, no. She's difficult to approach."

"Difficult how?"

Dr. Poznanski sat back and rubbed his chin. "She keeps her head pressed to the wall, like she's listening for something. When someone speaks, she tells them to hush. That's all we get from her. We're concerned she might be unstable."

"Unstable?" Candace said. "Sounds to me like she's trying to find birds. When I'm cut off from water, the only thing I can think about is finding it again. Trust me, that can drive you a little batty. When HEX was holding me, they originally had me stashed somewhere that was completely dry. Made me nuts."

"Interesting," he murmured.

"Any others?"

"Tori Drake has a healing ability."

"That would explain why I didn't die after Aspen," she said.

"Miss Drake has been amenable enough to us, if only a little reticent. I think she's more upset about being locked up than about who's holding her."

"Then why not let her out if she's not a threat?" Candace asked. "Put her to work in the clinic."

"We're still evaluating her. We don't want to be too hasty."

"So I can see her then?"

"I don't see why not. How's your head?"

Candace chuckled. "That's most of the reason I wanted to see her. I'd do nearly anything to get rid of this headache. It's not bad, just constant."

"Why didn't you mention this to your physician?"

"Because I'm tired of getting pumped full of radiation any time I get a bruise," she said. "It could be stress, lingering dehydration, or maybe I'm just healing. Do you have proof of Tori's ability?"

"Some. The girl is compelled to treat every nick and scratch."

"So maybe we consider this a test run. If we show her trust, maybe we'll get some of that back," Candace said, shrugging.

"But you don't trust them."

"Nope," she said. "Not until I see proof. I'm only going to get that one way. So, Tori makes four, if we include Mica. You said there were five guarding me. Who's the other one?"

"The other one is more problematic," he said. "I'm afraid I can't let you in to see him alone. In this case, I'd ask Mr. Lawrence to accompany you."

Candace sat up straight in her seat. "I'm sorry?"

"Naveen Patil displaces heat," Dr. Poznanski explained. "It wouldn't be out of the question for him to attack you on sight. Mr. Lawrence can easily counter anything he'd try."

She tried to control the twitch below her eye, but couldn't quite stop it. "I think he's got his hands full with other babysitting duties."

"Someone else can see to Miss Burke, a move we've been contemplating anyway," he said. "Unless you have an issue with interacting with him in a professional capacity?"

Gritting her teeth, she shook her head. "No, sir. No issues."

"Good," he said. "He'll join you after lunch. If you take Miss Nasik with you, I see no reason to prevent you from seeing the others in holding this morning."

She really should expect to walk away with unpleasant work any time she had a meeting in there. She should be used to it. Was she being punished for being competent or proactive? Here, Candace, let's make everything as horrific as possible, shall we?

Sighing, she agreed to the plan, knowing from experience that any attempt to argue a point would only make it worse. With a reminder that she should see Dr.

Holtz about her headache, Dr. Poznanski dismissed her.

"SO YOU'VE seen these guys before, right?" Candace asked as the elevator descended to the holding cell level.

Deborah nodded. "When they first brought everyone in, yes. I did a quick evaluation on their stability."

Candace fidgeted with her nails. "And they all seemed fine?"

"Well, aside from being unhappy with being locked up, yes." She giggled. "They're all stable and seem surprisingly open to conversation."

"Dr. Poznanski says that's not the case with the bird girl. Lucie, was it?"

Deborah hummed. "Yes, well, that was the first day. If she's cut off from what she's connected to, that might contribute to whatever problems they're having."

"I thought we'd go there first," Candace said as they stepped out of the elevator. "Do you know which one is hers?"

Deborah led the way down the hall, pausing at the fifth door on the left side. "This one." Her hand hovered over the handle. "Oh my. She's not well, Candy. You may have to hold her until I can calm her some."

"Consider it done."

The moment the door opened a crack, the person inside let out a hideous screech. Instantly, Candace stopped her, locking her muscles in place mid-run. Lucie was a mess. Her short brown hair stuck out in places, as though she'd been tearing at it. Her wild gray eyes danced around the room, not settling on anyone or anything for more than a split second. Unstable? Wow. The girl was out of her mind.

"Oh no," Deborah said with a sad sigh. "They'll never let her out like this. She's done."

Candace snapped her head around, gaping at the empath. "What? What do you mean done? According to you, she was fine less than two days ago, and now she's like this? No way, Deborah. I refuse to believe she's not fixable."

Deborah stepped in front of Lucie and touched her face softly. "I don't know what to tell you, Candy Cane. She's one big jumble of emotions. I can't make any sense of it. It never settles."

Setting her jaw, Candace made a decision. "Then we have to get her out of here."

"We what?" Deborah said, horrified. "We can't do anything like that."

"We have to, Deb," Candace said. "It's the birds. Think about it. She's missing her connection. She's lost without it. We have to get her somewhere with birds. The only place that has them here is outside, maybe in the Quad. If that's what she needs, I imagine they'll come to her once she's there."

"They'll never let—"

"Oh, they can try to stop me, sure. That'll work about as well as it did that last stupid Mirror test."

Deborah paled.

"Can you endorphin her to sleep or something?"

"Uh..." Deborah stammered. "Melatonin, not endorphins."

"Right. Melatonin. Can you do it or not?"

She chewed her lip, but nodded. "I think so."

"Do it."

Deborah took hold of Lucie's hand and closed her eyes, concentrating. After a minute or two, she looked back at Candace. "You'll need to get behind her. When you release your hold, she'll collapse and we'll have to carry her."

Getting Lucie out of the cell was a challenge, especially since Deborah had to hold one of the woman's hands at all times to keep her asleep. Candace did the majority of the lifting, setting her down to open the door and through the elevator ride back up topside.

Mitchell, tell Mica to meet me outside the clinic ASAP. I need help carrying.

"You what?"

Just do it. Hurry.

By some miracle, Mica got the message and was strolling through the hallway past the clinic precisely when she needed it. Lucie was not a small woman, and Candace's arms ached by the time he came into view. As she passed some of the weight to him, Dr. Poznanski burst through the door.

"Miss Bristol! Why did you remove that woman from her cell? She's not stable!"

Candace glared at him. "She's not stable because she's cut off from her birds. I'm taking her to them. Are you going to try to stop me, or help me fix her?"

It had been quite a while since she saw someone turn purple with anger, and that had been General Jacobs.

Still, Dr. Poznanski didn't block their way, and they continued down the corridor, heading for the dining hall: the nearest exit to the Quad.

By the time they got outside, a large crowd of onlookers gathered, plastered to the windows as Candace and Mica set Lucie on the brown grass. They stepped back a pace or two, working out their arms and shoulders.

"Can you bring her around slowly, Deb?" Candace asked, readying her connection again should it go poorly.

Brushing away beads of sweat from her forehead, Deborah nodded. "I think so," she said. "Just keep a close eye on her, okay? I don't know how she's going to react when she wakes up."

Within moments, Lucie's eyes fluttered open and her breathing sped up, her chest heaving as consciousness returned. When she jerked to a sitting position, Candace stood ready to paralyze her, but the woman stopped. Her head tilted to the side and then up into the chilly gray sky, her eyes searching.

At first, nothing happened.

Then, a whooshing current of air caused Candace to duck. A hawk circled down to land carefully on Lucie's upward-pointed toes, mirroring the woman's cocked head.

They stayed that way for a long time, deep in some unspoken conversation. Candace watched on, mesmerized by the strange communing. Eventually, the hawk departed, two little brown birds taking its place. Twice more the winged visitors changed, until, at last, Lucie fell back on the grass, stretching out and smiling like she didn't have a care in the world.

Mica chuckled softly beside her. "That's one, Candy Cane. How many miracles do you need before you're considered a saint?"

Candace gave him a bland look. "The girl needs birds. It didn't take a miracle, just someone with an inability to give a shit when people tell her not to do stuff."

Deborah shook her head and giggled. "Well, lucky for Lucie, there's an ANGEL for that."

Lucie looked at Candace, still grinning. "Thank you," she said, glancing at Deborah. "Both of you. My brain was fried down there. I sort of forgot how to talk." Her gaze shifted to Mica. "Did you tell them?"

He shrugged. "I told them you talked to birds, but, dang, Luce, I had no idea you'd lose it like that. Candy Cane is the one you should thank." He slapped Candace on the back, earning him another glare.

Lucie got to her feet and stood in front of Candace, eyes brimming with tears. Candace opened her mouth to speak, but before she could say a word, the woman flung her arms out and hugged her so tightly that Candace couldn't breathe. Lifted off her feet, she watched the world spin as Lucie giggled and twirled them.

"Lucie, she needs air!" Mica said, laughing loudly.

Stunned, it took Candace a moment to find her balance once she was back on the ground.

"Thank you so much," Lucie said, squeezing her one last time before spinning away in a circle and lifting up an arm to catch another bird that flew in for a chat.

A familiar clearing of a throat wiped the grin off of Candace's face. Slowly, she turned to see a very unhappy General Jacobs and Dr. Poznanski focused on her with laser-like precision.

EVOLUTION: HEX

She crossed her arms and smiled as best she could. "Problem solved. Next?"

"You were not given permission to remove her from her cell, Miss Bristol," Dr. Poznanski said, the first to recover his ability to speak without screaming.

"Would you rather I have left her there to dissolve into a giant mess of crazy that couldn't be fixed?" she asked. "I might be wrong, but I'm pretty sure that helps no one. From where I'm standing, I just won us an ally."

"And where do you propose we keep her now, hmm?" General Jacobs said.

Candace looked back at Lucie, blissfully smiling at a robin. "Give me a room. I'll watch her."

"You already have a roommate, Miss Bristol," he said.

"You know damn well where I'm staying and it's not with *him*. Give me a new room. You can't keep her in that cell. She needs birds."

She wouldn't have been a bit surprised if steam started pouring out of the General's ears.

"You're ready to make that sort of commitment to someone you already told us you don't trust?" Dr. Poznanski said.

"Keep your friends close, your enemies closer," she said. "Look at her. She's harmless unless she tells a bird to peck my eyes out. In which case, so long birdy."

"Miss Bristol, I don't think—"

"She can stay with me," Deborah said, interrupting the argument. "There's no need to fight about it. I don't have a roommate, and I'll be able to tell if something changes with her. Candace is right. She's harmless. All she needed was a bird to talk to."

Candace snapped her mouth shut, stunned by Deborah's sudden assertiveness. The empath's smile was warm and soft, instantly placating the two very angry men.

"Are you certain about this, Miss Nasik?" General Jacobs asked.

"Very," she said. "Lucie seems very nice."

The General looked at Dr. Poznanski, not at all pleased, but unable to unleash a tirade out in the open. There were ANGELs watching on in every direction Candace glanced.

"Get her a bracelet. Same as the other one." Without further argument, General Jacobs turned on his heel and fumed out of the Quad.

Dr. Poznanski studied Candace for a moment, and she met his gaze head on. "Well, Miss Bristol, if you intend to keep your enemies close, you might want to consider moving in with the General next time."

Candace grimaced, but said nothing.

"Miss Nasik," he continued. "When you're finished here, bring your new roommate to my office. She needs a tracking bracelet and a badge."

"We'll be there shortly, Doctor," Deborah said pleasantly. "Thank you."

He gave Candace one last look of reproach before making his own exit.

When he was gone, Candace plopped down on the grass, rubbing her forehead. Stupid headache. She needed to see Tori, but it didn't look like that would happen any time soon.

Mica eased down beside her, leaning back to look at her. "Anyone ever tell you that you might have the biggest, brassiest balls on the planet?"

She huffed a single laugh. "They usually confuse it for sheer stupidity. At the moment, I'm inclined to believe that explanation."

"Well, whatever it is, you did something amazing today, Candy Cane."

Candace sighed and laid back on the cold earth. "We'll see. I might make a disaster out of it yet."

CHAPTER 10

"SO WHAT are you gonna do for your next trick, Candy Cane?" Gabe said over his lunch. "Pull a rabbit out of your sleeve or flowers out of your hat?"

"Why is this such a big deal?" Candace said, frowning. "It didn't take a genius to figure out what Lucie needed, just a little compassion."

"I was referring to how you handled Jacobs and Poznanski."

"I didn't handle anything. I did the only thing I could," she said waving him off. "Besides which, they weren't going to do anything out in the open like that. Aside from wounding their pride, what reason would they have to punish me? What can they do?"

"You disobeyed orders."

"What orders?" she said. "They didn't tell me not to take

EVOLUTION: HEX

anyone out of their cell."

"Yeah, but you didn't ask," he pointed out. "Around here, you know that's how they roll."

Candace chewed thoughtfully. "I didn't plan on taking Lucie out, you know. I just didn't see any other options once I got in there. Anyway, even if it didn't work, what was the worst that would've happened? She calls down a flock of ravens or something? She wasn't going to do anything I couldn't defend against."

"I guess, but—" Gabe started to argue when something behind her caught his attention.

She didn't need to look. Jackson's presence was constantly on her radar since they were in such close proximity. If asked, she could tell his exact distance from her at any given moment.

The awareness only made the ache in her chest worse.

"Duty calls. See you later, cuz," she said.

Standing, Candace picked up her tray and headed for the door, acknowledging Jackson with a grimace. He followed a few steps back until they got to the elevator.

The last time they were there, she was introducing him to Kristie, hoping to win the girl's trust. What a difference a month made.

He didn't speak on the ride down: no pleas for forgiveness or bargaining. Candace stared at the elevator doors, willing the ride to go faster, feeling the pull extending from her scarred shoulder to his.

You're here to work. Keep the rest of your problems topside.

Two cells down from Lucie's empty one, Candace readied herself to meet Naveen. Per Michele, he was completely stable, if not a little antsy. When she reached for the handle, Jackson stopped her.

"Better let me go first," he said. When his hand brushed hers, she yanked it back, fighting off the urge to forget everything about the past few weeks and give in to old passions.

Stupid hormones.

His pinched look told her he was fighting a similar battle, but he pushed through, focusing on the job they had to do.

"Anyone home?" he asked, poking his head around the door.

"Jus' chillin'!" a voice called from inside, a cold rush of air drifting out behind it.

She shivered, but nodded when Jackson looked to her for the go-ahead.

"All right then," Jackson said as he opened the door fully. "First thing's first, let's make this place a bit more hospitable."

When she stepped into full view of the cell, Candace gaped. Ice hung from every surface, more like a freezer than a prison.

"Hospitable?" The young Indian man lounging on the cot let out a shrill whinny of a laugh. "I finally got this place comfortable."

Jackson stepped into the center of the room and closed his eyes. A moment later, a wave of heat blasted out from him, instantly warming the air and defrosting every surface. "Comfortable for you, maybe," he said with a smirk. "But Candace here is a little more sensitive than we are."

"Sensitive?" she said, defensive. "That's hilarious,

Sunshine."

Naveen whinnied again. "Ah, so you're Candace. I've heard a lot about you. Who's this hunk of hotness?"

To his credit, Jackson barely flinched, but Candace couldn't resist sending a little verbal jab his way. "Looks like your fan club is growing, Jackson."

The muscles in his jaw clenched in irritation. Candace ignored it and strode forward, hand extended. "Candace Bristol. Former HEX prisoner. This is Jackson Lawrence."

"Naveen Patil," he said. When his fingers closed over hers, she shivered again. They were like ice. "Former prison guard, but I don't think I ever had the pleasure of attending you personally. Chuck certainly had plenty to say about you, though."

"I'll bet he did," Candace grumbled, dropping his hand.

He gave a nasally giggle. "But that's neither here nor there, Candy Cane. What's a guy got to do to get out of this cell and out amongst people again?"

Candace crossed her arms and frowned. Thanks to Chuck, a complete stranger was using that nickname. "It's not as simple as that, sorry. I can't just let you out when I don't know the first thing about you."

"So, ask," he said with a sly grin. How someone managed to be so slimy and so cold at the same time was hard to reconcile.

"Who's Chuck?" Jackson asked, his jaw muscles clenched so tightly that Candace was worried he'd break a tooth.

"No one you need to fret about, Sunshine," she said.

"I think I'd like to make that decision on my own, if you

don't mind."

Even though she knew better than to goad him, the words tumbled out of her mouth. "You shouldn't ask questions you don't want to know the answers to."

Jackson took a step toward her, the temperature in the room noticeably increasing. "Oh, I'm pretty damn sure I want to know."

"I want a lot of things," she said, glaring at him. "Doesn't mean I get those either."

"Candy, if you don't—"

His words got lost in one of Naveen's high-pitched giggles. Both she and Jackson stopped and stared at him, completely embarrassed to be caught airing their problems in front of a stranger.

"Oh, don't mind me," Naveen said, waving them on. "This is better than TV."

Candace pinched the bridge of her nose and sighed. Her stupid headache was getting worse. "Look, Naveen, here's the thing. You seem fine and all, but I've got nothing to go on with you. Aside from a free pass out of here, what is it you're looking for? If you had to pick a side, where would you fall; with HEX, or with us?"

Naveen shrugged and examined his nails, picking at the cuticles. "Depends."

"On what?"

"On whether or not you'll let me fight in the field," he said. "Dr. Ferdinand never did, and I was with her for a year. Can the ANGELs do better for me?"

"You want to fight in the field?" Candace asked. "Why?"

Naveen puckered his lips and looked her up and down

like she'd lost her mind. "Because I want to be a badass superhero, Candy Cane. Why else?"

"So you're in it for the glory then?"

He snorted. "Aren't you? I thought that's what ANGELs did. You know, kill the bad guy, then do a PR tour. That kind of thing."

"That's, uh…" How to put it? "That's not exactly it, but I guess I see your point. Regardless, I still don't have proof that you won't start killing everyone the moment we let you out, so you see why we're kind of stuck."

Naveen shifted his focus to Jackson and sniffed, his eyes studying every inch of Jackson's heat-radiating body. "Let me have a go with him. We should be pretty fairly matched."

Jackson rolled his eyes. "Not happening. I'm more than you can handle."

"Oh, really now?" Naveen said, a playful gleam in his eye. "Then what's the harm in it?"

Man, Naveen was really odd. "That's not something we can agree to immediately," Candace said. "We'll have to take it higher up for approval."

"Whatever you say, Candy Cane," he said with a sigh. "Not like I'm goin' anywhere. You let me know when you're ready to see me in action." It was so quick, she almost missed it when he winked at her.

"In the meantime," she said, ignoring the overtones. "Is there anything I can get you? Maybe a book or two?"

"Oh, you could bring me piles of ghost stories," he said, completely giddy. "That or cozy mysteries. Or Westerns, those are good too. I wouldn't mind a magazine or three if you've got 'em."

"So what you're saying is that you're not overly picky," Jackson said.

Naveen gave him another of those head-to-toe looks of appraisal. "Oh, I have standards. I'd be happy to tell you about them any time you like."

Candace was at her limit of weirdness. "I think we can find you something," she said. "We'll let you know on the other thing." Backing away, she eased towards the door. "Can't make any promises, though. Anything else you need?"

"A shower would be nice," he said, wrinkling his nose.

"I'll see about that too," she answered. "Come on Jackson. I think we've done about as much damage as we can for one day."

"Oh, I don't know about that," he said as he pulled open the door. "All the walls are still in place."

"You're just full of jokes today," she said with a flat look. "It was good to meet you, Naveen. I'll see you later."

"Ta!" Naveen waved as they left.

When the heavy door closed and locked behind Jackson, he turned, his mouth open and poised to start another argument. Candace held up a hand, stopping him. Her headache was more than an irritation at that point. "Just, don't yet, okay? There's something else I have to do while we're down here, and I'm not ready to deal with whatever you're about to say, so save it, Sunshine."

He closed his mouth, but didn't look happy about it.

Before Deborah took off to settle Lucie in, Candace asked her about the other HEX prisoners— specifically, which cells they were in. The cell before Lucie's was

Michele's, and the one after it was Tori's. That was where she headed.

"I thought we were just seeing Frosty today?" Jackson said as Candace reached for the handle.

"I was supposed to come here this morning, but other stuff happened and everything flew out the window," she said. "Tori's supposed to be some kind of healer. I need her help."

His normal look of agitation dropped away, instantly replaced by concern. "Are you hurt? Why didn't you—"

She held up a hand again, wincing at the sound of his voice. "I have a bad headache. Just follow and shut up and make sure she doesn't kill me or something, okay?"

"Lead the way, Sugar Plum." His words were so soft, so gentle, Candace had to close her eyes and swallow past a pang of regret that stole her breath.

Recovering, she pulled open the door and stepped inside.

Tori sat bolt upright on the cot, looking a little panicked. "Closer," she said. "Hurry. I can help."

"Help with wh—" Candace winced and dropped to her knees as sudden, stabbing pain ripped through her skull.

"Candace?" Jackson said, instantly beside her. "What's—"

"Quickly!" Tori yelled. "Bring her here! I can help! I can fix it!"

Unable to fight beyond the pain, Candace felt herself being lifted off the ground and pressed tightly against Jackson's chest. The contact barely registered past the nightmare inside her head. Fingers closed around her forehead and pushed into her hair, against her scalp.

One searing flash of light, and everything was gone.

SQUINTING, CANDACE tried to focus. It was too bright to see anything clearly.

"There you are," a female voice said. "Thought we lost you for a minute. Welcome back."

Candace shut her eyes against the light. "Am I dead?"

When Jackson laughed, she knew she was still alive. The sound tingled down from her ears to her toes, filling her with warmth.

"You're not dead yet, Sugar Plum, though not for lack of trying."

"Where am I?" she asked.

"In the clinic," the woman said. "Jackson and I brought you up, and they let me stay to make sure you didn't need anything else."

Cracking an eye open, Candace looked in the direction of the voice. Tori perched on a stool, grinning. "They let you stay?"

"Mmm hmm," she said, her head bobbing happily. "And look." She held out her wrist and wiggled it, the silver tracking bracelet catching in the light. "They said since I saved you I'm good to go. They're going to let me work here."

"They what?" Candace said and tried to sit, but a wave of dizziness pushed her back to the mattress. "Oh my God, what the hell happened to me? I feel like I'm gonna puke."

EVOLUTION: HEX

"Head trauma," Tori chirped. "Residual damage from Aspen, I think. Coupled with... Uh..." she trailed off, glancing up at Jackson nervously.

"Coupled with what?" he asked, crossing his arms, feet planted.

"Oh, nothing. Just side effects of your treatments I think."

Tori was a terrible liar. Candace knew damn well that wasn't what she was going to say, but whatever it was, she wasn't willing to talk about it in front of Jackson.

"It was a burst blood vessel," Tori said. "An aneurysm. Did you have a headache or anything before?"

"Since I got back, yeah," Candace replied. "But they didn't find anything during my checkup so I thought it was just stress or dehydration or something."

Tori wobbled her head from side to side, thinking. "Well, yes, it was pretty small so it might not have shown up, but if you'd been a minute later in getting to me I don't think you would've made it. You were lucky."

Candace laid an arm across her eyes and snorted. "Yeah, lucky me. It was only a brain aneurysm. Woo hoo."

"You're lucky Jackson was there too," she continued. "I couldn't have gotten to you with those restraints on."

"Restraints?" Candace asked. "What for?"

"They didn't want me inadvertently touching anyone and reverse healing them. They're very suspicious. But it doesn't matter. Jackson took care of the restraints and you." Tori smiled.

"How noble of him," she deadpanned.

"You realize I'm standing right here, don't you?" he said.

Candace dropped her arm and looked at him. "Yeah,

why is that? I'm fine. You're excused from princess rescuing duty now."

He set his mouth in a hard line and met her scowl with one of his own. "Everyone needs help sometime, Sugar Plum."

She replaced her arm and sighed. "Stop calling me that. You don't get to any more."

"And you plan on stopping me how, exactly?"

"I have my ways. Maybe I'll make your tongue swell up so you can't speak."

Tori cleared her throat. "Do I, uh, need to give you two some space?"

"No," Candace said, at the exact moment Jackson said, "yes."

A knock at the door interrupted the argument. Dr. Poznanski ducked inside, his smile placid, revealing nothing about his feelings on the current situation. "Satisfied with the results of your experiment, Miss Bristol?"

Did she detect a hint of smugness in his words? "It's been a pretty productive day, aneurysm aside, so, yes."

"Perhaps you'll consider taking the rest of the afternoon off then."

"Sounds like good advice," she said, matching his humorless tone of voice.

"Miss Drake, Mr. Lawrence," he said, not taking his eyes off of Candace. "Would you give us a moment, please?"

Well, crap. Whatever was coming wasn't going to be fun.

Tori left without protest and Jackson only hesitated at the door, looking back at her with an unspoken question: would she be okay?

She answered by looking away.

Dr. Poznanski didn't waste a second once they were alone, not even bothering to sit. "Were you aware of the severity of your condition before you went to see Miss Drake?"

"No." It was the truth, and she tried to stress it. "If I knew how serious it was, I never would have waited."

"You were unaware of fluids leaking within your own body?"

Candace tried not to scowl. "Are you? It's not like I sit around scanning myself all day. I had a headache. I'm not one of those people who jumps to the worst possible conclusion any time they're a little uncomfortable."

He watched her, his face unreadable.

"Are we playing games again, Dr. P?" Candace said, sighing. "You know I don't like doing this dance. Ask whatever it is you're really after. Though, I'm not sure why you'd think I'd ignore a brain aneurysm to prove a point."

"You have a new scar," he said, motioning to her arm.

"Yes, and he has one to match. Next question."

"Any others I should know about?"

Well, there it was. "You want to know if they turned me."

Dr. Poznanski waited, silent.

Tired and cranky, Candace was nearing the end of her patience. "I'm not HEX, no. I don't agree with what they do. Their methods make me sick."

"Your behavior of the last few days has raised suspicions," he said.

"Why? Because I want to help people? HEX or not, everyone deserves a chance to be better. As far as I can tell, the worst of the batch you took from there is Naveen, but he's just a little weird for all I know. I have no idea what to make of him." Candace rubbed her eyes and wished she wasn't so dizzy when she sat up. "I don't know how to convince you I only want what's best for everyone. Keeping others safe, super *or* human, will always be my top priority."

"And your decision to separate from Mr. Lawrence?"

She winced. "Different issue. That's personal."

"You're upset about his relations with Miss Burke, even though they resulted in your safe return?"

"You could say that, yes," she said through gritted teeth. "I don't agree with *his* methods, either."

"Yes, well, I imagine you'll be out of your cousin's room soon enough."

"What's that supposed to mean?"

Rather than answer, Dr. Poznanski pulled a pen light out of his lab coat pocket and clicked it on. He ran a few tests on her vision before entering data into a computer.

"I think I'll send Miss Drake back in to see to you again. I'm concerned about the lingering dizziness," he said, his hand on the door. "Now that she's had some time to regain her strength, she should be able to fix whatever damage remains."

He disappeared out into the hallway.

Tori was back a minute later. She scooted a stool up beside the bed and slowly scanned every inch of Candace's body. As the visual sweep crept back up, Tori paused, staring at Candace's right shoulder: the place Jackson left his mark.

She cocked her head to the side. "I can get rid of that, if

you want."

Pinching her lips together, Candace looked away. "No, it's fine. Leave it."

"Hmm," she murmured, then fixed her gaze on Candace's forehead. "I think you'll be okay once the residual swelling goes down and some of the leaked blood disperses, but I can speed that up a bit if it'll make you more comfortable."

"Please," Candace said. "I'm not used to getting dizzy. I kind of hate it. My whole equilibrium is off right now. It's hard to think straight."

Tori smiled and rested a palm above Candace's eyebrows. "No problem. Just relax. This will only take a minute."

CHAPTER 11

THEY KEPT Candace under observation until dinnertime. After Tori's second treatment, she finally felt like herself again. She strode out of the clinic, taking a deep breath, glad to be rid of the headache that plagued her for two days.

"You should know," Jackson said, suddenly by her side. How long was he waiting in the hall to ambush her? "I've been relieved of babysitting duty. Bradley Pryor got the job, so he can turn her ability down."

"How nice for you," she said, not pausing in her walk to the dining hall. "It'll free you up to pursue your lofty aspirations of writing the great American novel."

"Very funny. Aren't you the least bit happy about it?"

"Does it change the fact that you slept with her? On multiple occasions, no less."

He missed a step, unable to respond.

Candace glanced at him from the corner of her eye. "Then I don't see what there is to be happy about."

"Okay, I get it, but can you at least give me a chance? I'm trying, Candy. Tell me what to do and I'll do it."

She stopped and leaned up against the wall, tired and not even sure where to begin with him. "It's more complicated than that, Jackson. Don't tell me you don't have your suspicions about her. Everyone's concerned she'll lose it."

He raked a hand through his hair and sighed. "I know. I've been treading carefully with her." He ignored her derisive snort. "But I'm not going to fake it with her to keep her stable. I can't. It'll kill me, Sugar Plum. I can't pretend to be with her when it's you I want."

"I'm not... I'm not ready for that. At this point, what you want is irrelevant." It was harsh, but it was true. No matter how much she loved him, the images, the lingering feel of him in his moments of betrayal, they needed time to fade. "Besides, even if being cut off from you doesn't break her, seeing us together might. I'm not willing to put everyone at risk that way."

Jackson's eyes searched hers, his eyebrows pulled down into a frustrated frown. "How can I fix this?"

Closing her eyes, Candace tried to let go of some of the hurt. "I don't know that you can."

His arms shot out, pinning her against the wall, and he pressed his forehead to hers. "No," he said, his breathing ragged. "I will never accept that, Candace. Don't tell me there's nothing I can do. I'm not going to give up on us. I won't let you, either." His voice broke, the cracks in his armor raw and visible.

The dull, constant ache in her heart twisted in on itself, doubling up and tearing at her emotions. Candace choked back the tears and gently pushed him away. "I can't, Sunshine," she whispered. "I can't let it go. Not yet. It's killing me, but no matter what I do, the memories of you..." She took a breath to steady herself before meeting his desperate gaze. "Stop pushing me. I need time to process, to think about all of this."

His shoulders dropped, the hope in his eyes crumbling away as his expression strained. "I don't know if I can do that. Telling me to stay away from you is like telling me not to breathe. I don't want to be with you, Candace, I *need* to."

"I..." she said, the first tear escaping even as she brushed it away. "I know. But I can't. I *can't*, Jackson. I haven't made peace with this thing yet." She took a few steps down the hall, then turned her head to leave him with two last words. "I'm sorry."

SHE FLOATED on the surface of the water, trying to settle her thoughts into something resembling coherent. In a single day, Candace managed to free two of the four held HEX members, but what to do about the others?

Mitchell, I dunno what else to do here. Got any ideas?

"Candy! You all right? Tori said there was an emergency earlier."

Fine now. She fixed me. Did she tell you what happened? Part of the problem was what happened in Aspen, but there was more she wouldn't say.

"Yeah, sorry. I think it was partially me."

What?

"Remember when I said you'd get rewired for talking to me like this?"

You gave me an aneurysm? Are you kidding?

"When things get pushed around in your head, it can exacerbate existing conditions. I didn't think about it. You were all healed up when we started the process. I forgot Tori was going to reverse that for the raid."

Tricky details. Whatever. It convinced them to let Tori out. But that brings me to my problem.

"What problem?"

I've freed Lucie and Tori, and might have a possibility for Naveen, but I don't have a clue what to do about you. Got any ideas there?

"For what?"

For how to get you out. Unless you're fine with being locked up for however long. Basically, Tori and Lucie were released because of the circumstances at the time. They might be convinced about Naveen's apparent desire to get his picture in magazines and stuff and think they can buy his loyalty with promises of future glory. So how do we prove you're okay? They'll think anyone that can read minds will know exactly what they want to hear and see. I can't find an angle around it.

Candace got nothing back for several minutes. Maybe Michele was thinking.

Mitchell?

"Don't worry about it, Candy Cane. I think it's covered."

Covered? Covered how?

"Well, if it works, I'll let you know."

That's super reassuring, Mitch.

"You worry about Naveen. If we need you, we'll let you know."

We? Who's we?

"Plausible deniability, Candace. You focus on Naveen."

Fine. Just don't do anything stupid, okay? I kind of need you on this whole thing.

"Aw, that's sweet. Are we BFFs now?"

Candace snorted out loud, then rolled her eyes, realizing Michele couldn't hear the derisive grunt. *I consider this a relationship based on mutual survival. Don't act like you don't need me too, Mitchell. We're stuck together, whether we like it or not.*

"Symbiotic frenemies?" There was definite laughter in that thought.

We'll start there. Candace couldn't help smiling to herself. Despite everything, she had to admit Michele was kind of growing on her. Then again, with the woman's voice in her brain, it was difficult not to get used to her presence.

"Good night, Candy Cane."

The contact broken, Candace resumed swimming laps. After a while, she paused. Someone was watching her, but Jackson was nowhere nearby as far as she could tell. She scanned the room, then turned her attention to the windows lining the pool. No one was out there, either. At least, no one she could see.

Focusing inwards, Candace called to her connection, taking stock of all the water around her. There was the pool, the pipes…

Someone was there; she could feel them, but couldn't see them. Was that Gabe? No, the body was too small to be him, and besides, Gabe had no reason to spy on her, he'd simply ask.

Then who?

Rather than wait to find out, Candace snapped the cord taut, immobilizing whoever it was. She opened her eyes.

"Time to drop the camouflage, mystery guest," she said, her gaze resting on a lounge chair not twenty feet away. "I'm not gonna hurt you, but I expect an explanation."

A figure shimmered into visibility on the chair. When it clarified, Candace was stunned at the person sitting there, hugging her knees. The girl, the one from Aspen, she was the one spying on her? What was her name again?

She dropped her hold enough to allow speech. "I'm not going to hurt you," she repeated. "I know what Gabe told you, but it's not like that. I'm not a threat, I promise. So what are you doing here?"

The girl gulped, staring out at Candace from behind a curtain of straight brown hair. "Just watching," she whispered. "You're pretty when you swim."

God, the girl couldn't be more than thirteen, fourteen at the most. "What's your name?"

"Mindy," she answered.

"Mindy what?"

"Lansky."

Candace nodded and lifted herself out of the pool. She approached the girl cautiously, not wanting to scare her any more than she already was. Her towel was nearby, and Candace dried off, wrapping it around her torso before sitting in the lounge chair beside Mindy's.

"Hi, Mindy. I'm Candace Bristol," she said. "If I let you loose, will you promise not to run away?"

"I promise."

With a sigh, Candace let her go. Mindy inched back into the seat, but stayed put.

"You don't have to be afraid of me," Candace said. "I just want to talk."

"About what?"

Candace shrugged. "Whatever you like. You. Me. The weather. Your choice."

Mindy gnawed her lip nervously. "Um, okay."

When the girl lapsed into silence, Candace smiled softly. It was going to take time. "How old are you?"

"Thirteen," she said.

Candace sighed. "So young. Can I ask you a question?"

Mindy nodded.

"Did you want to be a superhero?"

She nodded again.

"Why?"

"So no one could hurt me again."

Her simple statement tugged at something inside Candace: a deep, empathetic sadness. "I'm so sorry."

Mindy frowned. "Why?"

Candace leaned back in the chair, releasing a slow breath. "Lots of reasons, but mostly because I think you've already learned that just because you're a superhero it doesn't mean you don't get hurt anymore. There's more ways to hurt someone then by making them bleed."

With a small nod, Mindy acknowledged the truth of the words. "Why did you want to be a superhero?"

Closing her eyes, Candace tried to think back, to remember who she was before she came to California. "I wanted to be good. I wanted to help people, to protect them."

"You don't anymore?"

"I do," Candace said. "But it's more complicated. Good and bad, it's not always easy to figure out which is which. It's more like..." She paused, trying to put it into simple terms. "It's more like figuring out what I stand for, and trying to help as many people as I can, regardless of whether or not others think they deserve it. I'm not perfect, though. I make mistakes just like everyone else. The difference between us and normal people, however, is that when a superhero messes up, everyone sees it. Nothing we do is small. The tiniest of decisions, hesitations, failures to hesitate... the repercussions are huge. I spend every day wondering if something I do is going to end up hurting another person. Our hands can heal as much as they can bruise."

Candace chuckled a little. "Sorry. I get philosophical when I'm around this much water. Deep, if you will." It was a stupid joke, but Mindy cracked the smallest of smiles.

"Do you swim at all?" Candace asked.

"A little. Not like you."

"I usually swim before breakfast, around five or so," she said. "If you want, you're welcome to join me. You don't have to hide. I promise I won't bite."

Mindy nodded again, but didn't commit to anything.

Candace stood and stretched, yawning. "Well, I've had a long day, so I think I'll call it a night." She headed for the locker room, but turned to wave. "See ya, Mindy."

A few of Mindy's fingers flickered back at Candace in response. "See ya."

"SHE DOESN'T want you, Sunshine," Kristie said, her fingers curling up into Jackson's hair. *"You heard her. She doesn't think she can be with you any more."*

"I don't know, Princess," he murmured, staring into Kristie's eyes. *"I don't know that I can give it up that easily."*

"Shh," she whispered. One of her hands untangled from his hair and brushed his lips. *"I can help you forget all about her. You don't have to wait for someone to decide if you're good enough."*

Jackson's eyes shone, that smoldering flame flickering slightly. *"Am I good enough?"*

"Let me show you how good," she said, lifting up and pressing her lips to his.

Candace sat up, gasping, choking on tears. As she covered her face with her hands, the sobs shook free, rattling in her chest. She wanted to vomit.

Another heartbeat passed, and Gabe was there, his steady arms wrapping around her shoulders. "Easy, easy," he said, stroking her hair. "It was a nightmare, Candy Cane. Just a dream."

But she couldn't breathe. Her lungs expelled the air as quickly as she took it in, forcing it out in strained cries. "I'm losing him," she managed between them. "I'm losing him, and I can't fix it!"

"Candace, you gotta calm down," he said, holding her tighter. "You're not losing him."

"He won't—" she broke off in a gasp. "He won't wait for me. He won't and then I'll be alone!"

"Jackson will wait forever if he has to," Gabe said. "He's as stubborn as you are. Maybe more, if that's possible."

Candace shook her head and buried her face in his chest. "What can I do? I can't... I can't..." She dissolved into hysterical tears again.

No matter what Gabe said to her, nothing helped. The pain ran too deep: the nightmare too close to the truth. Eventually, she cried herself to sleep in his arms, waking a few short hours later to nauseating emptiness in her stomach.

Earlier than normal, Candace dragged herself to the pool. If nothing else, maybe she could soak away some of the horrible dread plaguing her. She needed to calm down enough that she could figure out some way forward, some words to say that would start them down the road to healing.

She barely noticed when someone else slipped into the water. The presence of another stirred her connection, drawing her out of her malaise. Candace surfaced at the edge of the pool and looked down the line. Two lanes over, Mindy was treading water, watching her with marked uncertainty.

Pushing away her own problems, Candace offered up a smile. "Good morning."

"Morning," Mindy replied, sheepish.

"Sleep well?"

The girl shrugged, her slight shoulders barely causing a ripple. "You?"

Candace faltered for a moment, but recovered. "Not as well as I'd like, but it happens." What next? It wasn't like the girl could race with her and hope to win. "I usually just swim laps for an hour or so. Nothing fancy. Don't feel like you have to keep up with me or anything. There aren't many who can. Float when you're tired. Quit when you prune. That's about all there is to it. Sound good?"

Mindy bobbed her head, then pushed off from the side, setting off at a moderate pace.

Surprisingly, Mindy toughed it out for a full sixty minutes. She wasn't overly strong or fast, but her endurance was stunning. After the hour, the girl ducked out with a quiet "thank you," and went on her way.

What concerned her at the moment, however, was that Candace didn't sense a thing from Jackson. He normally swam in the mornings, but he wasn't anywhere nearby or even on his way. In fact, the more she focused on it, the more she realized that she couldn't feel him at all. If he was anywhere within a five mile radius, she would know it.

But there was nothing.

Nothing? How could that be? Panic surged inside her. Was her nightmare becoming reality?

Candace bolted from the pool and back to Gabe's room, but her cousin wasn't there. Lingering warmth from the shower told her he hadn't been gone long, but she had no clue where to begin looking for him. She was being ridiculous. She couldn't keep running to him that way every damned time she freaked out. *Get it together, Candy Cane.*

Taking a deep breath, she decided to clean up before she went in search of Gabe. Maybe he'd be back by the time she got out of the shower. If she failed to find him, she decided to spend the day in the clinic, either visiting with Tori or reading medical textbooks. There was less need for

EVOLUTION: HEX

Candace's abilities in the clinic with a dedicated healer available, but more hands helping when people were hurt couldn't possibly be a bad thing.

When she emerged from the bathroom, Gabe still wasn't there. With a sigh, she decided to go about her day. He couldn't avoid her completely, after all.

She found him at breakfast, catching him as he sat down with Amir and True.

"Hey, you left early this morning," she said to him as she sat her tray down and slid onto the bench. "I needed to talk to you."

"Oh yeah?" he asked as he stuffed a bite of french toast in his mouth. "What about?"

Candace glanced at Amir and True, uncomfortable with having the discussion in front of them, but it wasn't like True didn't know what was going on. And since True knew about Jackson and what he'd done, that probably meant Amir did as well. "Uh, we can talk about it after breakfast. So how come you're up so early?"

Gabe rubbed his eyes, and a stab of guilt cut her. Candace was the reason he didn't sleep well the night before. "There was a situation. I almost had to go out east, but they decided to send someone else."

Candace frowned. "A situation? What? Who did they send?"

He shrugged. "They didn't tell me the exact details, but it was something to do with an accident in the caves in the Shenandoah Valley. They needed to shed a little light on the rescue. Because he's got heat and light, they sent Jackson instead."

Her stomach dropped. "They sent him... out east?"

"It's not permanent, Candy," True said, reassuring her. "One mission only. He'll be back in a day or so."

Breathe, Candy. Breathe. He's coming back.

Gabe nudged her leg and she jerked, suddenly aware she was staring into space.

"Huh? What?" she said, blinking at him.

He gave her an understanding smile. "I asked what you had planned for the day."

"Oh," she said, trying to remember what she decided. "I think I'll go to the clinic, do some studying. I thought I might check up on Trevor, too. Has anyone heard anything about how he's doing?"

Amir shook his head sadly. "They've still got him under lockdown. One of the corpsman told me he's not healing well. They don't want to wake him until the worst of it's over, but I don't know how much longer they'll give him."

Candace picked at her toast, pulling off the crust. "Think they'll let me see him?"

Gabe shrugged. "Probably. You've been to see him before and he's probably only alive because of your intervention, on two separate occasions, at that."

In reality, it wasn't her she was concerned they wouldn't allow. Maybe Tori couldn't fix him in one go, but she could at least make significant progress. Would they trust her to try?

There was only one way to find out.

CHAPTER 12

TORI PACED the waiting room when Candace walked into the clinic. Immediately, the healer ran up, looking frantic as she grabbed Candace's hands.

"There's someone here I can help, but they won't let me," Tori said, talking a million miles an hour. "I can't keep still, Candace. It's calling me, but I can't do a thing about it. Can you get me in?"

Startled by the behavior, Candace tried to calm her down. "Whoa. Hang on," she said. "Who won't let you in where?"

Tori motioned to the hall leading to the ICU. "Someone back there. I tried to go in this morning, but the control desk said no. They said I can't go by myself."

"Ah, right." Candace nodded. "I think I know the patient

in question. I was actually going to see him this morning. They needed my help with him before, so I think they'll let me back there. Come on."

As Candace led the way, she explained to Tori who Trevor was and what happened to him. "Trevor Ching was wounded in the Portland attack. He suffered severe electrical burns and probably only survived because of his super strength. However, that same strength has been a problem in his treatment. When he woke up, pain medications didn't work and they had to induce a coma while he healed. I haven't seen him since I've been back, but from what I hear, it's not going well."

They bypassed the control desk with a wave from Candace and a nod from the corpsman seated there. The closer they got to Trevor's room, the more agitated Tori got, and the woman was practically vibrating by the time Candace opened the door. Tori rushed into the room, her hands instantly going for the bandages covering Trevor's left side.

"Hang on, Tori," Candace said, touching her shoulder. "Before you start, you need to explain to me what you're going to do. They may have given you a pass for the time being, but I expect they'll ask me to report on whatever you do here."

Tori twitched, her fingers rubbing together as she tried to control her impulses. "I have to remove the bandages. I need skin to skin contact for this to work."

Candace nodded. "Let's at least wash our hands and put gloves on first, okay?"

"But," Tori argued. "Skin to skin—"

EVOLUTION: HEX

"I know." Candace smiled reassuringly. "We'll get there."

Scrubbed in and gloved, the two of them set to work removing the gauze protecting Trevor's wounds. Candace clamped down on her urge to gag as she saw what lay beneath the dressings. The skin grafts the doctors put in place mostly took, but looked loose, unhealed. It was a month since Candace saw him last, and almost nothing had changed.

Tori's face contracted in anguish. "This is awful."

"This was done by one of Dr. Ferdinand's *mistakes*," Candace said, gritting her teeth. "He wasn't the only one hurt that night, either. Dozens were killed, I don't even know how many were injured. It was horrific."

"I'm so sorry," Tori whispered, a few tears running down her cheeks. She looked down at Trevor and lifted an ungloved hand, gently resting it against his cheek. "I want to make it right where I can."

Candace tensed, unable to do anything but watch as the healer worked. It was nothing like in the movies or comic books. There was no blinding light or even so much as a soft glow around her hands. At first, Candace couldn't tell if anything was happening or not.

She got a little closer, squinting at Trevor's face. Like watching a time-lapse video, Candace finally saw progress. Gradually, the separations in the skin grafts closed up, sealed to the point of invisibility. They were still red and raw, but the improvement was undeniable.

Tori pulled away, gasping, and sank to her knees. Candace rushed around the side of Trevor's bed. "Are you all right?" she asked.

Her breathing quick and jerky, Tori nodded. "I'll be fine. It's just that there's a lot of damage. I tried to…" She broke off and took a few gulps of air. "I tried to fix as much as I could, but it's really extensive."

Candace helped her to her feet and walked her over to a chair. "I don't think anyone expects you to completely heal this kind of thing in one go, Tori. I see a huge difference already. Your ability is amazing. Mine has a few medical applications, but nothing like yours. What you can do is incredible. If I could, I'd trade you in a heartbeat."

"I'm not all that amazing, Candace," Tori said, staring at the floor. "If Asia were here, she'd have him up and running laps already."

"Who's Asia?" Candace asked. She vaguely recalled Mica mentioning the name before.

She shrugged a little. "Another HEX healer. She's first string. Very powerful. She never let me do anything. Always called me Lil Bit."

"Lil Bit?" Candace asked. "Why?"

Tori chewed her lip and wouldn't meet Candace's eyes. "Because, compared to her, I can only do a lil' bit."

Candace grunted in disgust. "That's awful, Tori. She sounds like a bitch."

Another shrug.

Kneeling in front of her, Candace smiled and lifted Tori's chin. "Know what I think?"

Tori's lip quivered.

"I think you're a lil' bit awesome. Seriously. No one here can come close to what you can do," Candace said. "I mean, look at what you did for me, what you're doing for Trevor.

Don't let anyone tell you that's not significant. It's not a competition, it's a team effort."

"You really think so?"

The emotion in Tori's eyes was so familiar. Mica looked at her the same way when they discussed his ability. Why? Wasn't the HEX goal to make everyone feel like a family? Family shouldn't devalue the strengths of its members. Family shouldn't make you feel less important than anyone else; it should be the opposite. Family should hold you above anyone else and love without condition.

"Of course I think so, Tori," Candace said. "It kind of pisses me off that anyone would make you think otherwise."

The shyest of smiles crept across her lips. "Thank you, Candace," Tori said.

"You don't need to thank me for treating you with respect, Tori," she said with a chuckle and stood. "That's baseline for me. Besides, by my estimation, I still owe you for saving my life."

Tori giggled. "That's like owing the broom for sweeping the floor. I did what I was made for."

"Ah, but here's the difference," Candace said as she searched around for clean bandages for Trevor. "A broom can't choose not to do its job. You can. I'm thanking you for making the choice to help." She frowned at the inside of a cabinet, not finding what she was looking for. "I'll have to tell a corpsman to come in and fix him up." She turned back to Tori. "Can I walk you back to your room? You look like you could use some rest."

They headed out, stopping at the control desk to let them know about Trevor. Assured they would take care of it,

Candace steadied Tori as they reached the waiting room again.

"So who did they stick you with for a roommate?" Candace asked.

"No one, since my room is back there," Tori said, motioning down the main medical hallway.

Candace stared at her. "They're making you live in the clinic?"

She shook her head. "No, I asked to. I'm right where I want to be."

Candace shrugged and let it go. She supposed she'd choose to live in the pool if they'd let her, so it probably wasn't any different for Tori. Being close to the thing you were connected to brought a comfort like nothing else could.

Well, except maybe one other thing.

Candace flinched as memories of Jackson's arms invaded her thoughts, socking her in the gut with longing. She didn't think it was possible, but him being all the way across the country without her made it worse. Even if he had done something terrible, he'd done it for her.

Honestly, Candace didn't have any idea what was going on in his head. The knowledge of his actions kept her from even being able to talk to him about it. So far, every moment she was with him was spent trying not to scream or cry or punch his stupid face.

"Candace?" Tori said, giving her a concerned look.

"What?" she said, shaking her head to clear it. "Sorry. I got distracted. What did you say?"

"I asked about his condition."

Candace blinked. "Who's?"

EVOLUTION: HEX

"Trevor's. You said you had to help him before. What did you do?"

They stopped in front of a door and Tori swiped her badge in the card reader. Candace collected her thoughts as they went into the office-turned-bedroom. It really wasn't much more than that. A few bookshelves had been removed to clear space for a fold-up cot, but aside from that, it looked exactly like Dr. Poznanski's office.

"The last time I saw Trevor was when he first regained consciousness after the attack," Candace explained. "I had to paralyze him and talk him down. He woke up in pain and with no memory of what happened. The more I talked to him, the more a few things came back, but it wasn't for long enough to tell how serious or permanent the memory loss was."

"Hmm," Tori said, easing onto the edge of the bed. "I don't know that there's anything I can do for that. I can only repair physical wounds, not restore memories. That's more Michele's area of expertise. Have you talked to her at all?"

Aware that the room almost certainly had hidden surveillance, Candace went into acting mode. "You mean outside of them interrogating me at the HEX compound? No. I haven't. I didn't really know what her ability was until they told me after I got rescued." She crossed her arms and cocked her head to the side, thinking. "Do you know much about what she does?"

Tori shrugged. "Not in a lot of detail. Like I said, I was second string for HEX. Michele was first string with Asia and others. I know she's a telepath. I know she can talk inside your head. She can read your thoughts like pictures and intents, but not like verbatim words, from what I gather. I dunno much, really. She's a little standoffish. Not like Mica. I know they're twins, but Michele was always more like a protective big sister. Mica's the friendly one."

"Do you think she's in a hurry to get back to Dr. Ferdinand?" Candace asked, almost hoping the ANGEL Project was listening in.

"Could be, but I don't think so," she said. "She'll stick with Mica. If he's happy, that's where she'll want to be, too."

Candace considered that before continuing. "And what about you?"

"What about me?" Tori said, skimming her shoes along the carpet as her legs dangled over the edge of the cot.

"Are you in a hurry to get out of here?"

Tori snorted. "Not at all. Not if you guys let me work. I never got to do anything important back there. Dr. F might've found me and made me what I am, but it was pretty clear I was never really important, not with Asia around. At best I was backup."

As much as Candace wanted to press Tori for information, even things about her background, the woman looked exhausted. "Well, if it means anything, you'll be first string around here."

Tori stared at the floor, biting her lip, but unable to hide her smile.

"I'll let you get some rest," Candace said, opening the door. "Come find me later if they won't let you in to see him again."

"Sure," Tori said, her gaze still firmly fixed on the floor. "Hey, Candy?"

"Yeah?" She paused and looked back.

Tori's dark eyes lifted. "Thanks."

Candace smiled and nodded, then closed the door as she left.

SHE TOOK a deep breath, one hand resting on the handle, the other holding her badge above the card reader.

She was being stupid. It was her room, too. If anything, she should boot *him* out. She could do it while he was gone, and he wouldn't be there to argue with her about it.

Releasing the air from her lungs, Candace swiped the badge and pushed open the door. Before she could talk herself out of it, she went in and shut the door behind her, leaning back against the cool metal with her eyes closed.

Breathe. Just breathe. He's not here.

Slowly, she opened her eyes. The memories were on her instantly, as heavy as his scent lingering in the air: something warm and earthy, like burning leaves on an autumn day. Jackson was everywhere: in the pristinely made bed, in the carefully ordered office supplies, in the bookshelves so meticulously organized. She wandered over to the desk, seeing her pile of medical textbooks stacked on the corner. They were mixed up in size and shape, exactly how she left them. He hadn't touched them. He left them there for her, as though she'd be back at any moment to pick up where she left off in her reading.

Pulling out the chair, Candace sat, needing to catch her

breath. She ran her fingers over the surface of the desk, touching the various cups and holders keeping everything in its place. She stared at one of them, a light blue cup filled with pencils in various states of sharpened and dull. It never occurred to her to look before, but as she studied them, they didn't look like average Number Two pencils.

She picked one out, looking at the label. Gold embossed words told her what she needed to know.

They were drawing pencils.

Candace never assumed she knew everything there was to know about Jackson, not by a long shot, but that? Shouldn't she know about something like that?

Her curiosity on high, she opened one of the desk drawers beside her and pulled out a pad of paper resting on top. The bright orange cover was smudged in places, smeared fingerprints stating ownership. Hesitant, she flipped the cover up.

All of the air whooshed out of her lungs as she stared at her own face.

No. Not her face. Her face the way *Jackson* saw it.

The lines were soft, her expression relaxed and eyes closed in sleep. Candace studied the marks, following each one and the pure emotion behind it. How long had he studied her face to know it in such detail? He even captured the feeling of movement in her hair, in the way the light seemed to hit every strand as it shifted in unseen currents.

Hands shaking, she turned the page.

Candace was swimming, her legs so close together they were more like the tail of a fish than human limbs. Currents wrapped around her body, obeying her unspoken commands as she twisted within.

In the next drawing, her head was emerging from the water, hair flowing behind her, lips slightly parted, and eyes wide.

At the fourth one, Candace couldn't go any farther. She stared at the paper, overwhelmed by the image. Naked, she floated in a whirlwind of fire and water. Her face was turned, a hint of pain in her expression as flames licked her bare skin. Candace covered her mouth, holding back a sob. That was Jackson's fear, that he would hurt her. It was the nature of fire to burn.

As the first tears rolled down her cheeks, Candace closed her eyes. For him to draw her that way... how didn't she know? Why had she never noticed that in him?

After a few calming breaths, she glanced back at the notebook. In the bottom right corner, he scribbled in the date.

Less than a week ago.

Choking on sobs, she flipped the book closed and carefully replaced it in the drawer. It told her everything she needed to know.

The problem was, how could she get those visions of him, those flickers of betrayal, out of her head?

Jackson loved her above all others. He knew he was hurting her, but had to save her. Someone like him wasn't capable of doing nothing, of trusting others with what he held most dear. Not Jackson. Not ever.

Candace pushed away from the desk and collected a few of the textbooks to take with her. She needed to get out of there. If he came back unexpectedly and found her in their room, she wasn't sure what would happen. If she could find somewhere quiet, free of distractions, at least she could calm down, maybe sort through some of it.

Torn between the hurt and the longing, Candace hurried out into the hall. The confused mess in her heart wouldn't allow her to think, not while she sat there, surrounded by his things, his memories.

Only one place could offer her the peace she needed. Water understood. Water would never question. Water was the one thing she would never doubt.

CHAPTER 13

AFTER ANOTHER night of restless dreams that woke her with shuddering sobs, Candace was exhausted. She was bone tired and sick of not sleeping well. Half-seriously, she wondered if Mica had any of that knock out gas of his hanging around. Maybe then she could get a few hours of shut-eye without waking up terrified.

Gabe was curiously absent from breakfast, and Amir and True didn't stay long after Candace sat down. Maybe they could sense Candace's foul mood and wanted to steer clear. She didn't give it much thought.

As she dumped her tray, someone touched her arm. Candace jumped at the unexpected contact. Turning, Deborah stared at her, surprised by the reaction. "Sorry, I didn't mean to startle you."

Candace smiled and caught her breath. "Don't worry about it. What's up?"

"Do you have plans for today?" Deborah asked as they left the dining hall.

"Clinic stuff," Candace said. "I'm stalled on Naveen until you-know-who comes back from out east."

"Oh, good." Deborah linked her arm through Candace's and led her away. "I need your help there anyway."

"My help?"

Deborah nodded. "Mmm. After Tori finishes another treatment this morning, they think Trevor will be healed enough they can wake him up."

"And you want me to play bodyguard?"

"That, and I thought, based on what happened last time, you might be able to help assess his memory loss, or help his recall."

Candace shrugged. "I guess. I'm not sure how useful I can be there. I mean, I haven't known him for all that long."

"But you were in Portland with him. You know what happened." Deborah pulled open the clinic door and let them both in.

"Do you think it's smart to tell him about all that right away?" Candace asked as they collected Tori from the waiting room and headed for the ICU. "Especially the part about Gil... and Allen. Does he need that kind of bomb dropped on him the minute he wakes up from a coma?"

Deborah smiled at Tori and continued talking. "Not the minute he wakes up, no. But I think he'll want to know everything once he's coherent and his pain is managed. Wouldn't you?"

Candace conceded the point and looked at Tori. "All rested up?"

She nodded, her same twitchy mannerisms back. The healer was in a hurry to get back to work.

They filed into Trevor's room. Dr. Poznanski looked up from a tablet as they entered, his expression pleasant enough, though he didn't seem overly glad to see Candace. She ignored it.

"Good morning, ladies," he said. "Are we ready to help get Mr. Ching back amongst the living?"

Tori bounced from foot to foot. "Absolutely."

Candace prodded her towards the sink to wash up. Deborah stayed to the side and out of the way as they worked to remove Trevor's bandages. As much as Candace could tell, his burns looked even better than they did when she left yesterday, as though the healing continued rapidly without further assistance from Tori.

"He's so much better today," Tori murmured as she worked.

"I told you," Candace said, grinning. "A little bit awesome."

They repeated the process of the day before, with Tori gently resting her palm against the left side of his face. Several minutes passed, and the redness in his skin was all but gone when she was done, with hardly any traces of scarring. Dr. Poznanski caught her when she collapsed, carefully guiding her over to a seat. While Tori caught her breath, Candace turned her attention to Trevor, feeling the water in his body to make sure everything was where it should be. Carefully, she shifted fluids around, reducing some of the residual swelling around his injured tissue.

"Excellent work, Miss Drake," Dr. Poznanski said as he examined the healed skin. "What do you know about the internal damage?"

"Most of it was surface damage, fortunately," she said. Her voice sounded like it was being dredged up from the bottom of her lungs and forced out. "There was some damage to his internal organs, a bit to the lungs, a little to the heart, but I think I've fixed most of that. He's lucky he's so strong."

"And your assessment, Miss Bristol?"

Candace nodded. "That's about as much as I can tell. Everything seems to be flowing the way it should, water-wise. There's a little bit of scarring around the inside of his ribs, but otherwise he'll be okay."

"Excellent," he said. "How about we wake him, then?"

Candace gulped, nervous. She readied herself should it not go well.

Dr. Poznanski approached the controls for the IV drip and made his adjustments.

When he finished, he backed away. "And now, we wait."

"How long?" Candace asked.

"Could be a few minutes, could be a day or more," he said. "Likely as not, it will probably be today. It depends on any brain trauma he suffered and what remains as far as injuries go." Dr. Poznanski turned to leave. "I trust you ladies will keep an eye on him. Make sure you let me know when he's awake."

"Thank you, Doctor," Deborah said as he left.

They waited in silence for several minutes, unsure of what to expect. Candace focused on his heart rate monitor, watching the numbers gradually tick up. Twenty minutes after stopping the drugs, Trevor let out a soft groan. She pulled up a stool and sat, positioning herself at his eye level, ready to paralyze him should he show any signs of violence.

When his eyes opened, her face was the first thing he saw, much as it had been the last thing before he went to sleep. He blinked slowly, trying to place her.

"Hi, big guy," Candace said, smiling softly. "You with us again?"

"Candy Cane?" he croaked, his voice strained after a month without use.

"That's me," she said, grinning. "Glad you remember me this time. How do you feel? How's the pain?"

His eyes traced her face. "Better than the last time I saw you. How long has it been?"

She looked back at Deborah. It would probably be a shock if Candace told him straight out.

Taking that as her cue, the empath came over, gently taking his hand. "Hey you," she said quietly. "Remember me?"

It took him a minute, but a small smile pulled at the corner of his mouth. "Deborah. How could I forget?"

It was a good sign he remembered that much, and Candace breathed a little sigh of relief. They spoke with him for a while, filling him in on his injuries. At one point, Candace glanced back to Tori, only to see her fast asleep, her head leaning against the wall.

When he asked about why he was in the clinic, what put him there, Deborah deflected. "Hang on to your question for a bit, okay?" she said. "Dr. Poznanski wanted us to tell him when you were awake." She smiled again and went for the door. "I'll be back in a minute."

Trevor's brow wrinkled when he caught sight of Tori. "Who's that?"

"Her name is Tori Drake," Candace explained. "She's the reason you're better now. She heals."

"Is she from out east?"

Candace shook her head. "No. Not exactly."

His eyebrows shot up. "I was out long enough for a new round of ANGELs to go through?"

Sensing his panic, Candace touched the side of his face. "No. She's not a new recruit in the normal sense. She's..." She frowned and dropped her hand. "It's a long story. And complicated. We'll fill you in gradually. A lot's changed recently. I don't want to overwhelm you."

Trevor was watching Tori again. "Is she nice?"

"Very, yes," Candace said, fighting back a grin. "I'm only just getting to know her myself, but she seems very sweet."

His gaze stayed on the healer until Deborah returned with Dr. Poznanski and a corpsman. The rest of Trevor's questions would have to wait.

CANDACE'S DAY was completely filled with Trevor. At Deborah's suggestion, they took their lunch with him in his room, constantly talking to him, filling in the gaps of his memory where they could.

The hardest part was telling him about Allen and Gil.

Deborah held his hand through it all, and Candace made

sure to break the news herself. Their deaths still weighed heavily on her, especially Allen's. Tori was silent through most of it, listening to the stories and getting to know Trevor through shared ANGEL experiences. Even with reliving the grief, Candace couldn't help noticing the small, shy glances between the healer and the giant. She wondered if he was drawn to Tori because of their connection through her ability. It wasn't easy to pin down for herself. Tori was nice the first time Candace met her. Still, she wondered if her opinion was colored by any healing Tori might have done while Candace was unconscious. She gave up trying to analyze it eventually. There was no way to go about it objectively.

It was a little awkward when they came to the part explaining who Tori was. Telling Trevor that their new healer was so recently a part of the organization responsible for the deaths of two of his close friends was rough. His internal struggle to reconcile it was visible on his face. He glanced from Candace to Tori, unsure about how to feel.

"I wasn't understating when I said it was complicated," Candace said, apologetic. "It's going to take time for everyone to adapt. I don't think it's impossible, though."

Trevor let out a heavy sigh. "You're probably right."

Tori was twitchy again. "I know this is a lot to take in, but would you mind if I..." She trailed off, losing her nerve.

"If you what?" Trevor asked, his deep voice kind, rather than judgmental.

Candace noted the way Tori rubbed her fingertips together, as though they itched. "Ah, I think I see. Trevor, there's still a bit of damage from the attack. She wants to fix it. Well, needs to, really. She gets antsy when someone's hurt and she's not allowed to help."

Tori blushed as Trevor's gaze rested on her again.

"You've done this much for me," he said. "If you want to, you're welcome to patch up the rest."

The way he said it, it sounded like he meant much more than healing his physical wounds.

Afterwards, Tori was completely wiped, barely able to shuffle her feet as Candace helped her back to her room.

"He seems nice," she mumbled sleepily.

Candace hefted Tori's arm across her shoulders and grinned. "He is. He's also single."

At that, the other woman stumbled. Candace chuckled as she helped her back up, and they finished the walk to her office bedroom. "Sorry, I couldn't resist."

As tired as she was, Tori was still red-cheeked as she sat down on her bed. "That wasn't what I meant, you know. I wasn't fishing."

Candace giggled. "It's okay. It doesn't take an empath to see he's interested in you. I just thought I might help things along, you know, in case you were curious."

Tori rubbed her eyes and yawned. "I'm too tired to be curious, but, thanks," she said.

"Sure thing," Candace said, already at the door. "Get some rest. I'll see you later."

Tori was passed out before Candace even flipped off the light.

Deborah met her in the clinic waiting room and hooked her arm to lead her out. "Hungry?" she asked.

"Uh, I suppose," Candace said. "What's on tap in the

dining hall tonight?"

She waved a hand dismissively. "I had something else in mind."

"Something else? Where else would we eat? It's after six already and it's not like we can get pizza delivered or anything."

"Actually," Deborah whispered, leaning in close. "I may have talked a staffer into bringing a special treat, but we have to be sneaky about it."

Candace narrowed her eyes, suspicious. "What?"

"Do you still have that outfit True loaned you the other day? That gorgeous sweater and jeans?"

"Outfit?" What was all that about? What did that sweater have to do with anything? "Yeah, it just came back from the laundry. Why?"

Deborah giggled. "You'll need something warm for the walk."

"For the walk?"

The empath shoved her down the hall in the direction of Gabe's room. "Just do it. Trust me. Go get yourself prettied up and meet me here in an hour, okay?"

"Deborah, what—?"

She shooed her away. "Just do it," she repeated. "You'll see."

Confused as hell, Candace wandered away. Whatever it was, it was something different, which was kind of nice. Besides, it might be fun to do something under the radar that didn't involve possible mutiny.

DEBORAH WAS all giggles and no answers as she led Candace away from the compound and out through the Quad. The most she would say was "you'll see," which really did nothing but cause suspicion and wild speculation on Candace's part.

After walking for half a mile in the dark, she caught the faintest hint of something burning: a wood fire.

Another quarter mile, and the source came into view.

The sight of the bonfire stopped Candace in her tracks. If there was fire involved, Jackson must be, too. For the first time all day, she realized she could feel him again. He was back and he was close— dead ahead if her gut was right.

"What are we doing here?" she asked, determined to get an answer. "If this is some sort of setup he's planned, I'm not going over there."

"He who?" Deborah said, the picture of innocence.

Candace crossed her arms and leveled her with a look. "Don't play dumb with me. You know damn well who, and you know damn well why I don't want to go."

Deborah's face softened and she reached for Candace's hands, pulling them free as she urged her onwards. "Just trust me, okay? It's not what you think. I promise."

As the endorphins kicked in, Candace tried to hold on to her irritation. "Not cool, Deb. Why does everyone have to use chemical weapons on me to get their way?"

Releasing her hands and taking up a cozy position on Candace's left arm, Deborah giggled. "Because you're too stubborn to listen to people otherwise. It'll be fun. I swear."

The sounds of music coupled with the scent of burning wood, and people came into view as they got closer. A secret party? That's what it was? What for? And why didn't she know about it?

They came to a halt inside a circle of tiki torches, a haze of citronella mingling with the smoke from the fire. Deborah let out a shrill whistle, abruptly ending all conversations and silencing the music. Almost every ANGEL was there, parting as Deborah led Candace around the fire to a set of tables on the other side.

Cake.

Pizza.

Soda.

A bowl of candy.

Balloons?

"Happy birthday, cuz," Gabe whispered in her ear.

Candace turned to look at him, stunned. "This is... for me?"

Gabe chuckled. "You forgot your own birthday?"

She crossed her arms and huffed. "I've been a little busy."

"Good thing I'm looking out for ya then, huh?" His grin spread across his face, showing how thoroughly pleased he was with himself.

She couldn't really be mad at him. Dropping her arms, she grinned back. "Comes in handy sometimes." She laughed at herself. "I can't believe I forgot my own birthday." With a few steps, Candace closed the distance and hugged him tightly. "Thank you," she said.

"You're welcome," he said. "But I can't really take all the credit."

Candace pulled away and turned back to Deborah, holding out her hand. When she took it, Candace pulled her in for a hug. "You're smarter than people give you credit for, empath," she said, chuckling. "Thank you."

"You're so welcome, Candy Cane," Deborah said, squeezing her tightly. "But the surprise wasn't my idea, just how to keep you busy all day."

"Is this a party or what?" Gabe yelled, starting up the conversation again. "Let's get this thing rolling!"

The whole thing left Candace speechless and overwhelmed. Between slices of cake and pizza, her fellow ANGELs offered birthday wishes and hugs, and there was even a table of gifts. With the portable speaker and the guitar someone brought out, the air was always filled with music and laughter. They even sang the Happy Birthday song, much to Candace's embarrassment. She never knew how to act for that, and settled on awkwardly smiling at everyone who gathered around.

Two hours in, they finally cajoled her into opening her presents. There were comic books and graphic novels, new clothes from True, the sweetest little friendship bracelet from Mindy, and a blank journal labeled "Life Lessons" from Gabe.

"It's pretty big," he said, shrugging. "I figured you'd need plenty of room to write down all the stuff you have yet to learn."

"Funny," she said, nudging him with an elbow. "I'll remember that next time I have to correct your grammar."

Candace giggled and reached for the last package.

EVOLUTION: HEX

Wrapped in plain brown craft paper, it was about twelve inches square and three inches deep, and heavier than it looked. There wasn't any indication who it was from. Curious, she peeled away the paper, revealing a very familiar-looking binder, the silver ANGEL logo emblazoned on the black cover.

Her mouth went dry.

Shaking a little, she opened the front cover, revealing the card collection she brought with her from home. Faces of friends and colleagues stared back at her, as familiar as family.

And they were all signed.

She flipped the pages one by one, pausing at the few that were without signatures: ANGELs that were no longer with them. Even cards for the Superheroes at the Virginia compound were autographed in silver ink.

Only one person could have made that happen.

It didn't take her long to find him. Jackson pulled at her like a homing beacon. He stood away from the group, back amongst a clump of trees, watching her. When Candace met his eyes, her throat constricted. She couldn't breathe.

"This was all his idea, Candy Cane," Gabe whispered in her ear. "Not mine."

As she stared at Jackson, the lines of his sketches floated through her mind. The intensity of the emotions on those pages — the longing, the adoration, the regret, and fear — they were all there in his eyes, burning hotter than the bonfire behind her.

Gabe touched her back briefly, breaking her concentration as he left to have a seat on a log beside Mica. She watched them for a moment as Mica settled in with the guitar and strummed the opening chords of a song she didn't recognize.

"How about a dance, Sugar Plum?" Jackson's words fluttered across her skin, softer than a butterfly's wings.

Unable to speak, Candace turned slowly. Her gaze fixed on his face, the rest of the world faded away. They swayed to the music, close, but never touching. As Mica's voice mingled with the notes from the guitar, Jackson slipped his fingers into hers, and her thoughts ran circles around everything between them.

Jackson rested his forehead against hers, closing his eyes. "I never wanted to hurt you, Sugar Plum," he said softly. "But fire—"

"Fire burns," she said, completing his thought. "And water can drown you. That's the chance we take."

He sighed, his eyes pinched tight.

"But," she continued. "That power can take away the bad things, the impurities. Burn them away, wash them down the drain. It can make a fresh start. Both can renew as much as destroy. It's up to us what we choose to do."

Jackson lifted his head, meeting her gaze. "Candace…"

She shook her head, the barest of smiles touching her lips. "I'm not saying everything's all right. That's going to take time, but I think I've realized something. There isn't enough time in the world for us, Sunshine. Even if I had eternity, it wouldn't be enough."

As they stopped their sway, she pulled her hands from his, resting them against his chest. His heart thudded against her palms, matching hers beat for beat. Candace lifted up, her face tilted, welcoming him home.

Searing, sharp pain burst into life, shooting through her lower left side. Gasping, she collapsed against Jackson, fingers clutching at his jacket as the agony spread through her abdomen.

"Candace? Candace, what's wrong?" When his hand touched her side, she cried out. He jerked it away, and she caught a glimpse of crimson staining his palm as she sank to her knees.

Before she knew what happened, Candace dove into her connection, calling to the water within her own body to save her. Fluids leaked from her, all but stopping as she took command of their movements.

"See?" Kristie's voice behind her almost broke her concentration. "I told you I wasn't giving up."

Candace focused on her breathing, on keeping the water within her. Somewhere she heard ANGELs yelling, raising the alarm.

"What did you do?" The heat rolled off of Jackson as he rose to stand.

"I fixed it, Sunshine," she said, her voice high and laced with deranged giggles. "If she's gone, there's nothing standing in our way."

Glancing up, Candace couldn't see much of what was happening. All of her focus was inward, on staying alive, but a quick look at Jackson stopped her heart. Blue flames danced around him, winding through his hair and fingers. Calm, but undeniably furious, Jackson was both beautiful and terrifying.

"I lost her once," he said, his voice hoarse. "How dare you try to take her from me again."

"But… I thought…" Kristie said, confused. "But you want me! I know you do! You were just pretending not to so she wouldn't hurt me!"

"You don't get it," he said, barely audible. "It was never *her* you had to worry about."

When Candace heard footsteps rushing towards her, she turned to see Kristie, her face contorted in rage as she charged forward, knife in hand. She howled as she raised the weapon to strike again, but froze, pain replacing anger in her expression.

Candace stared. Blackened cracks spread across Kristie's skin. As they grew, small pricks of light seeped through, escaping from her body in small, violent explosions. She burned from the inside out, charring, unable to even scream. Her skin crackled and turned white until, at last, she crumbled away into a pile of ash and smoke.

Stunned at the display of power, Candace slammed back into reality with a fresh round of pain flaring from her wound.

"Hang on, Candy Cane," Gabe said, gently lifting her and passing her into someone else's arms. "Tobias will get you to the clinic."

As the wind rushed through her hair, her last coherent thought almost made her smile.

Happy birthday to me.

CHAPTER 14

CANDACE AWOKE to the feel of ice in her veins. Trembling from the cold, her teeth chattered, and her breath came in shaky pulls. Gradually, she opened her eyes.

The clinic. Again. Maybe she should just move in and be done with it.

"Candy?" Jackson's warm fingers slipped between hers, but even he couldn't drive out the chill inside her.

"H-hey," she said, shivering. "We really g-gotta s-stop meeting this w-way."

His dark eyes lifted from hers, his eyebrows scrunched together. "Why is she shivering?"

Dr. Poznanski bent over her, resting the back of his hand against her forehead and frowning. "She's not running a fever. Miss Bristol, how do you feel?"

As she shifted slightly, she winced, a jolt of pain reminding her to keep still. "As-s-s-side from like I was stabbed?" When he responded with an impatient look, she continued. "Like someone's p-pumping dry ice into my arm."

Dr. Poznanski's expression shifted from vague concern to keen interest as he turned toward her IV drip. Candace followed his line of sight, taking in the half-empty bag of blood hanging beside her.

He stepped back and crossed his arms, letting out a thoughtful hum. "Between Miss Drake and the surgical staff, we were able to patch you up, but you lost quite a bit of blood in the process. Given the genetically altered nature of ANGELs, normal blood donations aren't an option, and we have to draw from within our ranks. Furthermore, we're still restricted by blood types on top of this. You presented a challenge as there are only two individuals here that are a match for you."

"Wh-who?" she asked.

"Your cousin and Mr. Patil. We took one pint from each."

"S-so wh-why am I c-cold?"

"Any reasons I give would be pure speculation," Dr. Poznanski said. "But I believe you're feeling the effects of Mr. Patil's donation at the moment, though I've never seen an ANGEL be physically affected by a transfusion this way. It may have something to do with your ability or his, or some combination thereof. As I said, it's pure speculation at this point."

"B-but you think this w-will wear off, r-right?"

"As you process it, I would think so," he said. "But it's possible that won't happen until those cells are completely out of your system, replaced by your own body."

Candace searched her memory, paging through everything she was learning in her medical studies. If the average woman had six to seven pints of blood, each taking about four to six weeks to create, she could be looking at a minimum of twenty-four weeks of feeling frozen inside. "So p-possibly half a year or m-more like th-this? Awesome," she said, groaning.

"Consider yourself fortunate, Miss Bristol," Dr. Poznanski said. "Without Mr. Patil's willing participation, you might have died."

Jackson's grip on her hand tightened. "Anything I can do to help?"

"I would think twice about that, given your demonstration on Miss Burke this evening," Dr. Poznanski said.

Candace sucked in a sharp breath and closed her eyes. Visions of Kristie's crumbling face burned behind her eyelids, eliciting another shiver. Jackson's grip on her hand loosened, prompting her to hold on tighter and look at him. She knew what it meant to take a life on purpose. Now, he did too. No matter what he'd done in the past, she wouldn't have wished that on him.

"Well, it's late, Miss Bristol. Should you need anything else for the pain, feel free to use the call button. The on-duty physician will see to your needs." Dr. Poznanski opened the door to leave. "Your cousin wanted to see you once you woke. Should I send him in?"

"P-please."

It took Gabe less than fifteen seconds to get in the door. "You really need to get a handle on your drama, Candy

Cane," he said as he eased onto a stool. "I'm kinda ready to be bored again."

"You s-say that as though I'd d-disagree with you," Candace said, smiling.

He frowned. "Why are you shaking?"

"R-reaction to d-donated blood," she said. "Not yours. Th-thank you for th-that, by the way."

Waving it off, he glanced up at Jackson. "Who's blood?"

"One of the prisoners from the HEX raid," Jackson explained. "Naveen Patil. He displaces heat. Sort of my opposite."

"Ah," Gabe said, then looked back at Candace. "How are you otherwise?"

She sighed. "I'll s-survive. As always. In c-case I d-didn't say it enough already, th-thank you, b-both of you," she said, glancing at Jackson. "For tonight. K-Kristie aside, it w-was very th-thoughtful."

"Yeah, well, I didn't intend for you to end up in surgery by the end of it," Gabe said, running a hand through his hair. "We're lucky Tobias is so fast."

"I could've taken her," Jackson grumbled.

Gabe snorted. "Are you kidding? She'd have been barbecue after thirty seconds if I let you."

Jackson didn't argue, but he didn't look happy about conceding the point.

"Look," Gabe said, his expression earnest. "No one else would've been able to take on her level of crazy the way you did. With Candace unable to fight, you did the only thing anyone could. We knew it was a matter of time before she snapped, Jackson, but no one expected her to attack

Candace. That was probably the most insane thing she could have done. I know I already said this, but thank you for what you did."

Jackson was quiet, staring at his hand holding Candace's, his thumb absently brushing against her skin. Candace squeezed his fingers, prompting him to meet her eyes. She smiled softly, hoping to reassure him.

After holding her gaze for a moment, he looked up at Gabe and nodded once.

Candace closed her eyes, flinching as another wave of discomfort passed through her abdomen. The whole pain thing was really getting old.

"You should put this button to good use," Gabe said, handing her a small, black device with a white button on one end. "It'll come in handy until you're all healed up."

She took it, but held off. There were things she needed to say before her brain scrambled from painkillers. "Thanks. I w-will."

Sensing it was time for him to go, Gabe stood and placed a kiss on her forehead. "Get some rest, Candy Cane. I don't know if I'll be able to check on you tomorrow. They're starting up the next SAGEs first thing in the morning."

Candace gaped at him. "They are? Wh-why didn't you s-say s-something? G-get out of here and g-go g-get some s-sleep. I'll be f-fine."

Gabe smiled, but it faded when he glanced up at Jackson, a tiny crease of worry forming between his eyebrows. "You should get some rest too, Candy Cane."

"I will. D-don't worry."

He gave her one last skeptical look, wished them

goodnight, and saw himself out.

Jackson stood, letting go of her hand. "I should probably—"

She grabbed for him, stopping his retreat. "W-wait." The sudden movement made her wince again.

Jackson sighed and sat back down again. "You need to rest. You don't need me here to—"

"Yes, I do," she said, forcing her teeth not to chatter. "I always will. D-don't be stupid."

He leaned on the edge of the bed and reached out, the back of his fingers gently caressing the side of her face. "I'm not good for you, Sugar Plum. I'm not good for me either."

"That's n-not your call," she said, scowling. "And I th-think we've established wh-which one of us has all of the g-good judgement h-here."

Fighting back a smile, he smoothed out the wrinkle in her forehead. "It's very hard to take you seriously with your teeth chattering like that."

"D-don't p-piss me off, S-sunshine," she growled. "I g-got robbed of the only b-birthday p-present I wanted."

"You didn't want the cards?" Worry crept into his voice.

She pushed his hair out of his face and smiled. "That w-was a beautiful gesture, b-but not what I w-would've asked for."

"What then?"

Candace met his gaze and beckoned him closer, curling her finger towards her. Flames danced in his eyes as he leaned in to her. She stopped him with barely a breath between them.

"W-we have a lot to talk about, Sunshine," she said

softly. "But this will d-do for now."

When he kissed her, heat erupted inside her, banishing the ice from her body. The unreserved love in his touch kindled something in her that she hadn't felt in a month, a piece of her brought back from the dead. Old desires flared, though dulled by the protests of her wounds. Tears of pain and relief eased down her cheeks, and it took all she had to pull away from him. It wouldn't do her any favors to reopen what little Tori and the doctors managed to fix.

"I love you, Candace," Jackson whispered against her mouth. "I don't deserve this."

"Not up to you," she said. "It's gonna take time, but I'm willing to let you try to make it up to me."

"Why?"

She brushed a kiss against his cheek. "Because I love you, too."

"Did you push that button already?"

"No, why?"

Jackson smiled and wiped away her tears. "I just wanted to make sure you weren't operating under the influence."

Chuckling a little, she lifted the device to dispense the painkillers and pressed her thumb against the button. "Not yet, but I am totally ready for a good night's sleep."

"You haven't been sleeping?" he asked, the worry returning.

Candace eased into her pillow a bit more, already feeling the effects of the drugs. "You know how it is."

"Anything I can do, you know I will, Sugar Plum," Jackson said, smoothing her hair behind her ears.

"I'll be fine," she said with a yawn. "It takes time."

"Candace?"

"Hmm?" she murmured, drowsy.

"I'll see you in the morning."

Too tired to reply, she drifted into the haze of sleep, content with knowing he'd be there tomorrow.

PAIN STIRRED her from sleep. Candace's eyes flew open, unsure of where she was or why she hurt. When she took in the white walls of the clinic, the events of the night rushed back.

The feel of his hand in hers pulled her attention away from her own discomfort. Jackson's head rested on his arm beside her on the bed, his fingers still intertwined with her own. He slept there? Like that?

Not wanting to wake him, but not wanting him to spend the rest of the day with a sore back, Candace closed her eyes. Rather than attempt to go back to sleep, she called to her connection, focusing on the water in Jackson's body. She began with soft ripples, sending a gentle massage from his scalp down to his toes, eventually concentrating her efforts on the tension in his neck and shoulders.

"You don't have to do that," he said. Candace opened her eyes to see him lift his head and rub the blur of sleep from his vision. "I'm fine, Sugar Plum, but thank you."

"You stayed all night?" she asked. "That wasn't necessary. I'm not going anywhere."

"Not a risk I'm willing to take." He strengthened his grip on her hand, lifting her fingers to his lips with a gentle kiss.

Candace watched him for a moment. It was a sweet

gesture, but it didn't elicit the smile from her that he was probably hoping for. "Jackson, we're not all better yet. You know that, right?"

He sighed and lowered her hand, resting it back on the bed again, but still not letting go. "I do. But I'm going to take whatever it is you're willing to give me, Candy. Since you didn't tell me to leave last night, I stayed. Even if all I get to do is hold your hand while you're sleeping, that'll be enough."

"I don't know how to not remember those feelings, Jackson. You with her, me unable to do anything about it. I don't know how much I can give you. That kind of betrayal... it doesn't go away with a few big romantic gestures."

His shoulders drooped, and he refused to meet her gaze. "I know."

"You know, then, that I need to hear about it."

"What?" Jackson's eyes snapped up, dumbstruck. "You don't mean... *those* parts, do you?"

"What? Ew, gross. No." She pulled her hand away and shooed him back. "Yuck. Definitely not what I meant." Candace sighed and dug under the blanket for the medication release button. "I'm talking about *you*. Like what kind of batshit crazy idiocy made you think that was a good idea. Why you apparently made a habit of it. Why the hell they decided to let her out. That kind of stuff." She located the device and pushed the button, sighing in relief as the painkillers hit. "No, I have no desire to find out those other details, Sunshine. You just keep those to yourself."

A few frantic raps on the door preceded Tori's sudden

appearance. She didn't spare them so much as a "good morning" or even glance at Jackson. Candace stared at her as Tori blurted out a request for Candace to expose her midsection for treatment.

Candace giggled, half because of the drugs, half at Tori's flustered bedside manner. With a nod, Candace pushed back the blankets and folded up the bottom of her thin cotton shirt. At least they dressed her in something more like scrubs than a stupid patient gown. She barely got a look at the bandages taped around her side before Tori was peeling them away, revealing the tail end of a nasty, stitched up incision.

Jackson sucked in a shocked breath, his attention riveted on the wound.

"I'm going to be fine, Sunshine," Candace said with a sigh as Tori's hand touched her belly. "Tori's a little bit awesome."

"I half wished I hadn't killed her," he growled. "Just so I could do it again."

Pushing aside the strange sensations of tissue growing back together, Candace frowned at him. "Don't say that, Jackson. I don't for a second believe that's true. You did what you had to, but don't *ever* let me think part of you enjoyed that." She glanced at Tori, whose brow was beaded with sweat. "You need to help her. Make sure she gets back to her room."

"Candace," Jackson said, his face pinched. "I didn't mean—"

She stopped him with a wave. Tori looked pale. She was going to collapse if she pushed it any more. Candace grabbed her hand, pulling it away from her stomach. Instantly, the healer's knees gave out, but Jackson was fast enough to catch her.

"Sorry," Tori mumbled sleepily. "I tried to fix it all, but..."

"Don't worry so much," Candace interrupted. "There's no rush." She looked down at her stomach. All that remained of the exterior damage were the threads of her stitches. "I feel much better already. It's amazing, Tori. Really. You do fantastic work."

"Thank you," she said as Jackson gathered her up in his arms. Her head dropped against his shoulder. "There's still some..." she said, interrupted by her own yawn. "There's still some left on the inside."

Before Candace could reaffirm that she would survive, Tori was passed out.

She sighed. "Poor girl," Candace said. "She doesn't need to try so hard. I hate that they made her feel second rate."

"Who?" Jackson said, shifting Tori's weight.

"HEX." Candace took a deep breath and leaned back into her pillow, closing her eyes. "I don't think they valued her at all. Sucks. She's really sweet."

"Hard to tell while she's out cold. Where do I take her?"

Candace explained where her room was, ready to get back to sleep herself.

"I'll be back in a few minutes then," Jackson said.

"Not necessary," Candace said. "I'd rather you spend some time with Naveen. See if he's ANGEL material. Maybe bring him those books, and see if you can find somewhere he can shower and get some clean clothes."

"But—"

She grimaced. "Sunshine, his blood is partly why I'm still alive. Dr. Poznanski said he willingly gave it. I'm asking you to do this for me, if for no other reason at all. Can you or not?"

He hesitated, but nodded anyway. "For you."

"Thank you." She let out a slow breath and relaxed again. "I'm going to take a nap. If anything happens with the SAGE treatments today, let me know, okay?"

With an unhappy sigh, Jackson opened the door, pausing to look at her one last time before he left.

"Go," she said, giving him a reproachful look. "I'm fine."

"I'm coming back later."

"You've got stuff to do. Do that first."

"You're going to make this as difficult as possible, aren't you?"

"Is that a complaint?"

"Just a question. I want to set my expectations."

Candace rolled her eyes. "You're stalling, and I'm tired. Get going or I'm revoking your visitation rights."

A smile flickered across his face and he winked at her, letting the door close behind him as he left.

Unable to fight off the effects of the medication a second longer, Candace closed her eyes, satisfied he'd do what she asked.

SHE WAS alone for most of the day, but Candace found she didn't mind one bit. Dr. Holtz came to check on her once, making sure Candace had everything she needed and to see how she was healing, and a corpsman dropped off food. Other than that, she was left to herself with nothing to do but watch mindless television for hours. It was heavenly. When her stomach grumbled, she wondered how much longer she'd have to wait for dinner.

Almost immediately, there was a knock on her door. Candace turned off the TV as Tori walked in the room, Jackson close behind her carrying two trays of food. Knots of indecision twisted in her stomach as he smiled at her. As much as she wanted to forgive him and move on, it wasn't as simple as that.

Candace turned her attention to Tori instead of thinking about it any more. When Tori set her hand on Candace's stomach, she focused on what the healer did. She closed her eyes, letting her connection speak to her about what was going on within her body. Cells pulled and split, regenerating damaged tissue, knitting flesh with flesh. Candace used water to guide extra resources of blood and molecules of proteins to the problem areas, hoping to make Tori's job easier.

She felt Tori pull away. Candace opened her eyes, expecting to see the other woman dead on her feet from exhaustion. Instead, Tori's head was cocked to the side, a curious expression on her face.

"What did you do?" she asked.

Candace shrugged. "Not much. Moved some things around, rounded up extra building blocks. Did it help?"

Tori blinked, amazed. "That was fantastic, Candace. It made my job so much easier. Half of my energy is spent looking for new materials to use in the healing. Not having to do that means I can focus on putting things back together."

"Really?" Candace said, hardly believing what little she did had that much of an effect.

"Really." Tori nodded. "In an hour or two I'll be recharged enough that I can fix the rest of you. You'll be back in your room tonight."

Candace winced reflexively. Tori didn't know a thing about her current room situation, and hadn't meant anything by it. With a nervous glance at Jackson, Candace saw his shoulders tense. He caught it too.

"There's no need to rush on my account," she said. "I'm totally fine vegging in front of the TV for a little while yet. There's a really terrible B-movie coming on at seven, and I had grand plans of killing brain cells tonight. Besides, the doctors will probably be too busy with the new SAGEs to clear me."

"Speaking of," Jackson said, picking up on the change of subject. "They already let Marissa, Christian, Tobias, and Leigh out."

Tori grabbed one of the dinner trays and set it on Candace's bedside table, swinging it over the bed. "That's right," she said. "I saw them leaving. They seemed fine, but tired."

Candace frowned at her food. "No word on Gabe or Valerie though?"

"I'm sure he's fine, Candy," Jackson said. "Some of us take longer to recover than others. You know from experience, if memory serves."

Nodding, Candace conceded the point, but couldn't help worrying. Gabe told her he had light sensitivity his first time through the treatment process, so she shouldn't be surprised he was taking longer to recover, much as she always did.

Tori yawned and stretched. "Well, if it's all the same to you guys, I think I'll cut out for now, maybe go get dinner, too. I'll see you later, Candy?"

Not wanting her to leave, but unable to find a good excuse for her to stay, Candace nodded and smiled. "See you later."

When she was gone, Candace and Jackson ate in silence, and she used the distraction of food to keep the conversation at bay. It worked, for a while.

"What movie?" Jackson asked quietly.

"Hmm?" she mumbled over a mouthful of chicken, then swallowed the bite. "Oh. Just some Godzilla knock-off. Nothing special."

The awkward silence made her squirm. He was fishing for an invitation, but didn't want to come right out and ask.

"I didn't know you liked those movies."

She nodded. "Yeah, Gabe says he hates them, but he never complained when I made him watch with me back home. That used to be our Thursday night tradition. Pizza, crappy movie, and planning our study and training schedule for the next week."

His forehead creased. "Training schedule?"

"Training schedule," Candace repeated. "When we were still trying to get into the ANGEL Project, we'd make lists of what we needed to study up on and plan out our running routes and strength routines. That kind of stuff."

He chuckled. "Wow. You took it really seriously, huh?"

"You didn't?"

Jackson shrugged. "I read some, sure. But I didn't actively

work at it like that. I had a construction job that kept me physically active, so that kind of prep wasn't really necessary."

She stared at him. He was good enough on his own to get in? Suspicion gnawed at her. "What was your score in the testing?"

Damn him, he was fighting back a grin. "Ninety-eight."

"Ninety-eight?" Her mouth fell open. "Without studying?"

Even though he tried to shrug it off, he was totally failing at the whole humility thing. "I do okay."

Candace rolled her eyes. "Okay? Come on, Sunshine. Why didn't you tell me before?"

"You didn't ask," he said with a chuckle.

"So, what you're saying is that you're pretty much a genius?"

He grinned and shoved some food in his mouth, not even trying to hide it anymore. "Your words, not mine."

She snorted. "No wonder they hung on to you so long. I always wondered about that."

"Yeah, well, they almost cut me loose, in case you forgot," he said, frowning at his tray.

Wincing, she nodded silently.

He was quiet for a moment, not looking at her. "Ever wish you could take it back?"

Her head snapped up, shocked he would even think that. "What?"

"Speaking up for me," he said, clarifying. "Do you ever wish—"

"Not for a minute."

When he lifted his eyes to hers, he didn't look convinced. Sighing, she pushed the table to the side and motioned him closer. Jackson set his tray on a chair and scooted his stool up beside her. Candace took his hands, taking a deep breath as she tried to put her thoughts into words.

"Jackson," she said. "No matter how messed up things are right now, don't assume that means I'd go back and change it if I could. At least, not that part. I've never thought twice about what I told Dr. Curtis about you, and I never will."

"But you're not coming back to our room, are you?"

She pinched her eyes shut. "Sunshine…"

"It's okay," he said, his voice barely above a whisper. "I get it." Jackson pulled his hands away and stood. "I wasn't really expecting it."

"Jackson, don't—"

He held up his hand and backed towards the door. "No, I told you how I feel. I'm not going to ask for more than what you'll give me. It's fine. If you want me to move your stuff to Gabe's room, that's what I'll do."

Candace pinched the bridge of her nose, frustrated. "I didn't say you had to do anything like that, Jackson. Stop jumping to conclusions."

"I'll see you tomorrow, Candace," he said, refusing to listen as he flung open the door and left.

"Seriously?" She stared at the door, a little stunned. "What the hell just happened?" Realizing she was talking to herself, she leaned back on the pillow and let out a tired sigh. "Why are boys dumb?"

Clicking on the TV, there wasn't much she could do about any of it at the moment. Hopefully, bad acting and cheesy special effects would take her mind off of it — off of him — for a little while at least.

CHAPTER 15

AFTER BEING given the all-clear by Dr. Poznanski, Candace decided to take Tori to breakfast the next morning. Candace's muscles ached with the memory of her wounds, but she was sure that would clear up with a long swim in the pool.

Making quick introductions between Tori, Amir, and True, Candace waved off concerns that she was anything but back to normal. It took flashing them the place where the knife sunk into her side before they believed her. There was little more than a tiny pale scar remaining as evidence of the attack.

"I don't know what happened to it, but I'm pretty sure that sweater you loaned me is toast, True," Candace said with a sigh. "Sorry. I'll totally get you a replacement if—"

"Candy Cane," True interrupted. "While it's sweet you'd offer, that crazy bitch stabbed you. I'm pretty sure we can file it under forgive and forget. It's a sweater. I'm just glad you're okay."

"Can I ask you something?" Amir said.

Candace nodded and waited for the question.

"Have you talked to him about what happened that night?"

"Talked to who?" she asked, pretty sure she knew, but needing confirmation.

"Jackson."

"You mean about what happened to Kristie, right?"

He nodded.

"Not really," she said, sighing. "A lot's happened, and we're just getting to the point where we're talking at all."

Amir grimaced. "Yeah, I get that. Still, if you get a chance, you might want to bring it up with him. The first kill is the worst, and he's not the type to talk it out with anyone. You know how much taking a life messes with your head. Since he's not likely to talk to anyone else, you should think about asking how he's doing with it."

She added one more item to her endless list of things she needed to discuss with Jackson. Amir was right. That one might be more important than almost anything else.

"What are your plans for the day, Tori?" Candace said, switching topics.

The slight color in Tori's cheeks said more than her words. "There's still more to do with Trevor," she said. "They told me I can visit him on my own now. You don't have to go with me anymore."

Candace shot knowing looks to True and Amir, but didn't say anything to embarrass Tori.

"What about you?" Tori asked. "You're supposed to take it easy."

"I have grand plans of swimming and curling up with some of those awesome birthday presents I got." Candace couldn't help but be excited. New comics and graphic novels? Pure bliss. "That and making sure Gabe's okay. Have you guys seen him yet?"

"No," True said. "But I don't think he got out until late last night. Let us know how he's doing when you see him?"

Promising to report back at lunch, Candace excused herself and headed for her cousin's room.

She opened up the door and poked her head inside. "Any survivors?" she called out to him. "Hey sleepyhead, you awa—"

Her question was cut off by a flash of light and a small explosion beside her head. Dropping to her knees, she checked herself for any damage, but only a small, fried lock of hair paid the price for the surprise attack.

"What the hell, Gabe? Cease fire!" she yelled through the doorway. "I just got out of the clinic and I'd like to avoid going back for at least a day if I can."

"Candace?" Gabe said. "What? What happened? Are you okay?"

Blowing out a breath, Candace eased the door open again. "I'm fine, but why are you asking *me* what happened? You're the one shooting at me."

"Shit," he grumbled, flopping back onto his pillow, an arm draped over his eyes. "I'm sorry. I don't know. I was asleep. You scared me."

"So is it safe to come in or what?"

With his free hand, he waved her inside. "Yeah, it's safe. Sorry. Unexpected side effects."

Candace stood and walked in, stopping a few feet away from the bed. "Unexpected side effects?"

Rather than tell her, Gabe pointed up at the ceiling. "I've got a little control issue."

When she looked up, she did a double take. Easily a dozen holes were burned into the ceiling tiles, none bigger than a quarter and crispy around the edges, and always in pairs. "What the hell? Did you do that?"

"Yep."

"How?"

He sighed and lowered his arm, his eyes still closed. "No sudden movements or sounds, please. I'm kind of on a hair trigger."

"Oookay," she drawled out, waiting for an explanation.

Slowly, he opened his eyes. Resisting the urge to gasp, Candace took in the mirror-like surface of his irises. They gathered and dispersed light, giving them a soft glow even in the morning sun.

"So, about the burn marks?" she asked softly.

"Snap your fingers or clap or something. Startle me."

Confused, she did as he asked. Rather than a noise he'd expect, Candace pulled a handful of water from the glass on his bedside table and splashed it on the side of his face.

Instantly, two shots of pure light fired from his eyes, straight up to the ceiling.

"Holy shit!" she yelped, jumping back a foot. "Your

eyeballs shoot lasers?"

Heaving another sigh, Gabe put his arm back over his face. "Could be worse. At least I didn't turn into a shark or something too. I'd be fodder for one of your terrible monster movies then."

"Are you gonna be able to get a handle on that?" If he couldn't, that would be a huge problem and incredibly dangerous for anyone around him. "I'm having visions of you becoming a hermit and collecting lint from lizard belly buttons or something. You can't walk around like that."

"Lizards don't have belly buttons. And you have a knack for stating the obvious sometimes, Candy Cane." The irritation in his voice made her cringe. "How about suggesting something helpful instead?"

"Sorry," she said. "I didn't come prepared to be brilliant this morning. Hmm." Candace crossed her arms and considered the problem. "Do the higher ups know about this yet?"

"No," Gabe said. "It didn't happen until I was back in here. I couldn't risk going out by myself and hurting anyone."

"Well, I can help with that much for sure," she said. "But how are we gonna get you out to see Poznanski? I don't think a blindfold is gonna do the trick."

"Too bad we don't have a laser-proof head bubble handy," he grumbled. "I hear there's a nationwide shortage on those, though."

Candace snorted. "Damn. You're cranky after treatments, huh?"

"It's been a long twenty-four hours, Candy Cane. Don't start."

EVOLUTION: HEX

"All right, all right. Let me think." Candace paced the room, wracking her brain for something they could rig up in the way of a deflector shield. Nothing she thought of was going to help, though. Any normal object wouldn't stand up to Gabe's ocular weaponry. They were all made of materials that would burn up.

She stopped pacing. Materials.

"So, here's the thing, cuz," Candace said. "Everything I can think of is made of stuff that might take the heat for a while, but probably won't last long enough to do us much good."

"Again, not helpful."

"I'm not finished, jackass. Stop interrupting." When he piped down, she continued. "Since normal materials won't work, we need something new."

"That had better not be it, Candy."

"Well, up until about a week and a half ago, that would've been a huge problem. Now, however, we have a very special friend that might be able to solve your problem without having to wait years."

Gabe went rigid.

"Uh huh," she said with a chuckle. "That'd be him."

"Candace," Gabe said, straining. "I don't know that seeing him is a good idea for me right this second."

"Look, I know where you're at, but do you see any other options?"

When he spoke, it was only a whisper. "But, what if..."

The vulnerability in his voice was almost painful to hear. Candace sat on the bed beside him and took his hand. "What if what, cuz?"

"What if… what if he doesn't, you know, want me?"

It was a little awkward, but Candace wasn't about to let him flounder in self-doubt. "Two things, Gabriel. One, I think we've got bigger problems at the moment, and you probably shouldn't worry about that until we get your laser eyes under control. And two, everything I've seen between you and him the last few days tells me that won't be an issue."

He squeezed her hand tightly. "I really don't want you to be wrong, Candy Cane, but what if—"

"Gabe, just stop. Seriously. If you two were any cuter together I'd go into a diabetic coma. Now, can I go get him, or are you gonna fight me on this until you successfully fry your eyelids or bring the ceiling down?"

Releasing her hand, Gabe nodded. He told her which room was Mica's, and she left without any more arguments from him.

Several doors down and across the hall, Candace knocked, hoping he was in. A moment or two passed before she heard movement on the other side. She knocked again. When he answered, he was still groggy from sleep.

"Candace?" Mica said, rubbing his eyes. "What's up? What time is it?"

"Almost eight. I need your help with something."

"My help? Really? With what?"

She took in his bare chest and sweatpants with a smirk. "You, uh, might want to get dressed. Not that he wouldn't appreciate the eye candy, I'm sure, but there's other stuff we have to deal with first."

Mica's ears went pink and his shoulders pulled in self-consciously. "Um, all right. Give me a minute?"

"Sure," she said, chuckling. "I'll wait."

He must've dressed in record time, because it wasn't more than five minutes before he emerged refreshed and ready to go. All in all, Mica was pretty damned good looking. Gabe had excellent taste.

"So, where are we going?" he asked as she led him down the hall.

"Gabe's room," she replied, fighting back a giggle when he missed a step. "Just here."

Candace stopped, her hand resting on the handle. Mica shifted uncomfortably.

"Hey, not that I don't trust you or anything, but, uh, what is this exactly?" he asked.

"I told you, I need your help with something," she said. "I can't really explain out here, though."

He didn't look convinced. "Help with what? I'm not going in there until you tell me what it is I'm expected to do after you open that door."

Mica was oddly weirded out. What did he think was going to happen? It wasn't like Gabe was going to…

When realization hit, Candace's eyes went wide. "What? Oh my God. You think this is some kind of freaky booty call or something? Whoa. No. Absolutely definitely not that. Nope. I don't do that. No way." She shook her head fiercely. "This is totally outside of anything like that. I'm talking about your ability, Mica. Full stop."

His shoulders relaxed, and he let out a small sigh of relief. "Oh. Yeah, of course. Sorry. You were just being so secretive I wasn't really sure… I mean, I know he had that treatment yesterday, so…"

Candace lifted a hand to stop him. "Dude, not what I do, not what I want to know about. Gabe and I are close, but certain lines you don't cross, man. So, are we cool?"

He chuckled and shoved his hands in his pockets. "Yeah, we're cool."

She nodded once, then gave a warning knock on the door before opening it. "Shields up?" she called through the cracked opening.

"Very funny," Gabe grumbled at her.

Candace ushered Mica in and closed the door behind them. "So, here's the problem," she said, motioning to Gabe, duly noting his white-knuckled grip on the blanket. She pointed at the ceiling above him. "He's having some vision problems and control issues."

"Huh?" Mica said.

"You're gonna have to show him, Gabe," she said, sighing. It couldn't be easy for him. "He won't know where to start if he doesn't know what's happening."

"Fine," Gabe said. "You know the drill."

Candace crouched down beside the bed at face level, waiting for her cousin to open his eyes. When his lids cracked, she whispered a single word in his ear, scrambling back when the lasers fired.

She giggled at him. "Wow. Bit sensitive, are we?"

"That was messed up, Candy," he growled, replacing his arm over his eyes.

Standing again, she turned to Mica, whose eyes were wider than saucers. "So, that's the problem. Any little thing triggers it. Nothing I know of is any help, so I thought you might have an idea. Got any laser-dispersing space age materials hiding up your sleeves? Preferably something he can see through, probably a temporary fix until he gets this under control."

Mica crossed his arms and chewed his lip, thoughtful. "Maybe, but it's a little more complex than throwing a shield on his face and calling it a day. I need to know some specifics, like the frequency of light shooting out of his face and the size of the beams. If I can talk to Dr. MacClellan, he might have the equipment we need to test all that. Not to mention the raw materials I'll need to create what I have in mind."

Candace blew out a breath. "Well, I suppose that makes sense. Problem is, what do we do with him in the meantime? He does any more damage to the ceiling and it won't last the day. How do we get him out and protect everyone while we move him?"

"I'm right here, you know," Gabe said, frustrated.

"Hush. The grownups are talking," she said back. Man, he was cranky. "Anyway, your thoughts?"

Mica bit back a chuckle. "His arm seems to be doing the job for now. Maybe we should just duct tape it there until something better presents itself."

"You guys are hilarious," Gabe said. "Can we get serious? I'm hungry, and your jokes aren't getting the food here any faster."

"I see your snark runs in the family," Mica mused. "I know that tone of voice."

Candace giggled and picked up Gabe's badge from the nightstand. "Okay, cuz. How about this? I'll go get your food. Mica hasn't eaten yet anyway so he can get breakfast, too. After that I'll come back here, drop it off, and then go talk to Poznanski and MacClellan to see what we can do about all this. Sound good?"

"Sounds like I'm in for a long wait."

"Like you had a busy day planned or something?" She stuck her hands on her hips. "Relax. I got this." Pushing his hair back, Candace brushed a kiss against his forehead. "Try not to burn anything down while I'm gone, okay?"

"Yes, Mom."

With a smile and a shake of her head, Candace grabbed Mica by the arm and steered him out.

"Is he gonna be all right by himself?"

She waved off the concern. "He'll be fine. Besides, he's all kinds of bitchy. Highly unpleasant to be around. I think once he's had some food he'll feel better, but until he's free to move around again, he's going to be a pain in the ass."

Leaving him to his thoughts, she walked the rest of the way to the dining hall in silence.

"Can I ask you something?" Mica said as he reached for the handle to open the door.

"Sure." She stepped into the doorway and looked at him.

"What did you say to him to get him to fire?"

Giggling, Candace turned away, but gave her answer over her shoulder with a wink. "I whispered your name."

She'd never seen someone turn that shade of pink before.

HER HOPES for the pool were completely dashed, as she spent the morning taking care of Gabe's problem.

Between meeting with Dr. Poznanski about the situation, tracking down Dr. MacClellan, guiding Gabe down into one of the practice rooms for safe keeping, and helping Mica arrange equipment and materials, Candace was lucky she even had time for lunch.

She sank down on the bench across from True and heaved a tired sigh.

"I take it your grand plans didn't amount to much?" Amir asked.

"Yeah. Not exactly," she said. "Did you guys hear about Gabe?"

True shrugged. "A bit, but you know how rumors are. We were hoping you could clear it up some."

Candace rubbed her face and walked them through her morning, filling them in on the specifics of the laser problem. Amir and True both looked worried.

"But they think they have a solution, right?" True asked. "I don't know how much longer the Pavo Team can go without him."

"Well, for the time being, Jackson and I can fill in for him," Candace said. "That was likely to happen anyway since, you know, Allen." She closed her eyes and took a deep breath, flashing back to memories of their fallen teammate. "But Mica seems pretty confident he can create something that will..." She trailed off, trying to remember his phrasing. "Refract small portions of the beams at various angles, kind of breaking it up and scattering it into smaller, harmless fragments. He wants to make a special glass with microprisms or something inside." She chuckled at herself. "Honestly, it was a bit over my head, but Dr. MacClellan seemed to understand it, so that's really all that matters."

"Can we get in to see him?" Amir said. "I don't want to be in the way or anything, but I'd like to make sure Gabe's doing all right."

Candace nodded. "That shouldn't be a problem. Fair warning though, he's in a foul mood. If poor Mica sticks with him through this, Gabe better count his lucky stars."

The joke didn't elicit the reaction she thought. Instead, both True and Amir were frowning, concerned.

"Did I miss something?"

They shared a look and Amir leaned forward, lowering his voice. "Gabe never told you about his first, did he?"

"I didn't push that issue, no," Candace said. "I figured he'd tell me when he was ready."

"Candy Cane," True said, starting slowly. "You should know. What happened with Sebastian wasn't that much different than what happened with Adrian."

Candace's breath caught. "Meaning..."

"Unstable, yeah." True sighed and scrubbed a hand across her forehead. "Only difference there is that they got to him before he killed anyone. Gabe watched the guards drag him off in a gibbering mess when Bas attacked. It was awful, Candy. Gabe was crushed. Honestly, he didn't smile much after that. Not until you showed up."

Candace couldn't imagine Gabe without a sense of humor. Well, she could, but she hated the thought. She caught a glimpse of that when he was laid up in the clinic after Adrian's breakdown. No wonder that situation affected him so much. Not only had Adrian been Gabe's friend, but all of the memories of his own pain were heaped on top of it.

But something else nagged at her.

True said the guards dragged Bas away.

Candace knew what the ANGEL Project did with unstables.

She shut her eyes and swallowed. Chances were that Sebastian— Bas, as True called him— was still alive, chained up and drugged somewhere in the depths of the compound.

What would Gabe do if he knew? She couldn't imagine he'd be okay with it. And what if Mica found out about Gabe's first love? Would he be the one to break the news to her cousin?

Questions swirled around in her skull, and none of their answers made her feel any better.

"What are you thinking, Candy Cane?" Amir interrupted her ruminations.

Candace sighed. "I think I need a nice, long soak in the pool. I need to clear my head so I can think straight. Why does everything have to be so damned complicated?"

"You're a superhero, Candy," Amir said with a small laugh. "Everything is bigger for us."

She grimaced and focused on shoving food in her mouth instead. The sooner she could get to the pool, the better.

CHAPTER 16

IT WAS NICE to get a bed for herself for once, but Candace had more trouble sleeping than she anticipated. Maintenance didn't get around to fixing the tiles Gabe had damaged, and she spent several hours staring at them, wondering if they were going to come down on her, before she finally drifted off to sleep.

The next day was spent alternating between swimming and helping out with Gabe. He was even more agitated than the day before. Spending so much time with Mica wasn't making it any easier on him. The internal struggle was visible on her cousin's face every time Mica was in the room. Still, there was nothing to be done until they solved the problem of his laser eyeballs.

When she got tired of listening to Gabe complain, she

decided a walk in the cool evening air might do her some good. In her wanderings, she spotted movement on the ballfield and went to investigate. Standing apart from the small crowd on the bleachers, Candace leaned up against a tree to watch the impromptu baseball game. It was funny to see superheroes doing something so normal. For a moment, she could almost imagine they were just like everyone else. Well, until one of them hit the ball so hard it rocketed into the distance, looking like it might be on fire.

"Hey, Candy Cane," someone whispered in her ear.

Startled, Candace spun to come nose to nose with Christian Markov. She let out a relieved breath and leaned her back against the tree. "Hey, Chris. What's up?"

With a casual smile, he set his hand against the bark, almost a foot above her head. "Oh, nothing. Saw you standing here and needed to come say hi."

While suspicion gnawed at her, she wasn't about to jump to conclusions. "Uh, okay. Hi."

"So," he said, drawing out the word. "Still in Gabe's room?"

"Mmm hmm," she said, raising an eyebrow.

"Then, uh..." He inched closer. "Things not going well with... Jackson, was it?"

If she said she was surprised by the question, she'd be lying. After all, Christian witnessed the showdown in the dining hall personally. It wasn't shocking he'd think she might be available. Still, it wasn't like she gave him any indication she was interested in looking elsewhere for that sort of companionship.

"I think you should probably back up, Christian. I get

antsy when people invade my personal space."

"Hey," he said, his steely blue eyes sparkling and shifting in the evening light. "I'm just chatting with a friend. That's all. Is that allowed?"

Candace uncrossed her arms, letting them dangle at her sides freely should she need to react quickly. "Oh, it's allowed, so long as chatting is all you have in mind."

"Just chatting?"

She nodded.

Christian hummed, his gaze settling on her lips. "And nothing else?"

"You're in dangerous territory, Chris. I'm considering you warned."

He was closer, his breath warm on her face. "You should know, there's not much I wouldn't do for just a little taste of—"

Whatever dumbass line was about to come out of his mouth was cut off as someone slammed into the side of his body, tackling him to the ground. Sighing tiredly, Candace couldn't make herself feel bad for him.

Jackson and Christian rolled across the grass, both taking swings at one another as they went. When that had little effect, both men scrambled to their feet, almost snarling at one another as they faced off.

"She said she wasn't interested, Markov," Jackson seethed at him.

"Jealous, are we?" Christian spat back. "Just because I got closer than you have in days to—"

A clean right hook to his jaw shut him up, but, surprisingly, Christian barely flinched. Instead, he smirked.

"Nice try, but you forget that I've gotten a power up. You can't hurt me, hot head."

Christian charged, but Jackson was too fast for him, appearing two feet behind Christian in the blink of an eye. "Still no match for me, GQ." His right leg shifted back, and Candace knew what was coming. That was his pre-fireball stance.

Christian sneered and prepared to charge again. "We'll see about that."

Tired of the whole situation, Candace put a stop to it. Two streams of water blasted up from the ground, hitting each man square in the chest and knocking them back ten feet, flat out on their backs. To further ensure the fight was over, she pulled at her connection, paralyzing both of them where they fell.

"If you two are about done, you should know that I'm extremely bored here." She walked over to Christian first, looking down at him with clear disapproval. "I did warn you, although, I think you got off light. You can ask Jackson what happens when someone gets closer than I'd like them to. He's experienced that firsthand."

Not willing to waste any more breath on that, she crossed over to Jackson.

"And you," Candace said, shaking her head. "You need to get a grip. I was fine and totally capable of getting rid of him on my own, Sunshine. As evidenced by how you're both laid out right now."

Stepping away, she released her hold, waiting until they were standing before continuing. She looked from one to the other, thinking of what she could do that would punish them both equally.

"Shake hands," she said, crossing her arms.

"No," they said in unison.

"Do you two need another lesson?" Candace raised an eyebrow. "I said, shake hands. I'm not above making you."

It took them a minute of grumbling, but they relented nonetheless, grudgingly shaking hands.

Her need for a walk ruined, Candace turned away, heading to the dining hall for dinner. Maybe she'd just go to bed early and be done with the whole stupid day. Without solid rest the night before, plus Gabe's constant state of irritation, coupled with making no progress on much of anything else, in addition to dumb male posturing, she was done.

"Candace, wait!" Jackson called after her, jogging to catch up.

"Not a good time, Sunshine," she said, casting him a sidelong glance. "I'm so not in the mood right now."

"So you're not going to let me apologize?"

She stopped and faced him. "Fine. Apologize."

Jackson floundered for a moment with the full brunt of her agitation on him. "I'm... I'm sorry."

"For what?" she said, hoping to prompt something a bit more heartfelt from his end.

"For not letting you handle that situation."

"And?"

His eyebrows bunched together. "And..." He trailed off, apparently not sure where to go next with it. "For attacking Christian?"

Candace gave him a flat look. "Nope. Wrong answer."

Without further explanation, she strode off again.

"For not letting you make your own decisions?" he asked when he caught up to her again.

"Closer, but still no."

"Can I get a hint?"

Stopping again, Candace set her hands on her hips. "Seriously?"

Jackson blinked at her. "I've got nothing, Sugar Plum."

"Think back to your last visit to the clinic," she said. "That ringing any bells for you?"

The tension drained from his face as realization set in. "Oh."

"Yeah. Oh." She turned to walk away again, but he stopped her with a hand on her arm.

"I'm sorry I got upset, Candy. Really." His face pinched as his eyes stared into hers. "And I should have apologized to you yesterday, but..."

"But what?"

"I was busy. And when I wasn't busy, you were. I did look for you. Three times, actually." Jackson let go of her and sighed. "And then it got to be too late, and I didn't want to wake you. I'm sorry I left that way. I should've stayed to listen to you."

"Yes, you should have." As much as she tried to hold on to her anger, she couldn't, tiredly releasing a breath instead. "Look, I can only try so hard on my end, Sunshine. You're going to have to do a lot of the work here. When you pull crap like that, I'm less inclined to try because it gets me nowhere. If you're going to walk out when it gets tough, there's no point. You have to trust me to work through what

I need to work through, and be there when I'm ready to go forward. Can you handle that or not?"

He took a deep breath and nodded. "I can."

"Good." She turned again and took a few steps, but looked back at him when he didn't follow. "Are you coming, or not?"

"Huh?"

"Dinner. I'm going to go eat. I guess you don't have to come with me, but—"

Jackson jerked forward, almost leaping to her side. She tried to hide her smile, but couldn't quite manage it. As they started forward, Candace gave him a little ground, softly slipping her hand into his. His grip was hesitant, his shoulders tense, as though he was afraid to move in case she changed her mind. Squeezing his fingers, she offered a reassuring smile.

"Next time you want to defend my honor, do me a favor?"

"Sure. What's that?"

"Make sure I need defending. It's kinda cute that you're jealous, but, really. I feel a little robbed that I didn't get to clock him myself."

Jackson chuckled. "Well, if it makes you feel any better, I don't think it would've done you any good. Whatever changes the SAGE treatments made, apparently getting a bone structure made out of titanium was one of them."

Candace giggled. "Hurt yourself a bit?"

"I'll survive. You could always offer to kiss it and make it better."

"Baby steps, Sunshine," she said, smiling. "Baby steps."

EXHAUSTED FROM the day, Candace was asleep the moment her head hit the pillow. However, she woke several hours later, breathing ragged and heart hammering. While she recognized terror when she felt it, it was different. When her nightmares hit, they always lingered, their images lodged in her brain like apparitions, intangible but fully felt. But there were no memories of nightmares to explain the fear clinging to her. What she felt was something else. It wasn't her fear.

It was Jackson's.

Before she knew it, she was out of bed, standing in front of his door, debating on the wisdom of being there. She couldn't control the impulse. He needed her, and she knew what it was like to be haunted the way he was. Taking a deep breath, Candace slid her badge through the card reader and peeked inside.

Something in her heart cracked when she saw him. Jackson was in bed, his back to her, but visibly shaking. Quietly, she slipped inside and shut the door. She didn't ask, didn't speak, only eased in beside him, curling up against his back. Candace closed her eyes and snuggled against him, hoping her presence would be enough to calm him some. At her touch, Jackson stilled, holding his breath as she settled in.

When he let out a long sigh, she reached up, laying a hand against his arm. Jackson let out one choked sob, and she pulled back on his shoulder, prompting him to turn and wrap his arms around her, burying his face in her neck. Each shudder of his body pulled at her heart, aching for him and the pain she knew all too well. He clung to her like a man drowning. Candace held him, allowing him the release he'd provided for her on so many terrified nights of her own. Whatever was still broken between them, it didn't change the fact that she would be there when he needed her.

Eventually, he drifted back to sleep, still holding onto her like a lifeline. Candace resigned herself to another night of less than ideal sleep. Being used as a pillow by someone considerably larger than herself wasn't exactly comfortable.

What little rest she managed to get was disturbed the moment sunlight peeked through the blinds. It took her a minute to remember where she was and why she couldn't move. Jackson's weight pinned her in place no matter how her muscles protested, begging for motion. She didn't want to wake him. If there was some way she could slip out quietly, maybe she could avoid the awkwardness that was sure to follow the moment he opened his eyes.

"Good morning, Sugar Plum," he whispered against her skin.

Damn it.

Candace sighed into his hair and pushed the loose strands off of his face. "Good morning, Sunshine."

Rather than release her, he pulled her closer. "Thank you."

"Mmm," she murmured. "Wanna talk about it?"

"No."

"You should, you know. It'll help."

Jackson didn't answer, burrowing deeper into her

embrace.

"Can I guess?"

"Can I stop you?"

"That's a dumb question."

Silence again.

She shifted a little, as much as his iron hold would allow. "Kristie?"

A small nod was his only response.

"I'm so sorry, Sunshine. I know how hard it is. I can't tell you it'll get easier, but I'm here for when it's too much."

Jackson was quiet for a moment, and she felt his first tears as they cooled against her chest. "Please, don't leave me."

Candace closed her eyes and kissed the top of his head. "I'm not going anywhere. And if I do, I'll always come back. Don't you know me at all?"

"Better than I know myself," he said. "Which is why I can't believe you're here."

"Don't be dumb. Where else would I go? This is it for me, Jackson. I told you. For as long as I'm breathing. I don't say things I don't mean."

The silence stretched out for several minutes, and she wondered if he'd fallen back asleep.

"I died every time, Candy." His voice was strained, choked with sorrow. "Being with her... it killed a piece of me because I knew how much it was going to hurt you. I couldn't think. I couldn't breathe knowing you might be... that they might have... that I was responsible for..."

Jackson swallowed hard. Candace didn't think it was possible, but he held her even tighter. "When Gabe told me about your marks, something in me snapped. I went crazy, like a hysteric combination of relief and determination to get you back, to see you safe again. She was the only way I thought I could find you. She knew where you were. I knew her weakness. I just didn't know what it would cost me to get that information. Because of what I did, I nearly lost you twice. Once by being with her, once when she tried to kill you. I don't know how to fix that. I don't know how to forget it. I don't know how to give myself forgiveness, never mind how to beg yours."

"Oh, Sunshine," she said, holding him to her. "You don't have to beg me, just love me. That's it. It's the most simple thing in the world. We all make mistakes. You, me, everyone. Loving someone means accepting them and their choices."

"I can't ask you to accept what I've done, Candy. If this were reversed..." he shivered. "But I can't imagine you losing it the way I did. When it comes to you, I can't think straight. That's what makes this worse. You would've found another way."

"You have no idea." Closing her eyes, she sighed. "I knew, Jackson. I knew what that situation would do to you. The last thing I heard before they took me was your voice. I heard the guilt, the pain, the fear... I knew you'd put that on yourself. I knew you'd let it eat you up. I hated every second because I couldn't tell you, couldn't convince you it wasn't your fault. And I knew you'd do something, whatever it took, to get to me. I just wish you'd held out a little longer."

"Candace, I—"

"Jackson," she interrupted. "Look at me, please."

He lifted his head, tears shining in his eyes.

"What happened in Aspen wasn't your fault."

"But—"

"It wasn't your fault." She laid her palm against his cheek, thumbing away a few tears. "Don't be sorry for things you couldn't control."

Jackson lifted a hand, brushing hair from her forehead. "Candace?"

"Hmm?"

"I need your permission."

A smile tugged at her lips. "Permission for what?"

"Right now? To kiss you."

"And then?"

"I suppose that depends," he said, the hint of a grin forming in the crinkles of his eyes.

"Uh huh. Depends on what?"

"On how much you're willing to let me make up for after I kiss you."

"I think I like the sound of that, but that better be one hell of a kiss to completely convince me to let you try."

Jackson lifted up on an elbow, hovering above her as he stared into her eyes. Tiny, glittering embers burned in his pupils— red, the color of desire. He lowered himself slowly, pausing a breath away from her face.

"I love you, Candace," he whispered. "And I'm going to spend every day of the rest of my life showing you how much."

The kiss began slowly, gently, his lips brushing hers with featherlight touches, gradually building to a heated embrace that fanned a raging fire in her heart. The taste of him reminded her of days when things were simpler, when every move she made was for him, and not part of some larger plan. He drifted from her mouth, his lips trailing small kisses along her jawline, down her throat, across her shoulder.

As he pushed aside the strap of her tank top, he paused, breathing against her neck. "Only with your permission, Sugar Plum. It might kill me, but say the word and I stop."

A little frustrated that he even paused at all, she tried to catch her breath. "Forget about that, Sunshine. You stop now, and I'll never forgive you."

She heard the grin in his words as he nuzzled her ear. "Then I suggest you get comfortable. Hope you weren't planning on breakfast this morning, because I have no intention of letting you leave."

"For someone who thinks actions speak louder than words, you sure do talk a lot," she said.

His kisses started in again, behind her ear. "Then I hereby forbid you to talk any more," he said, pausing to tease her. "Unless it's you screaming my name."

"That's pretty presumptive on your part, Sunshine."

He chuckled, sharing her memory of their first time together in his room. "I prefer to think of it as realistic. Now hush, Sugar Plum. Let me show you how well I know you."

Jackson picked up where he left off, slowly exploring her body, leaving little explosions of sensation in his wake. His hand drifted up, under her shirt, teasing as he stripped away the garment. Candace bit her lip as he made his way down her body, watching him, feeling his intense focus in every caress, every kiss. He paused at the waistband of her shorts, asking the question again when he met her gaze.

EVOLUTION: HEX

Do I have your permission?

With a single nod, she gave away all rights to her sanity. The sensations he stirred in her with the feel of his mouth against her flesh chased away anything resembling coherent thought. He worked slowly, methodically, bringing her to the height of bliss as his name tumbled off of her tongue.

Tingling from her toes to her nose, Candace closed her eyes, struggling for air as the ripples of pleasure spread through her body. Shuddering, she felt his kisses moving again, down her thighs, then back up, tracing patterns along her belly. Everywhere he touched, he left behind a small prayer of gratitude, of love and dedication meant only for her. Jackson took his time, eventually coming back to gaze into her eyes.

"I almost forgot how beautiful you are," he said, smoothing her hair. "Not that I could ever really forget, but I never remember how amazingly stunning you are, Candy. Every inch of you. I can't get enough. It will never be enough."

Candace wound her legs around him and held his face in her hands. He bit back a gasp, holding his own desire at bay. "I'm yours, Jackson. All of me. Everything you can see and everything you can't. My heart, my soul... they belong to you. Trust that. Take it. Only one person on this planet can break me, but that's because he owns me. You, Sunshine. Always you."

His lips crushed against hers, stealing her breath as he entered her, completing her. They rolled and twisted together, neither able to contain the weeks of longing, of heartache, of need a moment longer. Everything he was flooded into her. Jackson let go, pulling her into the cracks in his heart, sharing both sorrow and elation. With him, she was whole. With him, she could face whatever terrors haunted the night, or the disguised horrors that came at her in the unyielding light of day. He was her strength, and she was his.

So long as she had him, she could fight off anything the world threw at her.

And she would win.

CHAPTER 17

THE ONLY reason Candace managed to pry herself away from the bed was the incessant rumbling in her stomach. Jackson chased after her as they raced down the hall to lunch, and she erupted into fits of giggles when he caught up and tickled her mercilessly. Despite the torture, it was easily the happiest she'd been in weeks, and she relished every moment.

Gasping, she finally fended him off, grinning at him from her position pinned against the wall. "You are so gonna pay for this later," she said. "No fair tickling."

"I have ways of making it up to you," Jackson said as he closed in for a kiss.

The clearing of a throat stopped him before he made contact. Jackson made an exasperated face and pushed off the wall, giving Candace a clear view of who interrupted them.

"Not to, uh, ruin the moment," Mica said, smirking. "But I was just on my way to find you. I think we've got a solution to Gabe's problem."

"You do?" Candace asked, stepping out in front of Jackson. "Already?"

Mica chuckled. "Already? I've been working on it for two days, Candy. I don't think it's ever taken me that long to create something since I got my ability."

"Impressive," she said. Her stomach protested loudly, reminding her of where she was headed moments ago.

"Tell you what." Mica grinned at her. "You go eat before that monster tries to claw its way out, and I'll meet you at one. I still have a few adjustments to make, so I'll be in the room with him anyway."

Jackson tried to hide a chuckle, to which Candace elbowed him in the stomach. "Sounds great," she said. "I'll be there."

"*We'll* be there," Jackson corrected.

Candace rolled her eyes. "Subtle, Sunshine."

Mica stood there for a moment, fighting back a smile. "All right then. See you both at one for the trial run."

"Sure we won't be interrup—"

Candace silenced Jackson with a look, then turned back to Mica. "One o'clock."

Looking slightly ruffled, Mica waved and headed back to wherever he came from.

"You shouldn't tease him," she scolded Jackson as they continued their trek to the dining hall. "I don't think he's comfortable with that yet."

He slipped an arm around her waist and kissed her temple as they walked. "Yes, dear. I'll try to be more sensitive."

Candace frowned. "I mean it. You need to ease up. I don't want either of us to ruin Gabe's chances with Mica. Let it go, okay?"

He sighed and switched to holding her hand. "All right. I'll try to behave."

"Thank you."

They hurried through lunch, Candace actively avoiding the curious glances of the other ANGELs. Half an hour later, the two of them entered the training room set up for Gabe. Everywhere she looked, scorch marks marred the padded walls, ceiling, and floor. Either Gabe had been practicing, or he totally lost control. The room was nowhere near that condition when she left him yesterday.

Gabe was laid out on a cot, much as he was every other time she was in there, but something was different. Giant goggles protruded from his face, extending up nearly a foot from his eyes. Each eyepiece was a series of stacked metal cylinders and must have weighed ten pounds together.

"Nice look, cuz," she said with a giggle. "They couldn't get you a pair in pinstripes?"

"Not fucking funny, Candy Cane," he growled at her.

Stunned by the harsh response, she wasn't sure how to reply.

"Good to see ye lookin' well today, Miss Bristol," Dr. MacClellan said from a small work table at the far end of the room. He switched off a few pieces of machinery before walking over to join them. "Try not to let his foul mood get to ye." He motioned to Gabe with a smile.

The door opened and closed as Mica entered and joined them, holding a black box under his arm. "So what did I miss?"

"Nothin' yet," Dr. MacClellan said. "Let me show you." He herded everyone over to Gabe. "What we've rigged up fer the moment is a series of lenses designed ta break up the emitted beams. But, as ye can see, this version is too heavy and impractical."

"Gee, ya think?" Gabe grumbled.

Candace scowled. Frustrated though he might be, that was no excuse to be so rude.

Dr. MacClellan coughed. "As I was sayin', this version provides the correct amount of refraction, but it isn't really useful as it's too heavy to—"

"I think we've established that much," Gabe interrupted. "Can we get on with it?"

When Dr. MacClellan opened his mouth to speak, Candace held up a hand.

"I'm sorry, Dr. MacClellan, but I think I need to speak with my cousin for a moment." She broke off glaring at Gabe to look at the other men. "If you wouldn't mind giving us some privacy, that is."

Dr. MacClellan nodded briefly, an amused grin turning up the corners of his mouth, and ushered Jackson and Mica out. When they were gone, Candace turned her full attention to Gabe.

"I am going to say this once," she said. "I know what you're fighting through right now, but so help me, if you can't control your mouth, I will do it for you."

"You don't even—"

"No. You don't get to talk right now." Candace wasn't about to excuse him. "I've been in your shoes more than once. I fought with every fiber of my being to keep from giving in to those hormones. Yes, I know it's uncomfortable, but if you don't knock this shit off immediately, you'll lose him for good. He already seems a little nervous about all this. You push him too hard, too fast, and he'll run the other way even faster, Gabriel."

Sighing, she smoothed the hair away from his forehead. "He's spent the last two days doing nothing but trying to help you, cuz. I can only do so much. Quit being a jerk and try to think of his feelings, okay? He's gotta be overwhelmed by everything. I know you're having a rough time of it, but Mica is too."

Gabe took a long, deep breath and released it slowly. "I know. You're right. I'm sorry for being a jerk."

"You ever talk to me that way again, and I won't be so nice next time," she said, chuckling.

He snorted. "You call that being nice?"

"You wouldn't like me when I'm angry, Gabe. There's a big difference between giving you a kick in the pants out of love and kicking your ass because I'm pissed off."

"Right. I'll remember that."

"You'd better," she said. "Now, if you think you're ready to be civil, I'll give them the all-clear."

Gabe took another deep breath and nodded.

She left him laying there, and stepped out into the hall. After sending Jackson and Dr. MacClellan back inside, she stopped Mica.

"Can I talk to you for just a minute first?" Candace asked.

He shifted his weight nervously. "Uh, sure."

Candace considered him for a moment, weighing her words carefully. "I don't want to put you in an awkward position, and I would normally stay out of this, but, well, it's Gabe. That said, I need you to make a decision."

Mica fidgeted with the box. "About what?"

She smiled softly. "About him. If you like him, that's fantastic. If not, you need to tell him. It'll hurt, but it'll hurt him less now than it will later on. He really likes you, Mica, but if you don't feel the same way, you need to let him know before it goes any further."

He didn't say anything, and he frowned at the floor, his lips pinched together.

"Are you okay?"

He nodded faintly, then sighed. "Candy, see, the thing is…" He paused and glanced up at her before looking away again. "The thing is, I've never, you know, been with anyone before. Like that."

Unaware she'd been holding her breath, Candace released the air from her lungs in a relieved rush. "Oh. That's all?"

Cheeks the color of cranberries, he nodded again.

"I mean, not that that's not a big deal, but you like him, right? That's not the problem?"

Mica looked up at her, eyes wide. "What? No. No, I like him a lot, Candy." A shy grin eased onto his lips. "Got a weakness for blonds and all that."

Candace chuckled and took his arm, pulling him towards the door. "Well, I think the two of you need to have a little talk, then. Seriously. Just tell him. He's a little messed up at the moment, but that's the hormones screwing with him. The Gabe you met before is who he really is. I've known him all my life. He's maybe the kindest, most understanding person I know. I mean, he'd have to be to put up with all my crap." She paused as she reached for the door handle. "If you don't want to talk to him, I can, if you'd rather. But, I won't say a word unless you want me to."

"Thanks, Candy, but I think I can handle it," he said with a grateful smile.

"Okay," she said, pulling open the door. "I'll leave it to you, then."

When they went back inside, Dr. MacClellan was carefully unscrewing cylinders from Gabe's goggles. After setting each on a small table beside the cot, he helped Gabe to sit and removed the base, pulling the strap off of his head. Mica stood to Dr. MacClellan's right, fidgeting with the box again.

"All right, Mr. Reynolds," Dr. MacClellan said. "Let's see if your material works the way we've planned it."

Mica shifted the box into one hand, opening it with the other. Candace bit back a giggle as he produced a pair of black-framed glasses straight out of the 1950s. The lenses had a holographic look, with the slightest rainbow shimmer on the surface.

"Here we go," Mica said as he slid the glasses onto Gabe's nose. His hands pulled away, his fingers lightly grazing Gabe's face, eliciting a barely-controlled shudder from her cousin.

"Open your eyes," Mica said softly, still standing in front of him.

"Not until you move away," Gabe said. "I don't want to

hurt you."

Candace fought back the urge to squeal over how damn sweet they were that way.

"You won't," Mica said. "Have a little faith in me."

Oh lord, she'd kiss him herself if Gabe didn't do it soon. She chewed on her thumb to keep from doing anything to spoil it.

His breathing shaky, Gabe's eyelids slowly opened, taking in Mica's face. "Hi."

"Hey," Mica answered back with a shy grin.

Dr. MacClellan cleared his throat and Gabe jerked. There was a flash of light from his eyes, but the blast didn't make it past the lenses, exactly the way Mica designed them.

Grinning like an idiot, she grabbed Jackson's arm and squeezed, fighting back an excited giggle. He smirked at her and shook his head.

"Mission accomplished?" he said with a chuckle.

Candace rolled her eyes, then looked back at Mica. "Thank you so much for your help. You as well, Dr. MacClellan. This is more than I thought would be possible in a few days. You guys are amazing."

"Mr. Reynolds is responsible fer most o' this," Dr. MacClellan said. "He's got an amazin' gift."

Mica ducked his shoulders and blushed again. "Well, eventually I'd like to get rid of the frames, maybe some sort of contact lens." He glanced at Gabe out of the corner of his eye. "But I kinda like the glasses. Like a hipster alter-ego or something."

Candace couldn't control her giggle. "Oh my God, I have so many inappropriate responses to that I don't even know where to start."

Gabe turned and fixed her with a look. "Watch it, Candy Cane."

She bit down on her lip and stared at the ceiling.

"Well, this has been fun and all," Jackson said, winding an arm around her waist. "But I think it's about time we got back to superheroing." He looked down at her, the smoldering flames in his eyes catching her breath. "Ready to go?"

Candace nodded, absolutely ready to get back into his arms.

Feeling ten feet tall, she floated out of the room, hopes high that the rest of the day would be as wonderful as the morning had been.

SHE LAID there, motionless, her bones like jelly. Unable to wipe the satisfied smile off of her face, Candace stopped fighting it, saving up her energy to stretch and snuggle closer against Jackson.

"Are we even for the tickling, then?" His voice rumbled in his throat, his deep chuckle sending shivers down her spine.

"What tickling?" she said with a sigh.

Jackson's fingers drifted up and down her arm, further soothing her as she edged towards sleep.

"Candy?" he said softly.

"Hmm?"

"Will you stay tonight?"

The uncertainty in his voice made her wince. She sat up, propping herself on an elbow. Candace studied his face, tracing the lines of his worry with her fingertip. "Do you need me to?"

"Always."

While she planned on staying anyway, there was no sense in passing up a golden opportunity. "Then answer a question for me first."

"Why do I not like the sound of that?"

"Because you have an intense dislike for divulging your personal secrets," she said, folding her arms on his chest and resting her chin.

"Personal secrets? Well, now I'm curious what it is you're going to ask."

Candace idly traced little circles on his skin. "I was wondering about those drawing pencils you have."

Jackson chuckled and pushed her hair behind an ear. "You've been snooping, haven't you?"

"We're not talking about me," she said with a sniff.

"Let me guess," he said. "You saw them when you took your books, didn't you? The day I was gone?"

She blinked at him. "You knew I was in here?"

"I stared at those things for weeks, Candy. You think I wouldn't notice some were missing?"

Her heart melted a little as he watched her, the look in his eyes a mixture of longing and regret. "I suppose I'll buy that," she said. "Yeah, you caught me. So, why didn't you tell me you draw?"

"You never asked."

"Were you ever going to show me?"

Jackson laughed again. "What, and destroy my carefully cultivated gruff exterior of masculinity?"

Candace rolled her eyes. "Carefully cultivated? Wow. No ego there, Sunshine. But you know, the whole artist thing is kind of sexy. Lends you an air of mystery." She winked at him.

"Ah," he said, touching the side of her face. "So that's what gets you going, huh?"

"Gets me going?" Giggling, she slid back to his side. "I don't know about that, but it was a definite reminder that I don't know you as well as I should. At least, as well as I think I should, anyway. Does that make sense?"

"It does." He kissed the top of her head. After a minute of silence, he spoke again. "Do you want to see what I've been working on?"

"Of course, but…" She hesitated. "Would you be mad if I told you I peeked already?"

His chuckle reverberated through her body. "No. I already assumed you had."

Candace lifted up again, leaning down to kiss him softly. "Then, yes. I would love that."

Jackson reached over and clicked on the lamp on the nightstand. Sorry to lose his warmth, she let him slide out of bed, admiring the view as he stepped into a pair of boxers. Giggling at herself, she sat up and tucked the sheet around her body. Jackson returned after fishing the orange pad out of the drawer, and slid in beside her.

"Some of these aren't finished yet, but you can see what's here so far," he said as he handed her the sketchbook.

Her fingers shook as she touched the cover, already

knowing what she would find when she opened it. As she lifted the front, Candace held her breath.

The drawings were as beautiful as she remembered them. Each line swept her emotions to new heights of admiration and understanding. The raw feelings on display in his works of art overwhelmed her.

Gently, she touched her fingertips against her face on the page. "You really see me this way?"

Jackson kissed her shoulder. "No, but I think it's lack of skill, rather than intent."

"Lack of skill?" Candace turned her eyes to him. "Sunshine, these are beautiful. There's no lack of skill here."

"Keep looking."

Frowning, she flipped past her sleeping face, on to the one of her swimming, followed by her head emerging from the water.

"I keep drawing you because I can't get it right. I've never been able to capture everything you are."

When she got to the fourth one, the swirling vortex of fluid and flame surrounding her, Candace closed her eyes.

"This is the one, Jackson," she whispered. "This was how I knew how much you were hurting."

"From the moment I saw you, Candy," he said, resting his forehead against her bare shoulder. "This is what I've been afraid of. You're too good, and I don't want to take that away from you."

She closed the pad and set it aside. Where to begin? She wasn't that perfect person, some paragon up on a pedestal. "I wish you didn't think of me like that."

He lifted his head and cupped her cheek, turning her face

to his. "Why? Everything you are, everything you do—"

"I'm not." Candace brushed his hand away and pulled her knees to her chest. "I'm not this ideal vision you have of me. I make mistakes. I hurt other people. I don't always see the truth until it's too late. I…" Tears clouded her vision, and she pinched her eyes shut. "If you keep holding me up so high, Sunshine, there's nowhere to go but a long fall down. And then what?"

Lifting her chin, Jackson brushed his lips against hers. "Then I fall with you."

When he kissed her again, she couldn't hold back the tears. He couldn't possibly know what he would face if he stayed with her. Everything, with HEX, with the ANGEL Project, it was all in the way, and she didn't know if she could shield him from what was coming. Candace chose that fight for herself, not for him. If he knew, what would he say? Would he understand? Would he try to talk her out of it, or stand by her and support the path she chose?

When he pulled away, Jackson gently wiped the tears from her cheeks. "Why are you crying, Sugar Plum?"

She swallowed. She needed to tell him, but that wasn't the place for it. She couldn't trust their room wasn't bugged.

"Because you don't know how wonderful you are, Sunshine," she said. "For other reasons, too, but those can wait. It's late." Picking up the sketchbook, Candace passed it back to him. "Put this away, and let's get some sleep."

When the lights were off, she settled back in against the side of his body, treasuring the warmth he radiated. In the morning, there would be much to discuss, but for the moment she would be content to be at his side.

CHAPTER 18

CANDACE CLOSED the door behind her with a sigh, leaning back against it. She smiled to herself, happy.

"Does this mean I get my room back?" Gabe grinned at her as he emerged a few doors down: Mica's room.

She answered him with a smug look of her own. "Doesn't look like you need it."

"Yeah, well..." He shoved his hands in his pockets, the hint of a blush creeping up his neck. "Your stuff takes up a lot of space." He set off towards his room, passing her.

Candace giggled. "Were you trying to sneak out of there before anyone caught you?" She trotted up beside him.

"No," he said, lifting his chin.

"Such a liar," she said, nudging him with her shoulder. "You're totally doing the walk of shame."

EVOLUTION: HEX

"I'm not ashamed of anything," he insisted, pushing his glasses up on his nose. "Why are you up so early anyway?"

Candace shrugged. "I usually am. I always go for a swim about this time, you're just never awake to see me."

"Uh huh."

They stopped long enough for him to unlock the door and let them both in.

"I'm guessing things went well with you and Mica then?" she said, rummaging around for a clean swimsuit. "You're not nearly as bitchy as you were yesterday."

When he didn't answer, Candace looked up. Gabe was trying to hide his grin behind a shirt he was unfolding. She chuckled and went in search of clean clothes to take with her.

"So, I know you usually swim and stuff," Gabe said. "But how would you feel about a run this morning instead?"

In a single question, her cousin obliterated her lingering good mood. Going for a run meant he wanted to talk.

Sighing, she tossed her suit back in the drawer and nodded. "Sure. Let me go tell Jackson about the change of plans."

When everyone was dressed and ready, they gathered outside in the cold morning mist, stretching out their muscles. Mica and Gabe took the lead, while Candace and Jackson followed their pace. No one said much for the first two miles, and Mica slowed to a walk.

"I need a bit of a breather," he said as he propped a heel on a tree stump and stretched. "You Physicals are tougher than you look."

Knowing the break for what it was, Candace nodded and

eased herself down onto a nearby rock. "So I suppose it's time for a chat, then," she said, sighing. "We should be safe out here."

"Yup. No man-made materials within half a mile," Mica said. "Well, except for what we're all wearing."

Only Jackson looked surprised at the turn of conversation. "Safe? Safe from what?"

Candace tried to smile, but couldn't completely hide her dread. "Safe from being overheard. There are things you need to know, Sunshine, and I couldn't tell you before."

His expression shifted from concerned to completely guarded. "About what?"

Standing, she walked over to him and took his hands. "You trust me, right?"

"Should I not?"

Her forehead bunched as Candace looked into his eyes. He searched her face for an answer to some unspoken question. Sighing, she dropped his hands along with her gaze. "I guess that's for you to decide, isn't it?"

"What's going on, Sugar Plum?" he said, gently lifting her chin. "What is it I don't know?"

Frowning, Candace chewed her lip and went back to the rock. "That's kinda what I've been asking myself for weeks, Sunshine."

"So I'm finally going to get the truth, huh?" Gabe said, crossing his arms as he looked back and forth between her and Mica. "I knew there was more to this than you were telling me."

"In as much as I know it," Candace said. She wiped the sweat from her forehead and detached one of the water bottles from her belt, downing half of it in a single drink. "I wasn't lying when I said HEX drugged me for about two weeks. The first week, I don't remember anything. I was totally out cold. The second, I was so high whenever they took me out for questioning I could hardly see straight."

"I'm still sorry about that, Candy," Mica said. "You know if I could've—"

"I know," she said, cutting off his apology. "You were a good soldier." She nudged him with her shoulder, eliciting a half-smile. Turning her focus back to Gabe and Jackson, she took a deep breath and got down to the hard stuff. "The first time Chuck took me out of the cell undrugged, he brought me to see Dr. Ferdinand."

She waited, gauging their reactions before beginning again. "Do you remember what Dr. P told us about her? About what happened when they were working together?"

"He said she used herself as a test subject and went crazy," Jackson said. He didn't move from his stance, feet planted and arms crossed in front of his chest.

Candace nodded. "That was the first lie. She's not a genevo. She's a completely normal human being."

"The first lie?" Gabe asked.

Candace swallowed hard. There was only one other thing she knew for sure wasn't true, but it would be the hardest for her cousin to hear.

"Dr. Ferdinand wasn't a test subject." Mica picked up the story, sensing her hesitation. "Dr. Poznanski used her son."

"That may or may not be the case," Candace said. "All I have is her word on that."

Mica's head snapped toward her. "You don't believe her?"

"I believe what I have proof of, Mica," she said. "I haven't seen her son. I don't know if her story's true. I think it might be, given how desperate she seems, but that's not enough for me to risk my life for."

"Wait," Jackson interrupted the argument. "Why would you have seen her son? She thinks he's alive?"

Candace bit down on her lip as she winced. "Well, that's the thing. She might have good reason to."

"Explain." A single glance at Gabe told her everything she needed to know: he already suspected what she was about to say next.

She took a deep breath. "That's the second lie. The ANGEL Project doesn't kill unstables, unless it's done by an ANGEL in the field. Even then, I can't speak for everyone, only myself."

Candace watched her cousin, seeing the emotions on his face as the information hit home. He knew what it meant.

Gabe's arms slowly dropped to his sides. "What proof do you have it's a lie?" His voice was little more than a whisper.

Candace held his stare. "You've been through the Gauntlet, Gabe. You know what proof I have."

His eyes pinched closed, and his breath came in shaky jerks of his shoulders.

She stood and took a step toward him. "Gabe…"

Before she could get to him, Gabe bent over onto the grass and retched. In another few steps, she was beside him, rubbing circles across his back as another wave of vomiting shook his body. He coughed and choked, a few sobs breaking through.

"I know, cuz. I know," she murmured as she draped an arm over his shoulders, resting her forehead against his hair. "I know what that means for you."

Gabe clutched at the dry, dead plants beneath him. "He can't be. He can't be, Candy. I would know."

She pushed his hair behind his ears and did as much as she could to soothe him. "No, Gabe, you wouldn't. Not if he was unstable. That part of him is gone, just like it was with Adrian, remember? Bas isn't Bas anymore."

At the sound of his name, Gabe's back curled up, pulling in on himself.

"I know it hurts, cuz. I know it, believe me," she said. "You gotta fight through this, though. I need you." She lowered her voice, her mouth barely an inch from his ear. "Mica needs you, too."

At that, he stilled beneath her. Every muscle in his body tensed.

That last statement was either a very poor choice, or the perfect one. Whichever it was, Candace released him and backed away, waiting for Gabe to make his next move.

She blinked, and he was gone.

Startled, she searched the dirt or grass for any sign of movement. After a moment, Candace returned to where her cousin was only seconds before, reaching out to see if she could feel him.

Nothing. Only empty air met her fingers.

Well, shit.

"On the bright side," she said with a sigh. "At least he didn't blow something up."

"Yet," Jackson added. She shot him a peeved glare, and he shut his mouth.

"Who's Bas?"

Mica was so quiet, Candace almost didn't hear the question. Slowly, she returned to her seat on the rock, giving him a gentle smile. "Amir and True told me about him a few days ago. He…" She trailed off and frowned at the dirt. "Bas and Gabe were together during their first round of treatments. At the end, Bas lost it and attacked Gabe. From what I know, guards dragged Bas off, and that was the end of it. I've known for a while there was someone else before I got here, but Gabe never told me about him. I always thought he died or something." She scrubbed a hand across her mouth. "I can't imagine what this is like for him. It was different for me. Adrian… well, I know what happened to him. There was finality in it, as horrible as it was. For Gabe, it's been over a year of assuming he was dead, I guess, but not ever knowing for sure." Candace looked up at Jackson. "Did you know him?"

Jackson shrugged. "Knew of him, mostly. Being social wasn't really my thing then."

"Why didn't you tell me about him?"

He shrugged again. "You didn't ask. Besides, it wasn't my place to tell. I think your cousin would agree with me."

God. Were all men that dumb? Candace rolled her eyes and shook it off, turning back to Mica. His face was pinched, scrunched up in total uncertainty. She reached over and took one of his hands. "Mica, I don't think this changes whatever's between you two, but he might need some time to adjust. Knowing what I know about how it goes with this stuff when you start the second round of treatments, I can tell you he's not going anywhere."

"But you don't know that for sure."

She squeezed his fingers. "Yes, I do. I know Gabe. I also know, firsthand, about this imprinting thing. It's not a thing you walk away from. Trust me on that."

Mica finally met her eyes, flicking a brief glance at Jackson.

She nodded with a faint smile. "Like I said, it's not a thing you walk away from. I'm pretty sure it's impossible."

"But..." He lowered his gaze to her hand in his. "But what if it's different for us?"

Candace snorted. "It's not. I know my cousin. You can't get rid of him even when you want to. Once he decides he likes you, you really don't get any choice in the matter." She hurriedly amended her statement when she saw the worry in Mica's eyes. "Uh, not like in that creepy stalkerish way. As in, you can't help yourself but like him, too. You kinda have to."

Jackson chuckled. "Well, I'll give you that. I have to admit he's grown on me since he decided I was good enough for you, Sugar Plum."

While his statement brought up all kinds of arguments and points she could make, Candace decided to bring the conversation back around to the reason they were out there.

"So, to get back to the main story," she said. "I spent my last week at the HEX compound thinking about all of this. I came to two decisions."

"And those are?" Jackson asked.

"One, there are a lot of things I don't like about the

ANGEL Project. They keep us in the dark, Sunshine. They hide things. They lie to us. They almost completely shield us from the outside world, and I don't think their motivations for doing that are necessarily in our best interest."

She turned towards Mica. "Two, there are a lot of things I don't like about HEX. They unleash dangerous monsters on innocent people and cause havoc to further Dr. Ferdinand's selfish plans. They devalue the members of their team they deem less powerful, as though they aren't the least bit important. She was completely willing to sacrifice those perceived weaker links for her own purposes." When Mica opened his mouth to argue, she held up a hand. "Don't tell me I'm wrong. Outside of Mitchell, the rest of you here aren't as useful to her. I already know Tori thinks she's second rate, that *they* made her feel second rate, and I see the same look on your face when someone tells you how amazing your ability is. I don't think Lucie is bothered, but your sister told me all she cares about is her birds, anyway. I don't know much about Naveen, but if he's been HEX for a year and they never let him do anything, that tells me he's not even on her radar. It's horrible, Mica. She spouts all this garbage about being family, and then tosses you off like trash. Family doesn't do that."

"Naveen isn't much of a threat," Jackson said. "He can siphon heat, but it's slow. If he wanted to kill someone, he'd have to be touching them, and they'd have to stand completely still for several minutes at least."

Candace stared at him. "How do you know?"

He arched an eyebrow at her. "You gave me a job to do. I told you I would. It would've been nice to know why I was doing it at the time."

"Pardon me," she said, defensive. "Between aneurysms and stabbings, I didn't have a lot of opportunities. Not to mention a few trust issues I hadn't ironed out yet."

When he flinched, she knew that last remark cut a little too deep. Releasing Mica, she stood up and walked over to him, lifting up on her toes to kiss his cheek. "I'm sorry, Sunshine. That was uncalled for. This whole mess has been really stressful, though. I'm a little short on patience for people questioning my intentions."

Jackson released a deep breath and nodded. "I get why. It's okay."

She smiled up at him and went back to her seat.

Jackson started pacing, clearly deep in thought. Candace let him go, allowing him time to process everything they told him. After a minute or two, he stopped and looked at her again.

"So, what's the plan? What is it you're looking to do?"

She pulled out another bottle of water and fidgeted with the lid. "I suppose that's the big question, isn't it? Honestly, I don't have an answer. The biggest problem I had to tackle first was how to get the sacrificial lambs out of their cages, and I still haven't worked out what to do about Mitchell."

"Mitchell?" Jackson asked. "Who's he? I thought our other prisoner was Mica's sister."

At that, Mica managed a chuckle. "Mitchell is Candy's drug-induced nickname for my sister, Michele. But, speaking of, I don't think you should worry about that, Candace."

"That's what she said, too," Candace said. "But I don't

get why."

"Plausible deniability," Mica said. "It's being handled."

"Have you been going down to see her without telling me?" Jackson asked.

Candace looked at him. "No, why?"

"You're acting like you're in constant communication with her."

"Oh, that," she said. "I forgot you probably don't know what Mitchell does. She's a telepath."

"Wait, like you talk to her in your head?"

Candace nodded. "Yeah, that's about right. I mean, she can't get into my brain whenever she feels like it. Something about my wiring blocks her. I have to initiate the conversation myself."

"Lucky," Mica muttered. "She's been so bored since we got here I practically have a constant running commentary in my head these days. I finally told her to shut up so I could work on those lenses. I don't know who she found to bug, but sucks to be them."

"So," Candace said, hesitant. "This might be a bit of a sensitive issue, but where do you think she falls in all of this? She told me she agreed with me that some of what HEX does is wrong, and Tori said she'll side with wherever you go, but I'd like to hear what you think."

Mica shifted on the tree stump as he thought. "Well, despite what Tori says, I'm not completely convinced she'd stay with me no matter what. If she thinks I'm safe and happy, maybe she'd finally feel free to think about herself for once. No matter how many times I tell her I'm fine, she's refused to leave, but, then again, she doesn't believe a word

I say. Mich needs to see it to believe it."

Well, that was as clear as mud. Basically, the telepath could go either way.

"You know," she said. "I forgot to tell you something the other day."

"What's that?" Mica asked.

"She said to tell you congratulations, but didn't say what for. Do you know what she meant?"

A slow, enigmatic smile crept across his face.

"Mica?"

He stood and brushed off the seat of his pants. "We should probably think about heading back. If they're watching me," he said, flashing the bracelet around his wrist. "They'll know we've been stopped for a while."

At the reminder of his tracking bracelet, Candace froze. "Mica..."

"Hmm?"

"I don't suppose you know if there's more to that thing than a simple GPS, do you?"

Catching her meaning, he winked at her. "I'm smarter than I look, Candy Cane. Come on. Maybe Gabe will catch up with us on the way back."

THE RUN back was uneventful and absent of any trace of her cousin. Candace was worried. If Gabe was too upset, he might do something really stupid and get himself killed.

Worse, he could blow their cover and get *all* of them

killed.

She left Jackson at their room and went back to Gabe's to shower. When she opened the door, Gabe was laid out on the bed, staring up at the newly-replaced ceiling tiles.

Candace stayed where she was, allowing him whatever space he needed. When nothing seemed forthcoming, she grabbed her clothes and headed to the bathroom.

Emerging fresh and clean, she noted he was exactly where she left him. Sighing, she sat on the edge of the mattress.

"Do you remember what you told me when I was still fighting the Jackson thing?"

He responded with silence.

"You said it wouldn't be a betrayal if I moved on. You told me that's what Adrian would have wanted for me."

Still nothing.

Candace looked away and stared at the carpet. "I didn't know him, but if Bas loved you, I think he would want the same thing. Love means placing another person's happiness above your own. If you tell me he wouldn't want you to be happy, he didn't love you. Not really. And if he didn't love you, moving on shouldn't bother you. Life is too short to waste it torturing yourself over people who know you're suffering and don't care."

"This isn't the same as Adrian, Candy Cane."

"Isn't it?" she asked, turning back to face him. "If someone's heart dies, if they lose the ability to love or care, isn't that the same as dying? The person you know is gone. It's not a physical death, but who they are dies. I know what that looks like. I heard it in Adrian's voice. I saw it in his actions. My Adrian died long before his body did. I still blame myself for killing him, in both senses. My actions pushed him over the edge. My actions ended his life. I watched him die *twice*, Gabe. So, you're right, it's not the same."

He closed his eyes and swallowed. "I don't know what to do."

Candace gently took his hand. "I know. It's not an easy situation. I can't tell you what to do, and I won't even try. But, if you need someone to talk to, you know I'm here."

Gabe squeezed her hand, an acknowledgment of her support. She sat there, waiting for him to move away or dismiss her, but he did neither. Instead, he pulled her down and she curled up beside him as they'd done so many times of late. Candace slid an arm around his chest and squeezed him tightly, pouring every ounce of comfort she could into the hug.

"I don't like any of this, Gabe. I hate it. I hate that you're hurting and there isn't anything I can do for you. I hate that I can't fix it. Mostly, I think I hate that I'm the one that's making you face this."

He took a deep breath and wrapped her in a hug. "This isn't your fault, Candy Cane. You didn't cause any of it."

"No, but without my meddling you wouldn't be in this situation."

"Without your meddling, I wouldn't have Mica, either." He kissed the top of her head. "And that's a pretty big deal."

She laid there, thinking. "You need to talk to him about this, you know. He's worried you're not going to want him now, like there's a chance you'll walk away and do something… I dunno. Something you probably shouldn't do."

"It crossed my mind." Gabe released her and sat up, rubbing his face. "But fortunately I remembered there are people to think about besides myself. That, and…"

She propped herself up on an elbow and looked at him. "And what?"

"You and Jackson…"

"Mmm hmm. What about me and Jackson?"

Fidgeting with the messy blankets, he hesitated. "What was it like for you, you know, after?"

"You mean aside from the gut-wrenching feelings of guilt and nausea over getting involved with someone I didn't think I could stand?"

He nodded.

Candace sat up and swung her legs over the bed. "For starters, I could tell whenever he was nearby. It's this electric pull I can't ignore. Anymore I can tell you exactly how far away he is from me, how long it would take me to get to him, within a certain distance, anyway. I couldn't feel him like that when he went out east or when I was with HEX. Well, I couldn't unless something big happened. When his emotions are on high, I feel that too. That's how I knew he was in trouble for the second Mirror test, and what was going on with that Kristie situation. It was really weird at first. Now, it's unsettling when I can't feel him, like a part of me is missing. I don't know if that'll be the same for you. Jackson and I had a little bit of history before we got together. There was always a strange love-hate thing between us, I think, and those extremes carried over to the imprinting." She chuckled a little. "Regular people would think we're nuts, you know. Funny what becomes normal for you when you're anything but."

After taking a deep breath, Gabe slid off the bed and stood. "Yeah, I get that. And you're right, I need to talk to Mica. I think he's pacing his room." He grabbed her hands and pulled her up into a hug. "Thank you, Candy Cane."

"You're welcome," she said, squeezing him back. "Just be honest with him, okay? Do that, and I think you'll be fine."

He pulled away and headed for the door, leaving her with a small smile and a nod. After he was gone, Candace took a look around. It was time to pack her things.

CHAPTER 19

"YOU WANT me to what?" Gabe stared at her, incredulous.

"I want to test my shields," Candace explained, dropping into a fighting stance. "Better to do it in controlled practice than risk it in the field, don't you think?"

Gabe shook his head and adjusted his glasses. "But what if you can't defend against it, Candy? I'm not exactly an expert at this yet. My aim might be off, and then you're screwed."

Candace gathered water from the fountains of the practice room. "Then it's your job to get me to the clinic. Come on. Don't wuss out on me. We talked about all this already."

"I don't—"

"Gabe," she said. "I'll be fine. You gotta do this sometime."

Done talking, Candace threw up a wall of water five feet in front of her and ten feet wide. She tensed, ready to jump away the moment he fired.

Sighing, Gabe lowered his glasses. His line of sight drifted to her left, aiming elsewhere.

"That attack is only useful if you try to hit someone, Gabriel," she called to him.

"I am, Candace," he shot back. "Water bends light waves, remember? Now shut up and focus. I'll be aiming for your head so be ready to drop if it goes through."

Aiming for her head? Damn. Okay then.

Candace kept her eyes on her cousin, but her concentration on her wall.

"Three... Two..." he counted down. "One!"

Light flashed from his eyes, but it barely registered before she felt it hit her defenses. Reflexively, she closed in on the attack, making the wall denser where she felt the breach.

The blast never got through.

Candace blinked, stunned at the new sensation. It wasn't that it passed through the shield, or that it was reflected back.

The light was trapped, bouncing around between molecules of water.

"Gabe," she said, cautiously approaching the glowing spot in the wall. "Did I do what I think I just did?"

"Holy shit, Candy Cane," Gabe whispered. "How can you do that? You can't control light."

She tapped into her connection a little deeper, probing it for an explanation. When she found the answer, it left her with more questions. "I'm not," she said. "I'm controlling how the water interacts with light, not the light itself. What the hell? How is that possible?"

"You mean you've never done that before?" he asked from the other side of the wall.

Candace shook her head. "As often as I've sparred with Jackson, I've never been able to do more than block his attacks. His fireballs are at least partially light, and nothing like this has ever happened."

"So what changed?"

"I have no idea. The only time I've had an ability expansion is when I started feeling steam right before Aspen. I figured it had something to do with imprinting or something, but maybe that's not right? Or maybe it's because you and I are related I can alter something from you."

"Uh, what happens when you drop the wall, Candy Cane?" Gabe said. "You can't hold that forever."

"Hmm," she said, considering it. "Well, if I can control where it stays, maybe I can control where it goes, too."

Closing her eyes, she called to the water, rearranging molecules in patterns, effectively creating a channel of reflection for the laser blast to exit. "Better stand back," she said. "Let's see if this works."

Releasing her hold, a beam of light shot down the length of the wall, emerging at the far end to hit the padding at the back of the room. She dropped the shield.

"Huh," she said. "That was an unexpected turn of events."

"So you had no idea you could do that?" Gabe asked. "Really?"

"Really." Candace chewed her lip, frowning. "Though I haven't used my ability much since Aspen, to be honest. It's been really quiet around here the last week. I mean, even the Pavo Team has only been called out once, and that was just a dirty gen-evo lab in Chinatown."

"No other changes that you've noticed then?"

She shook her head. "No. Nothing."

Gabe shrugged. "So run through everything. Check it out to see if the rest is the same. Maybe it's just that you've never been attacked with pure light before."

"Could be," she murmured, then shook herself. "Okay. Let's give it a look."

Candace ran through all her attacks on a practice dummy: ropes, waves, bubbles, bullets. Nothing was any different than before.

"All good there," she said as Gabe examined the hole left behind by her droplet bullet. "So far, it's just my shields."

"What about that other thing you do," Gabe said. "Your camouflage?"

At the reminder, Candace got a little excited. No matter how much she tried before, she was never able to make her camouflage useful outside of the water. The way her body shimmered and reflected light rendered it useless in the open. But if she could control those reflections…

She dove into her connection again, covering herself in a thin film of liquid. It bent to her will, the molecules arranging themselves in reflective patterns as she told their many voices what the goal was.

Candace opened her eyes, noting she couldn't see so much as her nose. Holding up her hands, those too were transparent, showing through to her cousin where her fingers should be.

Gabe was staring, speechless. Testing out movement, Candace left her position, walking around until she was behind him and tapping him on the shoulder. He whirled.

"Not a trace of you, Candy Cane," he said, excited. "I at least expected wet footprints or something."

"If I'm holding the water against me, why would there be footprints?" she said.

His face scrunched up. "Uh, that's weird. If you're going for stealth, I'd recommend against speaking. I can see the inside of your mouth when you open it. Like teeth and a flapping tongue. Kinda gross."

Giggling, she dropped the camouflage. "I'll remember that next time. Although, that might make a killer haunted house prank."

The experiment concluded, they adjourned for the day. As they walked through the hallway, Candace shivered. The temperature dropped twenty degrees as they passed by another practice room.

"Must be Naveen and Jackson," Gabe said. "Has he been spending a lot of time training that guy?"

Candace nodded. "Yeah. Almost every day. Jackson thinks they're ready to let Naveen out, but I don't know much outside of that. I can't imagine they'll give him a roommate. I mean, I don't think I'd feel comfortable sleeping in the same room with him. Although, I tend to wake up if I'm cold so maybe it'd be fine."

"Mica says he's okay," Gabe said, shrugging. "He's a little odd, but not crazy or anything. He's just one of those people that takes some getting used to."

"Aren't we all?" she said, chuckling.

As they left the training hallway, True exited the elevator and approached. "Good, you're done," she said. "I'm supposed to collect you and Jackson."

"Collect us?" Candace tensed, instantly worried. "Was there an attack? There weren't any alarms, so..."

True shook her head. "No, nothing like that. You need to get to the Gauntlet. It's photo shoot day."

"Photo shoot day?"

"Of course," True said with a smile. "For PR stuff. Did you think you were going to be invisible to the public forever?"

Photo shoot? As in, for a collector card of her own and press releases? No matter how hard she tried, she couldn't fight back her grin. "Guess they didn't forget about me after all, huh?"

Gabe chuckled at her. "Oh boy. There'll be no living with her once she sees her face on one of those cards."

True snorted. "I guess that runs in the family then, eh?"

Candace giggled. "I can only imagine what he was like. How long did it take his ego to deflate enough to fit in the Showcase again? A week? A month?"

"Very funny," he said, rolling his eyes. "But you'd better get going. Makeup always takes longer with girls and I imagine they'll want their crowning jewel of a SAGE to be the pinnacle of perfection for this."

"Crowning jewel? Please. Maybe for now, but I thought Hayden and Markov were the poster kids." She waved off the exaggeration and headed for the elevator. "I'll catch you guys later."

THE PHOTO shoot was a whirlwind of bright lights and people buzzing about. It was strange to be the center of all that attention, and yet very detached from it at the same time. Candace had little say over poses or what she was supposed to do with the water they wanted spraying up around or behind her. She did put her foot down with the pink lighting. Really, why couldn't they give up on trying to make her some girly princess? When they finally capitulated and gave her blue backdrops, she was much more amenable to whatever else they asked of her, but she had no idea how the shots themselves turned out.

As she stood in front of a mirror, wiping away the heavy makeup with a damp cloth, Dr. Poznanski came up behind her. Candace turned, unsure of what the passive look on his face meant.

"You'll be headed to LA in three weeks," he said, his voice as unreadable as his face. "Mr. Lawrence will go as well. You'll be presented at an unveiling as part of a seven-day publicity tour with stops in Aspen, Colorado; Des Moines, Iowa; Portland, Maine; and finally Washington, DC."

Candace blinked at him, completely unsure of what to think about it. "A PR tour? Already? Isn't it usually a year before stats and such are released about new ANGELs?"

"Yes, well, your recent activities have made the public curious about you. Rather than allow speculation and rumors to continue, we've decided it's best if we introduce you and Mr. Lawrence to your new fans."

"New fans?" she said, staring at him incredulously. "What fans?"

"Internet conspiracy theorists, mostly," Dr. Poznanski said, crossing his arms. "There's been some questioning about the ANGEL Project's intentions and effectiveness, especially given the high profile nature of the incidents in Aspen and San Jose." A slight look of displeasure creased his forehead. "Had those been handled as well as the attack at the Hoover Dam, I doubt we'd be forced to go public with you two so soon."

Bristling at his insinuation, Candace opened her mouth to defend herself, but he stopped her. "As it stands, we can't change those events, but we can clarify them some."

Glancing away to the current flurry of excitement that was Jackson's photo shoot, Candace relaxed a little. If nothing else, it would provide her with an opportunity to spend more time with him. However, it also meant Jackson was going to have to put on a "plays well with others" face, which would certainly be a challenge.

"You'll need to meet with Miss Clemmons and Mr. Jones, as they can guide you some in how to handle yourself and what to expect of the tour. General Jacobs will also be along with you, so most of the press's questions will be fielded by him."

She sighed. "So, basically I'm just there for show."

He smiled slightly and turned away, retreating. "Perhaps you should take some time to practice your wave. How does it go? Elbow, elbow, wrist, wrist? I'll leave it to you to inform

Mr. Lawrence."

Biting back the urge to retort, Candace fumed silently. She wasn't even on the trip yet, and already she understood Amir's irritation with PR tours.

And Jackson would probably like it even less.

Wonderful.

AS THEY left the Gauntlet, Candace was quiet, considering everything that was going on and everything that could possibly go wrong with the PR tour. Jackson filled the silence with numerous complaints about the photo shoot, most of which was about the makeup and hair products they forced on him.

"I smell like a damned chemical weapons factory," he grumbled. "What the hell is the point of all the smoke and mirrors, anyway? We're superheroes. Do we need more special effects?" When she didn't reply, he nudged her with an elbow. "What's with you? Not up to soothing the savage beast today?"

"Hmm?" she said, glancing over at him. "What now?"

Jackson frowned. "Did something happen?"

Candace took a deep breath and tried to shove her worries aside. "We'll talk about it later. How about we grab showers and take a walk?"

His eyebrows lifted, curious, but he didn't question her further.

After Jackson decided to join her in shampooing her

hair, Candace was a little more relaxed. Thanks to his attentive hands, she was pretty sure every inch of her body was cleaned three times over. Less anxious than she was before the shower, they dressed and headed into the Quad, her arm slipping into his as they walked.

She was about to start telling him their plans for the coming weeks, when a familiar voice made her stop.

"Focus on my words. Let the sound of my voice guide you."

Beneath the branches of a wide tree, Trevor sat cross-legged, eyes closed, Deborah and Tori to either side of him. While that wasn't all that interesting in itself, the person sitting in front of Trevor left Candace a little stunned.

Michele was motionless, her focus singular, not so much as blinking as she stared at the massive man across from her. What was going on? What was she doing? Even more, why was she out of her cell, and who managed that particular feat of insurmountability?

"Let's go back slowly," Michele continued. "Tell me about waking up in the clinic. What do you see?"

"Candace," Trevor answered, his deep voice carrying over the chilly breeze. "Candace is there to help me. She helped me before."

"How did she help you before?"

Candace turned away from the conversation. Someone persuaded Dr. Poznanski to let Michele help recover his memories, and she was walking Trevor backwards through them. Who's suggestion was it to bring her in? Tori's? Deborah's? Frowning, Candace hooked Jackson's arm and led him farther out, strolling through the Quad as she collected her thoughts.

"So, they've decided to put us on display," she said as they passed the above-ground edges of the compound.

"On display?" Jackson asked. "Meaning what?"

"Meaning you and I are going on a PR tour in three weeks."

He stopped walking. "We're what?"

Candace sighed and pulled him along. "That was kind of my reaction, too. Poznanski says they're doing it earlier than normal because of recent things like Aspen. People are asking questions and aren't thrilled with the lack of explanation, I guess. Aspen is actually one of our stops, along with LA, Des Moines, Portland, and DC."

"They want you to go back to Portland?" Jackson asked. "To visit survivors or something?"

She shook her head. "Not Oregon. Portland, Maine. I'm not sure why."

He stopped again. His face contorted, a pained expression taking over. "That's where I grew up."

While she never really pressed him to talk about his past before, Candace winced. She should have known that. Gently, she slipped her fingers between his and squeezed. "Are you gonna be okay? I think they're going for the 'local boy makes good' angle."

"Des Moines isn't local for you," he said, scowling.

"It's Iowa, Sunshine. Anything less than a state away is local, and even then it's up for debate. Besides, it makes sense to bring me back to where it started. It's a human angle, showing how events shaped me into what I am now. It gives people something to hope for, maybe. Although, I don't know that if they knew everything that's happened since, they'd be quite as inspired."

Jackson pulled her against his side and kissed the top of her head. "Probably more inspired, likely. You've been through a lot, Sugar Plum."

"Most of which I can't talk about," she said, pointing out the obvious. "And if they knew what comes with the territory, I doubt they'd be at all eager to sign up themselves."

"It's probably more to improve public opinion," he said. "After Aspen and San Jose, they're looking to polish up their image a bit. Give the people something shiny to distract them."

A sad smile tugged at her lips. "Something shiny, is it? Funny, I don't feel very shiny. Although, you tend to light up the room from time to time, so there's that."

"You're hilarious," he said. "I doubt it'll come to that. What are we supposed to do, anyway? Do they need their trained monkeys to do some kind of act?"

"You've been listening to Amir, I see." Candace nudged him. "Actually, that reminds me. Poznanski said we should talk to Amir and True about this business. He wants us to be prepared to face the press."

"I'm surprised he didn't suggest Hayden and Markov," Jackson grumbled, adding extra vitriol to Christian's last name. "They're old hat at this nonsense, after all."

She sighed and rolled her eyes. "Don't tell me you're still worried about that stuff with Christian, Sunshine. I told you before, and I'll tell you again, Christian Markov can't hold a candle to you." She giggled. "Literally, he can't."

"Oh, so you've got jokes, huh?" He poked her in the ribs,

turning her giggle into full laughter.

Batting his hand away, she tried to get the conversation back on track. "But seriously, Jackson, have you ever watched one of these superhero press conferences before?"

He shrugged. "Not really. Never gave them much thought. I guess I didn't figure I'd ever be someone they wanted in the spotlight."

"Well, I've seen a lot of them," she said, slipping her hand back into his. "Some of the reporters ask silly questions like if food tastes different or does blue still look like blue after the treatments, but then you get ones that ask what's it like to kill someone with your brain, or have you ever wanted your normal life back. And then you'll get ones like…" She trailed off, suddenly unsure of herself, though it was probably stupid to worry about.

"Like what?" Jackson prompted.

"Well," she said, frowning. "Every now and then people ask about personal relationships. I know more about True and Amir than any other ANGELs because True was always kind of my favorite. I think I've watched every video interview with her and read every article I could get my hands on. Every time she was asked about Amir, she'd give the same answer."

"Which was?"

Candace chewed her lip, thinking. She tried to remember the exact wording. "We have a very close, working relationship. We're members of a team and like family to one another."

"Ah, I see," he said, squeezing her hand. "You're worried we'll have to fake it, huh?"

EVOLUTION: HEX

She nodded.

Jackson stopped walking and turned her to face him. "You realize I can't do that, right?"

She grimaced. "Sunshine, if we have to—"

"No," he said, the humor gone from his voice. "That is one thing I will never lie about. Never. I don't care how many orders they scream at me, or even if you told me I had to, I would never tell anyone anything but the truth about us."

"Even if it was to protect me?"

Placing a hand against her cheek, Jackson stared down into her eyes. "I couldn't lie even if I wanted to. Not about that. No one would ever believe me."

Grinning, she lifted up on her toes and brushed a kiss across his lips. "Okay, Sunshine. Then we agree. Can I ask you for one favor?"

As he wrapped his arms around her waist, pulling her against him, he smiled. "Depends on what's in it for me."

"I can think of a few things to tempt you with."

"Do tell."

She grinned and shook her head. "You don't even know what the favor is yet."

"Then ask. I'll let you know what I think proper payment is."

"Promise me if they try to put me in anything pink, you'll torch it on the spot," she said, wrinkling her nose in disgust.

His loud laughter echoed off of the nearby rocks. "That's your favor?"

"Mmm hmm."

Looking up at the sky, he considered it. "Well, I suppose

there are a few things on my list I haven't checked off yet."

"Want to give me a hint?"

"Nope," he said, tilting her chin up towards him. "I think I'd rather surprise you."

Candace giggled again. "I don't know if I should be terrified or excited by the look in your eyes."

"Mmm," he murmured, lowering his face to hers. "Bit of both, maybe. Keeps things interesting."

Before she could respond, Jackson's lips closed over hers, effectively rendering her brain useless. When he'd kiss her that way, there wasn't room for anything in her head but him. Warmth flooded her veins, heating every part of her.

"So this tour," he said, his breath warm against her skin. "Anyone else tagging along, or is it just us?"

"Just us, as far as I know."

"Good," he said. "Then I'll get you all to myself."

As much as she wanted that to be true, Candace couldn't help deflating a little. "This isn't a vacation, Sunshine. Everyone will want a piece of us on this trip."

"You think I'm going to let that stop me?"

She sighed and pulled away. "Jackson, you know you'll have to be on better than your best behavior for this. They're going to expect you to be perfect. You don't get to say you don't want to. You *have* to."

"I'm always on my best behavior."

Giving him a look, she nodded. "I know. That's why I said better than your best."

"Are you asking me for another favor?" He lifted an eyebrow with a mischievous expression.

"In this case?" Candace set her hands on her hips. "No.

I'm telling you that if you're not, I'm going to ask for separate hotel rooms. Even if that means I have to wear pink the whole damn trip."

Jackson chuckled. "I think you're bluffing."

"Are you willing to risk it if I'm not?"

Shaking his head, he shrugged it off. "I'm smarter than I look. I know you don't bet unless you know you can win."

Triumphant, Candace snuggled up to him again. "I knew you had a brain in there somewhere. Good choice."

CHAPTER 20

AS CANDACE emerged from the bathroom of her hotel suite, True gasped.

"Oh, sugar," she whispered. "You look amazing."

Candace looked down at the shimmery silver fabric draped around her body and smoothed it out self-consciously. "Are you sure? I mean, maybe it's too sparkly. Won't it attract too much attention?"

True chuckled at her. "That's kind of the point, Candy Cane. This is your big debut. You and Jackson are the main event. They've seen me and Amir tons of times. They're ready for the next big thing."

Stepping in front of the full-length mirror, Candace barely recognized herself. Glittering from head to toe, everything from her shoes to her eye makeup was silver, including the tiny flowers pinning her hair in place. If the ANGEL Project was looking for something shiny, they were definitely going to get exactly that.

True tugged at the wisp of a sleeve covering Candace's right shoulder, frowning. "I forgot about that. I should've made these longer to cover that scar of yours."

"I'm not worried about it," Candace said. "Who cares if someone sees?"

"You know you're going to get asked about it."

She shrugged. "And if I do, I'll tell them it was for personal reasons."

"You think they won't be able to guess?" True rested her hands on her hips, the red satin of her gown wrinkling slightly. "It doesn't take a genius to guess what, or who, that J stands for."

"So let them guess," Candace said. "I'm not going to lie."

"We went over this, sugar. You go public with your relationship, and you're going to open yourself to all kinds of questions that will make you want to punch the people that ask them. Are you ready for that?"

Candace picked up her handbag from the table in the entryway. "It's not like either of us is going to announce it or anything, True. We decided together that we're not going to deny it, and that's what I'm sticking to."

"You're aware that it might make trouble for those of us trying to hang on to what little privacy we have?" True said softly.

Candace turned and offered a smile. "I can't control whatever conclusions people jump to outside of myself. For what it's worth, neither of us will comment on anyone else's relationships. We'll respect your choices, but try to respect ours too, okay?"

"Fine, but don't say I didn't warn you," True said with a sigh. "You think you're good with the rest of the prep we've done the last few weeks?"

Candace tilted her head to the side and mentally reviewed what she learned from True and Amir leading up to the PR tour. "I think so. Basically, if it's about me, answer vaguely with something positive. If it's specific to ANGEL Project goals or operations, direct them to General Jacobs or quote from the brochure."

"You got it." True nodded. "Come on. We'll go collect the boys, and then it should be about time to head down to the party."

Amir's room was the mirror image of Candace's suite, though his was decked out in stainless steel and black marble, where hers was warm wood and creamy travertine. Candace followed behind True as they entered the lounge area where Jackson and Amir sat, chatting. All conversation ceased as the men realized who was joining them, and they rose from their chairs. Amir strode around the furniture with a wide grin on his face, but his expression was only for True.

"I never get tired of seeing you like this," he said, brushing a kiss against her cheek. "You are stunning."

Watching them, Candace wondered how they'd managed to hide their relationship from the public for so long. Sure, there were rumors and fan fiction about the two of them together, but not so much as a picture of them holding hands existed anywhere she knew of.

Smiling, she looked away from them, waiting for Jackson

to join them. When she looked at him, she couldn't remember ever seeing him completely speechless. He stared at her as though he'd never seen her before. Embarrassed, Candace's face heated and she fidgeted with her purse, unsure of how to take his reaction.

"See?" True said, smirking. "I told you it wasn't too much."

Candace giggled. "Well, if he doesn't regain the ability to speak soon, that could be problematic for tonight, don't you think?"

Jackson shook himself and slid up beside her, snaking an arm around her waist. He bent low to her ear and whispered, "I hope this thing doesn't go too late, because I don't know that I'll be able to behave for very long with you looking like this."

Blushing again, she laughed and extricated herself, taking him by the hand and pulling him to the door. "Come on, then. I have a week of General Jacobs ahead of me and I don't want to start it by ticking him off because we were late."

On the elevator ride down, Candace busied herself with straightening Jackson's deep red tie. Paired with his sleek black suit, she had to admit the look was fantastic on him. He wasn't the only one ready for the appearance to be over. It was going to be a hell of a lot of fun taking it all off of him.

They stopped on the fifth floor, reporting as instructed to a staging room. From there, they proceeded to the staff and freight elevator, then through back passageways towards the outdoor presentation space. Precisely at seven, General Jacobs was announced, along with True and Amir, leaving Candace and Jackson to wait for their cue.

Candace eyeballed the NSA detail guarding the entrance and stage exit. What on Earth was the purpose of having bodyguards for superheroes? She reasoned that it was probably more of a deterrent to any members of the press that worked up the courage to try their luck and get early pictures. That, or maybe they were concerned they'd try to bolt. Judging by the way Jackson was pacing, that might not be out of the question.

Smiling, Candace took his hand and did what she could to calm him. All it really consisted of was giving him a wink, as they had to be quiet so they would hear their names being called.

"In their short tenures as ANGELs," True said over the speakers. "These two heroes have faced unprecedented danger in multiple altercations, helping to avoid excessive fatalities when the risk to lives was greater than ever. Most recently, they were seen in action in Aspen, Colorado, where they took out one of the most organized, ruthless threats the ANGEL Project has encountered to date. Their teamwork resulted in the capture of not one, but six genetically enhanced combatants, who are now all undergoing rehabilitation to wild success."

Candace snorted. Well, that wasn't a total lie.

"First," Amir said, taking his turn at the microphone. "Hailing from Portland, Maine with the ability to manipulate fire, Jackson Lawrence!"

Candace squeezed his hand and practically shoved him towards the stage entrance. He emerged to thunderous cheering from the crowd she couldn't yet see. A sudden burst of heat hit her, evidence of pyrotechnics to punctuate his ability.

After a moment, the crowd settled. Candace's stomach knotted, knowing that she was about to be called.

"And now, from Hospers, Iowa, commanding the power of water, Candace Bristol!"

Swallowing past her nerves, Candace stepped out of the tent, the curtain blocking the stage parting instantly to allow her passage. Bright lights pointed at her from every direction, but she tried her best to focus on where she was going. She barely located her stage marker and turned to face the crowd with what she hoped was a pleasant smile. Behind her, streams of water arced through the air, splashing down on opposite sides.

It was unnerving to stand in front of what she knew must be a few hundred people but not being able to see any of them past the spotlights. She did as they practiced earlier in the day, standing and trying to look confident, allowing the guests their chance for photos. Strange to think that some of the guests were actors, rock stars, Hollywood studio execs, and Fortune 500 CEOs. To them, *she* was the celebrity. At least, that's what her cousin always liked to say.

After what felt like forever, General Jacobs took the podium.

"Thank you, Miss Clemmons, Mr. Jones. Honored guests, there's been some speculation about the current status of the ANGEL Project. You are all aware of the devastating attacks on Miami, Florida; Myrtle Beach, South Carolina; Portland, Oregon; San Jose, California; and, most recently, Aspen, Colorado. You have seen the amount of damage these events resulted in, and you may have wondered what happened to the good old days of fighting unstable back alley mutations. In truth, we have a new enemy, and it has caused us many losses. This new enemy goes by the name of HEX, and they have achieved stability in their genetic evolutions on par with the ANGEL Project. It is because of this threat that we've initiated a new stage in the program."

Candace tried not to gape at him. He was announcing them as SAGEs? There? That night? Why weren't they told?

"The two ANGELs you see before you are the first of a new breed. This stage, dubbed SAGE, or SecondAry Genetic Enhancement, has resulted in heroes mightier than any we have seen before. SAGEs are faster, stronger, their abilities expanded beyond all expectation. They are the reason Aspen was not a complete massacre. Their abilities are invaluable in the fight against our enemies."

While Candace was trying to locate Jackson, to see if he was as shocked as she was, the General spoke again.

"I'll now ask our SAGEs to demonstrate these new abilities. If you could please clear the center spaces."

Confused and trying not to show it, Candace floundered as a walkway extended from beneath the stage. The spotlights dimmed and she finally saw the crowd as they parted. A small crew of workmen sprang into action, pulling up thick panels of flooring in the center of the presentation space to reveal a full-sized swimming pool below. Looking up, a giant fire brazier burned against the night sky. What the hell was she supposed to do, fight Jackson? In a dress? Surely not.

EVOLUTION: HEX

Backing away from the edge, Candace felt a hand on her arm. True led her to the center of the stage where Amir and Jackson conferred with General Jacobs.

"What is this?" Candace said, turning away from the crowd. "No one said anything about any of this."

"Relax, Miss Bristol," the General said. "Consider it a Showcase demonstration without the destruction. Give them something pretty to look at, since it seems you have a talent for that as well."

She bristled. "Excuse me?"

Jackson grabbed her arm and pulled her aside. "Ignore him, Sugar Plum. We have a job to do."

"Ignore him? But he just said—"

"I know what he just said, and I don't like it either, but there's not a damn thing we can do about it right now."

Candace took a deep breath. "Fine. You're right. So what do we do?"

The hint of a smile crept onto his lips. "I have an idea. Let me start and follow my lead." He turned to go.

"Wait, what? What are you going to do?"

Jackson winked. "I'm going to give them a peek at the monsters inside us."

Her jaw sagged open. What did that mean? The monsters inside them? That sounded like a nightmare, not a show for the Hollywood elite.

Before she could get any more answers, Jackson was stepping down onto the catwalk. With prompting from True, Candace followed his example and walked off the stage, taking up a position across the pool from him. Aware of the eyes on her back, she couldn't turn to look at the crowd.

Focus on the job. Focus on him.

Every light in the place dimmed to nothing, save for those in the pool. Taking that as his cue, Jackson began.

The fire in the brazier shot up into the air, twisting, shaping itself into a terrifying figure as it looped and descended. Jaws gaping, the flaming Chinese dragon plummeted down, pulling up ten feet from the heads of the crowd, eliciting gasps and shouts from the onlookers.

A dragon, eh? She grinned. She could play that game.

Candace stilled herself, plunging into her connection, forming her own monster in her mind. There were so many ways that she was horrifying, and rather than pick one, she gave them all faces, lifting a slender, winged hydra from the contents of the pool. When the dragon came close again, the hydra twisted, wrapping itself around the fire beast, a mid-air wrestling match of mythical proportions. Their dance was fierce and frightening and beautiful. The creatures rolled and spun, eventually spiraling into one another in a breathtaking cyclone of liquid and light. Steam billowed in the sky, until, at last, that's all there was.

Candace watched the clouds for a moment, then called to them. The voices of vapor whispered back, following her commands and bending to her will. When she was done, Candace opened her eyes, smiling at the symbol left behind.

C. Swirls. J. Swirls.

With a wave of her hand, the clouds dispersed. As the lights came up, so did the applause, startling her slightly. She forgot where she was.

"Candace Bristol and Jackson Lawrence, ladies and gentlemen!" General Jacobs said into the microphone.

EVOLUTION: HEX

Taking that as her sign they were done, Candace turned and tried not to wobble on her heels as she made her way back to the stage. A look from True and Amir told her she did well, but it was only Jackson she wanted to see. He met her at center stage and took her hand.

Turning back to the crowd as the walkways retracted and the workmen recovered the pool, he whispered to her. "Take a bow, Sugar Plum. We earned it."

Chuckling, she dipped a small curtsy to the audience. "Was it good for you?"

"Let me get that dress off you and I'll show you how good."

"Shh," she said over a giggle. "Show's not over yet, Sunshine. Until then, you behave."

"You started it."

"Well done, you two," the General said, coming up behind them. "Ready to mingle?"

Candace sighed. Playtime was over.

AFTER THE most bizarre and uncomfortable evening of her life, Candace finally slunk back to her room, carrying her shoes to offer a little respite to her aching feet. True and Amir said those things were exhausting, but Candace wasn't prepared for the level of in-your-face questions and outright adoration heaped on her from all sides. Thanks to the constant bombardment of attention by celebrities and reporters, she barely made eye contact with Jackson the whole night, and he was nowhere to be found when she finally got away from the party.

But she thought it went fairly well, all things considered. The questions she got weren't that surprising, and what she didn't prepare for, she easily sidestepped or flubbed her way through. The strangest event of the evening was when a blogger for the LA Times asked her to sign the early-released collector card featuring her. Apparently, they were passed out in goodie bags for the attendees. It was the first time she laid eyes on it, and her internal reaction was not what she always thought it would be.

"Now everyone knows my face," she murmured to herself as she stared out the window at the LA skyline.

She felt him before she saw him.

"It's not like you could hide before, Sugar Plum," Jackson said, his arms wrapping around her waist as he brushed a kiss against the base of her neck. "People would notice you even if you weren't a superhero."

Candace smiled and rested her arms on top of his. "Where did you disappear to?"

"I was looking for something."

"And did you find it?"

"Mmm," he murmured as he kissed her neck again. "I did, but it was missing something."

Turning, her eyebrows lifted. "Oh really. What might that be?"

Jackson's hands drifted up her back, coming to a stop below her jawline. As he lowered his face to hers, he whispered, "You."

His kiss was slow and deep, burning through her like

embers of a smoldering fire. Her hands wandered up his chest, grabbing hold of the silky red tie around his neck and pulling him closer. Jackson growled against her mouth, then broke away suddenly.

"You're trying to get me to change my mind," he said with a smirk. "But I won't let you."

Confused, Candace released him. "Change your mind about what? I thought—"

Fingers under her chin, he tipped her head up to him and ran his thumb across her lips. "Oh, we'll get there, Sugar Plum, but I have something else in mind first."

Taking her by the hand, he led her out the door and to the hidden freight elevator. But instead of going down, he took them up.

"The roof?" She giggled. "Are you planning to get rid of me once and for all?"

As he brought her fingers to his mouth and kissed the tops of her knuckles, he shook his head. "I intend the opposite of that, Candy."

"Like you have a choice," she said, grinning.

When they stepped out of the elevator, Candace's breath caught. A wide circle of candles surrounded a blanket on the open rooftop. There, a small spread of fruit and finger foods greeted her, more than enough to make up for having little to eat at the non-stop social event of the past few hours.

"Where did you get all of this?" she asked as he urged her forward.

"The concierge here is very helpful," Jackson said. "He was more than happy to lend a superhero a hand."

She snorted. "I bet. How much did this cost you?"

He shrugged it off. "A photo and an autograph. The rest was comped by the hotel."

Standing inside the circle of light, Candace circled her arms around him and lifted up on her toes. "You'd better be careful. I could get used to this and then you'll end up spending all your time thinking up new surprises for me."

As she leaned in to kiss him, someone cleared their throat and she jumped, startled by the unexpected presence.

"Hate to interrupt this little romantic interlude," Chuck said as he emerged from behind Jackson. "But I thought now might be a good time for a chat since your entourage is elsewhere."

Reflexively, Jackson spun and pushed her back, blocking her with his body. With the heat rolling off of him, Candace was hesitant to touch him, but she set a hand on his arm and gently lowered it.

"Easy, Sunshine," she said. "Chuck's only here to talk. Don't crispify him yet."

Chuck's smirk rankled her, and she tensed, automatically dipping into her connection.

"Yeah, Sunshine, don't—"

The moment he used that nickname, she yanked on the cord, paralyzing him, and then stepped around a ready-to-explode Jackson.

"You'd better watch your mouth, Precious," she said. "If you want to talk, talk. I won't tolerate any bullshit, though. Am I clear? He already doesn't like you, and if he has a mind to show you how much, I can't stop him. Now," she said, dropping her hold. "You wanted to speak with me?"

Chuck snapped his mouth closed and scowled. "I'm

supposed to ask for a status update."

"A status update?" Candace asked. "She should be getting plenty of those from our mutual friend, shouldn't she?"

"Yeah, well, those have been less than forthcoming lately." He crossed his arms and stared at her from the other side of the candle circle. "And that's a little suspicious, don't you think?"

Well, that was interesting. Was Mitchell holding out on Dr. Ferdinand? To what end?

"I have no idea what that's about, Chuck, so stop giving me the evil eye. As far as I know, nothing's changed. I told her it would take time and I couldn't promise anything in the way of a schedule. These things don't happen overnight."

"It's been six weeks, Candy. We expected a bit more progress."

She sighed. "What do you expect me to do? My hands are tied. Especially with this tour going on. Every eye in the country is on the two of us right now, so I have to be careful."

Chuck sniffed and dropped his arms. "Right. The tour. Okay, Candy Cane. You have fun with your little parties. Just remember that we're not going to wait forever."

With those words, Chuck vanished, shifting away to somewhere else. Hopefully far, far from her.

Fingers closed over her arms, and she jerked, spinning away into a fighting stance. Jackson stood behind her, palms flashed in surrender. "Whoa. Just me, Sugar Plum."

Her shoulders dropped and she blew out a breath. "Sorry. That guy just puts me on edge. I can't believe he showed up here." Looking around, Candace frowned. "I'm sorry he ruined your wonderful surprise, Sunshine."

Stepping up to her, Jackson smiled. "Who said he ruined anything?"

Candace idly straightened his tie, forehead wrinkled as she replayed the conversation in her head.

"Jackson?"

"Hmm?"

"Do you think I'm in over my head?"

"Well, you aren't the tallest of people, so…"

She slugged him in the arm. "You know what I mean."

Setting a palm against her cheek, Jackson kissed her lightly. "Aren't you always? I have yet to see that stop you, though."

Smiling, she tried to push her worries aside. Dwelling on them wasn't going to change things, and she couldn't do anything about it that second anyway. "I suppose if I can handle you, I can handle whatever else they throw at me."

Jackson chuckled and pulled her tight against him. "Sugar Plum, you can handle me as much as you like. I promise not to complain. So, are you ready to pick up where we left off?"

"Absolutely," she said.

But as she followed him down to sit at their picnic, Chuck's words nagged at her.

HEX wouldn't wait forever.

CHAPTER 21

CANDACE AWOKE to pounding on the bedroom door and a startled yelp from Jackson as he fell out of bed. Heart hammering, Candace tried to clear her head as she pulled a t-shirt on and scrambled out from under the covers.

"Suit up," True said as she shoved two black skinsuits through the door. "We have a situation."

"A situation?" Candace repeated as she fumbled with the items. "An attack or…?"

"Yeah. In Burbank. Hurry."

With a quick nod, Candace closed the door and turned to Jackson, tossing him the larger suit. "Time to get to work, Sunshine."

Jackson grumbled and rubbed the sleep out of his eyes. "Good morning to you, too."

Ignoring him, Candace stepped into her gear and threw her hair into a messy bun. They emerged from the bedroom moments later and were promptly escorted to the roof. A helicopter waited, its blades whipping the wind around them in readiness for flight as the ANGELs were herded into it. Someone shoved a pair of headphones into Candace's hands as she took her seat and strapped in.

"What's going on?" she said as the helicopter door closed and they started to move.

"An unstable at one of the movie lots," Amir said. "Super strength, super speed. He's tearing up the sets. It's pretty early, and no casualties reported yet, but emergency personnel can't get in to assess the situation. The helo will drop us nearby."

When they arrived on scene, Candace gaped. Entire warehouse buildings lay in collapsed ruins. Above the din of sirens and people yelling, the crunch of ripping metal and an inhuman howl led them to their target.

Shredded clothing hung from the man's thin frame, and Candace could see his ribs through the gaps in his t-shirt. Dark, stringy hair hung past his shoulders as he bent to grab the wheel of a golf cart and fling it towards the large bay doors of an unmarred soundstage.

With a giant gust of wind, True prevented the damage, lowering the cart harmlessly to the ground. Amir clapped his hands in front of himself and sent a wave of pressurized sound at the man, knocking him face down on the concrete.

"Now that we have your attention—" Amir started, but his words died as the man scrambled to his feet to face them. "Amal?"

EVOLUTION: HEX

Snarling, the man ran at them, faster than Candace could react. Jackson slammed into his side, knocking him away as they skidded into the side of a trailer. The unstable recovered first, hitting Jackson so hard he flew into the sky. He landed on a cushion of air thanks to True, but Candace was focused on Amir and the unstable.

"Amir, do you know him?" she asked, the enemy ready again.

Amir stood, motionless, staring at the man as he seethed and crouched, growling at them like a cornered animal. When Amir took a step forward, the other man leapt to his feet, fists ready to fight.

"Candace," Amir said quietly. "I need you to paralyze him."

Uneasy, Candace reached into her connection and did as he asked. The unstable froze, his face contorted in a mask of anger. She looked at Amir, concerned about his reaction.

"Are you sure, sugar?" True asked, resting a hand on his arm. "It's been years since that happened. It couldn't be him."

Without speaking, Amir approached the unstable and studied him. Candace eased up beside True.

"Do you know him? Who's Amal?" she whispered.

True's face tightened as she watched Amir's progress. "Amal was Amir's twin brother. They were in the program together. Amal didn't make it and snapped before the final testing. We thought he was dead."

Candace felt sick. "Oh God. True, I had no idea. If I had..."

Amir whirled around. "If you had what?"

His expression was dangerous, muscles clenched like he was ready to explode. Candace shrunk back, finding herself pressed against Jackson's chest.

"You need to tell them, Sugar Plum," Jackson said. His hands rested on her shoulders, supporting her.

"Tell us what?" True asked.

"The ANGEL Project." Candace closed her eyes. "They... they don't kill their unstables. They lock them up. Use them for other things."

Amir ran at her, but True stopped him, holding him back. "That's not true! It can't be! I would have known!"

Candace shrunk back against Jackson, frightened by the violence in Amir's eyes. "I'm sorry. I... I didn't believe it at first when Dr. Ferdinand told me, but after everything I've seen..." She choked as Amir shook with rage. "I'm so sorry, Amir. I didn't know you had a brother. If I knew, I could've warned you. But I didn't know, I swear!"

"Easy now, sugar," True said in Amir's ear, trying to calm him down. "This isn't Candy's fault. She didn't do this."

Amir focused his gaze on Candace. "How do you know what HEX told you is the truth? Maybe they've had him all along."

While that never occurred to her, Candace shook her head. "Too many things point to the truth, Amir. I don't know about your training group, but everyone that's been through the Gauntlet as far back as Gabe has faced an unstable in there. Where did they come from? After Adrian died, Deborah warned me if I didn't get better, they'd do worse than drug me. She said I didn't want to know. And then at the second Mirror test, Poznanski said they'd neutralize Jackson if he couldn't get a grip. Not kill, *neutralize*. And then when they started torturing Kristie before I stepped in..." She swallowed and shook her head. "They lied about Dr. Ferdinand, too. She's not a gen-evo. She told me Poznanski used her son in those first tests. I can't say that part is true with total conviction, but I do know she's searching for him. You don't look that desperate when you're lying."

"Why didn't you tell us this before, Candy Cane?" True asked.

Candace looked at her mentor, helpless. "How? When? They've been watching me like a hawk since I got back. I only barely managed to tell Jackson and Gabe. Deborah and Chloe know, too, but not because I told them. They've seen things I don't think I want to know about." Amal let out a strangled cry and Candace adjusted her hold. "I don't know how to fix what's broken, True. HEX doesn't have it right, either. They unleash their unstables for us to kill. No one in this mess is out for anyone but themselves, and I don't know how to fight that. So you tell me, what would you do?" Suddenly aware of her anger, Candace unclenched her fists and took a deep breath. "I'm sorry. There's more to this than any of us know, and more than one side to the story."

"Candace," Jackson said quietly. "If this is Amal, what's he doing here? The ANGEL Project wouldn't have let him out after all this time. That's not what they do."

As his words registered, Candace gagged. "Oh my God. Chuck."

"Who's Chuck?" True asked, her hands still on Amir's arms.

"Chuck's the one who took me from Aspen," she said. "He sort of shifts himself to travel from place to place. Like teleporting or something. He came to see me last night and said they were getting impatient."

"Impatient for what?" Amir said, his voice strained.

"I..." Candace swallowed. "I told them I wanted to try to change some things about the ANGEL Project. Things like..." Her gaze drifted to Amal, still firmly in place. "Things like this. It's not right. You can't treat another human being like this. It's worse than keeping an animal in a zoo. Who knows what they do to them besides using them for target practice? I..." Her words ended in a chokehold of threatening tears. "It's not right. None of it is right."

Amir stilled, and True released him. After seeing Gabe's reaction to the idea that Bas might be alive, Candace couldn't imagine how Amir was coping with having it shoved at him that way. He turned to face his brother, his arms hanging limply by his side.

"I always assumed he was dead, I guess. After he snapped, I couldn't feel him anymore." Amir said. "I didn't think about it. I didn't want to."

True reached for him again, but he stepped away, closer to his brother. "All this time, and he's been locked away in some dark cell, having who knows what done to him." Amir's voice broke. "I can't... how could they do this?"

Candace shifted and refocused her concentration. Whatever Amir decided, she needed to give him time to make a choice.

"Can I..." He hesitated a few feet away from Amal, glancing back towards her. "Can I talk to him?"

"You want me to let him speak?" Candace asked. "I can, but, well, I don't know how much you'll get out of him. He's not..." She sighed and nodded. "If that's what you want."

She gave him a minute. If Amir wanted to say anything to his brother, he needed to do that before she loosened her hold.

Amir stood in front of Amal, tentatively reaching out to push the hair from his face. "I'm so sorry, Mal," he whispered. "If I knew..." He dropped his hand, his shoulders slumping. "Tell me what you want me to do. I can't stand seeing you like this. I'm so, so sorry. I didn't know."

Looking away, Candace eased up, allowing the unstable man the freedom of speech.

"Kill..." The word came out in a frothy slur. "Kill them all... Huuurrrttt."

She pinched her eyes tight, clamping back down on Amal's ability to speak as Amir dropped to his knees. She knew what it was like to live through. It was the same when Adrian went. There were few options, and none of them had happy endings.

"Sugar," True said as she knelt beside Amir. "We can't give him back to the ANGEL Project like this. You know that."

Head hung low, Amir nodded.

Setting a hand on his shoulder, she continued. "If you don't think you can, I will. You need to decide, though. I won't make the choice for you."

After a few shaky breaths, Amir got to his feet again and turned to Candace. "How?"

She blinked at him, confused by the question. "How

what?"

Tears shone in Amir's eyes, reflecting the early morning sunlight. "How did you do it? How is your heart still beating? I don't know if I can... How did you make yourself do it?"

Jackson's arms closed around her, lending her his warmth and strength, and she took a deep breath.

"Because no one else could," she said. "Adrian was already dead before I got there, his body just didn't know it yet. It took me a long time to realize that. No one should have to make that decision alone. Whatever you need, Amir, just ask. I can't hold him much longer, though."

He gave a shaky nod, then turned back to Amal. The two men stared at each other for a long time before Amir made his choice. Wrapping an arm around his brother's neck, Amir pressed his forehead into his brother's hair and closed his eyes. With Amir's whisper, Candace felt the water in Amal's body slow to a halt. Gradually, she released him, and as she did so, Amir lowered the dead man to the ground.

He killed him with a single word.

Candace turned away from the scene, taking Jackson with her as they left Amir to True's care. Not wanting to show it in front of Amir, the moment they rounded the corner of a building Candace broke down into tears within Jackson's embrace. He rubbed her back and held her as she cried, knowing how her past haunted her in that new death.

After a few minutes, he spoke. "There's going to be serious consequences with this, Sugar Plum, and not just for Amir. He'll get through it, but there's something else we need to think about."

She wiped her eyes and nodded. "I know. I'm worried, too."

Jackson kissed her forehead and pulled her tightly against him. "Are we thinking the same thing?"

Candace swallowed hard and gave voice to the fear they shared. "If they got one, when will they get the rest?"

A silent response was all the agreement she needed.

CHAPTER 22

ASPEN WASN'T any warmer than she remembered it being, and after the events in LA, Candace wondered if any place on the planet would feel warm. The looks that passed between Amir and General Jacobs as Amir carried his brother out of the Hollywood movie lot chilled her to the core. The General's eyes held a dangerous warning, Amir's held the threat of retaliation.

The site of the disastrous X-Games was completely unrecognizable. There were no burned-out tents or ruined event courses anymore. The debris was cleared long ago, and only a small, makeshift shrine told the story of what went before. The victims were primarily competitors and musicians, with only a handful of spectators listed amongst the dead.

EVOLUTION: HEX

Still, even one death was too many.

That afternoon, Candace and Jackson met with a few survivors of the attack, listening to their stories and hearing of their recoveries. One man, a snowmobiler hurt in the initial attack during the interrupted practice run, nearly lost his leg and would be fortunate to walk normally when he was healed. A young woman suffered severe burns during Stephanie's attack on the stage and would be forever scarred because of it.

Candace apologized to every one of them individually for not being faster in rooting out those responsible. When a ten-year-old girl quietly spoke of the nightmares that still haunted her, Candace couldn't hide her tears. As she held her hand, the young girl broke down into sobs, and it was all Candace could do to hold her until the hysterics subsided.

Of course, camera crews were present the entire time, filming every reaction, every handshake, every shared moment that Candace would rather have been private. Those people didn't need glitz and glamour; they needed someone to listen to their fears, to assure them they'd never have to live through something so horrific again.

If Candace had her way, they never would.

After dinner in the chalet's restaurant, Candace all but crawled her way back to the room. She was bone weary, but more mentally drained than physically tired.

As she tossed her key on the table inside the door of the cozy room and peeled off her coat, she stifled a yawn. The living area glowed in the light of the blaze from the fireplace, but something pulled her onward, through to the balcony at the far end of the room. It was a familiar feeling, yet not. She slid the balcony door open.

Freezing wind blasted her in the face as she stepped out to find the source. Snow whirled through the air, resonating with a low hum against the backdrop of the mountains. A million voices, deep and slow, wound around her as she stared, realization dawning.

The voice of ice thrummed in her mind.

"What are you doing out here?" Jackson said as he wrapped a blanket around her shoulders.

"Investigating," she said, still staring out into the darkness.

He kissed the side of her neck. "Investigating what?"

Pushing aside the flap of the blanket, she held out her palm, a few snowflakes drifting toward it. Zeroing in on the frequency of the frozen water, she concentrated. As she focused, the flakes halted in their fall, hovering inches from her hand as more collected, bunching together, building something, pulling more flakes as though they were magnetic. Before long, she had a large, floating snowball.

Jackson gaped, a glance at his face showing he was as confused as Candace. "How are you doing that?"

Sending the sphere shooting over the edge of the balcony, she shook her head. "I don't know. It's like before, with the steam, and then a few weeks ago I discovered I can trap light and control how it reflects. Now this? How is this possible? Why is my ability evolving like this? Have you ever heard of something like this happening before?"

He shook his head. "No, but no one in the ANGEL Project had a water ability before you came along."

Thinking, she leaned back against him. "The first time I heard steam, it was in the pool with you. I figured it was the imprinting bleeding over into my ability. Sort of like since we were so close, I learned how to talk to water with more heat. With the light, I thought it had something to do with being related to Gabe. But this? I've never felt water in the solid state before, and I'm out of superhero relations. So why can I feel it now?"

"Candace…" Jackson whispered. "Do you remember what happened when you were in the clinic? After your party?"

"Of course. Why?"

"Think, Sugar Plum. When you woke up, your teeth were chattering."

She stilled in his arms. "Naveen."

"Mmm."

"You're saying you think I absorbed some of his and Gabe's ability from their blood?"

Jackson shrugged as she turned to face him. "I think it's more like you learned a new language, if that makes sense. We talk about our connections being like a form of communication, right?"

"Yeah, but…" Candace trailed off as she thought. "Well, I suppose that makes sense. My ability learned the dialect of other states of water, when they have more or less energy?"

"Can you think of any other explanations?"

She frowned. "But I don't have your blood in my body. How does that explain the steam? The imprinting still?"

Jackson bit back a laugh. "Maybe not blood, but I think we're still talking bodily fluids here."

"Huh?" she said, confused for a moment, but as the implications of his comment registered, she flushed. "Oh.

Right."

Chuckling, he wrapped an arm around her and drew her to him, kissing the top of her head. "Yeah. Oh, indeed. Your body absorbs things, Sugar Plum. Like a sponge."

Candace sighed. "Well, this sponge is exhausted. And cold. Can we go inside and warm up?"

Without any argument, he led her back inside, and she snuggled down against Jackson on the couch in front of the fireplace. Between the fire and him, she finally defrosted a little and quickly fell asleep on his shoulder.

Some time later, her eyes fluttered open. Gentle fingers pushed the hair from her face, and she turned, looking up at Jackson from his lap.

"What time is it?"

"Nearly midnight," he said.

"Midnight?" Candace sat up. "You've been sitting here for three hours like this?"

Jackson smiled softly. "I didn't want to wake you. You looked like you could use the rest."

Curling her knees up, she smiled back at him. "Maybe, but you need to sleep, too." When he shook his head, Candace straddled his thighs, her arms draped over his shoulders. "How are you with all this? Really. Being here again... I know it can't be easy for you."

He shrugged and kissed her forehead. "I'm all right. It's not as bad as I thought it might be. Not that I want to revisit that one particular spot, but I'm dealing with it."

She fidgeted with the blanket hanging over the back of the couch. "Jackson..."

"Hmm?"

Candace looked him in the eye, searching for any hint of hurt. "You don't still blame yourself for that, do you? I mean, you know that wasn't you out there, right?"

He pulled her against him and she rested her head in the crook of his neck, the scent of smoky, warm earth filling her senses. "Not really, no. I think maybe a little part of me always will, but I know you're right. None of us knew what was happening out there. I'll be okay eventually."

She played with the buttons of his black shirt, slowly opening it. "Good, because I hate the thought that you might still be beating yourself up over that. I don't want you to hurt."

A chuckle rumbled in his chest. "You keep doing what you're doing and I'm going to forget all about it in thirty seconds."

The last of his buttons undone, Candace lifted her mouth to his ear. "Bet ya I can do it in half that."

"I'll take that bet."

"Start counting, Sunshine."

The moment he said "one," she ran her tongue along the edge of his earlobe, slowly tracing a path down his jawline. She stopped long enough to peel off her sweater and toss it aside before pushing open his shirt. As she leaned in to kiss him, she grinned.

"You stopped counting," she said.

"Hardly matters," he replied. "You had me at one."

Jackson ran a hand into the back of her hair and pulled her down to meet his lips. Crushed between his heat and the warmth from the fireplace, Candace lost herself in the embrace, submitting to the fire in her veins. They freed themselves of their clothing, eager to be closer, stripping away the thin barriers between their bodies. His hands drifted over her skin, fluttering across her most sensitive places. She urged him on, pressing him into her with unreserved need. As his lips met her throat, she moaned, her back arching in pure pleasure. They moved together, clinging to one another as if keeping the other whole.

Holding her face between his hands, Jackson stared into her eyes. "If Heaven were on fire, Candy, it couldn't shine as brightly as you."

"For you," she said, breathless. "I'd burn it down if you asked me to."

Jackson kissed her again, his desire fervent and absolute as he laid her on the rug before the fire. Her legs wrapped around him, drawing him deeper, filling her, aching for more of him. Illuminated by the orange glow from the hearth, Jackson looked more god than man as he kissed her again. Each movement, each tiny touch, sent her body surging to new heights of pleasure. When she gasped his name, he answered with hers, his voice strained as he pulsed within her one final time.

Shuddering, he gathered her in his arms, struggling to catch his breath.

"Everything I am is yours, Candace," he whispered into her hair. "Everything."

She closed her eyes and held him against her. "And that's all I'll ever need, Sunshine."

"HERE," JACKSON said, handing her a steaming mug.

Candace took it, surprised. "You made me hot cocoa?"

He settled in beside her, adjusting the blanket to cover both of them. "You don't like cocoa?"

"Oh, I do," she said. "It was unexpected is all. Aren't you tired?"

"I caught a few winks while you were sleeping." He chuckled. "Wasn't easy with your head in my lap, though."

"Thanks for restraining yourself," she said, rolling her eyes, and took a tentative sip of her drink. "Wow. Perfectly drinkable temperature and everything. Impressive."

"I aim to please," he said, grinning while he drank from his own mug.

As she smiled over the rim of her cup, she nearly dumped it on herself when pounding on the door ripped through the moment.

Dread crashed down on her as if the ceiling collapsed. "Oh God," she whispered as Jackson jumped up to answer it. "This can't be good."

General Jacobs strode into the room looking as serene as the sea in a hurricane. "What did you do?"

Confused, Candace set her cup on the side table and stood. "Do? I didn't do anything. Why? What happened? Was there another attack?"

"Get your suits on immediately," he barked. "The shuttle leaves in five minutes." A soldier dropped a duffle bag on the floor as the General spun on his heel.

"Wait," Candace called after him. "What's going on? Where are we going?"

General Jacobs stopped in the doorway. "Back to the compound," he said. "There's a problem."

While Jackson grabbed their suits out of the bag, Candace stared at the closed door. What happened in California? Did Amir do something because of his brother?

"Get changed," Jackson said, tossing her skinsuit on the couch. "They'll explain on the way."

Her stomach rolled, but she forced herself into motion. Whatever it was, it was bad enough to pull them from the PR tour. And by the look on the General's face, he was placing all the blame for it on Candace's shoulders.

As the shuttle took off, General Jacobs explained some of what was happening, never once taking his eyes off of Candace. "The compound has been breached. Unstables are everywhere, and the ANGELs are having trouble getting people out."

For the first time on any shuttle flight, Candace felt sick. "How? Where did they come from?"

"I think you know exactly where they came from, Miss Bristol."

She pinched her eyes shut. There was no denying what she knew, not after what happened with Amal. "So it's somehow my fault that all the unstables you've locked away over the years are now loose in the compound?"

"I didn't say it was your fault. Should I?"

"Don't talk to me like I'm stupid, sir," she seethed. "You think I had something to do with this. Why? Why would I put everyone in danger that way?"

"Why, indeed."

Frustrated, she tried to calm down, but not even Jackson's

touch could subdue her anger. "I'm not the one who's been doing God-knows-what to those poor people for years. Don't you dare try to pin your mistakes on me."

"I'm not trying, Miss Bristol. We know you've been holding out on us, we just didn't know to what end."

Candace's jaw hit the floor. "You seriously think I had a hand in this? Have you lost your fu—"

"Candy," Jackson's hand closed over hers. "Don't. Not now. We have things to do before we can straighten any of it out."

"Oh, so now you're the calm one?" She glared at him. "Are you telling me you wouldn't lose your shit if someone accused you of this? Are you serious?"

He leaned in to her and softened his tone. "Candace, stop and think for a minute. We can straighten everything out later after we fix this mess."

"You mean after we get rid of all their mistakes? What if there are too many for us, Jackson? What then? Do you know how many unstables are locked up in the basement? Because I don't."

With a frustrated sigh, Jackson sat back in his seat. "No, I don't know. I always suspected quite a few, though. At least six of the last few batches of ANGELs went haywire, including Adrian. Out of the three training groups I've seen go through, that's not great odds. For us, it was one in ten. The one before that, three of ten. And your cousin's group lost two, including his boyfriend. I never asked, Candy Cane, but that was a question I didn't want to know the answer to."

And there it was. The cold calculation she always knew lurked in his heart surfaced. "So all this time, you suspected and ignored it? How could you do that?"

Jackson closed his eyes. "I'm not like you, Candace. You know that."

"They're people."

"No, they're unstables," he said. "You've said yourself that who they were dies the minute that happens."

Candace gritted her teeth. "It's a preventable outcome," she said. "Look at Lucie. They would've discarded her, locked her up, and all it took was a goddamned bird to fix her."

"Candace, I don't want to fight with you, but you know that was a single case."

Her anger at his callous disregard for life boiled over. "And if I had stayed with Adrian, he wouldn't have snapped. He would've had an outlet. He wouldn't have built up all that power, and it wouldn't have eaten away his mind. If I had fought through my fears, he wouldn't have had to die. I could have saved him."

Jackson's jaw clenched. "You're right, Sugar Plum. You could've saved him. The two of you could have had your fucking happily ever after reading books and screwing until all goddamn hours of the night. Adrian could've healed Trevor in a heartbeat. Adrian could've saved Allen. But you didn't save Adrian. Instead, he's a fucking ghost that's going to haunt us forever and remind you exactly of who I'm not."

A shaky sob worked its way free as Candace covered her mouth. Was that what he thought she wanted? Jackson was holding himself up to the image of a dead man, and she didn't have a clue. She turned away, hurt by his words and unable to think of any of her own. Never once did she compare the two men that way. For her, there was no comparison; there wasn't any need for it. While she held on to some regret over what happened, she never stopped to think of what she would do if she could go back and change it.

Would she?

The shuttle ride dragged on, the silence stretching into miles between them. As the craft touched down, Candace realized she needed to say something to Jackson, but what? How do you bridge a hurt that deep?

There was no time left to think about it. They unstrapped from their seats as the back hatch opened.

And when it opened, there was no room to think about anything but the nightmare outside.

SHATTERED WINDOWS and crumbling walls greeted them when they exited the shuttle at the main doors of the compound. Shocked at the transformation, Candace compared the scene to the day she arrived. Gone was the brilliant white gleam of the paint, replaced by scorch marks and cracks in the plaster. The shiny metal tiles bent and hung limply from the edges of the roof. Glassless, gaping windows stared down at her, and she couldn't help feeling as broken as that place. Not so long ago, that building held every dream she ever had.

Risking a glance at Jackson's impassive face, she wondered if the one dream she had left would survive the night.

A platoon of soldiers, M-16s at the ready, charged over to greet them.

"Report," the General barked.

One of the men stepped forward and saluted. "Most of the fighting is still inside, sir. A few unstables slipped out to the Quad and a small group of ANGELs are tracking them. Lower levels three through seven are compromised, but we're making progress. The main concern is extracting civilians and building integrity, sir."

"They're fighting below ground?" Candace asked. "That's ridiculous. Draw the enemy out. Open the stairwells. If the building falls, the ANGELS will be safe and can take out any unstables that escape."

"Are you suggesting we abandon the complex?" General Jacobs fumed. "Preposterous. What would you know about strategy in battle? We can't lose the building!"

The ground shook, a great rumble from deep in the earth nearly knocking them all off their feet.

"You're going to lose the building anyway!" Jackson shouted over the din. "You want to risk losing everyone with it?"

"How many civilians still inside?" Candace yelled, ignoring the debate. She'd make her own call when she got in there, screw the General and his orders.

"At least twenty personnel unaccounted for," the soldier replied. "Including Dr. Poznanski."

Even over the cacophony of the earthquake, Candace could hear General Jacobs cursing.

"What's his last location?" she shouted.

"Not sure, ma'am. He was down below but en route to

his office at last check-in."

With a brief nod, Candace took off, heading inside the building. Avoiding a few falling ceiling tiles, she ran for the clinic, hoping to find the man there. Part of her wished she didn't have to rescue him, but as it was entirely possible the only person who knew all the secrets of the GEF formula was him, he was too valuable to lose. The quaking subsided as she reached his office and pushed open the cracked door.

"Dr. Poznanski?" she said as she entered.

"About time you showed up, Miss Bristol," he said from behind his desk, frantically packing up a large briefcase with file folders and external hard drives. "Welcome to your war."

That again? Jesus. "Look, I don't know why you and the General are so insistent this is my fault, but I have nothing to do with whatever's going on. I came to get you out. This building isn't going to last much longer, and—"

"Ah, but you're wrong," he interrupted, closing the case. "If not for you, Emily wouldn't have gotten so proactive and sent her little shifter in to cause chaos. You know who she's looking for, don't you?"

Candace let her shoulders drop, relaxed should the need for a fight present itself. "She's looking for your first mistake. Her son."

Poznanski laughed, tired and a little insane. "My first mistake was letting him talk me into it. The second was not telling her about it. The third was ignoring the signs of his mental instability. They're funny things, mistakes. You try to hide one and more just add themselves to the pile. They're like rabbits. They multiply."

"Not if you own them," she said. "I'm sure if you come

forward with the truth—"

His laughter chilled her. "Miss Bristol, at this point I'm so buried in mistakes it would take three lifetimes to dig myself out. I'm not like you. I'm not brave enough to be a hero, that's why I create them."

The conversation ceased as another round of shockwaves shook the building. Poznanski ran from behind the desk, snatching the briefcase away as a bookshelf toppled over where he stood moments before. He scanned the room for any last items. Lighting on something, the doctor went for a binder on a shelf at the back of the room, and Candace gasped. As the shelving teetered precariously before his reaching form, she dashed forward, knocking him out of the way as it toppled over. Arms flooded with her hydraulics, Candace stared up at the heavy furniture pinning her to the floor. She couldn't hold it that way for long.

A screeching howl echoed from somewhere down the hall. Candace tilted her head, looking for Poznanski, and spotted him near the door in a glance.

"Hurry and help me out of here," she hissed through her teeth. "Someone's coming and he doesn't sound friendly."

No reply.

She looked back again, and her stomach dropped.

"I'm sorry, Miss Bristol," he whispered, clutching the briefcase and inching toward the exit. "I have to go. I have to run."

"God damn it," she said, muscles straining under the exertion. "If you don't help me, whoever that is will get you for sure."

Another howl, much closer, rattled what little was left of

the glass in the windows.

"I'm... I'm sorry!"

Poznanski bolted out the door.

"Fucking coward!" she cursed after him. With her one chance for help gone, she dove into her connection, frantically grasping for any water source nearby. Pipes screeched as they tore through the walls, instantly dousing the room in liquid. With one giant wave, she knocked the bookcase aside, soaking herself in the process. Scrambling over the slippery floor, Candace slid out into the hallway, heading in the direction Poznanski went.

Before the first turn, a blood-curdling scream stopped her in her tracks. It wasn't the howl of the unstable she heard before, though that soon followed, along with what could only be the sound of flesh smacking violently against hard surfaces.

Candace closed her eyes and covered her mouth, trying not to vomit as she pressed herself to the wall. She was too late. Poznanski's cowardice cost him his life.

But she still had a job to do. She couldn't let the unstable go, and she needed to retrieve the briefcase Poznanski risked his life for. If someone like him thought those things were worth tempting death, they must be invaluable. Taking a deep breath, she called to the water once more, finding a living source.

She snapped the cord taut.

When it was silent, Candace steeled herself and rounded the corner. Gagging, she turned away. Every wall, every floor tile, was splattered with blood and gore. The monster was completely still, clutching what was left of Dr. Roger

Poznanski by a leg.

Horrified, Candace pushed through, locating the dropped briefcase a few feet from the unstable. She was so close to him that she could smell his rancid breath as it oozed from his mouth. Reaching down for the blood-slicked handle of the case, she kept her gaze trained on the man's crazed eyes. As her fingers closed around the it, she froze. That was no young man. He was at least in his mid-thirties.

Dark eyes.

Dark hair.

Definitely Hispanic.

As her gaze lowered, she caught sight of the pale scar branded just below his left ear. Amidst the tangles of greasy hair, she could barely make out the letters.

H

E

X

Shit and double shit.

It had to be him. There was no way it wasn't Dr. Ferdinand's son. What should she do? Kill him and be done with it, permanently making her Dr. Ferdinand's enemy? There was no way a person could come back from the level of absolutely gone the man was, but it felt wrong for her to end it that way. Still, the call had to be hers. There was no one else there to ask.

She paused. Actually, maybe there was.

Backing out to the end of the hall, Candace focused on her connection, on the paralysis, then slowly let a part of her mind drift away.

Mitchell, I've got a bit of a dilemma here.

EVOLUTION: HEX

The reply took a minute, but it finally came. *"Are you fucking kidding me, Candy Cane? All hell's broken loose, and you say you've got a little dilemma?"*

Mitchell, I don't have time to argue with you. I'm pretty sure I've got your boss's son here in the clinic, and I don't know what I'm supposed to do with him.

"Fuck me, Candace. Are you joking?"

No. Now you get Dr. Ferdinand on the phone or whatever the hell you need to do and then get me some help here.

"They're already on their way."

What? Who?

"HEX. When they found out Chuck flew the coop, they started moving. They're not far out, but we need to buy them time."

How much?

"Ten minutes, max."

Breaking the communication for a moment, Candace adjusted her hold. *Mitchell I don't have ten minutes. You either send me reinforcements or tell Dr. F to get the lead out. I need to focus on him or in five minutes I'm going to look a hell of a lot like what's left of Poznanski.*

"Shit. Fine, Candy Cane. I'll see who I can get."

Good answer.

Candace severed the connection and sank to the floor. At least the shaking stopped. Hopefully the building would hold long enough for help to arrive. If things got dicey, she wouldn't have a choice but to pull the plug on that man. Closing her eyes to avoid looking at the viscera-painted hall, Candace trained her focus on holding Dr. Ferdinand's son. He was incredibly strong, and his bulging frame, even after years of imprisonment, served as testament to that. The threat of what he'd do if he got loose was enough to keep her vigilant, though she didn't know how long her strength would hold out.

After what felt like hours, loud footsteps pounded down the corridor. "Candace!" Trevor's booming voice called out to her.

She turned towards him and opened her eyes. "Hey, big guy. Are you the cavalry?"

"I am," he said. "Are you all right?"

"Relatively speaking," she deadpanned. "I have a problem."

"So I'm told. Where?"

Candace inclined her head down the hall across from her. "I need him to sleep for a little bit. His mother is looking for him, and I want to give her some closure."

Trevor looked down the way and sucked in a sharp breath. "My God. Who was that?"

"You mean what's left of the victim?"

He nodded, unable to look away.

"Dr. Poznanski. He didn't listen when I tried to stop him, and he left me pinned under a bookshelf in his office."

"Christ, that's horrible."

"Yeah, well, can you help me out? I'm running out of gas, and I don't know how long it'll take Dr. Ferdinand to get here."

Startled, Trevor took a step back and stared at her. "Dr. Ferdinand? The HEX leader?"

Candace sighed. "The same. It's a long story. Basically, they aren't who we were told they were. HEX has their own issues, so don't think I'm picking sides or anything. From what Michele said, this disaster isn't their doing, but I'm withholding judgment for now."

"I don't like this, Candy Cane."

"Well, on that we can agree." She took a deep breath. "So, as a favor to me, can you make this guy take a nap for a while?"

He frowned, but nodded. "As a favor to you."

"Thank you."

Trevor headed for the trembling unstable. In a single punch, the man was out like a light and Candace dropped her hold.

"Where do you want him?"

Candace considered it. "We can't take him out front. The General would have him shot on sight, and probably wouldn't mind if I got caught in the crossfire."

"The ANGELs are gathering in the Quad. Jackson's rounding them up, directing them out of the building."

"Sounds good to me," Candace said. "Do you know a shortcut out of here?"

Without any further conversation, Trevor turned, kicked in a door, and strode through. A giant crash followed, and she raced down the hall to see what happened. As she got to the door, Trevor reappeared, covered in white dust. "I made one," he said, grinning.

Slinging the unconscious man over his shoulder, he led Candace through a gaping hole in the wall and out onto the Quad.

CHAPTER 23

"I NEED a runner to get an update on sublevel five!" Jackson shouted above the din. "They should be out of there by now. Tell them to fall back."

"On it," Tobias said, then disappeared.

Candace stopped beside Trevor and surveyed the scene. It looked like most of the ANGELs were out of the building. Is that what Jackson did when she took off?

"So where are we with this?" Candace asked as she approached, setting Dr. Poznanski's briefcase beside her. "Do we have a headcount?"

Amir pressed a hand to his ear and held up a finger. "Got it. Leave the body for now. We'll figure out the rest later." He looked up at Candace. "Two left on the run outside. Gabe and three others are out tracking them. There were three unstables, but they found one and took care of it."

"We've got five ANGELs still in the sublevels," Jackson said. "I'm trying to get them out. The elevators are toast, and only two stairwells are usable. One of those might not be soon."

"Any hurt?" Candace said. She held her breath.

Amir's jaw clenched tightly. "Two ANGELs down. Kina Cross and Max Taylor. Ceiling collapse. Andreas got caught in it too, but Leigh got him out. He's banged up, but Tori says he'll pull through. Most of the casualties are civilian."

Another two ANGELs dead. Was that blood on her hands as well? Candace looked around at the twenty remaining Supers in the Quad. A few were nursing smaller injuries, but most looked to be in one piece.

A loud roar accompanied a fresh wave of aftershocks. The ground trembled as ANGELs jumped to their feet, steadying themselves on nearby trees or each other.

"We have to take out that unstable!" Amir yelled over the noise. "This whole area could become a giant sinkhole if we don't!"

Too late, the part of the building that was the dining hall shifted dangerously. Within seconds, the earth below it opened up, swallowing the structure whole as Candace grabbed the briefcase and ran with the other ANGELs from the encroaching chasm. Amir shouted into his earpiece as they fled, screaming orders to evacuate immediately. Two minutes later, the shaking stopped, and everyone turned back. The center section of the compound was gone, half of it flattened, the rest vanished below ground.

"Jesus..." Candace whispered. "Why? Why cause all

this?"

Another rumble preceded a small explosion from the far side of the building. Moments later, Tobias appeared, carrying someone in his arms.

"True!" Amir screamed.

Candace's stomach dropped. She ran to them as Tobias laid her down.

"She's still alive, but barely," he said. "She was the only one I could grab. The rest..." he shook his head.

Candace dove into her connection, looking for any way she could keep True stable. Tori knelt beside her, casting a glance at Candace before taking True's hand. Candace closed her eyes. Using the water in True's body, she shifted resources and fluids around, helping the healer repair injured tissues and set broken bones. In as much as she could, Candace tried to push aside her own fears about True's survival, to focus on the work. After several minutes, True groaned, but Amir kept her still.

"We've got incoming!" someone called, snapping Candace from her concentration.

She looked up to see the ANGELs gathering, all dropping back into defensive stances. Through the smoke and dust, figures appeared, maybe twenty by a quick count.

Tori met her questioning look with a nod. "I've got her. You go."

Standing, Candace stepped away, her anger rising as she recognized the people coming into view. Dr. Emily Ferdinand led the way, a placid smile on her face. Cold suspicion brewed in her gut.

"That's far enough," Candace said when they were twenty

feet away.

"We're here to help, Candace," Dr. Ferdinand said.

"Bullshit. You came to collect what's left of us."

She crossed her arms and smiled. Behind her, the HEX contingent shifted, several powering up with visible light from spheres of energy or fire. "Now Candace, you doubt my intentions?"

"Did you send Chuck in to let them loose?"

"I have no idea wha—"

Candace snapped the cord taut, paralyzing the doctor before she could spit out the lie. Turning, she searched the crowd of ANGELs for the face she needed. Deborah stepped forward, sensing the need, and stopped by her side.

"You'll know if she's lying?" Candace asked.

Deborah nodded. "It won't be easy with everyone else here, but I think I can, yes."

They walked over to where Dr. Ferdinand stood, frozen. Candace glared at the HEX members around her. "Any of you so much as sneezes and she's done, got me? Back off."

A few hesitated, but eventually all eased away from their esteemed leader.

"I'm going to ask you once," Candace said, toe-to-toe with Dr. Ferdinand. "Did you send Chuck to free unstables? Even just one?"

When she loosened her hold, Dr. Ferdinand swallowed nervously. "I sent him for my son."

Candace pinched her eyes shut, trying to keep her temper in check. "Why? How would you even know for sure he was here?"

"Roger would have kept him close. He would've wanted

to know where he was at all times. He was always paranoid."

"Where's Chuck now?"

"I don't know. I haven't heard from him since he left five hours ago."

Turning, Candace looked at Deborah, the empath's face streaked with dirt and blood. "Is she telling the truth?"

Slowly, Deborah nodded. "She is."

Considering the information, Candace relaxed her grip on her connection, but not completely. Pulling inward, she focused on Michele.

Mitchell, have you gotten anything from Chuck lately?

A touch at her elbow made her jump. Michele stood beside her, shaking her head. "I can't reach him at all, Candy Cane."

Returning her focus to Dr. Ferdinand, Candace continued her questions. "And the unstable in LA?"

"I had that one turned loose when no one would be around. I tried to be careful. You needed a push."

"A push?" Candace said, gaping. "Are you out of your mind? I told you it would be a slow progression. I told you I couldn't give you a timeline. And I also told you that the minute I didn't like your plans, I was done."

"Which is why you weren't told. You had nothing to do with it."

Candace backed up a few steps. Being so close to the woman, it was too tempting to beat her senseless. "You tell that to General Jacobs, who seems to think I did. You tell that to Dr. Poznanski who... oh wait. You can't. Your son used his skull to paint the clinic brain-matter gray."

The woman's words were faint. "I'm not sorry about

that. I would do whatever it takes to get my son back."

"Including putting everyone here at risk?"

"Whatever it takes."

Dropping her hold on Dr. Ferdinand, Candace looked around at the crowd pressing in around them. "Did you hear that? All of this," she motioned to the destruction. "All of it was done for one purpose. All she cares about, all she's *ever* cared about, is her own son and getting revenge for what was done, and, I might add, done with his consent. Her son *volunteered*. Her son talked Poznanski into it. He made that choice for himself, and she wants to punish everyone else for that."

A few HEX members shifted uneasily, some unsure of how to take the news.

Candace continued, pacing as she spoke. "You talk about family, and yet the person you would call mother uses you, repeatedly, for her own ends. Because of her, you've been labeled as dangerous. Hunted. Under her guidance, you compete for her attention, making the people she sees as less powerful feel unimportant, unwanted. She's put you in competition with one another, to see who can win at earning her affection. Family, *real* family, doesn't do that. Family wants the best for everyone, not to serve the purpose of one. Family realizes the importance of *all* its members. Family trusts each other." She paused and looked around again. "The ANGEL Project might not be perfect, but the ANGELs are a team. When one falls, everyone stops to help them up. I know. One loss is a loss we all feel. Tonight, we lost, what, four, five? And for what? Because one of yours wanted more attention from his mother?" Hands balled into fists, Candace tried desperately to hang on to what little self-control she had left. She leveled her gaze at Dr. Ferdinand. "I want no part of your twisted notion of family, but if any of them think they might be better off in a place where they are cared for as all members are cared for, I will gladly welcome them."

Dr. Ferdinand snorted. "You think the ANGEL Project would have them? With Roger gone, any HEX turncoats will be as good as dead."

Candace took a deep breath. Her next words might mean death for her. "I didn't say the ANGEL Project. I said *I* would gladly welcome them."

Silence hung over the group as each person interpreted her meaning.

A hand touched her arm and she turned. Amir stood there, face unreadable.

"You mean you're leaving?"

Candace nodded slowly. "Knowing what you know now, wouldn't you?"

"You know they won't just let you walk away. How do you intend to hide?"

"I don't intend to hide. I'm a superhero, Amir. I could never stop being one." She took another deep breath. "I might be able to negotiate something for myself, but if others were with me, if we worked together, they'd be more likely to listen. I don't want to stop helping people. I don't want to stop working, but I *do* want to start living. I don't want to be hidden away, untouchable except by those who made me into what I am. I don't want someone who has no idea what this life is like to be able to dictate mine. I don't want to have to ignore lies and horrors because if I don't, either me or the people I care about will suffer for it. I don't want to pay for other people's mistakes, but I will help fix them where I can." She scrubbed a hand across her face. "I don't have all the answers, but I'd like a chance to find them. Hopefully, with others to help me, we can figure it out. Together."

There was a long pause before anyone moved. When Amir extended his hand, Candace wasn't sure what to think. Was he wishing her goodbye and good luck? Hesitant, she reached out to take it.

"Then count me on your team."

Hope surged inside her. "You mean that? Even knowing they might—"

"I mean it. Because of Amal. Because I'm tired of being a trained monkey. Because I'm sick of not having a say. If you'll let me have a voice, I'm with you, Candy Cane."

"You ain't goin' nowhere without me, sugar," True said. Candace turned, shocked to see the woman on her feet, an arm slung around Tori's shoulders. They limped over to Amir, who took over for Tori. "I'm with you, too."

Touched beyond words, Candace hugged her mentor, trying to be gentle. "Thank you," she whispered. Backing away, she glanced at Tori. "You're welcome, too, if you want. But I understand if you want to stay."

Tori giggled. "Well, since I'm only here because of you, seems silly to stick around without you."

Relieved that even those three would step up, Candace couldn't hide her shock as every ANGEL in attendance followed suit. Mica didn't hesitate, neither did Lucie. Naveen shrugged and stood to the side of the group, content to go wherever, really.

As Gabe and the others returned from hunting down escaped unstables, someone filled them in on the current situation. Gabe approached Candace, looking absolutely beaten down.

He sighed tiredly. "All drama, all the time, huh, cuz?"

"Well, you know how it is," she said with a half smile. "I'm like a magnet for this stuff."

"So, you're basically asking me if I'm willing to sign up for more of that?"

Candace chuckled. "Well, I think your boyfriend made some assumptions there, so 'willing' might be the operative word."

Gabe looked over his shoulder to where Mica shrugged sheepishly. Chuckling, he turned back. "All right. I guess you've got me trapped then. I'm with ya, Candy Cane."

She scanned the group one last time before turning to the HEX members. "So there you have it. You can choose to stay where you are or come with us." Once more, she looked at Dr. Ferdinand. "There's a place for you too, if you want it."

Michele stepped up beside her. "You think that's a good idea, Candy? I mean, what's to say she won't—"

Candace held up a hand. "Everyone deserves a chance to be better. All I'm offering is the opportunity. She can say no, but I won't ask again." She stepped up to a pensive Dr. Ferdinand and studied her face. "Dr. Poznanski died trying to get a briefcase of hard drives and paperwork out of the building. I'm guessing it was his research. I'm not sure that anyone else knows the scope of his work better than you do.

If you're willing to work for and with us, not order us, I'm willing to bring you in."

"I..." Dr. Ferdinand said. "Why?"

"Because I think you need redemption as much as any of us do. Aren't you tired of running?"

Before Dr. Ferdinand could answer, a hand closed over her mouth, and another wrapped around her waist.

"So this is the thanks I get for saving your son?" Chuck hissed in her ear. "You're walking away from us? From your family?"

The crowd tensed, everyone drawing in on themselves, ready to act. Calmly, despite the situation, Candace held up a hand to stop them, internally tapping into her connection, searching for the source she needed.

"Hey, Chuck," she said. "Fancy meeting you here."

"Hey yourself, Candy Cane," he said with a sneer. "This is your fault, you know."

"Hmm. How do you figure?"

"If you just did what you said you would do, nobody would've gotten hurt."

Candace relaxed her stance, ready to react. "And what do you think I said I was going to do?"

Chuck's breathing was sharp, erratic. How much shifting did he do to tire himself out that way?

"You said you were gonna change things. Make it safe for us," he said, eyes wild. "Instead, I had to do it. I had to set those monsters free so everyone would see. One of them showed me... She showed me what you'd do. You'll kill everyone, Candy. You'll kill my family, and there will be nothing left for me!"

Candace balked, confused. "She showed you? Who is she?"

"She was in a cell. I don't know." He shook, jerking Dr. Ferdinand with him. "She showed me what you're capable of. She showed me what would happen if I didn't act. She showed me the truth!"

The truth.

Oh God.

At that moment, everything clicked into place.

"True," she said, not taking her eyes off of Chuck. "When you went through treatments, did you have the Mirror test?"

"No," True replied. "They didn't start that until the third training group. Two groups after mine."

"You wouldn't by chance know if there were any empathic unstables, would you?"

When True was silent, Candace risked a brief glance at her. Her face was slack and pale.

"True?"

"Just one," Amir answered for her, his voice hollow and distant. "Lynn was a powerful empath who could project feelings into something like movies. They didn't know she was unstable until the suicides started. That's when they figured it out. She was the worst kind of sociopath. When she was done with you, you were happy to die."

"Chuck," Candace said, taking a tentative step forward. "I need you to listen to me. What you saw, it wasn't the truth. It's what you fear to be true. That's it. That's what she does."

"No!" he screamed, yanking Dr. Ferdinand back two stumbling steps. "You're lying!"

EVOLUTION: HEX

Candace froze, not wanting to push him further. "Okay. Fine. What is it you want, Chuck? What do you want me to do?"

"I... I..." he stammered. "I don't know. I'm going to take her. She's coming with me!"

Without further hesitation, Candace pulled the cord taut, freezing his body in place. She loosened the tension in his muscles enough for Dr. Ferdinand to squirm free, bolting away from the shifter. When she was clear, Candace took a step forward. "Chuck, you need to listen to me right now. I don't want to hurt you, but if you try to disappear on me, I don't know what will happen." She freed him enough for speech. "How is this gonna go?"

He grinned, a slight insanity to the curl of his lip. "I think I shift out of here and pull your ability with me. Feel like gettin' the power ripped out of ya, Candy Cane? I wonder what that would do to you. Want to find out?"

"Chuck," Candace said, trying not to show her anxiety. What if he was right? "I don't think that's what's gonna happen. Why don't you take a few deep breaths, and let's talk about it, okay? No one else needs to die tonight."

"Candy," Jackson whispered, suddenly by her side. "Don't risk this. It's not worth it."

She couldn't chance taking her eyes off of Chuck. "It's not a choice, Sunshine. We can't let him leave. Not like this."

"You should listen to your man, Sugar Plum." Chuck laughed. "He knows what he's talking about."

"Chuck, please," Dr. Ferdinand said, imploring, trying to appeal to whatever was left of his loyalty. "Please, don't do this."

He didn't reply, keeping his mad gaze trained on Candace. "It's superhero chicken, Candy Cane. I say you flinch first."

"Don't do it," Candace said. "Don't throw it all away. We can fix this, but you have to let us help you."

"I'm not sticking around to watch you kill everyone, Candace," he said. "I don't need saving. They do." When he spoke again, he was screeching. "Save yourselves!"

Candace felt her connection snap tight, the water reaching toward her as he started to shift. "No! Stop! Don't—"

Too late.

Chuck was gone.

A puddle marked the last place he stood.

CHAPTER 24

THERE WAS no saving the building. California was riddled with fault lines. With all of the underground seismic activity caused by the unleashed unstables and the battle to get them under control, it wasn't long before the ground beneath their feet gave up its struggle for stability and swallowed the compound whole. There would be no recovering the bodies trapped in the wreckage below.

After Dr. Ferdinand and most of the Supers cleared out, taking her unstable son with them, Candace stood near the edge of the crater that was the ANGEL Project headquarters and tried to feel something — anything.

But she was numb, unable to fully comprehend everything that was buried under hundreds of feet of rock and rubble. She didn't know how many bodies lay buried in the wreckage. She heard a few names, Gabe mentioning Sebastian along with the dead ANGELs she already knew.

"It's time, Sugar Plum," Jackson whispered, touching her elbow.

She stared into the pit, her brain sticking on the one thing she thought she knew for sure.

"Jackson."

"Hmm?"

"I wouldn't change it."

He was quiet for a moment. "Change what, Candy?"

"Adrian. I wouldn't change it," she said quietly. "That's not to say I'm glad he's dead. Not that. I mean..." She frowned at the chasm before her. "I mean with you. I wouldn't change a single minute. You know that, right?"

When he didn't reply, Candace turned to him, swiping the hair away from her face. "That night, when I saw him on the verge of killing you... I think I knew then, I just didn't want to admit it. Nearly losing you, I think that helped me push through. Adrian isn't standing between us, Sunshine. He hasn't since the moment I chose to be with you. So don't let him haunt you, okay? Only one of us should have to suffer those nightmares, and I won't let it be you. You aren't the one that has to live up to someone else. Everyone else has to live up to you."

His hands brushed away the tear slowly trailing down her cheek. "I shouldn't have said those things to you, Candy. I'm so sorry. You're the last person I'll ever want to hurt. I only want to be the kind of person you deserve."

Lifting up on her toes, she wrapped her arms around his neck, holding him tightly. "Sunshine, it's not about what I deserve. It's about what I need. That's you, and it always will be."

"You make me a better man, Sugar Plum," he whispered into her hair. "Thank you."

"Don't be silly," she said, smiling as she pulled back. "I'm not doing anything but showing you what was already there."

Jackson opened his mouth to argue, but the screech of tires as five black hummers pulled up on what was left of the road cut the conversation short. As the contingent of ANGELs and HEX remaining in the immediate vicinity gathered around, the vehicles disgorged a small platoon of soldiers, including General Jacobs and two other four-stars Candace didn't recognize, neither assisting her with something helpful like a name tag.

"Miss Bristol," General Jacobs said. "You have two options. Surrender, or you will be forcefully taken into custody and tried for treason."

After the horrors of the night, Candace didn't have it in her to give the littlest damn about what he had to say. "So, if I surrender you'll still try me for treason, right? As the difference is probably in whether or not you'll try to shoot me first, I think I'll pass all the same."

"You've put me in a bad place, Miss Bristol," he said, his tone more dangerous. "This whole mess could be career-ending for me, but I intend to not let that happen. One way or the other, you will be coming with me."

The lightest of touches on her back and she knew he was there. They all knew it would happen, and planned accordingly.

"General, I don't give a flying flip about your career," she said. "In fact, I think that once your superiors and the press get wind of some of your policies around here, you're not going to look so great even if you do manage to bring me in. Torture, imprisonment, falsifying reports to those acting on behalf of the US Government... yeah. I don't think you're going to keep those shiny stars of yours when it's all said and done."

Even in the dark of night, his familiar shade of pissed-off puce was clearly visible on his face. "Company! Open fi—"

Pure power surged through her as Ryan Pryor lit her up with his aqua aura, boosting every cell in her body. Her connection blasted wide open, with every molecule of water singing in her head, all to the tune of her command.

They all stopped.

Every soldier, every Super, anyone within a mile yielded to her call. They dangled from her will by invisible puppet strings, waiting for a single word, immobilized until she was ready to let them go.

Ryan's ability surrounded her, engulfing her, seeping into every pore.

"At this moment," Candace said, her voice resonating through the people within her control. "I could kill you all with a single thought. We are done answering to the ignorant and corrupt."

She released a deep breath, clearing her head of the foggy haze of absolute control. "But I'm not going to kill you. Killing is the easy answer, and rarely the right one."

Keeping a firm grip on General Jacobs and the soldiers, she freed the mystery four-stars enough to speak.

EVOLUTION: HEX

"What are your demands?" One of the unnamed generals, the one with silver-white hair and the build of a lumberjack, said.

"Simple. We want what everyone wants. Freedom."

"All due respect, Miss Bristol," the other one said, more resembling an emaciated hawk than anything else. "You and your contingent aren't exactly regular citizens."

She rubbed her eyes, beyond exhausted by the situation. "Look, we're not out to start any fights, or take over the country, or whatever. We're superheroes. We want to keep doing that. We want to be a force for good. We want to help people. We want to do everything we were doing for the ANGEL Project and more, only…"

Frowning, she glanced around at the soldiers, all with M-16s pointed right at her. With a wave of her hand, the weapons fell to the ground. It was hard to think through everything with guns aimed at her head.

"Only what?" General Lumberjack prompted.

"Only, we want to do it on our own terms," she said finally. "We want to have the say over where we go and when. We don't want to be paraded out like pampered purebreds to do tricks for the elite. We want to use the talents we have between us not just to fight, but to make things better. I think, given the opportunity, we could build something truly fantastic, truly helpful. We're more than a destructive force." Candace stopped, smiling a little when she remembered something. "Our hands can heal as much as they can bruise."

"So, you're suggesting something more like contract work, correct?" General Hawk said.

"Contract, not mercenary," she clarified. "We won't be your personal assassins. We'd handle dirty gen-evo lab shutdowns, unstable containment, humanitarian aid..." Candace trailed off, her mind spinning off in a million different directions. "Other particulars to be determined later. There's a lot to think about still."

Looking back and forth between the two men, Candace couldn't tell how it was going. "I don't know who you are, but I get the feeling your say matters more than he-who-would-see-me-dead. You seem at least willing to listen to me, which is more than I can say for him. I'm not looking for a fight; none of us are. Don't confuse that for inability to do so if it's needed, though. There's little I wouldn't do to help the people I care about. So tell me, should I prepare for a fight, or can we make a deal?" Tentatively, she released the two generals but remained on guard.

"On one condition," General Lumberjack said.

"And that is?"

"You'll be subject to regulation on the number of new recruits you're allowed to take on," he said. "We can't allow you to build up an army. Whatever good intentions you might have, Miss Bristol, many a disastrous road has been paved with higher ideals than what you're proposing."

"That..." Candace considered it, trying to see down any possible path where that condition could come back to bite her. "That seems reasonable, but I'll need more specifics. Which I assume you'll need from me as well."

Ryan Pryor tapped her gently, indicating he was nearing the end of his reserves.

"What guarantee do I have that you'll keep your word?"

she asked quickly.

"We've kept our word to Dr. Ferdinand this long," General Hawk said. "When you get to her new hideout, she'll tell you what she knows. We allowed her to continue her work without much interference, so long as the ANGEL Project could keep her in check. We couldn't keep all our eggs in the Poznanski basket, after all. Seems that was a wise choice."

Stunned by the revelation, Candace dropped her hold controlling the people around her. Moments later, the aqua glow dissipated, and the power in her body ebbed to normal levels.

"Candace!" a tiny voice screamed as thin arms wrapped around her waist. Startled, Candace barely registered Mindy's small frame and protective shield before she heard the gunshot.

A metallic ting resonated inside the bubble, sending small ripples expanding outward from in front of her face as a single bullet ricocheted off of the shield.

General Jacobs wavered directly before her, a crimson stain blooming across the white shirt of his disheveled uniform.

Seconds later, he dropped to the ground, a pistol slipping from his fingers.

It took a moment for anyone to move, but the soldiers sprang into action first. Tori ran forward to help, but stopped within a step or two, her shoulders slumping. Glancing back at Candace, she shook her head, then retreated back into the group of waiting Supers. There was nothing she could do for a dead man.

Mindy still clung to Candace's middle, her eyes shut tight even as tears slipped from the corners. Candace hugged her tightly, smoothing down her wild hair strewn in every possible direction. How long had she been hiding beside her?

"Thank you, Mindy," she said, giving the small girl a reassuring squeeze. "You saved my life. It's okay now. It's over."

Hesitantly, Mindy cracked open an eye and peered around. "It's okay?"

Candace nodded. "It is. I promise."

The shield dropped and, gradually, so did Mindy's iron embrace. The girl was stronger than she looked. Handing her off to Deborah, Candace approached the two remaining generals.

"So, we have a deal then?" She stuck out her hand, hoping they hadn't completely fooled her.

General Lumberjack wrapped her hand in his beefy one and shook firmly. "I believe so, Miss Bristol."

General Hawk tipped his hat and backed away. "We'll be in touch."

The remaining soldiers gathered the body of General Jacobs, loaded up in the hummers, and left quietly.

Tired beyond words, Candace sank to the ground. The battle had been won, but there were still miles and miles to go.

EPILOGUE

CANDACE BATTED the cornstalk away, annoyed the plants kept getting in her face.

"How much further to the site?"

"Another quarter mile," Gabe called from a few rows over. "They'll work on harvesting this mess next week so we'll be able to get the new road in after that."

She couldn't help being a little nervous. Candace hadn't been to the construction site since they broke ground on the new headquarters in May. That afternoon, she hoped to get an updated timeline on how soon the building would be finished. Their temporary homes at the Colorado HEX hideout and the Virginia ANGEL compound were getting claustrophobic and she was more than ready to get down to business.

After the disaster in California, five months flew by in a blur of lawyers and hearings and press interviews. She felt like she spent half of her time defending the group from dangerous editorial columns and reporters looking for a new angle to attack her from. Fortunately, with Deborah taking over PR duties, it would be one less thing on Candace's overflowing plate.

As she broke through the cornfield, she gasped. What was supposed to be a gaping hole in the ground, maybe with a foundation in place, was a fully finished building.

A low, one-story structure stretched in front of her, maybe half a mile in either direction. Solar panels covered every surface, collecting the power needed to supply the highly advanced, specialized facility.

Outside the front double-doors, a small crowd stood, smiling and waiting for her response. Dr. MacClellan grinned and strode forward.

"Surprised ya, eh?" he said, laughing. "So what do ye think, Miss Bristol?"

"It's... finished?" She stared, disbelieving her own eyes.

Dr. MacClellan nodded. "For the most part, aye. There's still a bit o' painting to do on the inside, but all the important bits are in place and everythin's up an runnin'."

"There's one thing left to do, Sugar Plum," Jackson whispered in her ear as he appeared behind her. "We thought you should do the honors."

Glancing at the swath of fabric hanging from the wall beside the entrance, Candace chuckled. "Deborah will kill me if I pull that down before she can arrange some sort of ribbon-cutting ceremony. You have no idea how excited she

EVOLUTION: HEX

is to plan that."

"I promise we'll cover it up again for the public unveiling," he said. "We all decided you should see it first."

Candace tore her gaze away from the cloth to look at her friends. Mica was practically glowing with pride. He should be. Much of what the place was only happened because of his amazing ability to create new materials, both funding the construction with the sales of patents and making it the height of scientific achievement. Hector and Andrew were busy elbowing each other, still in constant competition, while Chloe sighed in exasperation. Marissa Hayden, with her surprising interest in architecture, collaborated on the blueprints for the building. Michele leaned back against the door, alternating between casting suspicious glances at Dr. Ferdinand and staring into space in boredom. Two people were missing that she wanted there more than anything, but Amir's duties training recruits and True's meeting with a New York-based clothing company had them tied up elsewhere.

"This is amazing," Candace said, stepping towards them. "I can't believe how hard everyone's worked for this. Honestly, it's more than I would ever have thought possible. Thank you guys so much for everything you've done. There are no words for this."

"So, not that I want to rush the momentous occasion or anything," Gabe said. "But your mom promised us her apple pie tonight, and I'm starving."

Laughing, Candace acquiesced. "All right, all right." She strode forward and took hold of the thick canvas covering. "Ladies and gentlemen, I hereby christen this…"

She yanked, the cloth falling to the ground to reveal gleaming silver letters mounted to the side of the building. The glow of late afternoon sunlight sparkled off of every metal corner.

"The ISLE."

I. S. L. E. The Independent Superhero LEague. Candace spent days wracking her brain for the right name to encompass everything the group was setting out to do. The longer she thought, the more complex the acronyms got. Finally, tired of waiting on her to come to bed one night, Jackson sighed in exasperation and told her she was overthinking the whole thing.

"It's symbolic, Sugar Plum. Save the explanations for your mission statement. Just say what the thing is and fill in the blanks later."

The name encapsulated in the very simplest terms who they were. They were autonomous, more than human, and a cooperative collection of individuals.

And yet, while they were aiming for integration within society, they would probably always be a little outside of it. By leaving the isolation of the ANGEL Project, they were no longer an island in the sea of humanity, but still a separate offshoot. An isle was precisely that. Accessible, yet still apart.

Candace stared at the signage for a moment, then sighed. "It looks wonderful," she said. "But we should probably cover it back up until we're ready for the press unveiling."

Andrew levitated the fabric and resecured it to the wall.

After making plans for a full tour the next day, Candace, Jackson, Mica, and Gabe headed back through the cornfield to the shuttle. Gabe and Mica disappeared up ahead, running off to have the pilot ready the vehicle for takeoff.

"You nervous?" Candace nudged Jackson with an elbow. "You know I won't let you off the hook this time."

Jackson sighed. "I know. I just have to get it over with. The first hit is the worst, right?"

Candace giggled. "The first hit? Jackson, it's only my mom. What do you think she's gonna do to you?"

"Parents don't tend to like me much," he said, scowling.

"And how many girlfriends' parents have you met since you became a superhero, Sunshine?"

He responded with a flat look.

Laughing, Candace took his hand and pulled him on, walking backwards. "I promise she won't bite. Just, don't mention our matching scars, okay? Though if your steaks are half as good as you say they are, she might not care that you branded her only child."

"So no pressure then, huh?"

Stopping, she tugged him close and lifted up on her toes, kissing him lightly as she wound her arms around his neck. "Don't worry so much. If you got Gabe's approval, you won't have a problem with my mom. She's already predisposed to liking you."

He smirked. "Oh really, and why is that?"

Candace kissed him again, slower, drawing him to her.

"Because I love you," she whispered against his mouth. "That's enough reason for her to love you, too."

Jackson leaned his forehead against hers and sighed. "I hope you're right, Sugar Plum."

"Of course I'm right." She giggled and broke away.

"Now hurry up before we're late for dinner. Since you're cooking, it would be rude to make her wait."

When they emerged from the cornstalks, Gabe hung out of the back of the shuttle, irritated. "Are you two about done with the kissy-kissy garbage? I've been promised steak and apple pie, and my stomach waits for no man... or woman, even if she is my cousin."

They climbed inside and strapped in, the shuttle door closing behind them. As they lifted into the air, Candace stared out the window, hoping for one last glimpse of the new building.

Sunlight sparkled off of the ISLE headquarters as they zoomed overhead. Closing her eyes to savor the moment, she felt Jackson's fingers intertwine with hers. Warmth settled inside her, filling her with hope.

So long as he was beside her, there was nothing they couldn't do.

ABOUT STARLA—

A GEEK of all trades, Starla Huchton has been crafting stories in various genres since 2007. She is a three-time finalist for Parsec Awards for her podcast fiction work, and was the first place winner for Science Fiction & Fantasy in the Sandy competition in 2012. Her work spans Science Fiction, Fantasy, New Adult Romance, Young Adult titles, Steampunk, Contemporary, and various other varieties of stories. She is greedy and likes all the genres!

When not writing, Starla trains three minions, a black lab, and a military husband whilst designing book covers for independent authors and publishers at www.designedbystarla.com.

Connect with the author on the Starla Huchton Author Page on Facebook, @starlahuchton on Twitter, or at www.starlahuchton.com. To be notified only for new releases, sign up for the mailing list at https://tinyletter.com/SAHuchton.

AUTHOR'S NOTE

I HOPE you've enjoyed this little journey with me and my superheroes. They took me for an amazing ride as an author, and I hope they've done the same for you as a reader. If they've brought even a little enjoyment to your life, please consider leaving a review for this title and the others in the series. It would amaze you how much something small like that can make a huge difference.

As a reward for sticking with me through this series, I thought I'd offer a little peek at what's coming later. There are hundreds of stories that could be told using this cast of characters, but something in particular pulled at me when I reached the end of *Evolution: HEX*. What you're about to read is the entire first chapter of the follow-on series to this one.

Happy reading, and I hope you enjoy the preview!

A

KEEP READING FOR A SNEAK PEEK OF...

The Chronicles of ISLE:
SPARK

PROLOGUE

It begins as a spark. The convergence of energy.

It grows, consuming, blooming into warmth.

It brightens, bringing light to the world.

That is who she is.

That spark, it was always there. She felt it from her earliest memories. It spoke to her in a voice she understood long before the sounds people made registered as words, as expressions of thought, as calls to action.

The spark knew her name before her ears recognized it on the lips of her mother.

But she would never tell. The secret was hers alone.

The spark was only the start.

ONE

"Tommy, we have to go. Can you give it a rest?" Phoebe nudged her brother with a foot. "Mom will kill us if we're late again and I'm tired of explaining why I can't keep you out of the mud."

"Shh," he hissed at her. "I've almost got it."

She rolled her eyes. "You say that every damn time, and not once have I seen you do it."

He absently brushed a hand across his forehead, leaving a smudge of wet dirt in its wake, darkening his white-blond hair. "Feebs, I'm serious. Shut it. Another thirty seconds and I'll—"

"What do you two think you're doing out here?"

Phoebe cringed. It was not her day. Turning, she gave her best sheepish smile. "Sorry, Auntie Deb. I've been trying to get him out of here, but—"

The flecks of gray in the empath's hair caught the fading light of sunset as she shook her head, exasperated. "I know, I know. You can't leave him. You shouldn't have run off in the first place, though."

Tommy stood and smeared his filthy hands down his

jeans. "We didn't run off. The building's right there."

Deborah gave him a look that shut his mouth.

"Come on, Tommy," Phoebe said with a sigh. "Let's go before we get in any more trouble."

"You two know how important this is," Deborah said as they walked. "You aren't kids anymore."

The past few weeks saw a definite change in their caretaker's mood. Deborah Nasik was always kind and patient, but of late she was always hovering, on edge with some unspoken anxiety.

"It's just a party. What's the big deal?" Tommy grumbled under his breath.

"You know exactly why it's a big deal, Thomas," Deborah said. "Eighteen is the magic number for you kids. Trish, Amal, Manny, Cheyanne, Dillon... It was the same with everyone. You might be special by society's standards, but you're not an exception to the rule amongst us."

Phoebe sighed. She hated the whole thing, but she understood. Because of her parents' choices, her life was practically written out for her.

Like it or not, she was born to be a superhero. Just once, she wished someone would ask her what she thought about things. Even if it was a simple matter of what she wanted for dinner, that would be something.

But no one ever asked her for her opinion on anything. Life was a series of non-choices, predetermined by nothing more than her genetics.

Tommy felt the same way, but he was far more outspoken about it than she was. Honestly, it was exhausting to listen to him sometimes. It was always the same story.

"Why don't we get a say? It's not fair."

They were both at the end of their tolerance with being told to grow up, so she let him rant when they were alone. Still, she wished her brother would ease up on complaining. Phoebe was all too aware how little control she had over her life; she didn't need his constant, vocal affirmations of it.

As the shiny, dark paneling of the building came into view through the trees, Phoebe steeled herself. The Independent Superhero LEague Headquarters, while being a constant presence in her life since day one, would probably always intimidate the hell out of her. Within those walls was more history than she thought she wanted to know, including that of her parents.

It wasn't always that way. ISLE was born only a few years before her, and as much a child to her parents as she was. She grimaced. In some ways, it was probably more so. That place and everything it represented took precedence over anything she was or had ever done, that was for sure.

"You know that isn't true, Phoebe," Deborah said softly. "You and your brother were always more important. They love you more than you know."

Irritated at the invasion of her private emotions, Phoebe scowled. "I'm entitled to my feelings. And please stop with that."

Deborah smiled. "You know I can't."

Deborah Nasik's empathic abilities weren't something she could shut off, Phoebe knew. It made her a perfect nanny, but damn was it annoying to have someone around who was constantly aware of any and every feeling Phoebe had. As a result, her and her brother, as well as the rest of the Superkids, were probably the most honest people on the planet. As they were raised around people that could see through every lie they'd ever thought to tell, it was impossible to learn dishonesty. Well, mostly.

Superkids. God, how she hated that label. Not only because she wasn't really a kid anymore, but because of everything it implied.

She would never be normal. She would never be anything but her parents' legacy.

The building cast its shadow over them as the main doors of the ISLE Headquarters opened. Every time she walked through them, it felt like she was being swallowed whole.

Beautiful cream-colored tiles stretched out through the entrance and down either side of the main corridors of the ISLE complex. They carried on straight ahead, proceeding through the large double doors to the conference room. The lights were already dimmed for a slideshow or teleconference or whatever nonsense they'd have to sit through for that night. Phoebe noted the large flatscreen at the front was already illuminated, ready to show whatever over-the-top preparation they had in mind for next week's big event. Phoebe took the lead, passing Tommy and Deborah as she headed past the rows of guest seats to the wide u-shape table at the front. Keeping her displeasure off of her expression, she lowered herself into a chair on the left end of the table, staying well clear of the center seats. Those were reserved for the faces of ISLE, the ones who made the final call in all business matters.

She did notice she wasn't the last to arrive for once. The most important seats were empty, the others filled with people she considered family: ones not bound by blood, but by purpose. There was one exception to that, and Phoebe couldn't help but give her uncle a small smile as he grinned at her from across the empty center section. He winked at her from behind black-framed glasses. Out of everyone in her strange, extended family, he and his partner knew her thoughts on the whole business, allowing her more than one long chat to get it all off of her chest.

The doors opened again, and the final two members arrived. Everyone brought their quiet conversations to a close, waiting for them to take their seats.

Phoebe's stomach tightened as they sat.

"Thank you all for coming tonight," her mother said, kicking off the meeting. "I know we're all extremely busy this time of year, so I'll try to make this quick. A week from Saturday, we'll be opening the compound for the birthday celebration, and we need to make sure everything's on schedule for the debut."

While Phoebe groaned internally at the word "debut," Tommy couldn't hold his in. She elbowed him in the side, prompting a look of irritation from him, which she returned with a glare of her own. Phoebe hated the whole idea of the public unveiling as it was; she didn't need him adding extra grief from their parents on top of it.

While her mother collected status updates from everyone on everything from compound security, to food, to fashion, to parking, Phoebe tried to stay focused and listen. Tommy wouldn't, and at least one of them needed to know what was going on if they were the main attraction. The only thing that made her smile through the whole meeting was the sketches True Clemmons showed of the design of her dress for the party. Finally, something she had input on. Even if it was only the color, a shimmery red-violet, it was a victory she would take. She wouldn't have her fitting until Wednesday at the earliest, but it was definitely something she looked forward to.

"Teams of two and three will take turns patrolling the perimeter," her father said, pulling up the schedule on his personal screen and throwing it to the larger one, replacing the sketch of her dress with the map of the compound. "We'll rotate so everyone has time to make an appearance at the event." He added with a smirk, "So everyone suffers equally."

Phoebe hid her chuckle at her mother's peeved face. Dad made no bones about detesting the public spectacles, even though he understood the need for them.

"Transparency, Sunshine," she'd always say. *"We have to keep the Normals happy."*

"Suffers equally," Tommy grumbled under his breath. "Yeah, right."

"Knock it off, would you?" Phoebe whispered at him. "Like you're the only one that has to do this."

"Just cuz you get a pretty dress doesn't make this any less bullshit," he said back. "Don't act like you care."

Her simmering irritation threatened to get the better of her. "It might be bullshit, but get over yourself. You know I hate this as much as you do."

"Did you two have something to add?" her mother asked from the center of the table.

Phoebe shrunk down in her seat. *Damn it, Tommy.* "No,

ma'am."

Their mother's unpleasant look of reprimand shifted to Tommy.

"No, ma'am," he said, sighing unhappily.

Her light aquamarine eyes moved between them as her expression softened from disciplinary to understanding. "Then we'll move on." She redirected her attention to the group at large. "The watchbill will be distributed accordingly once it's finalized. Make sure your teams have the information as soon as it's available."

The meeting proceeded on, dragging out well over an hour. As everyone collected themselves and wrapped up personal conversations, Phoebe hung back with her brother, knowing a lecture from their parents was coming.

But as they waited, someone else approached them. Dr. Emily Ferdinand, head of the genetic programs at ISLE, stopped in front of them and smiled, the wrinkles around her eyes bunching together.

"Big week for you two," she said. "Nervous?"

Tommy shrugged, still looking unpleasant.

"We're dealing," Phoebe answered for both of them.

"Well, how about you come see me in the morning?" Dr. Ferdinand asked. "There are a few tests I need to run, to make sure everything's as it should be. We don't want any surprises for your party next week."

As Tommy didn't look like he'd be answering, Phoebe nodded. "Yes, ma'am. Eight o'clock?"

She brushed away a loose strand of gray hair. "That will be fine. See you in the morning."

When Dr. Ferdinand left, Phoebe sighed to herself.

More needles. Like she hadn't had her fill of those in her almost eighteen years.

The last of the attendees departed, leaving only her brother and her parents in the room with her.

Taking in the look on her mom's face, Phoebe braced. *Here it comes...*

But instead, her expression changed, eyebrows bunching in concern. "Come on, you two," she said. "Let's get home. Dinner should be ready."

Phoebe and Tommy trailed behind as their parents, their fingers lightly intertwined, led the way. They wound down the sidewalks of the miniature town, passing vintage-style lamp posts that lit the pavement in the dark. Reflections of the lights glinted off of the solar panel roof tiles of every house, their colonial-style porches trimmed in red, white, and blue batting in preparation for the approaching Fourth of July holiday. Phoebe swatted at a buzzing mosquito, annoyed they never bothered her father that way. The scent of burning charcoal wafted through on the summer breeze, and somewhere a few people were laughing together, the echoes of their voices carrying from a backyard.

The smell of pot roast and potatoes greeted them as they strode in the front door of their home. While everyone else headed upstairs to clean up after a long day, Tommy most needing it, Phoebe went to the kitchen, taking plates and silverware from the cupboards and setting the table. Her thoughts drifted as she worked, her motions second nature to her.

Things were changing. The moment her secret was out in the open, her life would be even less her own than it was already.

A life of service, dedicated to helping those who could not help themselves.

As she took a glass from the cupboard, a knock at the back door made her jump. Setting it down, she answered the summons, unsurprised to see her best friend standing outside, shifting from foot to foot.

"So?" Samantha Hayden said, playing with her long, black braid. "What about tonight?"

Phoebe glanced around, checking for anyone within earshot. "Do you really think this is a good idea, Sammi? If we get caught..."

"We won't," she said, grinning. "I already worked it out with Amal. He'll make sure we're in the clear."

"I dunno, I mean, this is such a stupid risk to take. You know what next week is, right?"

Sammi leaned in, blue eyes gleaming mischievously. "All the more reason to do it now before the world knows your face. Come on, Feebs. You promised. This may be your last chance to be anonymous. Don't back out on me."

Well, she had a point. After next week, everyone and their mom would know who Phoebe was.

She sighed. "Fine. What time?"

"Can you be out by nine?"

It would be tough to get away, but not impossible. "Yeah, I think so. They usually go for a swim about then, so I'll be there as soon as I can, okay?"

Sammi giggled quietly and gave her a hug. "Thank you! I'll see you then."

As Samantha bounded down the porch steps, Phoebe

shook her head and let out a slow, tired breath. It could possibly be a big mistake, but, really, what was the harm in it?

"Phoebe?" her mother called from the kitchen. "What are you doing out there?"

She waved off the concern when she was back inside. "Nothing. Sammi wants me to come over and watch a movie after dinner."

A single, blonde eyebrow lifted into the air. "What movie?"

Phoebe made a face. "You know her. Probably some sappy, romantic comedy." Intensely grateful Deborah wasn't around, she went back to collecting glasses and filling them with water. "So can I?"

"Is Marissa home?"

Phoebe shrugged. "I dunno. Sammi didn't say. It's just a movie, Mom."

"Yes, and you have an appointment in the morning, if memory serves."

She closed her eyes and tried to be patient. Seriously, she was almost eighteen and she still had to ask permission to walk down the street to a friend's house? "I know. Dr. Ferdinand told us. I won't be out late. You know my tolerance for Sammi movies only goes so far. Two, max."

After a pause, her mother nodded. "Fine. But you're home by midnight, got it?"

She sighed. "Yes, Mom." It was the best she would get.

Dinner was quiet, as her parents rarely had much left in the way of energy for talking by nighttime. The wildfires in Colorado took up most of their time that day, and they'd both been out there, corralling the flames and extinguishing them before they reached the suburbs of Colorado Springs. Seeing their exhaustion, Phoebe took pity on them and offered to clean the kitchen after the meal. With a grateful kiss on her cheek, her mother wandered out and back upstairs to change for her evening swim. Tommy didn't stick around to help.

Only her father lingered by the counter, studying her quietly. Phoebe glanced up at him from the sink.

"Something you want to ask?" she said.

He rubbed his chin, the stubble there scratching at his calloused fingertips. "I know this is hard on you, Phoebe, but you know procedure."

She nodded as she scrubbed out the glass baking dish. "I know. When everyone here is a special snowflake, no one is."

"I hate these things. I'd abolish them if I could."

If anyone understood, it was her father, of that she was sure. Like Tommy, he was always very vocal about the publicity aspect of ISLE. "Yeah, I get it. But Mom's right. If people don't know about us, they won't trust us. It makes sense."

He was quiet for a moment, then touched her arm. Phoebe looked up, and he led her back to the table, sitting her down for a conversation.

"This isn't fair to you," he said. "You didn't choose this."

Phoebe frowned and folded her hands on the table.

"Your mom and I, we did. We signed up for this before we even met. We knew what was involved. We knew what kind of life it would be. While that's changed some from what it originally was, the commitment remains. Get superpowers, spend the rest of your time using them to help others. That was our choice. You kids…" He trailed off.

"Dad," Phoebe said, noting the pinched look on his face. She reached over to take one of his rough hands. "I know. You didn't think about kids back then. Who would? I can't imagine considering that right now, and you guys weren't much older than I am when you met. But you're people. People want families. Superheroes aren't immune to that."

Smiling softly, he lifted her hand and brushed a kiss across her knuckles. "It doesn't mean it wasn't a selfish decision. Superheroes give up most of their right to be selfish when they become what they are."

Phoebe chuckled. "You're superheroes, Dad. Not perfect. I think you're allowed."

"Are we?" he asked as he searched her eyes. "Everything we do is bigger, has more serious consequences. Often, it's not the superhero that pays the price. In this case, it's you and your brother."

What was he looking for, scouring her face that way? Forgiveness? "What's the matter, Dad? You think we hate you for making the choices you did or something?" His answer came in the form of a frown. Phoebe squeezed his fingers. "We don't. Tommy complains a lot, but he loves you guys. I do, too. You wanted a family. We are one. Whatever life this is, it's all I've got, and you and Mom gave it to me. So don't think we hate you for it. Yes, it's frustrating, but it's who we are. Complaining about it isn't going to change anything." She smiled and pulled away. "It's a puzzle, a challenge. We have to figure out the best outcome within limited circumstances."

At that, he laughed. "A challenge? You are so much like your mother sometimes."

Phoebe giggled. "I could do worse than take after one of the most powerful and respected superheroes of all time. I'll take that as a compliment."

"Jackson?" her mother called from upstairs. "Are you coming?"

Her father grinned and stood up from the table, planting a kiss on the top of her head. "I'll see you later, sweetheart. Don't stay up too late."

"Yes, Dad." She rolled her eyes.

"Jackson?"

"On my way, Sugar Plum," he called as his feet pounded up the stairs, taking them two at a time.

Not rushing with the dishes, Phoebe waited until everyone was out of the house. Even Tommy went along for the evening swim, leaving her alone at last.

She opened her closet door, considering. If she changed clothes, her parents would know something was up. If she so much as wore lipstick, she'd be busted. However, her flip flops had to go. She could play that off easily enough, as one could stub their toe in the dark. If she ended up where she thought she would end up, however, she would make sure to clean her sneakers before coming home.

After running a brush through her long, brown hair, she wound it up into a simple bun and headed out. One block, a right turn, and five houses down, she jogged up the stairs and knocked on the door.

When Sammi answered, Phoebe tried not to cringe. Her lips were redder than a fire truck and her eyes were more heavily painted than a clown's.

"What?" she asked, hands on her hips. "And why are you

still in those clothes?"

Phoebe sighed and stepped inside. "Because, unlike you, I have to go home to two parents that watch me like hawks and question every little thing I do. And what's with the makeup? Don't you think it's a bit much for a high school party?"

Sammi shrugged and adjusted the strap of her red tank top that displayed every last curve the girl had. "Depends on what your goal is. Maybe you're only going to look, but I intend to get the hands-on experience."

Phoebe pinched the bridge of her nose and closed her eyes. "Sam, that's maybe the worst possible—"

"Come on," Sammi said, grabbing her by the arm and dragging her through the house and out the back door. "You worry too much. We'll be fine."

Yep. Her mother would kill her for sure.

And Sammi was leading the way down death row.

OTHER BOOKS BY STARLA

AS STARLA HUCHTON

THE ANTIGONE'S WRATH SERIES
Master of Myth

FLIPPED FAIRY TALES
Shadows on Snow
The Stillness of the Sky

My Bittersweet Summer (standalone)

AS S. A. HUCHTON

THE ENDURE SERIES
Maven
Nemesis
Progeny

THE EVOLUTION SERIES
Evolution: ANGEL
Evolution: SAGE
Evolution: HEX

Lex Talionis (standalone)